THE DISTRICT GOVERNOR'S DAUGHTERS

D1553850

Camilla Collett

THE DISTRICT GOVERNOR'S DAUGHTERS

TRANSLATED BY KIRSTEN SEAVER

Norvik Press

Some other books from Norvik Press

Jens Bjørneboe: *The Sharks* (translated by Esther Greenleaf Mürer)
Jørgen-Frantz Jacobsen: *Barbara* (translated by George Johnston)
Kjell Askildsen: *A Sudden Liberating Thought* (translated by Sverre Lyngstad)
Christopher Moseley (ed.): *From Baltic Shores*
Janet Garton (ed.): *Contemporary Norwegian Women's Writing*
Fredrika Bremer: *The Colonel's Family* (translated by Sarah Death)
Suzanne Brøgger: *A Fighting Pig's Too Tough to Eat* (translated by
        Marina Allemano)
Kerstin Ekman: *Witches' Rings* (translated by Linda Schenck)
Robin Fulton (ed. and transl.): *Five Swedish Poets.*

The logo of Norvik Press is based on a drawing by Egil Bakka (University of Bergen) of a Viking ornament in gold, paper thin, with impressed figures (size 16x21mm). It was found in 1897 at Hauge, Klepp, Rogaland, and is now in the collection of the Historisk museum, University of Bergen (inv.no. 5392). It depicts a love scene, possibly (according to Magnus Olsen) between the fertility god Freyr and the maiden Gerðr; the large penannular brooch of the man's cloak dates the work as being most likely 10th century.

Original title: *Amtmandens døtre*. First published 1854-55.
Translation © 1992 Kirsten Seaver.

Cover illustration: Blue Interior, by Harriet Backer (1883).
Photo: J. Lathion, © Nasjonalgalleriet, Oslo.

British Library Cataloguing in Publication Data
Collett, Camilla
    District Governor's Daughters
    I. Title II. Seaver, Kirsten A.
    839.8236 [F]

ISBN 1-870041-17-8
First published in 1991 by Norvik Press, University of East Anglia, Norwich NR4 7TJ.
Reprinted 1998. Managing editors: James McFarlane, Janet Garton and Michael Robinson.

Norvik Press has been established with financial support from the University of East Anglia, the Danish Ministry for Cultural Affairs, the Norwegian Cultural Department and the Swedish Institute. Publication of this book has been aided by a grant from the Norwegian Ministry of Culture.

Printed in Great Britain by Page Bros. (Norwich) Ltd.

Contents

Translator's introduction   7

The District Governor's Daughters

    Author's Preface   27

    Part One   31
    Part Two   153

Translator's Introduction

[Jacobine] Camilla Wergeland Collett (1813-95) was Norway's first feminist novelist, and *The District Governor's Daughters* (published in two parts in 1854 and 1855) was the first Norwegian novel that addressed itself to social problems directly. As the author's preface to the 1879 edition makes clear, the book caused a tremendous stir when it first came out. Some reviewers missed the point of the book completely, while others found it too accurate for comfort. Of all Collett's works, it has remained the most widely read, and it is firmly placed among the classics in Norwegian literature.

In addition to giving a powerful impetus to feminism in Norway, this novel, as well as Collett's subsequent writings, had an acknowledged influence on such authors as Bjørnstjerne Bjørnson, Jonas Lie, Alexander Kielland and Henrik Ibsen.

Ibsen (1828-1906) and Collett were friends and saw each other from time to time during the latter's repeated travels on the Continent after her husband's death in 1851. Each admired the work of the other. Ibsen once referred to Collett's prose as 'the best to be found in Norway'. In her book *From the Camp of the Mutes* [*Fra de stummes Lejr*], 1877, a highly personal view of how literature through the ages has fixed women in an inferior position, Collett takes exception to several of the female characters in Ibsen's plays, but then goes on to say: 'But who has also created such female characters as he? We must go back to Shakespeare to find them.'

Ibsen and Collett did not actually meet until the winter of 1871-2. The Ibsens were living in Dresden at the time. John Stuart Mill's *The Subjection of Women* had just appeared in Danish, and Ibsen's wife Suzannah apparently took an immediate liking both to Mill's book and to Camilla Collett, with whose work both she and her husband were familiar. Collett found herself equally at ease with Mrs. Ibsen, but for the playwright himself she felt less than wholehearted admiration at first. In a letter to her son Alf, dated 23 February 1872, she described her initial impression: 'He is from top to toe an egotist, especially as a man in his relationship with women. His domestic situation has surely been one of the lesser influences upon him. Notice his heroes: *All despots vis-à-vis women.* Even that despicable creature Peer Gynt a noble woman is supposed to drag out of the mire, i.e. sacrifice herself for. Among our geniuses, he is the one who throughout life has least succeeded in obtaining that view of existence which is the true one, and who therefore, despite great talent, aims wrong. He has lived like a hermit always.'

Suzannah Ibsen had more influence over her husband's ideas than Collett gave her credit for in this letter, because at home she promoted the ideas of both Mill and Collett, and Ibsen did indeed take Collett and her work seriously.

Collett felt certain that Ibsen used not only her writing, but also her own life, as inspiration for many of his plays. Her strange, drawn-out love affair as a young woman with the Norwegian poet Johan Sebastian Welhaven was common knowledge, and Collett thought Ibsen had used this relationship as the basis for *Love's Comedy* (1862). Ibsen was very non-committal, but Collett nevertheless had some reason to claim that she had provided inspiration for this play. As the Danish literary critic Georg Brandes (1842-1927) was the first to point out, Ibsen had obviously borrowed from *The District Governor's Daughters* the poet Falk's long and lyrical speech about the delicate tea served to the Emperors of China.

When Ibsen's *The Lady From the Sea* was published in 1888, Collett was deeply moved, according to her Danish friend and biographer Clara Bergsøe. Collett saw her own life reflected in this play, with Welhaven being cast as the stranger, while her late husband Jonas Collett was the model for the faithful husband. She told Ibsen so in a letter, and Ibsen confessed: 'Yes, there are several similarities, many, in fact, and you have seen them and felt them. I mean things that to me might appear as mere suggestions. But it is now many years since you, by your spiritual passage through life, in one way or another began to play a part in my writing.'

Long before this, plays that showed the direct and acknowledged influence of Collett's life work had begun to appear. *Pillars of Society* was published in 1877, half a year after Collett's second visit with the Ibsens. Although the timid and ill-used Mrs. Bernick plays a prominent part, this play also gives us a new type of woman: the free-spirited, vigorous Lona Hessel, who Collett thought was directly modelled upon herself, but who is generally thought to have been inspired by the Norwegian feminist Aasta Hansteen. In the character of Consul Bernick's sister, Ibsen shows his new understanding of the difficult position of unmarried gentlewomen.

Pillars of Society was followed by *A Doll's House* in 1879 and *Ghosts* in 1881, both of which caused public reactions similar to those that had first greeted *The District Governor's Daughters*, and for very much the same reasons. In realistic dialogue exchanged by contemporary characters in a homely setting, Ibsen pointed to problems which were known to exist, but which were not considered fit subjects for public, or even private, discussion: the double sexual standard and the ravages of venereal disease; the written and unwritten laws governing women's lives, which in the end affected men's lives as well; and the devastating results of sacrificing honesty to the stranglehold of philistinism, provincialism, pettiness and prejudice. Those were precisely the problems Camilla Collett aired in her first book. Sexual promiscuity is just touched upon in the awareness the unhappy Louise has of her husband's infidelities, but the other ingredients are there in full force.

The District Governor's Daughters is the story of two young people, Sofie Ramm and Georg Kold, who in their separate soul-searching reached the same conclusion: The only love between a man and a woman worth having is one that is freely exchanged between two equals. Only such a love is a proper foundation for marriage. Because of her upbringing, Sofie hoped for such a love timidly, almost against hope, while Kold hoped for it actively, articulately and enthusiastically. Kold refrained from declaring his love for Sofie in order to give her love for him time to grow, but no sooner had *she* declared her love for *him* but he fell victim to the same fear of other people's opinions and interference that had almost paralysed Sofie. Overheard by Sofie, Kold denied his love for her in a conversation with his friend Dr. Müller. Sofie knew she had sinned against society's mores in telling Kold of her love before he had formally declared himself. Timid and reserved once more, she became the victim of family suasion and acquiesced in her 'proper' destiny: a marriage deemed desirable by the criteria of bourgeois comfort and respectability and measured by every yardstick except those of love and honesty.

Although the lives of women in all stations of life obviously have improved a great deal in Norway since this book was written, Norwegians — especially those past their first youth and familiar with rural or small-town life — have no trouble recognizing Collett's passionate description of how a sweet young girl is transformed into a drab Norwegian housewife. Furthermore, although there now are well over four million people in Norway, as opposed to a population of 1,400,000 (of whom only 163,000 lived in urban areas) in 1850, it is even now a fairly sparsely inhabited country. Norwegians are still familiar with the pressures brought to bear on those who live in small, often isolated, communities, where generations of stable, homogeneous populations have created a feeling of familiarity and social transparency. Here, people know a great deal about each other, believe themselves entitled to knowing even more, and feel practically honour-bound to comment upon each other's lives and behaviour. In that kind of social climate the fear of such comments may in a very real way govern people's lives.

A peculiar kind of humour, so hard to translate but so basic to the style of both Ibsen and Collett, has always been the Norwegians' defence against their often dreary and constricted world. Humour is the saving grace of social intercourse; it is the rudder one can tilt to steer around shoals suddenly looming up in the river of a conversation. How thoroughly Collett understood this is clearly seen in the tongue-in-cheek conversation between Kold and Sofie over the torn book, during which they re-establish their footing with each other.

Norwegian humour is a curious mixture of self-deprecation, understatement and exaggeration, with an element of gallows-humour running close under the surface. There is also a keen appreciation of the bizarre. Although the sometimes high-flown language of *The District Governor's Daughters* may strike the modern reader as melodramatic, it is well to bear in mind that in Norway, then as now, true pomposity has always triggered laughter, so that the sententiousness of Sofie's mother and the pedantic self-importance of the clergyman Brøcher have always seemed ridiculous, albeit true to a certain type.

But the restrictions imposed by the narrow provincialism of Norwegian society were no laughing matter. Ibsen never forgot the social ostracism he had felt during his childhood and youth in the small town of Skien, as a consequence of his father's bankruptcy. The thorn was always there. It is visible in *Peer Gynt*, in which Peer and his mother suffer not only financially, but also socially, because Peer's father lived above his income and went bankrupt. It is present with undiminished force in *Pillars of Society*, in Consul Bernick's passionate explanation of why he has to save the Bernick family from financial ruin at all cost. In the same manner, Camilla Collett's own experiences suffuse *The District Governor's Daughters*. That is not to say that the novel is autobiographical, but to any reader familiar with Collett's life, the parallels between her and Sofie are many.

Camilla Collett was born in Kristiansand, in the south of Norway, but when she was only four years old, the family moved to the rural parsonage at historic Eidsvoll, then more than a day's journey north of Oslo, because her father Nicolai Wergeland had obtained the living there. He had acted according to desires conceived just a few years earlier, when he had been one of the signatories of the Norwegian Constitution at Eidsvoll on 17 May 1814, during the brief, hectic period of Norway's seeming independence, as the Napoleonic wars in Europe drew to a close and Norway's centuries-long union with Denmark came to an end.

Like so much of Norway, the human world at Eidsvoll was dwarfed by the surrounding forests and mountains. In Collett's writing, as in that of so many Norwegians, descriptions of the natural landscape mirror or set the stage for accounts of the inner world of human feeling. She had plenty of time to be by herself and to reflect upon life, although she took lessons from her father and from the various tutors secured for her brothers. Her rogues gallery of tutors and curates doubtless comes from these years.

In 1826, when Camilla was thirteen years old, her father, who had high ambitions for his youngest daughter because of her beauty and many talents, enrolled her in Miss Pharo's school for girls in Christiania [Oslo], where she felt very much out of place. Her father next entrusted her to the educational institution run in Christiansfeld, Denmark, by the Herrnhuters, a sect of Moravian Brethren. Here she stayed from her fourteenth to her sixteenth year. Letters between her and her family, as well as from her father to the head of the school, make it clear that those were not very happy years for the shy country girl from Norway, although she did well in her studies. In the present novel, Sofie's references to homesickness while she was away in Copenhagen have the warm, full ring of Collett's own experience.

Those years were very important for Collett's future development. In 1828, a pastor named Roentgen joined the school and became young Camilla's religion teacher. He was a popular and inspiring teacher, and Camilla remained deeply religious all her life. Among the other adults associated with the school, it is amusing to note that the school's doctor, of whom Camilla Wergeland with her bouts of nervous stomach ailments was probably not very fond, was named Müller. One cannot help thinking that she chose the name deliberately for Kold's interfering medical friend.

In writing of the delight Sofie's father took in her letters home, Collett draws on her own awareness of the pleasure and pride her own letters from school had given her father, and when she describes Sofie's confusion and exasperation at suddenly having to be a young lady in dress and manner, she is recalling her own experiences upon returning to Norway.

In addition to spending two years away at school, young Camilla Wergeland also travelled to Paris with her father in the summer of 1834, returning home in the autumn via Amsterdam, Hamburg and Copenhagen — a trip undertaken chiefly because of her father's concern for her health and state of mind, both of which were suffering from her uncertain relationship with Welhaven. Also, her early biographer Bergsøe claims, Camilla was despondent at her family's refusal to let her become an actress. Although the journey did not cure her of her love for Welhaven, it probably whetted her appetite for the gypsy life she was to assume in her later years. A long visit with a cultivated Hamburg family, from 1836 until the spring of 1837, cemented her taste for German culture and literature. In her writing, this predilection is continually in evidence.

In Norway, the literary climate during Camilla's formative years was warmed by the autumn rays of romanticism, the general favourites being such German and Danish romantic writers as Oehlenschläger, Novalis, Tieck and Steffens. It took several years for a uniquely Norwegian brand of national romanticism in art and literature to grow out of the new national self-awareness arising from the dissolution of the Dano-Norwegian union in 1814. As a modern biographer of Collett, Aagot Benterud, points out, a growing admiration for the classical style ran parallel to the current of late Continental romanticism in Norway in the years after 1814. The new style stressed simplicity and virile strength, leaving little respect for traditional feminine qualities. The social style accompanying these literary developments also emphasized restraint and control — women were expected to be passive, and it was a terrible breach against etiquette for a woman to reveal tender feelings for a man before he had made it known that he had serious intentions. This 'Law of Femininity', as Collett called it, was the bane of many women's lives and almost of her own, and her awareness of the harm such strictures had done fuelled her writing of *The District Governor's Daughters*, which she referred to as 'the long-suppressed cry from my heart.'

In addition to the rival currents of late romanticism and neo-classicism, there were great socio-economic changes in Norway in the years after 1814. A new upper class of civil servants, including the clergy (and district governors), displaced the old mercantile aristocracy, and parsonages such as Camilla's childhood home became cultural centres. The general economic situation in Norway was steadily improving in the 1830's and '40's, and homes became more comfortable in the bourgeois style — witness Sofie and her sister Amalie redecorating the family sitting room.

With such rapidly changing and often clashing cultural and social impulses swirling around her, it is small wonder that Camilla Wergeland felt in an almost perpetual state of conflict. Added to these external forces was her own personality, which seems to have been a particularly warring conglomerate of qualities drawn from her elegant, beautiful and gay mother and her brooding, passionate father, whom she most resembled in temperament — a mixture of characteristics which was in no way mitigated by the rather haphazard discipline in the Wergeland household.

After 1833, when the farmers began to demand the use of powers granted them in the Constitution of 1814 — a struggle in which Welhaven and Camilla's brother Henrik were involved on opposite sides — the power of the civil servant class began to wane. There were also fresh romantic breezes from Denmark and Germany blowing across the literary stage, especially the current of the 'romantic realism' associated with 'das junge Deutschland', of which Welhaven became an exponent in Norway.

Although this new form of romanticism brought with it a different feminine ideal from the neo-classical one, women in Norway did not suddenly become any better off, for modern factory-based industry, with its emphasis on materialistic achievements, had also begun to have an impact on Norwegian society by this time, leaving little admiration for the sort of qualities in which women were supposed to excel.

During this post-1814 political and cultural ferment, the Norwegians were not only reacting to the various currents of Continental European thought, but also engaging in a unique struggle to re-define Norwegian life and language, which had been subjected to heavy Danish influence for centuries. Political and literary polemical writing commanded a large and enthusiastic audience, many of whom gathered around two opponents: Camilla's brother, Henrik Wergeland (1808-45), and her first love, Johan Sebastian Welhaven (1807-73). The feud between these two poets is mentioned several times in the present novel.

Henrik Wergeland was a reformer of the bastion-storming school and was in every way the temperamental opposite of the elegant, fastidious Welhaven. The impatient, fiercely nationalistic and democratic Wergeland wanted Norwegian language and culture to revert as far as possible to an unadulterated state. To Welhaven and his followers, who were grateful for the extended cultural contacts allowed them through the Dano-Norwegian culture, this seemed a call to return to primitive and barbarous conditions. Wergeland was the champion of, among other things, general education, plain and wholesome peasant-style living, and the admission of Jews to the kingdom — his efforts in the last-named cause bearing fruit after his death. He was a prolific and gifted writer and poet, who during his short and tempestuous life managed to exert a great deal of influence and to offend not a few, including Welhaven, who thought Wergeland's poetry crude and roughly hewn compared with his own carefully crafted verse. He was not really opposed to most of Wergeland's goals. He was just as committed as Wergeland to the preservation of the national cultural heritage, and his heart beat just as strongly for the glories of the Norwegian landscape. Essentially, the two men differed over tactics.

Although Camilla and her brother Henrik were temperamentally similar in many ways — stubborn, passionate, romantic, with strong likes and dislikes and a proneness to exaggeration — they were physically quite different. He was burly and strong, with a broad, defiant face, while she was a tall, willowy beauty with large, pensive eyes. Collett endowed her heroine Sofie with the same slenderness and also gave her the rich, lovely hair and the curiously floating walk for which Camilla herself quickly became renowned when she entered the social scene in Christiania, where her family connections gave her ready access to the circle formed by the wealthy bourgeoisie and the intellectuals of the day.

It was during a visit to the capital towards the end of January, 1830, when she was barely seventeen years old, that Camilla Wergeland met the handsome, reserved Welhaven. His romantic good looks and deep, expressive voice immediately captured her imagination, while her fastidious temperament as well as her firm grounding in Continental culture drew her towards his camp. She fell deeply in love.

Judging from contemporary accounts as well as from letters and journals that became accessible later, Welhaven was also strongly attracted to the beautiful Camilla, about whom he wrote many admiring poems published for all to see. He was not only poor and proud, however, but also cautious, and the stern moral climate surrounding him and Camilla, in which it was anathema for a young woman so much as to hint at an attachment unless encouraged to do so by the gentleman's prior declaration, must carry a good share of the blame for the agonizing, protracted and futile love affair that ensued.

A modern reader of old novels tends to be struck by the chasteness of the encounters between young people in love. Collett's letters and journals offer persuasive evidence that such chasteness was not only the proper literary ideal, but was in fact practised, obviously aided by the lack of opportunity for young people to be by themselves, but also resulting from what Jane Austen would call 'true delicacy of feeling'. Although Welhaven and Camilla Wergeland saw each other regularly on social occasions after first becoming acquainted in early 1830, it was not until November of 1831 that they had their first real conversation, when he helped her buy a copperplate print as a gift for a friend. He also wrote her a letter in connection with this transaction—the sealing wax of which she ate. But feverishly in love though she was, she went to great lengths not to have her feelings noticed by him or their friends. During 1832, as well, she took great pains to avoid Welhaven, keeping firmly in mind what she had been taught about the need for women to be careful. In *The District Governor's Daughters* one may certainly marvel at the perverse strength with which Sofie avoided Kold even when living under the same roof with him. Collett knew the process intimately.

We need to remind ourselves that Collett knew and loved Welhaven for seven years at a time when every young woman was under great pressure to be married and taken off her family's hands. Camilla's father, who for a long time had been concerned and understanding about what he sensed of Camilla's feelings for Welhaven, was growing impatient, but Camilla wrote in a letter to one of her brothers that she would rather be an old maid at home in solitude than 'lose herself' — a statement which takes on the hard sheen of defiance when one knows that her own older sister had been married off against her will, like Sofie's sister Louise in the present book.

In the spring of 1837, Camilla wrote to her close friend Emilie Diriks: 'My love for Welhaven is extinguished. I love him no more.' Although patently untrue, in the light of later events, it showed a changed frame of mind, in which she was becoming psychologically ready to form a new attachment; this time to the man she married.

Peter Jonas Collett, whose father had been District Governor of Buskerud near Oslo, was born in 1813. Although half a year younger than Camilla Wergeland, he must have seemed older because of his steady temperament, gentleness, and cool, inquiring mind. Furthermore, he was used to managing his own life. At the time he and Camilla Wergeland were becoming acquainted, in January of 1838, he had just completed his law studies in Christiania while living on a small inheritance. He was a well-known and articulate member of Intelligenspartiet, the pro-Welhaven faction, and his falling in love with Henrik Wergeland's sister did not deter him from continuing his attacks on Wergeland. Nor did the familiar conflict of loyalties frighten the equally strong-minded Camilla.

Since they were all members of the same social circle, Jonas Collett was well aware of her earlier attachment to Welhaven, and in order to make certain of her feelings towards himself, he waited so long before proposing that Camilla, who was truly in love, became quite impatient and worried, especially after she overheard, through a half-closed door, Jonas Collett denying his love for her before a friend whose business he did not think it was. The shock of that moment formed the nucleus of one of the most crucial scenes in *The District Governor's Daughters*.

On 14 July 1841, Jonas Collett and Camilla Wergeland were married. All of Jonas Collett's understanding and personal equilibrium must have been called into service during his and Camilla's ten years of marriage. With her bouts of melancholy, and with her frustration as she sensed her unused talents pressing from within while the demands of housekeeping and motherhood clamoured from without, Camilla Collett probably was not the easiest soul-mate. Her husband did everything in his power to help and comfort her, and he encouraged her to write. She produced some elegant essays and short stories in which, amid fairly light and conventional entertainment, one can glimpse the darkly moving shapes of the ideas that were to possess her completely later in life.

Four sons gradually joined this unusual pair, whose personalities and way of life continued to cause comments in Christiania society — comments of which they were aware, but which only drew them more closely together. Jonas Collett saw to many of the details of running the household, such as hiring servants, shopping, etc., for which his wife had neither the talent nor the inclination. In this aspect of life she clearly endowed Sofie Ramm with attributes she did not herself possess. But despite her shortcomings as a housekeeper, she was an excellent hostess, who knew how to create an atmosphere of ease and comfort, and their home was a gathering place for Christiania's intellectual élite.

Camilla Collett was fully aware of her own failings and of the strength and support she drew from her husband. In her preface to *From the Camp of the Mutes* [*Fra de Stummes Lejr*], published in 1877, she reflected:

Then *he* came and gathered up the exhausted one; placed her by his side; lovingly examined the full extent of her condition and told her that here was much to be salvaged. Yes, *he* it was who gave courage to the timid one; who untied the silent mind and tongue; he it was who turned her into a real person. And when he had completed this, his foremost task here below, he was called away and left her behind alone. My husband, the best friend I ever had — alas, could I but meet you again! If only it were true, what they teach us! If only we could meet happier than back then — could I but undo my sin against you! Because my transgression against you was my failure to bring joy with me into your house.

Jonas Collett had been appointed Professor of Law at the University of Christiania in 1848. His rapidly growing family made it necessary for him to take on more and more outside work as well, and, being overworked and having never had a strong constitution, he succumbed to typhoid fever just before Christmas of 1851.

Camilla Collett had not led a conventional life up to this point, so it is hardly surprising that she refused to enter into the secluded, penurious widowhood expected of a woman in her position. She refused an offer of financial help from two of Jonas Collett's brothers, but she did accept an invitation to send her eldest son to the one uncle and her youngest son to the other. Then she sold her house and went to Denmark with her two remaining sons. Benterud surmises quite reasonably that Camilla Collett intended this as a temporary arrangement. Nevertheless, the pattern of travel abroad became fairly permanent, and although she constantly wrote to the two sons she had left behind in Norway, she lost contact with them, and they were later adopted by their uncles.

She had already begun *The District Governor's Daughters* before her husband's death, although he had told her he did not think the time was ripe in Norway for such a novel. She finished Part One in Denmark in the summer of 1853. Part Two was partly dictated from her sickbed in 1855 — something to bear in mind while reading her description of what makes a good nurse.

In allowing her heroine Sofie Ramm to fade into a useful, unselfish, respectable existence as the beloved wife of Dean Rein, never again to be upset by the presence of Georg Kold, Collett in some ways dealt her heroine a kinder fate than she herself had been allotted. When Welhaven eventually got married, it was to a friend of Camilla's, Josephine Bidoulac, by whom he had six children and with whom he led a sober, bourgeois life. It is tempting to assume that this later development lent colour to Margrethe's description, in *The District Governor's Daughters*, of what eventually happened to the man she loved until she died.

Well aware of the strain generated in their tiny social circle by her husband's former relationship with Camilla, Josephine promoted a reconciliation between her widowed friend and Welhaven in 1859. Collett reacted in her customary emotional manner, which Mrs. Welhaven in the end found rather hard to take, and in 1860 she wrote and informed Camilla Collett that Welhaven would no longer visit her. Josephine Welhaven's feelings were still running high in 1863. After an unveiling of busts of Welhaven and Wergeland (who had died in 1845), Welhaven went over and thanked Mrs. Collett, who was present at the reception and who had been very active in collecting funds for the busts. He chided her for not visiting him and his wife. This brief exchange reportedly led to a furious confrontation between the Welhavens on their return home that night. Collett resumed her gypsy existence that same year and had only occasional, though friendly, contact with Welhaven until he died in 1873, seven years after the death of his wife.

Besides nursing the memories of her two loves, Camilla Collett had become increasingly occupied with the growing struggle to improve the conditions of women — a struggle she herself had helped lift out of the cradle by publishing *The District Governor's Daughters*. The Cause eventually became an obsession with her, and even her staunchest admirers, then and now, agree that her literary style suffered in her subsequent work as the ferocity of her feelings increased. Collett thought that, above all else, women must be educated to see themselves in a different light, and that they must be free of economic bondage — political privileges would then follow of their own accord.

In 1854, just after the publication of Part One of *The District Governor's Daughters*, Norwegian women were given equal inheritance rights with men, thanks in no small part to Jonas Collett, who had helped draft that law before he died. In 1863, unmarried women above the age of twenty-five were declared legally competent. By 1875, Camilla Collett had helped form a Women's Reading Society, which is still alive and well in Oslo and which still prohibits male membership.

In 1882, women gained the right to take the *examen artium*, the series of final exams from the Gymnasium that also serve as entrance exams to the University. In 1884, women were given the right to obtain University degrees. That was also the year the Women's Cause Association was formed, and Camilla Collett was made its first honorary member. Recognition for her work in securing women's rights had begun to replace her reputation for social and literary bohemianism. As early as 1863, King Carl Gustaf of Sweden and Norway had presented her with the gold medal 'Literibus et artibus', but that had not been enough to change overnight the opinion of respectable, conservative Norwegians.

When the Women's Suffrage Association was formed by Gina Krog in 1885, the Cause might be said to have gained momentum. The first women's journal, *Nylænde* [Newly Cleared Land], was started in 1887, and in 1889 the old marriage vows dating from 1688, which declared that a wife should be subservient to her husband, were changed. In 1901, six years after Collett's death, Norwegian women gained limited rights to vote in municipal elections. They obtained full suffrage in 1913.

A woman with Collett's powers of observation and elephant-like memory could hardly have failed to be angered by what she saw around her, quite apart from the lacerating effect she felt the prescribed feminine ideal had had on her own life. Her own sister's having been married off against her inclination, while loving another man, was not an uncommon occurrence at the time. From the Eidsvoll parsonage, she had observed how roughly and brutally the farmers treated their wives, who nonetheless were required to put up a good front. Women of all classes were expected to ignore open unfaithfulness in their husbands.

If the lot of a married woman was often bad, the fate of a spinster was no better. In her old age, Collett told her biographer Bergsøe that to her, the central figure in *The District Governor's Daughters* was Miss Møllerup, the demented old spinster who had lost her mind because of her shame at having revealed her love for a cynical young cavalry officer. This statement is deeply significant if we regard Miss Møllerup as not only a terrifying illustration of spinsterhood and of the punishment to be expected from a breach of 'The Law of Femininity', but as an embodiment of the contrasts and conflicts that permeate *The District Governor's Daughters*.

As the Danish scholar Elizabeth Møller Jensen has pointed out, Sofie Ramm had to choose between two extremes of femininity — the roughshod practicality of Mrs. Ramm and the commitment to ideal love and self-sacrifice practised by Margrethe D. Furthermore, 'the author is . . . juxtaposing the ideal and the real, the poetic and the prosaic, the internal and the external. . . .' Indeed, much of modern Collett scholarship has centred on this tension between fantasy and reality. If we look at the fate of Miss Møllerup in this light, we see that the poor woman suffered all her life for the one moment when she came out of her carefree butterfly existence to act according to the reality of her own feelings. Failing to notice the artifice and deception of her lover and the rest of her surroundings, she was in turn punished by them for having acted 'unrealistically'.

Considering Collett's obvious preoccupation with the problems that are bound to arise in any attempt to define reality, I think it is quite possible that she, being familiar with classical literature, was influenced by

Book VII of Plato's 'Republic' when she made Sofie's cave the locus of key events and epiphanies in the girl's life. [1]

According to Plato, Socrates made Glaucon understand that people who had been enslaved in a dark cave all their lives, chained so that they could only stare straight ahead to where shadows were moving, and able to hear only the echo of sounds, not the sounds themselves, would have a confused concept of reality. They would assume that what they saw and heard was real, while in fact it was only a reflection of reality, perceived in ignorance through their restricted senses. If one of those slaves escaped into the world outside the cave, what he saw and heard would be so painfully different from what he had known that he would be apt to think of his remembered impressions as real and his new ones as unreal. And what would happen if the former thrall went back into the cave to escape the confusion outside?

> Men would say of him that up he went and down he came without his eyes; and that it was better not even to think of ascending; and if any one tried to loose one another and lead him up to the light, let them only catch the offender and they would put him to death. [2]

I think Collett tells us that Kold's brief liberation of Sofie's mind brought the girl nothing but pain because she had been a slave to her world's definition of reality for too long.

Not surprisingly, Collett's symbolic use of the cave has been subjected to intense scrutiny by Collett scholars.

Jorunn Hareide calls upon modern feminist scholarship in her analysis of this symbolism and in her agreements and disagreements with fellow Collett critics. Her point of departure is that a book written by a woman about how women perceive their lives, cannot be properly analyzed and understood by people who insist on bringing a purely male-oriented critical or psycho-analytical tradition to bear on it. If one wants to insist

---

[1] *Emancipation som lidenskab*, p.48. (The translation of the quotation is mine.)

[2]. B. Jowett, tr., *The Dialogues of Plato*. Random House, New York, 1937, vol.I, p.776.

that Collett's recurrent use of the cave constitutes erotic symbolism, then the cave should at least be considered a symbol for the uterus, in which a woman quietly and privately nourishes new life, and not a symbol for the vagina, an organ which — despite Freud's insistence that vaginal orgasm was a litmus test for female sexual maturity — is relatively unimportant to a woman's erotic life.

Hareide cites the work of Ellen Moers[3], who observes that woman writers rarely use vagina-metaphors, but that they use 'feminine landscapes' with a clear symbolic function. These landscapes, which also mirror women's deep-seated need for a private place away from male dominance, feature high elevations with calm, undulating lines and perhaps a brook — such as in the present novel. Furthermore, Sofie's cave landscape is mysterious, challenging and attractive as well as secret, and it contrasts sharply with her family's carefully cultivated, conventional garden. According to Moers and Hareide, such a juxtaposition is common in women writers.

Sigurd Aa. Aarnes argues that those pure and true children of nature, Kold and Sofie, both had the same personal involvement with the cave, and that by serving successively as a pleasurable retreat, a school room, a cathedral, a fortress and a tomb, the cave symbol accompanies the novel through its various phases.

The critic Otto Hageberg suggests that Sofie and Kold were also similar in their passive approach to life. He points out that all the real action in the novel is provided by secondary characters — Margrethe D., Lorenz Brandt and Mrs. Ramm. Furthermore, he argues that there is obvious authorial approval of the main characters' passivity, because Collett came from a social class in which passivity was an inseparable part of being well-bred and deserving of pure and true love. This argument runs counter to the thesis set forth by Elizabeth Møller Jensen that Sofie Ramm and Camilla Collett were anything but passive. Collett did not actually want to marry Welhaven, and Sofie saw no benefit in marrying Kold; both women therefore saw to it that their first love relationships came to nothing. Møller Jensen thinks her interpretation is a logical extension of the claim made by the eminent Collett scholar Ellisiv Steen (Camilla Collett's great-granddaughter) that Collett deliberately clung to

---

[3] *Literary Women.* New York, 1977

the suffering produced by her dead-ended affair with Welhaven because it fuelled her creativity.

As these samples from various analyses of *The District Governor's Daughters* suggest, there is no danger of unanimity among modern Collett scholars. Their approaches and conclusions are as complex as the author herself. On one thing only do the critics agree: Collett's art and her carefully nourished memories are inextricably woven together. Writing *The District Governor's Daughters* may have been a catharsis, but for the rest of her life she nevertheless continued to scrutinize and explain her relationship with Welhaven as well as her intentions in writing her novel.

Admirers of Karen Blixen's fiction and epistolary art will recognize much that is familiar in Collett's writing — the same effort to step back and view herself from some distance (aware of cutting a figure); the same sense that a privileged background was not necessarily a good preparation for life; the same painful self-analysis and rehashing of the past; and, most of all, the same creative use of personal tragedy. But Collett differs from Blixen in at least one respect: none of her work has been accessible in English until now.

Kirsten A. Seaver
Palo Alto, California, U.S.A.

Bibliography

Aarnes, Sigurd Aa., ed., *Søkelys på Amtmandens Døtre*. Universitets-forlaget, Oslo (1977)

Amundsen, Leiv, ed., *Camilla Collett, Optegnelser fra Ungdomsaarene*. Gyldendal, Oslo (1926).

Amundsen, Leiv, ed., Camilla Collett, *Breve fra Ungdomsaarene*. Gyldendal, Oslo (1930).

Amundsen, Leiv, ed., *Camilla Collett, Frigjørelsens Aar. Brevveksling med P.J. Collett og andre 1838-1839*. Gyldendal, Oslo (1932).

Amundsen, Leiv, ed., *Før Brylluppet. Brevveksling med P.J. Collett og andre 1840-41*. Gyldendal, Oslo (1933).

Amundsen, Leiv, ed., *Peter Jonas Collett. Studenteraar. Optegnelser og Refleksioner 1831-1838*. Gyldendal, Oslo (1934).

Amundsen, Leiv, 'Camilla Wergeland i Christiansfeld.' *Urd*, no.2, February 1956.

Benterud, Aagot, *Camilla Collett. En Skjebne og et livsverk*. Dreyer, Oslo (1947).

Bergsøe, Clara, *Camilla Collett*. Gyldendalske Boghandels Forlag, Copenhagen (1902).

Collett, Alf, *Camilla Colletts Livs Historie*. Gyldendalske Boghandel, Nordisk Forlag (1911).

Hageberg, Otto, *Frå Camilla Collett til Dag Solstad. Spenningsmønster i litterære tekstar*. Det Norske Samlaget, Oslo (1980)lde, Jorunn, Grottesymbolet nok en gang. En polemisk analyse av Amtmandens Døtre.' *Edda*, Spring 1980, pp. 1-13.

Møller Jensen, Elizabeth, *Emancipation som lidenskab. Camilla Colletts liv og værk. En læsning i 'Amtmandens Døttre'*. Rosinante, Charlotten-lund (1986).

Steen, Ellisiv, *Diktning og virkelighet. En studie i Camilla Colletts forfatter-skap*. Gyldendal, Oslo (1947)

Steen, Ellisiv, *Den lange strid. Camilla Collett og hennes senere forfatter-skap*. Gyldendal, Oslo (1954).

'Diktning og demokrati. Camilla Collett 150 år — Full kvinnestemme-rettighet 50 år — 1813-1913-1963'. *Samtiden*, Hefte I, 1963. Asche-houg & Co, Oslo.

Wergeland, Agnes Mathilde, *Leaders in Norway*. Books for Libraries Press, Inc., Freeport, N.Y. (1966) [First published in 1916].

The District Governor's

Daughters

Author's Preface to the Third Edition, 1879

When this story was first published, more than twenty years ago, it was something new of its kind up here. Our domestic novelists, especially our splendid Mauritz Hansen, had occupied themselves almost exclusively with conditions among the common people in small towns. A description of social conditions among the Norwegian upper classes after our political rebirth* was as good as untried.

The uproar this effort occasioned at that time must principally be ascribed to its unfamiliarity. Both publicly and privately, this uproar centred on two objections. The first of these, that it was 'a novel with an objective', is now going to die of its own accord, because in our day and age it is just about impossible to write a novel that does not have an objective, a purpose. The second objection, which still remains and which says that this novel is the product of a pessimistic view of life that sees dark shadows everywhere, might perhaps be excused with the thought that in our time it is all but unavoidable to take such a view. It is mainly to counter this latter objection that I have found it necessary to say a few preliminary words of explanation.

The story retains its original title, *The District Governor's Daughters,* but it might more appropriately have been called *The Daughters of a Country.* In a *considerably toned-down manner,* the story describes the fate awaiting the daughters of the more cultivated classes, especially in our isolated rural conditions. Naturally, time has mellowed these conditions

---

* Referring to Norway's separation from Denmark in 1814, leading to the signing of the Norwegian Constitution and to a brief period of independence prior to a union with Sweden which lasted until 1905. [*Translator's Note.*]

somewhat, especially because communications have improved. Nevertheless, during my long life spent under such conditions, I have experienced nothing but tragedies among the various families; nor, for as far back in time as stories can reach, have I heard tell of anything else. Some of those stories were of an order that could have earned them a place in *Sophocles* or *Shakespeare*.

I therefore repeat: whatever I have said along those lines in my small contributions to a domestic 'History of the Female Heart' has been told with all moderation and due consideration, because I suspected, rather than knew, that it would be risky to tear away too suddenly the veil hiding conditions that people had agreed to ignore with their eyes open. People's store of beautiful, tender feelings had migrated almost entirely to the world of fiction, especially to the tear-jerking novels of that period which, with worn covers and in horrible translations, were to be found on nearly every family's table. With this sort of reading people sought to refresh themselves after the stress and prosaic conditions of everyday life; it was the comfort of a young girl's heart just as surely as it was relied upon to furnish material for social entertainment.

One might almost say that when confronted with the realities under their very eyes, people's sensitivity was dulled to the exact degree that their temperaments had been stirred by aesthetic sensitivity. After all, they had known nothing else for generations. They had grown accustomed to seeing these conditions, with their crises and occasional eruptions, in a class with other phenomena of nature such as droughts, cloudbursts, or the first frost that mercilessly wipes out the last of the flowers in the garden.

As I said, there had as yet been very little attempt at mediating between those two life forces, fiction and reality, in order to vindicate the right of the latter by the powerful aid of the former. *Mrs. Gyllembourg's* novels, which so salutarily succeeded and to some degree replaced those foreign sensationalist novels, certainly helped form a transition to a better understanding of our own life. But notwithstanding their more familiar appeal, they were based on cultural conditions and other assumptions that were too remote to affect us as much more than pleasant entertainment. The present story may, therefore, without arrogance and with the simple justification that it is dealing with facts, consider itself a first attempt at awakening such an understanding.

It is impossible to describe the astonishment occasioned by this glimpse through 'our own windows' to the inside. Before the second part of the book was yet out, its characters and their fates had given rise to the most heartfelt sympathies. What would happen to them? Nothing very bad, it was to be hoped!

The second part was, therefore, less satisfying. It caused all the reluctance to face the light to which a truthful story can aspire as the best proof of — its truthfulness. 'So close to happiness, those poor young people, and yet! . . . *Imagine having it all come to nothing because of a shabby coincidence, which could so easily have been avoided!* It is really too bad!'

In this last appeal — that the story's tragic turn depends on a few 'improbable coincidences' — the public has concentrated its weightiest accusation. We find it repeated in all the reviews; even the most sympathetic one is not without its 'improbable coincidence'.

And in precisely this appeal the critics, whose innocence stems from their lack of familiarity with the field, have touched upon the true, tragic, central nerve of the story.

It is called *fate*, but I wonder if in this case one had not better refer to it as the *vagaries of fate*? For truly the rules governing our society have been ordered and accepted in such a way that a woman's fate depends on a mere chance, a pure coincidence about as predictable as the result of a drawing in the great, guaranteed State Lottery when one has a number.

Marriage and a family have been decreed the destiny of woman; the 'true, glorious task of her life', 'her sacred, sublime calling' as the clergy refers to it. 'Therefore it is not so much through the talents of the mind, but through those of the *heart*, of *feelings*, that she gains her importance and fills her place in society,' etc., etc.

Fine-sounding words! One forgets only that the woman herself is helplessly shackled while confronting this sublime calling. After all, most women are in no way given the opportunity to fulfil their destiny, and if they do, scarcely one time in a hundred does their lot turn out to be something that makes this glorious task in life truly glorious, while everything external urges the woman to employ every means in fulfilling her destiny in such-and-such a way and no other.

And now for a woman's *feelings*, which are understood to contain a certain stubborn inclination and willingness to assume life's burdens for *him* only and for nobody else, and to find those troubles absolutely divine. Of what significance to society is this strongest explosion of her soul? How is it used? What sort of tender respect does society accord this treasure, which supposedly is so highly prized?

If you who ask this question want a serious answer, you must ask it of *reality*, the one and only reliable, incorruptible witness. Let it tell you its sad secrets, all those unpleasant, troublesome things that the world seeks to forget by stubbornly denying their existence. Reality will tell you, poor young girl, if you are the one asking the question; it will tell you that this same, most powerful force of your soul is merely extolled in speeches and poems, where it is given such names as 'the treasure of your heart,' 'the source of life's renewal,' and so on, but that on its home ground this treasure is held in very poor esteem as a miserable thing you must hide, almost as if it were something shameful. You must hide it and suppress it until it has consumed itself or, perhaps — if you are lucky — yourself. Reality can tell you that even when you win the big prize, even when the most wonderful thing happens and your affection is *returned*, and one of those quiet, quivering relationships arises which has not yet been sealed by words or made indestructible by trust, then this same society will have at its disposal a thousand means to interfere and to upset things. You are still obliged to remain silent and let everything take its course; you dare not seek an explanation if those words have not been spoken and the pact has not been sanctioned by the congratulations of relatives and friends. You must then remain on your guard; everything is hanging by a thread; some idle gossip, a badly timed joke, a crude friend, a thin wall revealing something that should have been interpreted differently — in brief, the most *pitiful coincidence* intervenes as fate and has the power to crush your happiness on the spot, while you — *you must silently let it happen.*

Reality, my early, dark, taciturn confidant, has told *me* all this. It has whispered it into my ear during long, cold, lonely days and has anxiously made me promise not to reveal it. Whether I have been able to keep that promise, I leave it to my story to decide.

Part One

One day towards the end of the 'thirties, a traveller from the south had alighted at Storemo Inn in one of the country's northerly counties, where drivers and fresh horses were provided for travellers. It was just at dusk. The traveller, in the small guest room at the back of the noisy rural parlour, showed every sign of having fallen victim to the indisposition and restlessness endemic to such rest stops; feelings which in his case were exacerbated by the complete dreariness of a dark and rainy October day.

There had already been an hour and a half's delay in obtaining the coach and its driver, who had to be fetched from three miles away under bad driving conditions. Meanwhile, the traveller had tried every means commonly employed under such circumstances to fight off impatience and to get the minutes to pass. He had brought out the last of his provisions without being able to eat a bite; he had turned the pages of an interesting book without being able to gather his thoughts sufficiently to read a single page; and he had, surely for the seventh time, examined the pictures on the walls, ranging from the Four Seasons in brilliant rainbow colours to two copperplate engravings on either side of the mirror, offering identical representations of *Christianus VII Rex* in apparent protest against the old saying that there can be too much of a good thing. Finally, he stretched out on that hard piece of furniture which, under the guise of sofa, is sometimes offered as an extraordinary convenience and luxury at Norwegian coach stops, and he pretended to be asleep.

The innkeeper's old wife had entered meanwhile and taken out of a corner cupboard some glasses and cups, which she began to polish eagerly. In the course of this labour, for which she seemed to allow herself more time than her duties as hostess and landlady would appear to permit, she examined the reclining figure on the sofa with undisguised curiosity. The traveller was quite a young man, and despite his physical fatigue and foul humour, he must have made a favourable impression on the old woman, judging from the expression on her face.

'The ride is a long time in coming; it's got to come from a long ways off, it has,' the landlady finally broke out.

Georg Kold — that was the stranger's name — looked up reluctantly without answering.

Relieved at having made a beginning, she added: 'Beg pardon, might he be the Assistant expected at the District Governor's?'

A brief and gruff 'yes' frightened her not at all; on the contrary, it apparently aroused her curiosity further, and whether our traveller wished it or not, he had to engage in conversation with her. He took advantage of the opportunity to gather some information about the District Governor's family, with which she was minutely familiar; he inquired about the situation of the farm; etc. Finally, he asked if the District Governor had many children.

'Indeed he has children, he has a son.'

'But no daughters?'

'Oh yes, God bless us, he has daughters, too; now, there was Miss *Marie* and Miss *Louise*, what got married, one to the Assistant, the other to the house tutor what later took orders and got a parish of his own. Now there is just Miss *Amalie* left at home.'

'Is Miss Amalie grown up?'

'Grown up? Oh heavens, yes, she's grown up enough; she's just the age of *Lisbet-Marie*; they two went and prepared for confirmation together — Lisbet-Marie, she's my daughter, she is, and she'll be two-and-twenty this Michaelmas.'

'Is she handsome?'

'What's that, now?'

'Is the young lady beautiful?'

'I should think so,' said the woman. 'Oh yes, that's a lovely person, that! You should see her when she comes to church; it's like she gives off a light far and wide, that's how beautiful she is.'

'I'll be damned!' muttered the stranger and jumped up. — 'Is that the driver arriving? — That will be a dangerous business, that!' he added, pursuing his own train of thought.

'Oh no, the road is not dangerous; if you drive nice and careful, you'll do those six miles in two hours,' the woman soothed him. 'Yes indeed, there he is!'

The calculation of two hours made by the innkeeper's wife proved too sanguine, however. With the weightiness of a specialist, Kold's young driver assured him that there was no possibility of putting the road behind them in fewer than three hours. Anyone the least bit familiar with our roads in their muddy spring and autumn state knows that this was no exaggeration. When the passenger heard this, he placed himself in God's hands and handed the reins over to the boy. Darkness soon enveloped them, and there were no other sounds than the heavy, splashing steps of the horse and the wind soughing in the wet trees. Deprived of external distractions, Kold abandoned himself entirely to the flow of his thoughts. His natural confidence and his longing to reach the end of his journey began to yield to the dismal dread that overcomes a person about to step into completely unfamiliar surroundings, especially if doing so in a state of fatigue and depression. How good it then is to come to a mother or to a kind, considerate aunt! One dreads the first impression of an environment of which one is to become a part for quite some time, and one fears the impression to be made by one's own person. To be honest, we must confess that the former worry, of how the family would please him, occupied Kold far more than the latter. Whether he also had a small, secret fear of Miss Amalie, we dare not say.

Sooner than Kold had expected, they turned into the treelined drive leading down to the District Governor's farm. In the deep dusk, our traveller could still discern the outline of a large, irregularly shaped building. After the driver had replied to a question asked from a door or a window, there was some stirring in the house. A light appeared and disappeared now in one, now in another window, and Kold, who had stepped inside, heard doors being banged shut and what sounded like fleeing footsteps.

As no human being appeared, he took it upon himself to pass through yet another door which stood ajar, and he found himself in a room that gave the appearance of being the family's sitting room. On the table was an overturned sewing basket, and on the floor a piece of knitting, which a half-grown cat was working over to the best of its ability. A burning candle was left on the table, while another, left behind on a bureau, flickered dismally by the opened door.

The District Governor now entered the room. He was a man close to sixty, small and of slight build, with a nobly shaped face suffused with a hint of bad health, fatigue or sorrow — at first glance it was hard to determine which. His greying hair curled in graceful locks. His accent revealed his Danish origins as he welcomed the new member of his household and begged him excuse the absence of the ladies due to domestic business; however, he hoped that at the supper table, etc. He then bowed, and after he very meekly had succeeded in disentangling the knitting from the reluctant claws of the cat, he picked up his candle and in a kind voice invited Kold to follow him to the room reserved for him upstairs. The old man's cordial manner immediately made Georg Kold forget his first unpleasant impressions, and his relief was complete when he was alone in his handsome, cheerful room, where he found all the comforts a weary traveller might wish for.

About an hour later he was called downstairs to the supper table. When he entered the sitting room, he found two well-dressed ladies whom the District Governor introduced to him as his wife and daughter. The lady of the house began a graceful speech to ask his forgiveness, but Kold only half listened, because his attention was fixed on the younger lady. He found the dreaded beauty less dangerous than anticipated. She was nevertheless a rather handsome girl, tall and plump, and blonder than her mother, who was smaller and of slighter build. One might mistake them for sisters, though one might perhaps be forced to pronounce the latter the prettier of the two. Having thus set his mind at ease with something uncannily resembling disappointment, Kold ate with the very best appetite at the plentiful supper table, with which the family wanted to honour the new member of the household.

We feel free to leave him there for a while. In anticipation of the observations which he himself would be able to make with some accuracy only after a considerable passage of time, we want to acquaint the reader with a couple of individuals in his new surroundings. Upon one of them we are forced to dwell in some detail, because this person will play a major part in the story, and because an analysis of this person in some measure serves to describe all the others.

The District Governor's wife, *Mrs Ramm*, was in certain respects a lady not devoid of talent. She had read much, experienced much, and she talked of it all in language both graceful and fluent. If, in the process, she was able to work in one or another beautiful little maxim, she gladly did so.

She had been 'romantic' in her youth. For those of our younger generation who do not quite know what this means, we shall state briefly that it was a home-grown concept retaining little or nothing of its original meaning. It was romanticism tamed and trained for our prosaic bourgeois life. Robbed of soul and content, it reappeared in grimaces and empty formulae — not the poetry itself, only a surrogate, its cast-off finery handed down to housemaids and ladies' maids. The most commonplace people yearned to be romantic, and they played their parts with sometimes very disappointing results. In the case of Mrs Ramm, however, time and the practical exigencies of life — she was an accomplished, efficient wife — had mercilessly ground down this side of her nature, so that the traces showed up only in fragments, like the gilding on an old piece of furniture. Mrs Ramm was hospitable and extremely gracious towards guests. In the art of arranging her home, of receiving and entertaining her guests, she had no equal, and nobody tried to compete with her. She also enjoyed an extraordinarily high degree of esteem in their neighbourhood. People turned to her in all matters involving taste; no festive occasion of any importance was possible without her advice and assistance. No doubt ever arose that she was a lady of most superior talents and the most exquisite breeding. She was one of those who might live for another thirty years without losing a single ray from the halo surrounding them, just so long as they are not removed from the safe distance and light in which they are placed.

Given an opportunity to watch her more closely, however, an impartial observer would soon discover the real nature of her breeding. It lacked a core. The graciousness with which she charmed strangers did not come from within; it was not the warmth of a benevolent temperament spilling over to include even the poorest and least important guest. It was a form of holiday vestments which she put on and took off as the occasion demanded. Such was mostly the case with her other enticements as well. Her exterior corresponded in a curious manner to her interior. Not many ladies of Mrs Ramm's age could pride themselves on being so successfully preserved. Mrs Ramm had a slight and delicate figure, which might still be observed with pleasure in a dance when, on grand occasions, she added to the festivity by opening the ball. She had a rich head of hair, lively blue eyes with a hard expression, and a blooming complexion, whose original rosy hue had by this time solidified into a standard red rather like the colour of bricks. She knew how to make the most of her appearance by dressing in a manner both tasteful and expensive when she was out among people. Her youthfulness was of the crystallized kind that makes one suspect it results from a chilling and a desiccation of the soul that act as preservatives against life's painful impressions. For when all is said and done, it is common knowledge that a truly soulful woman does not attain her full beauty save at the expense of her physical beauty. Only through such a blanching process can she obtain that expression which touches the soul, because it simultaneously tells of struggle and victory.

In her domestic life, Mrs Ramm was treasured as a woman who made her surroundings extremely happy. Her husband and children were fond of her in the manner of good people — out of necessity, out of the needs of their hearts. The District Governor had fallen in love with her, and, like thousands in similar situations, he had won her, and married her, without inquiring much about her love. 'It will no doubt come afterwards.' For this mistaken notion, that 'it will no doubt come afterwards,' he had paid with his prematurely grey hair and with that growing flaccidity of character which befalls men who allow themselves to be governed by a nature less pure than their own. His gentle, loving temperament had wrestled in vain with his wife's desire to shine and to command. One might blame him for not having resisted forcefully enough the unhappy marriages of his two eldest daughters. Yet he loved his children tenderly, and he might still follow those remaining at home with a look in which there was a fervent prayer for their future.

Not until Georg Kold had partially satisfied his appetite did he notice that the number of people at the table had been increased by one more besides his pupil *Edvard*, namely a half-grown girl. She was wearing the unbecoming clothing common to girls of her age; clothes that were, moreover, less than well-fitting and contrasting sharply with those of the two ladies. The girl did not participate in the conversation at all, but stared down into her plate, from which she occasionally glanced up with a look that was both shy and inquiring. After they rose from the table, she disappeared. Kold asked about her. As if he somewhat regretted the fact that the little one had not been introduced, the District Governor spoke up and said:

'That is *Sofie*, our youngest daughter. She is a little shy, but a good child. I want to ask you, Mr Kold, to look after her education a bit. There is little opportunity for her to learn anything here, and we have always been against sending our children away. You will find her somewhat neglected, but I hope the desire to learn will come. It is my wish that she share the morning lessons with Edvard.'

Kold bowed in reply and said nothing.

Having thus introduced the reader to the person who plays one of the major parts in the pages to come, we will leave Kold in his new position and allow two and a half years to pass. One winter's day, towards evening, we find him again in his room. He is not alone. Seated on the sofa is a short, powerfully built, swarthy, somewhat pockmarked man with piercing, not particularly friendly eyes. He is dressed in a casual, almost shabby travelling suit, and from a huge meerschaum bowl he is letting out immense clouds of smoke. This man is a doctor, and his name is *Müller*. At one time he had exercised great influence over Georg Kold. He had been his mentor and discharged him to the University, and, what was more, he had been Kold's friend when the latter was a friendless youth alone in the unfamiliar capital. Thus a relationship had grown up between them that, on the one side, was founded on the seniority of age and on the force of personality, and gratitude on the other. Of course, a few years had passed since that time. Müller was now on his way to another district, where he had secured a position, and as his route took him right past the District Governor's, he had paid his former pupil a surprise visit.

The room in which the two friends were sitting was almost too handsome for a house tutor in the country. As far as one could still discern through the tobacco smoke, all the articles belonging to Kold himself — a book cabinet, hunting instruments, a few art objects — were valuable and beautiful, and the somewhat antique furniture which at that time had not yet seen its renaissance, and which in the country tended to be pushed upstairs into bedrooms and storage rooms, was particularly well suited to the other articles in the room. Everything was in complete harmony with the person inhabiting the room. Even in his everyday dress, Kold's appearance revealed a meticulousness which is not very common among our people.

Müller let his eyes slide about the room in a probing manner and finished by measuring Kold himself with his small, penetrating eyes. Finally, he said with ironic resignation:

'I observe that in one respect, at least, you have remained the same.'

'Do you think so?' said Kold with a smile. 'That is certainly a good sign, dear Müller. You know it will never do to meet an old friend in a changed form. I really do still have the same incurable disgust for dirty linen and uncombed hair as six years go. I have once and for all given up any claims to originality in such matters.'

'Well, suit yourself! Just you dress up and perfume yourself for the alluring troll women and dairy wenches up here. To me it matters not at all, just so you don't do anything stupid. It *truly* gives me joy that you are comfortable. As you probably know, I thought it rather a desperate act on your part to go off to the country. I felt really uneasy when I saw the farm. "Good Lord, I wonder how things may be going here!" I said to myself. Now then, my poor Byron, are those lordly whims beginning to leave you? Do tell me in every particular how you really are.'

'Well, I assure you: much better than I had expected. I have seen for myself that a busy life is the very healthiest one for someone like myself, who has lived for some time in all sorts of tumult and confusion. As you probably know, I represent a sort of dualism here in this place; I am — that is to say, I was — both a tutor to the son and daughter and an assistant in the old man's office. In a way with which you perhaps will scarcely credit me, both forms of occupation have truly interested me.'

Müller shook his head. 'That is all very well, but in the long run it will not suffice. It is not really for you. It is also very fatiguing always to be doing the same thing. Youth needs to tussle with the world — it wants company, news. . .'

'I do not miss that. What is good about living in the country is precisely that there is none of the restlessness and self-consumption that constitutes part of life in a big city. In the out-of-doors I find enough to counteract the sort of fatigue you speak of. I wander about hunting and fishing, although hunting and fishing are the least of my intentions. Often I walk ten or twelve miles into the mountains with a book in my pocket. You cannot imagine how fresh and rejuvenating this life close to nature is; sometimes it spurs you on and awakens your spirit, and at other times it is as refreshing as a bath. After such trips up in the mountains, it is extremely restful and pleasant to carry on my usual occupations down on the friendly farm. Naturally, my relationship with the family also contributes to this feeling.'

'Ah, your relationship with the family,' Müller interjected, 'Do tell me a little about that.'

'With great pleasure,' replied Kold, unaware of the watchful look Müller at that moment fixed upon him. 'Edvard, my pupil, is a competent boy, although badly spoiled by his mother. It has been a pleasure to read with him. He is now finished and took his qualifying exams for the University this past autumn. Old Ramm is a thoroughly good, kind man. He treats me like a son, and I think he is as fond of me as if I really were his son.'

'Really!' exclaimed Müller. 'He is as fond of you as if you were his son! Is that so! Well, well! That is, by God, very nice of the man. Is he not Danish by birth?'

'Yes, but of Norwegian descent. The circumstances of his life in Copenhagen were most interesting. God knows what he wanted to do up here. What privations to have to teach oneself to put up with! His innermost being is, however, just as fresh to this day; in his appearance only do I suppose he is somewhat altered. He mostly stays in his den and is what is usually called unsociable, though he is far from inaccessible; towards me he is always very friendly and communicative.'

'No wonder! The poor man has finally met a cultivated person with whom he can talk. Your predecessors, however, if I know the species right, have been unfortunate, ignorant louts, have they not?'

'I almost think so. There has been a succession of such persons in the house who have functioned partly as Assistants, partly as tutors to the children, and whom the old man seems to shy away from mentioning. Yet it would appear that the ladies of the house have taken more pleasure in them. A couple of them even married daughters of the house.'

'A couple of them married daughters of the family! Bless us, my poor Georg, how many are there left of these daughters?'

'Only two,' replied Georg with a smile, 'that is to say, in reality just one; the other one is a child and has not been at home for a long time.'

'Only two and in reality just one,' Müller repeated. 'Oh yes, one is, by God, more than enough to cause misfortune. This misfortune has already taken place. You, my poor boy, are of all people the least capable of avoiding it.'

'Finally! There we have it!' said Kold and laughed out loud. 'Now it is my turn to say: "I see you are yet unchanged in one respect." I willingly believe that you would condemn all of humanity to celibacy if you could, leaving it to the good Lord to renew the race when the present generation threatens to die out. When I now say to you,' he continued in a tone of voice that showed little hope of convincing his opponent, 'when I now say to you that there is not the slightest hint of any particular relationship between Miss Amalie and myself, will you not then believe me? And if I have happily weathered the danger for two years now, I really do think I am safe hereafter.'

'Two years, of which you have spent the one travelling and in Christiania on behalf of the District Governor, while Miss Amalie probably spent the second one in visits to her mother's sisters. Now she has returned home, so that the novel may begin. Just you watch out — when next I come, you will have the noose around your leg, and farewell future, farewell all my dreams that at some point you would amount to something! Oh Georg, my Georg, you are done for!'

Müller had jumped up and was measuring the floor in long paces, while Georg in resigned anticipation assumed a comfortable position on the sofa.

'Good Lord, do have a look at her before you pass judgment. You have not seen her; she was out when you arrived, as you know.'

'Oh fiddlesticks; looks have nothing to do with the matter. She is one of the daughters of Eve, that is enough. Do you really not know that there is a power that is stronger than all will, all good intentions, all sensible conclusions? That is the power reposing in daily intercourse under one roof in the country — what is called "domestic warmth" in good Norwegian; a feeling of being at home. Don't you come and tell me about your mystical harmony ordained by nature, which pulls the souls towards each other with irresistible force! Don't talk to me of your predestinations and whatever nonsense it is all called. That has nothing to do with the matter. In this case, intelligence, will and taste cease to have power over a man, and he falls victim to narrowminded fate, the shabbiest of chances. She is ugly — in a short while you will find that some sweet irregularity of features is much more piquant than the cold features of regular beauty. If she is somewhat well along in years, you will dwell upon the advantages of maturity, and if she is a callow schoolgirl, you will make her into a Psyche. She has red hair — you cannot comprehend your past liking for brunettes and begin at last to see how beautifully her Raphaelite tresses reflect the light. Oh yes, you laugh, you laugh so sagely, so pityingly, as if you cannot understand how a thoughtful person can become a dreamer tilting at windmills. You suppose that one may take those tender, budding feelings and preserve them hermetically, like asparagus and green peas, until the time comes when you have better use for them? Don't make yourself believe that, my friend. Unfortunately, airtight containers have not yet been invented for such use. Whether you like it or not, those feelings will assume the shape of a *Hanne*, *Mine*, or *Thrine*; she will steal into your dreams at night, and her voice, which may be the only pleasant sound in the house, will echo in your lonely sitting room. You do not know, my dear Georg, how many unfortunate liaisons have been formed in this manner; how they swell the number of the many God-forsaken marriages in this country. Have you anywhere else heard of so many ill-considered engagements, so many broken ones! — Oh, if only they would break up again! — but a crazy system of duty prohibits the majority from doing what constitutes their only salvation under such circumstances. 'Domestic warmth' is a pure national disaster; it can only exercise its power in a society such as the Norwegian one, with its vast unpopulated stretches. It is as Norwegian as leprosy and hangovers. And the engagements that result from such insanities, those beery intoxications of the heart, are they anything more than a form of *delirium tremens*, the zenith of that madness?'

After a long pull at his pipe, which during this long speech had begun to go out, Müller continued in a dull voice:

'As you know, I myself fell victim to it. After my father's death had robbed me of all means of subsistence, I accepted, in my moment of need, a post as tutor in the county of North Trondheim. There was only one grown daughter in the family. I saw her with the eyes of inexperience — I was at that time younger than you are now — and it was not long before the situation began to take effect. Everything, indeed, conspired to it in the most peculiar manner. She had a sickly dragon of a mother; one of those vampires who literally sustain life by feeding on the lives of their daughters. The poor girl had never known the meaning of youth. Her mother did not permit her to stir from her side by night or by day. Therefore, I began with pity. In addition, the miserly witch who was their housekeeper had to slice the bread so thin and mix so much chicory with the coffee that *Bolette*, when it was her week, could show me all the more consideration. Nothing is more easily bribed than the appetite of a twenty-year-old. As far as my beloved's looks are concerned, I just wish to remark that the only young person in the house was a cross-eyed housemaid. I had not at that time acquired any special interest in tenotomy as a cure for strabismus, and I therefore had no particular reason to find that sort of eyes peculiarly interesting. In brief, the maid was cross-eyed, but Bolette was not. We then became engaged, and I remained so in good faith for a whole year after I had returned to Christiania. You know my principles in such matters. One must be as merciless as a surgeon. One must risk the operation, even if the patient might die in the midst of the pain.'

Kold remarked that it was not possible to set forth principles in such matters. In many cases a breaking-off would be barbarism. 'And Bolette, what happened to her later?'

'Yes, you see, she really did die from it,' said Müller, turning towards the oven to knock out his pipe. 'This tobacco is not the tobacco one buys at country stores, because with that I am familiar; that is precisely the weak side of rural shopkeepers. Where does the old man get it from? — It was a sad story,' he went on, sounding as if something had lodged in his throat. 'A breaking-off is a breaking-off, I thought; therefore I wrote my letter without embellishments; it was brief and easily understood. It was too sudden for her, poor thing! One must wait long for a letter that far north. She fell ill at once and died four days later without having spoken a word. Her mother wrote me a devil of a letter. Poor Bolette, it was better that way. Yes, it was, by Jove. I might have made her life miserable. She was such a gentle sort. At any rate, it was the salvation of me. When that business was over, I was thoroughly cured of any infatuation and whatever else all those kinds of youthful follies are called. With redoubled energy, I went to the hospital to take care of my business, and with scarcely the necessities of life I completed my medical studies. I have achieved what I never dreamed of. Whenever I succeed in saving a human life, I think that the gods in their mercy will accept it as a propitiatory offering for my poor Bolette.'

After a pause, Kold said: 'It is true enough that habit and chance proximity help form many unfortunate liaisons in our country, but, frankly, I think your own misfortune has given you a lop-sided view of the matter. You exaggerate the danger. You cannot know how many have escaped it.'

'Yes, I can,' replied Müller laconically. 'During a period of almost ten years, only five have escaped the danger, among the approximately thirty instances I have had a chance to observe.'

'Five escaped the danger!' said Kold, somewhat losing his composure. 'And by what miracle?'

'I can tell you that as well. In a couple of cases the disparity in age was too great; in a third *she* was stoop-shouldered; in a fourth *he* was saved in a strange way. Twice in a row, just as he was about to declare himself, he fell victim to an inflammation of the throat, and, as he is a fatalist, the fear of dying prevented him from making a third attempt. The fifth knight who survived the fairytale with the dragon was that *Nielsen* who became curate to the vicar in S. He was a bit of an original, as you probably remember; I had given him a bit of warning beforehand. He and a niece of the vicar's, a very beautiful girl who lived in the same house, began to detest each other in earnest, and by the time he left, they were practically at war.'

'Well, then, there you are!'

'But later they met each other in Sandefjord, and now they are married. I have just stood up as godfather to their first.'

'You must have kept an account book of all this,' said Kold, astounded.

'You are right, a small notebook would not be such a bad idea. So far I have kept the tally in my head, although the number is forever increasing. It is now up to — let me see — twenty-nine! Twenty-nine victims of the epidemic in fewer than ten years! I do not know what fatal notion tells me that you are to be the thirtieth.'

Kold laughed whole-heartedly. 'My dear, good Müller, do look at me. Do I look like a moonstruck, languishing knight?'

'No, you look well. Now you look less like Byron than you did before, when you were thinner and had acquired that sort of melancholy pallor. You have now become what you were when I first knew you. Then you were happy and radiant as a young faun. Later, you got into a sphere where I could not be bothered to follow you. But it was not difficult to see the gradual change in you.'

'Georg,' continued Müller, who noticed the discouraged expression of the other's face, 'you do know that I am not driven by curiosity in this matter. As profoundly as I am capable of taking an interest in anyone, I take an interest in you. God knows why, really! Perhaps because you are so different. Now you must tell me without reservation what you were up to a couple of years ago, and what drove you up here — now that we seem to have reached a confidential mood. This friendly room and the sound of that splendid old stove have really put me in a sentimental frame of mind.'

'Another time,' said Kold, visibly depressed. 'Let us not spoil these brief hours by ripping open old, destructive stories.'

'Another time is a tease, but — as you wish. If you want to put it in writing, so much the better, though try to do it briefly and without any extra coloration. As you know, I am no friend of lyricism.'

'Write? I write letters?' said Georg, laughing. 'A confession, in other words! I dare not promise you that, Müller.'

Here a maidservant interrupted them, announcing that the gentlemen were expected at the supper table.

Müller looked at his watch. 'A blessed custom here in the country! We are allowed the most unencumbered freedom for three or four hours, and the reminder of other people's existence intrudes only in the form of the fully laid table. We shall devote the rest of the evening to the family; besides, I wish to take a good look at Miss Amalie.'

Meanwhile, Kold had changed out of his jacket into a tailcoat and was gracefully tying a black cravat. 'Yes, you see,' he said in a somewhat embarrassed manner as he caught Müller's satirical expression, 'the District Governor always dresses for supper.'

In the doorway he turned and said in a serious voice: 'Perhaps I shall write to you some time. Until then, you may believe what you choose . . . that I am an enthusiast, the sort of immature boy as — the Georg you once knew.'

The next day, when the two friends again were together in Kold's room, their conversation stopped at the sound of a guitar or clavichord downstairs. They listened for a while.

'As far as that is concerned,' said Müller with a gesture of his hand in the direction of the sound, 'my mind is at rest. With her, you could remain for ten years under the same roof with no damage done.'

'It is not that she is not pretty enough or young enough; as I have said before, that actually matters very little. But something separates you and her which I had not taken into consideration. You are a child of our time; she is not. She is 'romantic', as people used to say in my youth. She bears the mark of an epoch of which you know nothing, but which is also often

44

called the period of Lafontaine, because it employed all manner of false and high-flown ideals which that author in particular made fashionable. Suddenly, a more judicious period arrived and created divisions within families. That is why older people now often walk around the pond like anxious hens and watch the ducklings frolicking in an element that is quite unfamiliar to them, and they cannot comprehend what sort of young they have hatched. But Amalie does not belong among them. She is her mother's daughter, one of the 'well behaved' children. I saw it at once in her manner of dress and in the way she looked up — like this! — and I became completely convinced when the conversation turned to one of her favourite writers. I am willing to swear that she has a favourite lamb, a favourite dove, or some such, and also that she is enamoured of "eternal, inviolable faithfulness", which one is compelled to extend to any lout who happens to be around.'

Kold wanted to contradict him, but secretly he had to admit to himself that the description was accurate.

'Miss Amalie is a thoroughly good, decent girl, despite a few notions derived from romantic fiction. The two of us have long had a clear understanding of each other. Someone must have described me to her as a sort of black traitor to her weak, unprotected sex, for in the beginning she was obviously ill at ease in my company. If we by chance were left alone together in the drawing room, a maidenly confusion would overpower her, and a couple of times when I happened to meet her out-of-doors, she let out a small scream and took off into the forest. But after a while I suppose she knew she had nothing to fear from me, and her manner became more trusting.'

'Finally,' Müller interrupted him, 'it was transformed into a sisterly, confidential relationship.'

'Exactly so; for a long time she confided to me all her musings about life and about the joys and sufferings which moved her, but I suppose I did not satisfy her in that role, because little by little her confidences ceased; she again became secretive and taciturn.'

'And now she finds you unbearable . . . enough about her. But you mentioned another one. Where is she? How old is she?'

'She is in Denmark with an uncle.'

'What does she look like? Is she coming back soon? You have as yet told me nothing about her.'

'There is not much to tell, either — of good, that is. That child has made my life rather difficult. She has practically done me harm. I was quite pleased when she left.'

'Dear me, harm! But in what way?'

'It is hard to say. She was a strange creature. I was so unfortunate as to have to teach her. May God preserve me! If anything in the world was ever a labour of patience, it was reading with her!'

'She was stupid, then?'

'Stupid?' said Kold, lost in thought. He looked at Müller absentmindedly.

'Well, yes, I asked whether she was stupid or intelligent?'

'That is the problem, you see, whether she was or was not. One could split one's head open about her. At times I fancied she had excellent abilities, but one usually was forced to believe she was not very gifted. She learned her lessons so poorly and appeared so ignorant that it was enough to bring me to despair. When I thought that perhaps she had trouble learning by heart, I tried with all sorts of oral lessons, but in vain; they left her just as absent-minded and inattentive. She seemed only to wait for the moment when she could leave like a puff of wind.'

'In your place, I should simply have excused myself from the job.'

'That was what I wanted to do as well. I wanted to tell her father that she was learning absolutely nothing, that I could think of nothing at all in defence of continuing the lessons, but I did not quite have the heart to do it. He simply had no idea. Because things had gone so brilliantly with Edvard, he had boundless faith in me. And then — and then, something drove me to exert myself to the utmost. One day she came to me and said she had such a desire to learn English. So be it, I thought; now I can try my patience on English for once. But there I was wrong again. She acquired that language in an unbelievably short time and with an ease that surprised me. Otherwise, everything went on as before. It was impossible to figure out whether I was dealing with stupidity, or unwillingness, or what.'

'The devil — should one not be able to figure that out?'

'Whenever I came down into the living room, there was always some to-do. Her mother was forever complaining of her. "I have succeeded in raising my other daughters to become nice, cultivated girls, but I have no control over Sofie." Old Ramm, however, is very fond of this daughter.

"My Sofie is somewhat wild, but I'm sure it will pass," he said. Towards me she exhibited a mistrust bordering on aversion.'

'One day, shortly before she left, I reproached her for this, and her reply then became a fresh riddle to me. At that moment she did not look like a child, and I was the one who grew embarrassed.'

Müller had listened to this account with a rather innocent expression. The last statement Kold had let fall so carelessly was nevertheless sufficient to awaken his indefatigable friend's teasing, although the latter tried to hide serious concern.

'There you are, thank you very much, now I know the lesson by heart. Watch out, here comes the metamorphosis — Nature's ancient, Heaven-sent, common, strange trick. The following day, as the wise pedagogue meditates over a new method of treatment for incorrigible, headstrong children, the door opens, and "mit schüchternen, verschämten Wangen sieh't er die Jungfrau vor sich steh'n"; oh yes, I, too, have read Schiller once.'

'That may well be,' said Kold, half laughing and half annoyed, 'but I was not at all so fortunate as to experience a metamorphosis. Right afterwards, by the first steamer, she went to Copenhagen to a sister of Mrs Ramm's — the wife of Cabinet Minister D., and there she has been ever since. Bon voyage! It is as if the mischievous house elf has left us; since then we have had peace in the house.'

'But by the next steamer the mischievous house elf will return. Do be on your guard, my boy, against this elf, which assumes many guises and many names.'

Müller's last words, as he grasped his friend by both arms, were: 'Georg, remain on your guard! Do not do anything stupid!'

* * *

Müller had left. Kold's first sensation was relief. His former mentor had acted with his customary arrogance and had claimed the confidence of former days, which Kold was no longer able to give him, but which he did not have the courage to withhold from him.

Though brief, this visit left marks on our friend's life of which he was unaware himself. The idyllic satisfaction he had considered himself so fortunate in possessing, had received a serious jolt. A sense of restlessness had crept into his mind. At times, his mind was drawn towards his earlier life, the memory of which had been laid bare in his talks with his old acquaintance, while at other times he was seized by a fear that Müller might actually have been right, and that the voluntary exile which suited him so well at the moment might nonetheless be dulling his spirit and preventing his further development. Through the prism of distance, the fresh events of the day appeared much more important than he might have found them up close. He felt a need for a livelier existence.

In such a mood he was pacing the floor in his room one afternoon, when the District Governor entered with a letter in his hand. Of course, Georg had noticed that Sofie's letters home were a source of extraordinary joy to the old man. On days when they might be expected, he showed an impatience resembling that of a most ardent lover. Even so, he had never told *Georg* directly about any of their contents; just this once his fatherly pride had not been able to resist the temptation. This he must show his dear Kold, in order that he might share his joy.

Kold was absolutely astounded by the letter, and he was seized by an emotion close to discomfort. He could not explain to himself just what confused him so. It was the letter in its entirety — its tone, its language, which had none of the turgidity and shapelessness so characteristic of someone in transition from schoolgirl to adult. Its singular language conveyed a perceptiveness that revealed a desire for a better grasp of the most profound causes and effects of life's phenomena, at the same time that Sofie's actual experiences seemed of little importance to her. She expressed herself as briefly as possible about her diversions, acquaintances, and whatever else her stay in her distinguished aunt's house might encompass, and then her remarks usually related to some observations she wished to make, and which again were not those of a young girl with a zest for life.

This understanding, this language, these profound remarks — where did she get them? Did studying, thinking, form their basis — was it *intuition*? Georg was tempted to believe in this mysterious ability of the female soul to acquire through an inner vision what men must learn by rote. Nevertheless, while the old father was merely revelling in the heartfelt devotion to himself and to her home that suffused Sofie's letter, to Kold it seemed that her letter was veiled in something sad and melancholy, which had the same effect upon her former teacher as a light morning mist over a landscape, surprising a passer-by.

Could it be Sofie who had written it? That strange child from the summer farm in the mountains, from the school room — that living test of his patience? He felt he could see her still, sitting there with her staring, abstracted eyes fixed on the clouds or on the road outside, while he was eagerly trying to explain something to her. He felt rather ashamed when the District Governor slapped his shoulder in a hearty manner and cried gaily:

'Well, does not your old pupil do you proud? Now, I also recognize the part you have played in this, Kold!'

It was an unmitigated pleasure to Kold to find the eagerness with which Sofie pursued her music, in which she had obtained the best teachers. On this subject she sometimes expressed herself joyfully, showing her delight in the art, and at other times with a dejection that sprang from a deeper source than mere dread of technical difficulties.

The District Governor's visit gave Kold just what he at that moment needed; it gave his vaguely flowing thoughts an object to which they could attach themselves. He could not get the letter out of his head, and in his mind he began to run through all his encounters with the peculiar creature who had written it. Among them there was many a detail he instinctively had kept from Müller, and which now appeared to him in a completely new light.

Kold had an older friend, a woman, with whom he had at a certain stage in his life exchanged thoughts about many things that were important to him. To this friend he had promised to send some little account of his present life. So far, that promise had not been fulfilled, and he had often taken himself to task for this. He had never thought anything good enough for the purpose. 'Now I shall try,' he said; 'I shall gather all these bits and pieces, and when I see them on paper, I shall be able to tell if it is something I can offer *Margrethe*.'

* * *

FROM GEORG'S NOTES TO MARGRETHE

This child confused me to a high degree. At times, my patience was at an end, and I remonstrated with her for being so lazy and inattentive. Then she might look at me so humbly, so beseechingly, that I could not say another word. Another time she might be so indifferent that it was as

49

if none of it concerned her. 'Perhaps she simply does not like me,' I thought. 'Downstairs, among her family, her personality will unfold in a more natural manner. There I might be better able to observe her.' But she was hardly ever to be seen downstairs. 'It is almost impossible,' said her mother, 'to get Sofie to sit still inside with a dainty piece of work. But so long as she may be on her hands and knees in the garden, digging in the soil and planting, or helping the dairy maids feed the animals, she is well pleased. Just consider what happened to me the other day. The Bishop's wife stopped by quite unexpectedly, and she asked about Sofie. I hastily got her in from the shed, where she was shaking flax along with the tenant farmers' wives, and I told her to change her clothes. She then entered, in her best dress, indeed, but with her hair full of chaff, and with such a desperate face! You may just imagine how pleasant that was!'

I heard such stories often. One day when the cowherd was taken ill, she begged to be allowed to take his place. In order to comprehend how she was allowed to spend an entire day in the wild and lonely outlying fields, you have to be familiar with the informality with which children are raised in the country. That was why I practically never saw her except at the table, where she would sit in silence. If she did say anything, her mother always seemed to believe it was something stupid, or that is was contrary to the good manners she sought to instill in her children. At such times, Amalie treated her with a protectiveness in which there was a mixture of silliness, precociousness and worry. I always had a great desire to defend Sofie in her petty conflicts with her family, and I tried by many a sign to make this obvious. She never would understand it. —

The cave was probably her favourite spot, her true refuge. For that reason, I seldom went there, although this spot held a great attraction for me as well. But Sofie did have a sort of proprietary right to it, and a couple of times when I had happened upon her out there, her expression had left me in no doubt that the surprise was little to her liking. All the same, once when I was coming down from the valley, I felt an urge to climb out on the cliffs that form this strange cave, because I wanted to see how it was closed off on the upper side. There, through a crack, I saw Sofie stretched out on the ground, immobile on the floor of the cave. Alarmed, I ran down, thinking that something might have happened to her. She was asleep, exhausted from her labour. Next to her lay a shovel that seemed much too heavy for her frail strength. Her face, garishly illuminated from above, was suffused with an expression of sorrow, which

I had never seen before. It came from the depth of her soul; in sleep alone could she look like that or, at any rate, maintain such an expression. Some faces are peculiar in that they assume, during sleep or a deathlike stillness, a beauty one does not otherwise perceive — perhaps because they have not acquired the harmonious expression that goes with it. For the first time, I realized that Sofie's features were regular and pretty. Seeing her head resting on a big book was an even greater source of wonder to me. It was not one of her usual books; I could see that at a glance. But what was it, then, that she was interested in reading? This was at a time when our lessons were in a particularly sad state. It was impossible to find out what book it was, because I did not want to wake her up. She encircled the book with her arms as if she wanted to protect her secret. —

Her distrust of me was boundless. Once only did I succeed in overcoming it and bringing her into a real conversation.

I was out hunting in the mountains on whose southeastern knee the farm's little summer dairy is located. I walked that way in hopes of seeing one or another member of the family, who often visited up there; at least I might take a rest on the beautiful cliff and get a little something to eat from the dairy maid. Even long before I reached the summer dairy farm, I heard a strange, echoing music, which sometimes sounded near and sometimes distant. At last I was able to distinguish two female voices taking turns calling home the cattle. But what a voice one of them was! Vibrant, full and pure as a bell, jubilantly strong and yet flexible, it echoed in the farthest ridges and filled every corner of the silent, forested depths below. I was now close enough to see the meadow around the summer farm without being noticed myself. It was Sofie who was singing. Who would have thought that this frail girl had such a Doomsday voice? Of course, *Marit* was teaching her, but it was obvious that she regarded her pupil with a sort of proud surprise. Attracted by all this calling, the tired and well-fed cattle were approaching the gate. Sofie ran down to them and climbed up on the gate, and while she patted the big, white lead cow on the other side, she sang yet another bit of an old folk song with that oddly flexible and vibrant voice, which assumed a tinge of comic melancholy as it was addressed to the cow. I was unable to suppress a shout of approval as I stepped out from my hiding place. Sofie turned towards me a face etched with the deepest alarm and made a movement that frightened all the cows into a hasty flight down towards the forest again, and she disappeared with them. I took off after her just as speedily. My dog picked up her trail, and after criss-crossing briefly through the thickest part of the forest, I found Sofie sitting on a rock sloping very steeply east towards the valley. She did not stir; she scarcely seemed to notice my sitting down beside her. In an uncertain manner, I began:

'What is the meaning of this flight, dear Sofie? How can my astonishment at your singing scare you so? Don't be so shy, so mistrustful. Is it so strange that your voice astounds me?'

Instead of answering, she burst into bitter crying.

'I don't understand you.'

'Just promise me that you won't mention it at home.'

'What?'

'That I can — that I have been singing.'

'But, dear God, why must those at home not know about it? After all, there is no harm in singing?'

'Because then I'll have to take lessons with the organist. He's so dreadful, so very dreadful. If only you knew what poor *Louise* suffered!'

'Louise?'

'Yes, my sister Louise; she who is married to *Caspers*, who was a tutor in our family.'

'I see,' I said, mechanically reaching for my hat.

'You ought to know,' Sofie went on, 'that when Louise was my age, she had a rather insignificant voice, but she was gay and happy, humming and singing all day long. Mother thought there was something extraordinary about her voice, and the old organist was sent for in order to train it. Since the business had been neglected for so long, it had to be done thoroughly, which meant starting at eight o'clock in the morning and keeping at it until twelve noon, just exactly for as long as they were threshing in the barn. The we would eat, and then they went at it again! And during that whole time Louise would be sitting there with the sheet of music in front of her, which she had a hard time understanding at all, and that disgusting old fellow sat next to her with his chewing tobacco in his mouth, and he would smack her fingers with a thin stick and thump the rhythm on her back. Louise always came away from those lessons exhausted with crying, and she often said, "Watch out, Sofie, lest you sing, otherwise you'll have to learn music." '

'Did your sister learn anything?'

'Oh yes, I'll tell you. After a year and a half she had learned to sing two pieces — "Beautiful Minka" and "Whence Do You come, Oh

Beautiful Star", and the teacher was let go. However, a fresh torture began for her. Every time we had visitors, Louise had to stand up and sing. No excuse would do. Mother said it was a shame, when her father had spent so much money on her, if she could not give them that pleasure. Oh, how many times did she sing "Beautiful Minka, End Your Complaint!" with such a desperate voice! When I just think of it!' Here Sofie burst into tears again. 'Louise was so frightened whenever she heard a carriage that she took off over hill and dale.'

'Don't cry any more now on that account, dear Sofie. Your sister probably never had any talent, but you so obviously do. Don't you think, then, that it is a sin to hide your talent as if it were something evil?'

'No, no!' she cried agitatedly. 'That is precisely how I avoid a great misery.'

'But such merciless treatment is not inevitable for everyone who wants to learn to sing. Your voice needs quite a different sort of training from what is available here; your parents will surely understand that.'

She gave me a wide-eyed look.

'Alas,' she said, 'even if I can learn how to sing ... in the way I imagine it to myself — how useful would that be to me? Louise never sings any more.'

The word 'useful' almost made me laugh, but I controlled myself. 'Oh yes, useful is just what it would be,' I said. 'In the first place, it is useful to be able to give pleasure to others, and I doubt not that you will soon be able to give your parents a pleasure that poor Louise apparently was never able to grant them, however willing she was to sing "Beautiful Minka". It will never occur to them to misuse *your* singing by turning it into a regular apparatus for entertaining strangers. Music will make you more free and trusting; it will enrich your soul. That is the most useful thing of all. Believe me, Sofie, everything beautiful is useful to a young lady, and she can never acquire too much of it. Her soul needs all the balance, all the independence it can get.'

Again she looked at me long and searchingly. Her look contained pain and wonder; she wanted to say something, but remained silent. I have never seen a more expressive face.

Fearing that such an opportunity would not soon return, I developed this theme further for her, talking as kindly and sensibly and with as much consequence as I was capable of.

Sofie kept walking silently by my side, a little ahead of me and half turned towards me. Once in a while, she looked up with wide eyes, as if she were drinking in my words. When we reached the summer farm, I asked Marit to find me something to eat, because I had grown very hungry, but Sofie assumed this responsibility with a friendliness and energy I had never seen in her before. By the time her horse came for her, we had become the best of friends. We walked down through the forest while I led her horse by the bridle, but when we reached the main road, she mounted before I had a chance to help her up. On her head was a small cap that had belonged to Edvard, and now she wrapped herself in a big cloak that covered up her usual unbecoming clothes. Seated on her horse, she held out her hand to me and said with an expression both beseeching and commanding:

'I am sure you will keep your promise — not a word about the singing.' At that moment, she again looked quite unlike a child. And then she took off like an arrow.

Had I been completely mistaken in her? Hidden beneath all those contradictions, was there not actually a wonderfully unique soul, endowed with strong instincts and fighting to be free, while she was ignorant of how to handle the reality around her? But what was it? What was stirring in her? What would happen to it in the end? Has it perhaps been extinguished in her new surroundings? She has been down in Copenhagen for two and a half years, now, and has been confirmed down there. Her aunt keeps an elegant, hospitable establishment. Suppose Sofie were to return perverted by urban life, devoid of distinctiveness and individuality? The other day, her mother confided to us that Sofie's aunt was very eager to keep her down there, because she might 'make her fortune' there. She has already had two serious suitors in addition to a few second-stringers. But all attempts at persuasion have stranded on Sofie's wanting to return home. And she is coming home. But she will most certainly not be the same Sofie as when she left; that gangling child in pantaloons and a dress made of dark blue cotton, and with braids down her back. Returning is the Sofie of seventeen, perhaps 'herrlich in der Jugend prangend wie ein Gebild aus Himmels Höh'n.' And what then? Alas, dear Müller, my old honest, awkward bear with your theories about 'domestic warmth' and with your fears! What I fear is that your predictions of disasters will not come true at all; I fear having no reason for fear. Never again am I to dive drunkenly, blindly believing, into those tantalizing depths where one imagines seeing pearls and treasures at the bottom. Schiller's *Taucher* was a hero, a young hero, the *first* time; the second time he was a fool. Alas, I shall never again be a fool! In our own time, they have invented diving bells that allow one to descend slowly and calmly observe everything without so much as catching a cold afterwards.

* * *

It was this mind-besetting vacillation between the past and the future, between old and painful memories and indistinct longings, that drove Kold to wander off out of doors one beautiful April day.

The terrain in which the farm was situated sloped down towards the river in a long terrace covered with grassy fields and sparse, deciduous forest. The far bank had a quite different character, consisting of a series of lushly overgrown cliffs that formed a base for the hills closing off the valley. On the other side lay the mill, and on the right a footpath wound between the cliffs. The path, which wound along the steep rock faces next to a creek, was extremely inviting already at this point, but it grew even more attractive as it approached the cave described earlier. At the end of the pass, the cliffs had formed a natural, wide arch, whose handsome shapes and symmetrical lines might almost make one doubt that it was a work of nature. Inside the arch, however, there were signs of human hands having come to nature's aid. Gravel and rock had been carefully cleared away; the ground had been smoothed and strewn with sand; and an irregularity in the cliff wall, as well as a couple of loose chunks of stone, had been covered with moss and made into seats. The vault, which was quite deep, would have been too dark, had not a crack in the rock above let in sufficient light despite a screen of shrubs and vines. Outside, by the right-hand wall of the cave, the creek rushed in a series of little falls down the cliffs and widened into a semi-circle in front of the cave before continuing its downward course. The view from this point was more welcoming and cheering than one would suspect from the general nature of the place; it provided a gentle corrective to the dark impression left by the vault. Through the widening passage in the rocks, the creek could be seen cheerfully coursing down towards the river, where the mill roof was visible beneath some ancient birches and the bright, fertile landscape beyond formed a most cheerful backdrop. As mentioned earlier, Sofie had since her earliest childhood assumed a proprietary right to the spot; a right nobody had tried to take away from her. Even as quite a small child, when access to the cave was often extremely difficult, she had found her way down there, protected by that unconsciousness of danger which is the invisible guardian of the very young.

Towards this spot Kold was now guiding his steps. Although the road was almost inaccessible, since run-off from the mountains made the creek overflow its banks both spring and fall, he succeeded in reaching the cave after some effort. From the entrance, he looked out over the landscape, to which the shimmering green moss, the splashing creek and the pure, blue sky lent an aura of spring that enchanted the observer. We may have seen a person or a place a hundred times, before one day it occurs to us to observe — that is, to examine with our inner eye — that person or place, which may then appear quite new and unfamiliar. When looking around the cave, Kold noticed for the first time that only the front part was smooth and regular, while the forces of nature had created a number of niches and recesses farther in, where the light from the radiant day fell with a blue sheen through the crack described earlier. Kold probed the cave with his eyes. It seemed to him that every stone, every tracing in the rock ought to be able to enlighten him about the being who was occupying his mind at that moment. Indeed, he thought he had found the imprint of a foot, the smallest foot on the whole farm. Where some dried moss had fallen away from the wall, a couple of rocks allowed themselves to be moved. He had found a secret hiding place. In vain he searched every cranny. While rooting around in the gravel, he finally hit upon something — a small, round, hollow article made of some hard substance and looking remarkably like a walnut shell. He studied it from every angle; he stared at the tiny, squiggly lines as if each one were a significant rune. It was and it remained a walnut shell.

* * *

TO MÜLLER

..... Farm, 29 March.

I have taken out an enormous sheet of paper; mended all the pens in my possession; and hastened to write 'Dear Müller'. I have locked the door, although I know that not a soul will disturb me — all in the faith that the old saying 'Well begun is half done' was coined especially for the writer of letters, this most capricious and difficult of all human exercises. Now I want to write to Müller; I shall; I will. One might have to wait a long time for such a confluence, both within and without, of all the prerequisites for writing a letter, a real, thorough letter, an outpouring of the heart in the old manner. Those prerequisites are: the month of March outside, which in the almanac is called 'the Month of Spring' — I myself would certainly give it quite another name, if I could not get rid of it altogether — and within doors there is quarantine and ill humour. But you must not think that we have no sun. It shines from the pale blue sky with a truly desperate perseverance, day after day, week after week. It almost blinds us with its reflection off the white roofs at the same time as it is powerless to do away with the masses of snow. The only bare patch I can discern up in the hills, the first thing my eyes see in the morning, has not grown any bigger for the last three days. If you are tempted outside by the sunshine, you are met by the piercing north wind, which chases you right back inside. Thus the day goes its monotonous way. The farm appears dead; the only sound is from the threshing in the barn, from early in the morning until late at night, as restless as the beats of an impatient heart. How sad this sound is! In truth, this time of year in the country is not to be — however, I do not wish to speak badly of the country. When summer comes, all is forgotten.

But I am supposed to be making a confession, and I am sure you are aware that with this long introduction, I am acting like a child who takes yet another detour if it fears it is late for school. Yes, to be sure, the confession I have to make is proving more difficult than I thought, and I am going to have trouble fulfilling my promise — not from fear of you, my dear Müller, do not think that for a moment! You are not going to have occasion for the least bit of ridicule; on the contrary, I shall be giving you pleasure. How shall I explain myself? . . . I have few events to relate; my misfortune lies with disappointments of a kind people like you never have to suffer, and which you therefore have a hard time understanding in others. You surely know the sorry illusions of my youth; you have tried to do away with them often enough. Later, our ways parted. There were years when I did not see you. I thought you had dropped me completely, until you suddenly surprised me with your visit up here in my isolation. That was handsome; that was faithful of you! In return, I can do no less than to keep my promise and tell you how I have spent the intervening time.

It is oddly moving to think back, in later years, to one's first youth, that happy period of green immaturity. You do not know whether to pity it or to admire it. Grandly, you want to throw away the happiness it offers, but you do it with a secret, gnawing sense of loss and with many a nostalgic backward glance.

I am sure you remember how I landed right in the middle of the worst uproar of our socio-political conflicts when I moved from my peaceful home to Christiania. The feud between *Welhaven* and *Wergeland* was at its zenith; it had just left the confines of the Student Society and become public. In every member of the educated class, right down to the youngest schoolboy, you could be certain of confronting a member of one or the other faction. It was enough to make a poor, inexperienced person quite dizzy. I also want to tell you, quite frankly, that I was too immature to judge clearly for myself about what I later realized were the central points of conflict: it has later seemed to me that their points of conflict centred on national improvement through general education, and on exchanging our own resources for the spiritual nourishment we were then still accustomed to getting from the outside. What mattered to me was that those questions were being debated between the bare, smoke-filled walls of the Student Society, to the accompaniment of raucous voices and the clinking of glasses. Boundlessly bitter personal polemics forced people to such glaring extremes that, in the end, any sort of compromise was unthinkable. The situation had to explode. Understandably, I joined forces with those who claimed to be the apostles of moderation and civilization. Such was the programme, at any rate. Moreover, I had just experienced another stormy evening in the *Student Society*, which had an aftermath down the street that had nightwatchmen running to the scene while the peaceloving citizenry was quietly disgusted.

The break leading to the formation of the *League* seemed to me an occasion of national importance, its purpose nothing less than the salvation of all bourgeois society. I saw in this separation only the victory of light over darkness, the victory of civilization over crudeness. So, there was a move, but as so often happens during a move, the mischievous house elf came along as well. We are all well aware that in addition to the leader himself, who at that time was the capital's *enfant chéri* and *terrible*, there were splendid people among those who moved out — persons whose mere name lent to this new society of Knight Templars an importance and respectability which it otherwise could not possibly have achieved. This fact may, however, have saddled the group with many supporters it would have been better off without. All told, I do not believe that the actual moral conditions were a particular improvement over the old ones; you only felt a need to behave with a little more dignity. But why do I tell you this, Müller! — you, who more than once described Welhaven's followers to my face when you knew I was a 'Troopist'* or a 'League Lionizer', and who ridiculed so viciously the terrible 'disparity between ideas and reality'! I do it because, for once, I want to make myself clear to you; you have never quite understood me in this matter.

So now I was a member of the League. Gradually, I began to see how onesided and decorously dead-ended its proposed programme was. Now, of course, its meetings, which mostly took place down at bookdealer *Dahl's* in Church Street, were carried out with all the jovialness of complete unanimity, since they were safe within their own camp; there was less noise and also less clinking of glasses. The polemicism filling the first columns of *Vidar* and later *The Constitutional Paper* was also more restrained than that of the opposite faction, but — I don't know — in the long run those juvenile judgemental airs, that cold, superior, irritating tone and that persistent maliciousness seemed more deadly to me than the most uninhibited discharges from the other side had ever been — at least the latter had shown heat and youthful excitement! Given some little time for reflection later on — and in my three years of rural isolation I have had plenty of quiet for such reflection — it is possible to see what can finally happen to a cause in the hands of fanatical partisans. The original champions, who really took their point of departure in some great new thought, might have been astonished indeed had they been able to foresee what friends and foes together could make of their cause, and to what they would then have to lend their good names. Not to mention the persons who happened to figure in those twisted representations. . . . Just imagine what a figure *Wergeland* would cut down in Copenhagen, or *Welhaven* in our coastal towns or inland hamlets! You will laugh at me, Müller, when I tell you that I ended as a rather lukewarm partisan, retaining a fondness for both of the poets at the head of their respective factions, although I must add that I stayed at a rather respectful distance.

---

* Term used to describe Welhaven's followers. [*Tr. Note*]

59

I became all the more absorbed in their poetry. Nobody has greeted each fresh poetic eruption more warmly than I. Perhaps I instinctively felt that in this case, the too powerfully personal might merely disturb matters.

Why, I often thought — why this bitter enmity between those two, who seemed more destined to form an alliance between themselves, something akin to the relationship between *Goethe* and *Schiller*? They seemed made to complement each other, not to destroy one another. It is not ideas that cause enmity, but partisans.*

My experiences in this business were not the end of my illusions.

The new League's balls and festivities were fresh additions to our city's social life, which now began to take a grander turn thanks to the frequent presence of the Court. All sorts of foreign réunions were attempted. Our jolly evening parties with ladies at the table — 'my full glass and the speedy tunes of song' — gave way to what seemed a race to find how, with the least grace and the greatest speed, you could gobble up what you had managed to scrape together amid crowds and confusion. We were given dinners and soirées and matinées and gouters and God knows what it was all called.

I am sure you also know that I was whirled into this social life, although I was the last to dream of such good fortune. I had practically become the fashion and had to be included everywhere. The amusing thing is that I supposed this distinction was offered to me in my role as a true 'Troopist', a real member of the *League*, while in reality I had little claim to such a description. I was a competent 'performer' and tied my

---

* Time, that great commentator, has in many ways confirmed the dimly perceived notions of our story's hero. Not only has time conciliatingly recognized the equal rights of both currents of thought, but it has almost reached the point of exchanging the parts, so that Wergeland is increasingly seen as the universal poet and cosmopolite, and Welhaven as the more specifically national poet. How the latter has perceived this, how he felt towards the adversary of his youth in his later years, must remain less certain. Nevertheless, a dream he had on the next-to-the-last night before he died seems to bear witness to his having gone to his Lord in a spirit of reconciliation — he dreamed that an irresistible force was driving him up to Wergeland's grave. [*Author's note in the 1879 edition.*]

cravat beyond reproach, as you so recently remarked. Nobody has any idea of the restlessness and excitement, infatuation and disappointment I suffered while making my way through it all.

I often recalled how, during my final weeks in secondary school, I had taken up my station by the driveway leading up to the Prefect's residence when the Vice Regent was giving a ball, so that I could watch the ladies getting out of their carriages. Please bear in mind how I had been affected by growing up in solitude in *E.*, where I devoured novels and poetry as a substitute for human company. My mother, beautiful and very talented, could only strengthen the notions I had formed about the other sex. My need to admire it, my enthusiasm for it, which may be said to run in my family and which has been the cause of many a romantic family event — perhaps I have told you about some of these, or perhaps I have not quite had the courage to do so — at any rate, if you were to go far enough back in time, in the end you might well come upon a dragon's tail or some other storybook item. No wonder, then, that I began to search with burning intensity for the ideal of my dreams, before I was worthy of being a part of that social world. If you only knew how I trailed after some the ladies who were touted as beauties. No troubadour, no faithful Knight of *la Mancha* could hold a candle to your Georg when it came to humbleness and perseverance. When I watched those ladies in their brilliant ballgowns, stepping out of their carriages or fluttering like visions past the lit-up windows, they appeared to me like beings of a higher order than the rest of us earthlings — crude creatures in boots. I was convinced that the joy of standing next to them, of speaking to them and dancing with them, would be more than a mere mortal could handle. My ecstasies contrasted strangely with the coarse and mocking remarks made by my comrades — how indignantly I sometimes stormed off!

Then I found myself inside the circle, and things turned out as you might expect — that is, just as I had not expected. I fell in love, by turn, with all the women called the 'queen of the season', and at each turn I realized, just a little less to my surprise each time, that beauty is deficient unless it is the harmonious expression of a matching soul. Otherwise, it would be an unreliable sort of beauty, most likely the sum total of dress and lighting effects. I don't know how it was, but all contacts with the owner of that kind of beauty left a strangely vague and empty impression on me. I am forced to think of *Julie R.*, in whose features I discerned the most devoted interest and sympathy for a tragically noble cause. Innocent young fool that I was, I told her how truly moved I was by her attitude. She then turned and made a face behind her fan to her friend, who in turn told the story and reproduced the grimace elsewhere!

Armed with this early wisdom, I long considered myself perfectly safe. I danced less eagerly; experimented with a certain sceptical, indifferent expression which at that time was coming into fashion; and wrote self-deprecating poems *à la Heine* in my solitary hours, until one day I again walked right into the trap, and this time in earnest.

A young lady had come to spend the winter with one of the families in town who at that time constituted something of a centre for the city's social life. Rumour had spoken of her long before she made her appearance. I was done for at once. I first saw her at a Lycée concert; our acquaintance grew throughout the various cotillions of the season; I proposed to her and was accepted during a lancers. This engagement lasted for one year.

Oh Müller, how beautiful she was! That creature, that face, held the richest promises of happiness a man could dream of — promises she broke every time she opened her mouth. I don't know the reason for this — her upbringing, an empty environment, her own person — perhaps everything combined. She was the incarnation of modern woman's educational mould, whose goal seems to be the complete extinction of all individuality and every spark of independence, and which in shallow natures produces dissimulation in everything: affectation instead of sensitivity, priggishness rather than modesty, and stock phrases instead of independent thoughts. Everything about my fiancée's lovely person was shiny, polished and smooth, reflecting only the petty futilities of the day. At times I tried to lift her thinking onto a higher plane and to egg her on to an independent opinion. I watched to see if I could perceive a spark of disapproval and anger when something really mean and hateful — but protected by current opinion — was allowed to spread unchecked, but no. The greatest moral disapproval I ever saw her exert herself to produce concerned a lady's ballgown, which was not in accordance with the rules.

And yet, Müller! . . . I could scarcely wait for the moment when I was to see her! . . . . One of those rare quiet evenings, perhaps at the end of a day when she had refused my entreaties to stay home from some diversion. How I would hurry to her. . . . Ondine, my Ondine! I wished I could close my ears and give myself over to contemplating her in silence. Müller, did you ever see her? . . . I wish I could be like the philologist in

Hertz's poem, who is moved by the beauty of his beloved to lift his voice in a hymn to her stupidity. Alas, in vain! I could not do it. Disturbed and utterly exhausted, on such evenings I would run rather than walk home, in order to — dream about her, and then I would start the next day exactly where I had left off. When that year of suffering was at an end, I felt as if I had gone through all the ancient Olympian punishments meted out as a challenge by the gods. I felt like every one of them, from he who perished in front of his drink or he who rolled rocks uphill that would then roll down just as fast, right to that unfortunate soul who came too near the sun on his presumptuous winged flight and plummeted to earth.

Only one thing more need be added to this description of my beloved, but that is also the most embarrassing confession of all: in the end I discovered that she did not love me. She did not love me, and yet she would marry me. (My material circumstances as the only son of the 'Mining King' would have permitted me to aspire to a small, domestic civil service position, despite my mediocre university degree.) On this point she was unassailable. Though able to produce an expression worthy of offended royalty because of a trifle, she suffered with a patience that brought me to despair any mention of the deep disparity of our natures and of the unhappiness this promised. She would laugh and fend off with a joke any indirect suggestion from me that we end our relationship. Finally, I took it upon myself to break the shackles, and I patiently endured the talk of the town. Naturally, I was the traitor, not the victim. Miss W. was considered one of the first ladies in the city, and the sad truth is that she probably was. She had the ability to be agreeable to everyone. Wherever she showed herself, at balls, concerts, the theatre, behind the raffle counter or in church on Sundays next to the assessor's wife, she was always the same — dressed with tasteful simplicity, friendly, well-mannered, proper in everything. She pleased everybody.

Therefore, the fault was mine and mine alone — the fault of the dreamer, the idealist with his nonsensical *demands* that he had acquired from novels and sagas about heroines. Yes, that is true; I did have some expectations that might have fitted that description, but I had not come by them the way people thought. I had cultivated those expectations in the innermost, deepest foundation of my soul. I imagined women to be what my mother had been — the soul of all her surroundings, the source of everything great and good around her.

Indeed, it is true that I had come to the big city imagining I saw in every lovely face, in each radiant eye, the promise of such a lifegiving soul. But in the big city, pettiness and blunted passivity had been laid down as the law governing feminine behaviour, and *Constance W.* was admired as the paragon of this beautiful womanhood.

After this sad story had been brought to an end, the magic of the stage on which it had unfolded was thoroughly destroyed. When there was nothing left to captivate me, the whole dreary emptiness of our social life was finally revealed to me. How could it be otherwise, when spiritual stimulation was lacking on both sides and a trifling infatuation was to be all that held two people together? Everywhere, you can see people struggling to be apart from each other. Wherever it is at all possible, the gentlemen tiptoe off and leave the scene to the ladies. You feel bored; you notice that something is amiss; and you cannot understand the reason why. In such an inner state of emptiness, you seek refuge in personal criticism, which is a euphemism for gossip, and ridicule is used as a simple expedient to hide the sadness of the personal shortcomings being discussed. For God's sake, let there be no hint of feeling or of admiration for anything; let us be as indifferent as possible and as polite as necessary in order not to be thought uncouth — that seems to be the keynote of our newly hatched social life. I have known people of a naturally friendly disposition who have forced themselves to be insufferable by every means at their disposal. I suppose the object is to be in keeping with current European fashion. Still, I believe that in our efforts to be *au courant* as Europeans, we are too quick to acquire the *drawbacks* and forget to include the *virtues*. We do not stop to reflect that many of the less pleasant phenomena of our times, which crop up in societies abroad, depend on assumptions and develop out of conditions that are fundamentally different from our own. We forget that such phenomena often arise as a reaction or protest against different worn-out, outmoded cultural forms; that they are fighting, changing, always renewing themselves; whereas they just appear as extraneous growths and caricatures if they are grafted onto our conditions. We, of course, have not even caught up with the old culture yet — much less with its degeneration. We have skipped it, as it were, although we could well have used plenty of the best it had to offer. We could use a little more idealism in our striving; a little more strength to love, as well as strength to hate what ought to be hated. We could use a little more respect for form, a little more regard for women, and a vision of what they really represent and what they could and ought to be. . . . Have we any of this?

I do not know. As for me, I felt as if I were congealing within, and I was so displeased with myself and with everything that I grasped at the slightest opportunity to get away. Nobody can wonder now that I avidly seized my current position. A total change of circumstances was called for in order that I might feel human again.

Still, I was not to leave town without a conciliatory gesture. In my hour of greatest need, the gods in their pity sent me my acquaintance with *Margrethe D.*

I had seen her at parties before, of course — or, rather, I had overlooked her. She was not exactly pretty, if you did not know her and had not talked with her. She was frail, with an expression of suffering, but she was infinitely fine and graceful. Her passivity — she almost always sat by herself among the others — was exactly calculated to arouse my interest, and this interest grew with every word we exchanged. Soon she was the only person I sought out; I had discovered her; and between us arose a beautiful friendship and confidence of a kind that is so little known between two young people in our social life that it could not fail to attract attention. We let people talk. Neither of us had any erotic designs. In our different ways, each of us had done with that. Since I was younger than she and inconsolable, I naturally became the confessing child. All I knew about her own fate was what I had learned from the talk of the town: that she had refused a very considerable match, and that she probably intended to remain a spinster for the sake of a whim. In her, I discovered everything I had failed to find in my previous inclinations: real feelings, a wealth of thought, perspicacity and understanding. She lacked small-talk, but talked with greater fluency on profound subjects than any person I had ever met. Her speech was flower-scented and full of originality — oh, so truly feminine! She was the first to criticize my behaviour, gently and cautiously, at the same time as she showed me the source of all my disappointments. Never have I found such independence of spirit in the face of surrounding pettiness. Margrethe D. was one of those rare natures who develop their uniqueness despite every obstacle, and who silently and quietly manage to endure the martyrdom of being different, because they are forced to seek refuge in their innermost selves. Nevertheless, there was a veil of sadness, or possibly of weariness with life, over her.

Had she herself loved?

'You have been both *demanding* and *prejudiced* at the same time; that is your misfortune,' she once said with slightly bitter emphasis, which was unusual in her. 'You have not looked in the right places for the one who ought to satisfy you. You have looked for her in the ballroom, beneath the chandeliers. You might have found her among the uncelebrated, the unnoticed, the hidden. The footprints of that sort of woman must be looked for in the darkest corners of a house, or in mental institutions, or in the *grave* . . . . The *grave*,' she added with emphasis, as if she wanted to impress upon me an address about which I must not be mistaken.

That was sad to hear; could she be right?

More gently another time: 'You complain about us, and with reason. But what are we to do? We grow only through pain, but unfortunately this also makes us unfit for living.'

Indeed, she herself was such a broken reed, from which the wind could still wrest melodic sounds, but also jarring ones. How much I owe to Margrethe! . . . She could not save my happy illusions, but she has salvaged my faith.

Georg Kold put this letter aside for some time, because he was occupied with other business that could not be postponed. Then he remembered about the letter; took out the small sheaf of papers; and read them through.

For a long time he sat musing with the papers in his hand. He had to ask himself if it was he who had written all this — and to Müller!

Yes, the letter was to Müller, indeed; it started off rather soberly, almost reluctantly, addressed to him. And then. . . .

Georg opened his desk; buried the letter in its innermost recess; and locked the desk carefully. He was like the trustworthiest of all trustworthy lock-keepers, who for the first time ever had been guilty of carelessness, and who now shamefacedly and hurriedly sought to do away with the evidence. Within half an hour he had finished another letter to his friend. On the first page he related as drily and precisely as a book-keeper all his unfortunate infatuations. The remaining three-fourths of the letter contained reflections concerning a public event which at that time had the newspapers and people's tempers in a state of ferment. He closed by saying that he had discovered two cross-eyed subjects in the parish and one in the annexe, whom Müller would have waiting for him when he next came to visit.

This letter was received by Müller, and he read it through with great attention. 'Look at that! My dear, idealistic, high-flown Georg! He is improving. He is beginning to descend to us ordinary mortals, who take the world as it comes. . . . One-two-three-four — he is still sincere — and followed by a "less-than-well-thought-out-engagement", and then he speaks as calmly about it as if it were a piece of pottery that can be riveted back together! . . . Disappointed — cured forever — illusions that cannot be salvaged. . . . Hah, I know how that is; it will last exactly until the next time a pair of beautiful eyes appear in front of him. Well, well! Two in one parish and one in the annexe! . . . No, he must go away; up there is no place for him. He must leave!'

* * *

(CONTINUED TO MARGRETHE)

20 May.

There is a terrible bustle in the house these days because of the daughter's return, I believe the day after tomorrow. I am the only person left in peace. A new room has been fitted up, and there is as much scouring and baking, polishing and tidying-up as if they were expecting a princess and not the pathetic child who walked around as practically an outcast before she left. At that time my sympathies were with her; now it may be the others' turn; perhaps — this is the last I have to say about her.

Spring has also arrived. It came last night. After the long, cold season with its sad, leafless trees and brown hills, the air all at once turned warm and damp; yesterday and this morning a warm rain fell. A glass of blue hepaticas and yellow primroses is on my dresser — I wonder if they are from Amalie? She is really a good sort, Amalie. The fields are a brilliant green; you can hear the leaves bursting out; and a pale green, translucent veil lies over the birch forest. I have opened all my windows facing the garden, where the yellow, sticky buds on the poplars are glistening in the sunshine. A strong scent fills my entire room, but there is something oppressive about the air. This transition from a long, depressing winter to our exuberant spring is almost too fierce for the nerves of an ordinary person; I feel out of sorts. No peace anywhere. I have tried to work, but it is impossible. What liveliness has suddenly descended on the peaceful farm! The gay voices of people and animals are sounding by turns. A buzzing outside announces the arrival of spring, and every moment a bumblebee comes grumbling in through the window to tell about it. The cattle are aware of it also; they are bellowing impatiently from stable and byre. . . . the poor things have to be kept inside yet awhile, to prevent them from eating the bad grass that first pushes out of the ground and that is supposed to be poisonous. May God preserve us from the evil grass! Amen.

* * *

Bad weather again delayed Sofie's homecoming for a few days, but it finally did take place and occasioned audible joy in the still night. Kold did not go downstairs until the following morning, with a pounding heart. He found Sofie in the living room with her mother and siblings. She greeted him, but she did not move towards him. Kold did not know whether to offer her his hand or not. When that becomes subject to deliberation, it is too late. Common expressions of welcome and politeness were exchanged; regrets were expressed about the weather, and Kold, whom tension had made quite depressed, soon withdrew. He hurried upstairs to his room; brought out *Ørsted's Handbook*; and read intently and uninterruptedly for a couple of hours. Then he finished a detailed proposal for the District Governor and went out for a ride.

Up to then, he had avoided paying attention to his own thoughts. His encounter with the recent arrival had been extremely brief, to be sure, but at any rate his impression had been most unsatisfactory. What had he expected? He could make no judgment about her manner. The ease and confidence with which she had given and received those meaningless phrases their conversation had consisted of, did not entirely please him. Whether she was pretty, he could not say, either. Sofie's cheeks had been swathed in a scarf, and a big shawl had enveloped her figure, which seemed slight and slender. Her face had been somewhat red and chapped. This should not earn the notice of anyone who knows how much damage a couple of days' journey in our sharp spring air can do to even the loveliest features. But either our hero was not as generous as the Danish poet who says:

> If north winds or conditions bleak
> Have hurt the roses on her cheek,
> Believe me, friend, it matters not.

Or — as seems more reasonable — Kold had simply given no thought to the air's effect on human skin. As other pockmarked and tattooed sons of Adam have thought before him, he probably assumed that a lady's complexion ought to be as pure and as delicate as her reputation, and Sofie's strongly coloured complexion displeased him.

For the next several days, the repatriate remained out of sight, because she had a toothache and kept to her room. Nevertheless, an invitation from a neighbouring family was accepted. It was Whitsun Day, and spring had reached its full glory. The whole family left early for the visit, while Kold did not join them until well into the evening. It was a rather large party; the front parlour was almost full. Since he was not looking for anybody and did not want to force his way through, he remained standing over in a corner, where the growing darkness almost concealed him. The dancing was about to begin. From the main parlour, where the furniture had been cleared aside, came the strains of a gay Strauss waltz, and the gentlemen — who included some guests from town, the young rural merchants, the local curate, and the sons of the house — were just hurrying forward to ask the ladies to dance. Kold caught sight of Sofie at a distance. It must be she; it could be nobody else; yet she appeared a stranger to him. It seemed to him that she was declining several invitations to dance. He stood in his corner contemplating this, while the room was emptying around him. Then Amalie came hurrying out of the main parlour. With an expression denoting business of the utmost importance, she pulled her sister towards the window.

There Sofie stood, three steps away from him, with the daylight falling sharply upon her.

'You must dance, Sofie; you simply must dance. For Heaven's sake, don't refuse; it will be interpreted very unfavourably. . . .'

'I never dance.'

'What, Sofie, you never dance?' exclaimed Amalie. 'You used to have a passionate love of dancing. . . . Can't you remember, when you were very little you would dance around for a long time, until you stumbled and fell against tables and chairs? . . . Besides, you have been taking lessons in Copenhagen. . . . Therefore, you are not serious.'

'I am completely serious,' answered Sofie firmly, but somewhat sadly.

'But, for Heaven's sake, Sofie! . . .'

'There are certainly enough ladies,' Sofie interrupted her, somewhat heatedly. '*Elise Breien* looks as if playing is quite a sacrifice; I might as well do that!' So saying, she was already in the main parlour, and during the first interval that occurred in the music, she assumed the seat at the piano, half by persuasion and half by force. She played steadfastly for almost the whole evening, waltz after waltz, country dances and galloppades. Perhaps she was hoping to placate the offended gods.

Out of a habit left-over from winter, lights had been lit in the main parlour, but they were barely visible. The clear nocturnal summer light from the northern horizon was pouring through all the windows. The piano was placed in a position where a bright light fell on the performer.

Just as every work of art requires a certain kind of frame and lighting, just as every jewel needs its own special setting and there are certain wines that can be appreciated only when drunk from green glasses, living beauty can manifest itself only when its own requirements are met. If people had a right understanding of this and knew how to disregard what is secondary, we would not so often do beauty injustice, and if beauty knew better how to avoid the accidental, it would be beautiful more often. Sofie confirmed the truth of this as she sat in front of the keyboard — set apart, free, merely reposing in her own youthful, graceful confidence. By its cut and colour, a dark silk dress, tastefully trimmed with white lace, which her aunt had given her, wonderfully accentuated Sofie's fine, slender figure. Those unnaturally tall hair arrangements were just beginning to yield to the Greek knot, which is so becoming to a young face. . . . Sofie's abundant, lovely hair was arranged in this manner, and since this fashion was not yet known up in that part of the country, it gave her a somewhat foreign appearance among the others. In the evening light her features had a brilliant, marble-like pallor, but someone standing close to her would discover that she did not lack the healthy glow of youth.

The hostess and Mrs Ramm had taken their seats on the sofa. The District Governor's lady was resplendent in silk and gold ornaments, and she had assumed her brightest party expression.

'I really do congratulate you on having got your Sofie back home,' said the short, fat Mrs Breien. 'I hardly recognize her; she has grown so pretty. She will have the lovely complexion that runs in your family, Mrs Ramm. Just watch; she will be even more beautiful than Louise.'

'Oh yes, indeed, she has improved. . . . When Sofie just gets a little more colour and becomes a little plumper,' said Mrs Ramm, who with such moderate expressions sought to keep her maternal admiration in check.

'Her former teacher must surely find her perfect as she is, because he has not taken his eyes off her since he arrived. There he is in the doorway, like a statue. My *Elise* had to sit out the last waltz; it would not have been so extraordinary if Mr Kold. . . ! But heavens, Elise certainly will not die of it, if Mr Kold does not know what courtesy requires. . . . Lord have mercy, now he is even taking out his lorgnette. Well, well, Mrs Ramm, do have a care!'

'What do you mean?' said that lady, with incomparable aplomb. 'Ah, . . . no, I would not hope for such a thing; that person has certainly made matters complicated enough in our house,' she added with a sigh. 'You see, my husband absolutely wanted Kold as a teacher for Edvard. He had been so extremely highly recommended to him. I don't doubt, of course, that he is a cultivated and competent person, which is enough to make my old dear appreciate him. But we women, my good Mrs Breien, we have more acute powers of observation; we judge a man's worth differently. Culture and talents are great advantages in a young person, but in my eyes they are no substitute for a lack of sensitivity, of character. Even before Kold arrived, I knew several stories concerning the young man that aren't exactly to his credit, and that are of a kind that certainly might make a mother's heart anxious.'

'Oh, I also know something about those stories,' Mrs Breien interjected.

'Indeed? Then do let us hear if your stories correspond with mine?'

'I can guarantee you that mine are absolutely reliable,' the plump lady stated. 'I have them from Elise, who corresponds, as you know, with her cousin in Drammen. I am well acquainted with Drammen; in that place they know just as well what is happening in Christiania as they do on the spot — indeed, at times even better. A lady was so much in love with Kold that she took poison. She later married someone we both know . . . but I mention no names. Two other ladies broke with their lovers, each convinced that the person we are talking about took a particular interest in her, and no sooner had they done so, but he retreated! That's how it goes when people want to throw out the dirty water before the fresh has been handed out!'

'I have been told the same story somewhat differently,' said the District Governor's wife, who was not quite pleased with the fat little lady's somewhat cynical mode of expression. 'But it all comes to the same thing. What is certain, is that his turn also came. He finally became mortally smitten by a Miss W., a very pretty, well-bred and in every respect excellent girl. They become engaged; everything is lovely for a while . . . then he grows cool and strange — suddenly he breaks it off. . . . Nobody can comprehend the reason!'

'*He* broke the engagement? He really did it *himself*? I call that shameful!' cried Mrs Breien in such loud indignation that Mrs Ramm looked worriedly around to all sides. 'Poor *Tilla Torp* was engaged for six years, and I do not wish to praise *her* lover in that relationship, but at least he let her have the triumph of breaking it off.'

'You may well understand, dear Mrs Breien, that I became anxious for my little girls when I heard that Kold was to come into our home. There was no need to worry about Sofie; she is practically a child still, and, besides, she could not stand him; there was always such a squabbling between the two of them. But Amalie, the poor, inexperienced girl . . . a heart that is pure innocence!'

'Well, yes! May I then hear how things really are between Amalie and him?' interrupted Mrs Breien, greedily moving an inch closer. 'I have more than once thought that everything was arranged between those two.'

'I shall certainly be pleased to put you wise. At first, Amalie was bashful and very reticent. She, too, had heard those rumours. Kold seemed to distinguish her, although I must say it was done in a modest, respectful manner. He never neglected to hand her in and out of the carriage, and once he walked her home from the *Meiers*, when it had been raining, and that could certainly not have been for the sake of the walk. When a young gentleman nowadays goes that far, one does not have to be very good at conjecturing to see what it leads to. But something must have come between those two young people. Amalie suddenly withdrew; her reticence — though this will remain between us two — turned into complete distaste. She simply cannot stand him. Pray notice, they never talk to each other. He gives nothing away; he must have a peculiar command of himself. But I do know that the poor girl has suffered in this relationship. Beneath that carefree exterior hides, I fear, a broken heart, Mrs Breien!'

Amalie, who was just then waltzing past with the curate, did not with her looks in any way confirm her mother's statement. Her somewhat large figure looked even more ample in a white dress, and her cheeks, to which dancing had lent an extra glow, competed in colour with the wreath of roses she wore at a slight angle on her hair.

'If I am not much mistaken,' observed Mrs Breien while she followed the dancing couple with her small, blinking eyes, 'our grave curate is very desirous of healing the broken heart. I have never seen him dance before, and this evening he is among the most eager!'

The pair had stopped just a short distance away from the two women. The way the curate was standing, with his hands tucked under the tails of his coat, while apparently entertaining his lady, he formed a rather peculiar contrast to the latter.

Brøcher, the curate, had a tall, thin, frail figure, which he carried very straight; a long, but all the narrower face; a sharp, birdlike profile; large, pale blue eyes framed by blond hairs; and a rather prominent lower jaw. A pair of voluminous sideburns might have maintained some degree of balance in his face, but nature had denied the curate this adornment. Nor did he himself seem to consider his face too long; at any rate, he took pains to add to its length by combing his heavy, flaxen hair upwards into a kind of coxcomb. His face had that reddish, indeterminate colour that is as far removed from the pink of health as it is from the warm, brown colour suggesting a strong, choleric temperament.

After this description, the reader will probably be in a position to conclude that Brøcher was not a handsome man. Nor was he. Still, he had a quality that completely made up for his lack of personal beauty. In well-bred country families, the sons leave the nest early in order to seek their fortune elsewhere. The daughters, on the other hand, do not take to their wings; they remain in the nest waiting for fortune to seek them out. In such a remote area, rich in families and daughters, the curate represented fortune. Truly, he was just about the only conceivable match in the entire neighbourhood. This, however, did not prevent the young girls from using him as the secret butt of their innocent fun, *for the time being*. The stiff, pedantic curate, extremely meticulous in both his clothes and his demeanour, walked among them like a huge blind man's buff, who for a while patiently allows himself to be tugged at and teased, but who suddenly may reach into the flock of people and grab one. This unpredictability is just what adds piquancy to the entertainment. But so far, nobody had seen any such tendencies in him. The erotic element did not seem at all familiar to him, and so far nobody had experienced anything resembling 'courtship' in him. Therefore, the symptoms discovered by the two matrons from their station on the sofa could not appear to them as anything less than very striking.

At this moment, the symptoms became cause for anxiety.

Amalie had in distraction pulled the petals off a flower and was now tossing aside the stem as she walked away. This stem was now hastily picked up by the curate, who put it in the pocket of his waistcoat.

'There! Am I right?' said the small lady and blinked her eyes. 'What do you say to that, my gracious madam?'

'Nothing, Mrs Breien, nothing,' said the other with a calmness of manner that surely might be called stoical. 'In such matters I leave everything completely to the young. I have endeavoured to bring up my girls in such a manner that they themselves know how to choose. I know nothing of compulsion, and we do not wish to know it in our house.'

While exchanging significant glances, the two ladies now observed silently how the old District Governor, coming out of the billiard room, approached Kold and, bringing his hand down on the young man's shoulder, awakened him from his reverie. Kold's dreamy expression at once gave way to respectful friendliness, as the old man took him confidentially by the arm and pulled him over to a window, where they entered into an animated conversation, which was interrupted when they were called to the table.

In this way, the evening and a good bit of the night passed quickly. People enjoy themselves in the country; they do not look at their watches as often as people do in the cities.

Without being aware of it herself, Sofie had the whole time been the centre of the small circle. Unconsciously, she was exercising her power over all of them, as her mother's approving looks and Amalie's sisterly doting showed. Still, while the older people at the party, who had known Sofie as a child, guilelessly showed their admiration, among the younger set curiosity was more in evidence than spontaneous good-will while they clustered around her.

Georg Kold was the only person with whom she had exchanged no word the whole evening.

Sofie had never had a confidante or a friend, but in her childhood she had kept a diary, in which she had conscientiously written down the small daily events of her life. In Copenhagen, she had stopped doing this. There were too many other demands on her time, and, besides, she felt she was in that state of transition in which one is apt to distrust one's impressions. After returning home, she again felt the old urge to confide herself, but the thought of keeping a continuous journal was distasteful to her, so she limited herself to jotting down, on odd pieces of paper, whatever had impressed her forcefully. We shall make public a few of those sheets of paper, written soon after her return home, which perhaps is the best way to obtain a faithful picture of Sofie.

* * *

24 May 1842

How strange it is to know that I am home again! Am I really in my home? In my dreams at night, I am again taken away; I have a vague notion of something unattainable; I land a hundred times on Norwegian soil; I see my home and enter under its roof; then everything is changed again and I am in completely unfamiliar surroundings, among creatures I do not know. Last night, I woke up in the midst of such a struggle.

'Is it not true, then?' I called out loud, and look! all the familiar objects became so strangely clear in the darkness. Great-Grandmother's portrait in the shadows above the dressers almost came alive within its frame. I really thought I saw her stern, rigid face twist into a smile at my surprise. Such is the consequence of our luminous Norwegian summer nights. I had to jump up and run over to the window, opening it in order to breathe in the scent of the flowering chokecherry below and to listen to the waterfall by the mill, which was singing its old song for me. How many memories that sound gave rise to! And then I had to look back at that wonderful, bright night sky, against which the outline of the mountains was so sharply and darkly drawn. Not long afterwards, the sun rose as red as glowing embers over the hills.

I cannot exist except in the Norwegian landscape; away from it I should waste away in the midst of all the joys and pleasures the world has to offer. Everything in this landscape is now new and fresh, and yet everything is so familiar. My immediate surroundings are just the opposite. Today, I walked into the sitting room that leads directly into the garden. It seemed so full of many things and yet so strangely empty and deserted. And the painting of Antioch and Stratonike, the sick prince who loved his stepmother, did not appear the same as before. Was it just the idea of it that used to enchant me?

On the other hand, the head of the old man in the copper print struck me as something I had never seen before. —

The reception I have been given here at home has surprised me. Mother and my sister and brother greeted me with such affection; as if they had been waiting for me with longing! . . . And Father! Had they made a note of an old wish, or had they just made a guess? I have been given a room of my own; the small chamber beyond Amalie's room has been redecorated and beautifully furnished. Oh, I had not expected all this! I certainly did not give them any pleasure when I was living at home before; was I not a dissonance in their lives? With hot tears I have often thought about this while living among strangers. But from now on, I want to give them joy. I shall gain control of everything about me that they do not understand; they are not going to be aware of it or made anxious by it. Alas, do I myself understand what it is? —

I have not yet been to the cave. Yesterday, when the visitors were going down there, I could not bring myself to go down with them. Is it possible to pray to God while surrounded by company, all laughing and dressed in their best clothes? —

30th.

We have been to a party at *Eng* — Father and Mother, Kold, Amalie and I. The whole neighbourhood was there; I got to meet everybody I know. In them also I saw this change, which I cannot understand, let alone describe. I was so glad to see them, especially the *Meiers*, my old playfellows. But it was as if they doubted that my friendliness was sincere; at times they would find a snide remark in my plainest words. *Vilhelm Meier* called me 'Miss' and addressed me by the polite form 'De', so I did not know whether to laugh or to be angry when I did not remember to return this courtesy. *Emma D.* was not nearly as pretty as when I left. The worst of it was that I almost got into a fight with young *Breien*, because I found his parents to be much more handsome than their portraits, which I happened to say I considered awful — not in the least intending a criticism. With a truly defiant expression, he asked me what I meant by that, and he begged me to be so good as to 'explain myself'. Several times in the course of the evening I was told: 'Yes, I suppose you have become so hard to please; — now that you have been abroad for so long, you probably think that nothing up here is good enough.' Something about most of the people depressed me, so I was actually glad when I was seated in the cariole with Father and driving with him in the lovely light evening of early summer. Father was so excited; we had so much to tell each other. I do not think they were equally lively in the carriage behind us. Kold had sat down next to the driver, and both Mother and Amalie woke up from a little nap when we stopped in front of our door.

1 June.

I did not go to the cave until this morning. The cave, at least, was not changed. To me it seemed moving, marvellous. The path to it through the gulch, the view, the river — everything was sweet and unique. How strange I felt when I again saw the spot where I had played and tumbled about as a child . . . . Played and tumbled! No, I have not played and tumbled, but I have worked, pondered and dreamed down there, and I have cried. —

Tiddle-tiddleho,
Tomorrow we shall go
High up to the deep dell.

As if in a far-away dream, I experienced afresh my very first visit down by the cave. It was on a summer afternoon. Being a very small child, I was out walking with my nursemaid. Although she had been forbidden to do so, she had taken me with her down to the mill. While she was deep in conversation with the miller, I stole away from her and found my way into the rocky pass. The view was soon closed off. The terrain was at that time quite impassable and overgrown, and I suddenly realized that I was alone among the steep rock walls. The old nursery songs had already awakened in me a concept of a mysterious, fairytale landscape that was different from the garden, and I had always imagined it to be in the dark forests on the other side of the river, which I could see from our windows. Now I was there; this must be one of those blessed places they sing about in the song:

There the cattle we may tend
Whilst no rains our pleasures end.
There the swallows sing
And in the pine tops swing.

My heart no doubt was pounding, but it drove me irresistibly forward. I slipped under the bushes by the creek and wandered through forests of bracken and sky-high monkshood. It seemed to me that I walked very, very far. Then I came to the creek crossing. A half rotted, mossy tree trunk — perhaps blown down at some point, perhaps put there by people — formed a very fragile bridge. Nevertheless, I crawled across it without fear and found myself standing in the clearing in front of the cave, which seemed to constitute a small, enclosed world of its own. Here, under the sheltering rock sides, strawberries were ripening in undisturbed plumpness. Every crack in the cliff was filled with flowers of many colours — I ran from one to the other and did not know which to reach for first. For a long time I peered cautiously into the opening of the cave, which was half concealed by flowering wild rosebushes. In those days I had only one word for all that was dreadful in the animal world. No, I could safely enter; there were no bears. — Three steps away from me, on the sand in the centre of the cave, lay a lovely black, shiny ribbon which I had to have. To my unspeakable surprise, it was no longer there when I arrived. I searched in the crevice — I shudder to mention it — feeling quite sad. The black ribbon was and remained gone. Was it a grass snake? I have never seen one there since.

The innermost vault was half filled with pebbles and gravel, which soon consoled me, because among the pebbles were rocks of such marvellous beauty. They were as white as marble and almost round; there were also some that glittered. I searched and searched, because I wanted to bring a pebble for everyone at home.

> One for Father,
> One for Mother,
> One for Sister,
> One for Brother,
> And one for the one who caught the fish.

All this took time, however, and before I knew it, it was growing dark. I ran happily off with my treasures — the strawberries, the flowers, the pebbles — in my pinafore. I was no longer restrained by fear. As if carried on invisible hands, I managed to get across the frothing creek and then through the forests of bracken and monkshood. Breathless, torn, without my shoes, but radiant with joy, I reached the house, where Mother came to meet me. . . . she was angry, and I was severely punished. The pebbles were thrown into the pond and my clothes into the laundry tub. The nursemaid was angry for a long time afterwards, because she had landed in trouble on my account. Father knew nothing about any of it.

The cave had been discovered, however. Once, long afterwards, when Mother was relating this incident to Kold, he said: 'Sofie will have to comfort herself with the thought that *Columbus* and *Magellan* fared no better when they came home with their trophies. They, too, were rewarded with punishment.'

Alas, they laughed, but they had no idea of how happy, proud and reverential I had been on reaching home. —

When I grew bigger, I busied myself down there all day. Nobody else as yet bothered with the place, and anybody witnessing my efforts would have found them as ridiculous as they were futile. But a child knows nothing of the leaden weight of calculation, which oppresses the courage of the grown-ups, paralysing their strength. Imagination carries the child across obstacles and impossibilities and sometimes accomplishes what cannot be achieved by wisdom.

As I started to clear away the colossal heap of gravel, the cave was already finished in my imagination and decorated like a small fairy palace. Edvard, who one day watched me tirelessly filling and emptying my little basket, asked derisively if I knew the story of *Mesdemoiselles Danaïds*. Scorn failed to kill my courage, however. With an air as grand as Edvard's own, I showed him how the drips from the mountain had hollowed out a groove in the rock. How happy I was when Father let me have the use of a farmhand, who in one day accomplished more than I had managed in months of hard work! Anyway, with the steady drip of water on the rock, the cave came to have its present appearance, and it has become our favourite spot.

10 June.
Yesterday I rode my clever little brown horse through the Stimann forest, and when I came so close to *Lilleholt* that I could see the bright white chimney behind the pine grove, I could not resist turning off to pay a visit to old Madam *Brandt*. She did not recognize me to begin with and at first thought I was a stranger, then Amalie, but when she finally had collected herself and brought me into the living room, where *Hans*'s old gun and shotbag were still hanging in their old place, she burst into tears, although she said she had used up all her tears. That the handsome, decent Hans should have died; this loving son, her one and only joy! I asked

about *Lorenz*. She sent me a look of unspeakable sadness and said: 'Do not ask me about him. I have no children any more.' I dared not ask; but I thought: 'Oh, why did it have to be Hans!' She told me in great detail about Hans's illness and death. Such accounts can be dreadful, that is for certain, but a mother's sorrow must be more eloquent than any other, because it elevated her at times to something so touching in her expression, so almost sublime, that I would never have thought it possible in that plain, ordinary woman! I was so moved myself that I could say nothing. Suddenly a smile flitted across her face: 'Just you have a look!' she said, pulling me with her into the bedroom. In this room, the large family picture with silhouettes had been moved from above the settee to another wall, and a portrait had been put up in its place. It was surrounded by a wreath of cottonweed— those delicate, pretty flowers that look like tiny miniature roses — which she said she had picked herself. The schoolmaster's son, who dabbles in 'doing likenesses', had painted this water colour portrait from memory. A hideous caricature! Just the same, there was a likeness. Something frightening struggled inside me, but it dissolved into crying. I felt as if I were about to choke. 'It looks like him, doesn't it?' she said.

'Extremely,' I said. Not for any price would I have destroyed her joy in this picture.

It is hard to believe that that childish episode, which catapulted me into fear and pain *without my understanding why*, left an impression on me which I could not get over! I became more serious. Just when I felt happiest, a fear would come over me, and I would steal into a corner and cry. Did there not lurk something evil underneath my gaiety, a sin — was it not to be followed by punishment?

The black, lovely, shiny ribbon I had reached for so greedily — had it been a grass snake? —

13 June

Today, Amalie comes and tells me that people had thought it 'affected' of me that I did not dance the evening of the Breiens' party. Incomprehensible! It is like accusing a poor man of wanting to distinguish himself when he is forced to have his leg amputated. Amalie was right when she said that I am fond of dancing. Indeed, I have loved dancing since my earliest days. As a child, I would give myself entirely over to this pleasure. At balls I danced tirelessly, violently, with boys, girls, big or little — it was all the same to me — so that Father often scolded me and was worried. For a long time afterwards, the skipping, fluting melody would sound in my ear. I danced alone in the forest and down in the meadow until I collapsed in the grass, my heart pounding. That unselfconscious, naive pleasure is now gone, however, and the magic with it.

In Aunt Charlotte's house I had more frequent opportunities to dance. I always looked forward immensely to each one. Once, when I returned from a ball, Aunt asked me with whom I had danced, and I said that I did not know, because I had been having such a good time that I had not noticed. This occasioned laughter, and I was teased to the point of despair. I assured them that I was serious; the gentlemen with whom I danced all looked alike, and they tended to ask the same thing, namely how I liked Copenhagen and how long I was going to stay. But now I decided to take more notice of them. From this moment, my pleasure went into a steady decline. I noticed that there was a great deal of difference among these gentlemen, and I told Aunt I had decided that from now on, I would dance only with those I liked. When she saw that I was serious, she explained that this was simply not possible; you had to dance with anyone who asked. A young girl ought not even to risk saying no and then having to sit out the dance. Cousin Ida illustrated the inherent dangers of such behaviour with a whole string of dreadful examples. Shortly afterwards, we were invited to a ball. I was restless and sleepless prior to this ball as well, but no longer from happy anticipation. The question of *with whom* I might dance filled me with dread. The music began just as we entered the ballroom, and the gentlemen crowded in to ask the ladies to dance. From a kind of fear, I managed to work myself into the front row, where I saw a couple of gentlemen I rather liked, and by whom I had some hope of being noticed. Nevertheless, a feeling of shame soon drove me to retreat, and I hid among the ladies in the back row, where I was not noticed at all. The dancing had long since started, when by chance one of the people with whom I had danced at the previous ball came and asked me to dance. He was a dreadful person who never opened his mouth save to say something embarrassing. Alas — I wavered for a moment, but the sound of the music was irresistible. It was as if I had been seized by a whirlwind, and I threw myself into the dance with him. Scarcely was the dance at an end, but another one followed. . . . By now I had regained my composure and wanted to decline, but just at that moment I saw my aunt's keen eyes resting on me. . . . I dared not.

Thus the whole evening passed without my having the strength to carry out my resolution. I returned to the house with an insufferable feeling of shame. I felt as if I had been deeply insulted, although nobody had offended me. —

* * *

A week or so later, in the middle of a beautiful, warm, sunny morning, there was much noise and bustle in the District Governor's house. There was to be an excursion to the mountains. Kold had gone hunting the day before and was to meet the rest of the family up at the summer farm, where they would go fishing in a nearby large forest pond. Dressed for the trip, Sofie was standing by the window, thinking: 'How strange that this outing is not taking place until now. For me it is as if it has already been.' So much had already been said, dreamed and discussed concerning the trip. Mrs Ramm, who usually directed such enterprises, did not at all approach them in that casual, improvisational way that always proves the most felicitous. The preparations were immense, and not infrequently the happy mood in which the plan had been conceived would disappear, leaving people half sick of it all by the time they were ready to set off. The whole previous day had been devoted to such frying and roasting as if an entire infantry regiment were to be supplied. Despite Kold's assurances that he would provide game, Mrs Ramm thought it best to prepare something 'just in case' luck would not be with him.

In the drawing room it was impossible to move one's feet, due to the travelling clothes and the loaded baskets. The long awaited, almost solemn moment arrived when it was declared that everything was ready, except that the mistress of the house remembered it might be a good idea to bring mustard. One person called for a riding crop; another for a parasol; then Amalie exclaimed with a look out the window:

'Lord! Here comes Lorenz Brandt!'

'Are you mad!' shouted her mother, but then added more daintily, 'That is just what we need!' Displeasure descended on all the faces. Sofie let out a deep sigh of impatience.

'Quickly, children! Away with the clothes!' said Mrs Ramm. 'He must absolutely not notice a thing. We cannot, in God's name, drag that person along; it would ruin the whole trip for us.'

In unspoken agreement, everybody was already hurrying to obliterate every suggestion of an excursion. The clothes were tossed outside and the baskets were pushed under sofas and tables. A moment ago so full of life, the entire company were now standing about as if petrified.

The person responsible for this unpleasant disturbance was meanwhile approaching the farm with firm steps, and then he walked without ceremony through the drawing room door. His figure and movements were still those of a youth, but it was difficult to determine his age. It was impossible to say whether time or dissipation had aged his features and etched them with furrows. He was dressed in a green, threadbare overcoat that appeared to have belonged, in happier times, to a heavy-set man. The rest of his costume consisted of homespun trousers, unpolished boots, and a cap with a wax-cloth cover decorated with a cockade whose colours — another lively theme in the student feud — could no longer be the cause of argument. A checked waistcoat of cotton-and-wool tweed, with shiny buttons, was buttoned all the way up to his throat and appeared, along with a blue plaid kerchief, to perform the kind office of concealing what was underneath. He was accompanied by a large, scrawny poodle of a dirty white colour.

'Ah, good day, good day, my friends, how are things here? Your most obedient servant, gracious madam! It is a long time since I have had the pleasure of seeing you. Always the same; just as young and flourishing! For you, the poet's beautiful words are suitable: "And Idun's eternal spring colours her cheeks." — The devil, how hot it is!'

'Good morning, Brandt, and how are you?' said the lady with tart friendliness. 'I suppose you are on your way to visit your mother? Amalie, get some breakfast for Brandt; he'll no doubt be leaving in a minute — there is a good distance yet to Lilleholt.'

'Oh, there is no hurry, with Lilleholt, I mean; time enough to embrace my mother this evening. — That will be a surprise! She has not seen me for a year. Brother *Hans* had to go the way of all flesh, poor boy! I am now her only support.'

A general desire to laugh died away in pitying embarrassment, to which Brandt was completely oblivious. Just then he caught sight of Sofie, who had retired to a corner.

'What is that! Is that Sofie I see! Have you come home again? Is it really Sofie?'

Sofie overcame her reluctance and held out her hand to him. 'Good day, Lorenz.'

'Well, I must say! One gets to experience many strange things in this insane world, but this, God forgive me, I would have sworn was an impossibility. Is it Sofie? You were quite a nimble little thing before you left, but damned skinny and pale; — I certainly remember I was stupid enough to reject you at the balls — '

'Please help yourself, Brandt!' Mrs Ramm interrupted him, in an attempt to cut the subject short. 'Have some breakfast. Amalie, fill his glass!'

'Many thanks,' he said and fell to his meal with vigour. ' — I did find you somewhat skinny and pale, as I said, but by God, you had something special about you. You were not like those other prigs — there, there, don't get angry; as you can hear, I was saying that I was a fool not to appreciate you properly and to understand that you were one of those who had an eye for me. — That was then,' — he emptied his glass with the speed of a conjurer, ' — when I was the handsome Lorenz Brandt.'

Sofie, who had retreated, just stared at him with a look expressing loathing and fear by turn. In vain she attempted to find the traces of his former beauty in those puffy, reddishly lead-coloured features, in which every base passion was trying to gain prominence. At one time, Lorenz Brandt had really been the handsomest boy one could see, and he had been the pride and hope of old Madam Brandt. In those days, he had often visited the District Governor's family, whose young and lively girls were always happy to see him. Showing exceptional promise, he had been taken under the protection of a relative who made it possible for him to study. It is not the province of this story to tell how he was sucked into the maelstrom of the wild *Sturm und Drang* period of student life, which brought so much wonderful talent towards the light while sinking others beyond salvation, and from which Lorenz had emerged in the debased condition in which we now encounter him. So far, all attempts to save him, on the part of the District Governor and his family and of other friendly people, had been in vain.

'Is it possible to distort a lovely, noble shape to such a degree?' Sofie wondered. What had happened to the pure profile and the finely chiselled mouth? And to those eyes, the deep, clear blue of which had exhausted her sisters' entire store of beautiful similes? Lorenz's blond, curly hair, which in its former abundance might have served as a model for a sculptor, now hung dishevelled and loose like the rigging of a sinking ship.

'Thank you, no more, Mrs Ramm! Definitely no more,' he said, draining his fourth glass. 'This colour is no good in such heat. No, the *brown*, that has a cooling effect! I do not know if you have noticed, madam, that there is no better antidote to heat than cognac. Old *Ole Holm*' taught me that, and it is remarkable, quite remarkable! If you have a little bit on hand, we might just try. No? But you ought to recommend it to the District Governor as quite effective. Are we not going to have the honour of seeing him downstairs?'

'Right now my husband is so overburdened with business,' said the lady; 'I doubt he is coming downstairs.'

'But of course, then we'll not put him to the trouble. Besides it is more fitting that I go upstairs and pay my respects to him.'

'Father is not quite *well*, either,' said Amalie.

'He is really very poorly,' added his wife with a worried expression.

'Terribly poorly and yet overburdened with business! . . . That is a great, bloody shame. But how can you, Mrs Ramm, who are tenderness itself, allow this? No, it must not be permitted; he is much too precious to us all for that. If nobody else will talk sense into him, I shall — I shall immediately. . . .'

Mrs Ramm well understood the crude irony concealed in these words. She was just about to invent a fresh excuse to avert the intended visit to her husband — which visit, she well knew, was for the purpose of what Lorenz called 'borrowing' money — when something occurred that turned Lorenz's thoughts in a direction she found even less to her liking.

Croesus, the poor starving beast, had sniffed out the basket underneath the table and begun conducting investigations in a way that immediately caught Brandt's attention. Before Mrs Ramm could prevent it, the basket had been discovered. Brandt pulled it out, while bottles and glasses clinked against each other.

'Ei, ei, was ist das! Bottles, bread, chocolates! Where is it going? And only now do I see that Miss Amalie is so curiously attired. You really look like Miss Guinivere ready for a spot of falconry! Two-three-four — ' he

---

'A well-known souse at that time; typical of his period. [*Author's note from the 1879 edition.*]

said, holding the bottles up to the light. 'I believe, may God strike me, that it is Rhine wine! Dare I ask whither the excursion is intended to be?'

'We are taking a trip to the summer farm in the mountains,' Sofie finally said.

'And,' her mother interrupted her, 'when you came, we were just discussing how we were to be conveyed. As there are so many of us, we are a little short of transportation. I am sure it is best to postpone the whole thing.'

'Nay, why so? You have a stable full of horses; what, then, can be wanting?'

'We have only three,' said Amalie. 'Mother's carriage horse and the two browns, which are for Sofie and myself. The other horses are up at the summer farm. Brøcher was also supposed to come along, but he has no horse.'

'There is Brøcher coming up the drive with two horses!' Edvard shouted. 'One lady's horse; it's for you,' he said to Amalie, who blushed.

'You see!' said Brandt. 'The splendid, blessed curate! And, by God, he's in his hunting clothes; yes, I'll be damned if he's not as green as a parrot! And with spurs on. That, Lord help me, I want to watch! If you manage to get off your horse properly while wearing those, I'll eat both you and your spurs for breakfast tomorrow. But it does not matter; you are just as dear to us regardless. — Then we are all set! Now I'll take the old dun-coloured mare.'

'The old dun-coloured is lame, is it not, Edvard?' said Mrs Ramm desperately, winking her eye.

'Is it lame? Wait, we shall soon find out!' and Brandt ran out so fast that he almost knocked down Brøcher, who was just entering.

At that point, a chorus of lament broke loose.

'What do you suppose, Brøcher!' cried the mistress of the house. 'Everything was ready; we were only waiting for you when that drunken person appeared as if fallen out of the sky. . . . We must take him along; that will be the end of it.'

'What a dreadful thing!' moaned Amalie. 'And that was a fine idea of yours, Mother, to offer him breakfast. . . . Was he not cheerful enough beforehand? What a heavenly trip it could have been!'

'Just ask him to come along, why don't you,' Sofie begged.

'Yes, by God, that is best; we may just as well leap into it as crawl,' said Edvard. 'Never you mind about him, the rest of you. I'll assume responsibility for him myself,' he added with an air of self-importance.

Brandt came rushing in. 'Victoria! It's clear sailing! The dun-coloured mare is no more lame than you are, madam. That is what I call a stroke of luck. Besides, you are short of escorts for so many ladies. I don't see Mr Kold. Where is His Grace?'

The parade set off. The lady of the house led the way in a cariole with the housekeeper, in order to arrange everything ahead of time for the comfort of the rest of the party. Then followed the two sisters on horseback, accompanied by the curate. Edvard and Brandt, likewise on horseback, completed the procession.

From an upstairs window, the District Governor was nodding to them in his friendly fashion. Just like frightened game listening by the cave exit to see if the danger is past, he had not showed himself until now. On such occasions, when the whole household was turned upside-down, he was never to be seen downstairs; he ensconced himself as best he could behind his desk.

Brøcher and the two ladies had already left the main road and had covered a good distance of the narrow, but well-cleared forest lane, which for about six miles cut through the northernmost stretches of the district. They had completely lost sight of Edvard and Brandt. The curate was entertaining himself exclusively with Amalie and seemed scarcely to notice that Sofie was with them. The latter fell farther and farther behind. A small adjustment to the bridle delayed her a little, and perhaps Brøcher used this opportunity for a perfect *tête-à-tête* with Amalie — at any rate, he coaxed the horses into a steady trot, and soon Sofie found herself alone in the dark forest. She stopped for a moment and abandoned herself with indescribable pleasure to being by herself. She took off her hat and perched it on her saddle horn, and moving forward at a slow, swaying step she let the cool forest air flow freely about her head. Those soothing breezes seemed to have a similar effect on the brown horse. It shook its headgear as if it would rather be rid of it, but failing in this, it made do with a leisurely search for the few blades of grass that stuck out from the moss along the ditch. As time wore on, it became too late for Sofie to consider catching up with Amalie, and she decided to wait for Edvard and Brandt, who were coming up behind. Soon she heard hoofbeats on the hollow, booming rock surface. It was not without fear, however, that she discovered Brandt to be alone.

'Where is Edvard?'

'Edvard turned off at the Jokum farm. He wanted to pick up a bridle and bit at the blacksmith's, but he'll catch up with us at the summer farm, by another road. And you, Sofie — why are you alone?'

'I was delayed a little, and then I thought I might just as well wait until you caught up,' said Sofie, hiding her fear behind her calmest face. She sensed that like certain animals, Brandt would be most dangerous when confronted with fear or distrust.

'Did you? That was certainly nice of you. You will not regret it, by God, I shall protect you.'

'But now let's try to catch up with the others.'

'What's the hurry? It's so long since I have seen you. I must really thank the fortuitous occasion that makes me your champion,' he added gallantly, while a considerable slackness in his features and a certain dejection in his eyes suggested that he was about to become sober again.

'Yes, it is a long time since we saw each other — almost five or six years, I think.'

'I cannot believe it's you — you, who used to be the sort of delicate little bit of fluff one could blow away with one breath. It's true, by God, whether you believe it or not — I dared not dance with you because you were too slight. I was afraid you might get hurt. Now you look quite like Louise! . . . Seeing you puts me in mind of so many funny incidents she and I went through together. Can you remember the time we overturned in the Tom hills? The shafts broke, and there we stood in the most awful weather and didn't know what to do!'

'Yes, but you didn't hesitate for long before you picked up Louise and carried her home for more than a mile and a half in the deep snow.'

'Tut, that was not much to brag about. Louise was the prettiest girl in the whole countryside, and many would have envied me that walk.'

'And then you rushed off again to fetch poor *Broch*, who had remained on the battlefield and crawled under the fur rug. . . .'

'And you sent along a muff and foot-warmer for him — how furious he was! . . . No, but do you recall, Sofie, when I put on a cassock and delivered a wedding sermon in the manner of Broch? *Marie* and *Vilhelm Meier* were the bride and groom. At that time, Marie certainly had not the least suspicion that Broch himself would play a part the next time, and that the part of the groom, ha! ha! ha!'

'Oh, don't laugh at that,' said Sofie with aversion. 'Nobody can know what the future may bring. . . .'

'No, by God, you're right. No mother's son can know that. Surely nobody knows that better than I do.'

'And can you remember, Brandt,' Sofie interjected, anxious about having said something he might think referred to himself, 'the day you won the prize as the Ladies' Favourite, by jumping three times over the Major's big horse?'

'Do I remember! As you know, that was the time I had passed my university entrance exams with the highest mark. Your father gave a party for me, and in the evening we danced! — What would I not gladly have done that day! — What gaiety! What joy! "Es waren schönen Zeiten, Carlos." Times have changed.'

'Yes, it seems that much has changed,' said Sofie, painfully agitated.

They rode along in silence for a while.

'I don't know why I happened to think of the old days just now. It's strange enough . . . when I see you on horseback like that, slim and straight as a queen, and with those long tresses flying in the wind, I am taken ten years back in time, and I am on my way to the summer farm with your sisters. The sun was playing in just the same way over the green hillocks; the heather was blooming; and we heard the noise of the river coming closer and closer. I might almost believe that the ten intervening years are a dream. . . oh, a dream!'

Again he fell silent, as if distracted in some way. Another embarrassing pause occurred, and when they arrived at a fork in the road just at that moment, Sofie exclaimed, just to have something to say: 'Which way shall we take now? Do you know the way, Brandt?'

'The right way —! Yes, the hell I knew it; I just took the wrong one,' shrieked Lorenz with a peal of laughter. Sofie made a startled move.

'How you frighten me,' she said, and coaxing her horse into a gallop, she left Brandt a little distance behind. When she reached the top of a steep slope, she halted and let her voice ring out over the quiet hills. A faraway shout answered. Then she turned to Lorenz, who was following slowly.

'Forgive me, Sofie, if I have frightened you,' he said humbly. 'From now on you may relax.'

Sofie looked at him in surprise. He was as pale as death, and his eyes shone with a strange light. At that moment, he still showed a trace of the beauty that had once distinguished him.

'Aha!' shouted Lorenz in quite a different tone of voice. 'There, it seems, comes St. George the knight, who is to deliver you from the dragon.'

'Oh, thank God I find you alive!' said Kold and deftly manoeuvred his horse between the two others without greeting Brandt. 'The party is in a terrible uproar of worry. . . . Nothing has happened to you?'

'Nothing at all, not the least bit; I know the forest so well that it is impossible for me to get lost.'

'But I thought I heard you shout, or was I mistaken?'

'I just wanted to try the echo against the Giants' Wall. You really have troubled yourself for no reason.'

She was met with a grateful look from Lorenz, who said with some self-consequence: 'Mr Kold does not at all seem to notice that Miss Sofie had an escort.'

'I beg your pardon, Mr Brandt; I really had observed it, and I assure you all due notice was taken of the fact that Miss Sofie was accompanied by you.'

'And yet I say,' said Lorenz angrily, 'that Miss Sofie was just as safe in my care as she would have been with three "Troopists" such as yourself. If there were ten such here, I would stand by what I have said.'

'But, as I at most could be said to be one "Troopist", a brave man like yourself had best not get involved with me.'

'I shall hold you accountable for your taunts another time,' said Lorenz, pale with anger.

'Taunt you! Poor man! It's a long time since any man found it worth his trouble,' Kold continued mercilessly, turning towards Sofie.

'What do you mean by that?' shouted Lorenz, incensed. 'Now you'd damn well better explain yourself . . . '

'For God's sake, Mr Brandt, control yourself; be calm!' cried Sofie. 'Or I shall have cause to complain about you! I assure you, Mr Kold, I have had no reason for fear until now.'

'And that is *my* fault, Miss Sofie,' said Kold, somewhat hurt by Sofie's words.

'I call that spoken like an angel!' said Lorenz, suddenly gentle. 'For her sake it shall be forgotten. I forgive you.' He solemnly gave Kold his hand.

'Oh, many thanks!' said Kold with a most peculiar expression, while he urged his horse in front of the others. They soon reached the summer farm, where the entire company halted for a repast.

We rejoin everybody by the big pond — a pond so deep and so hidden in the embrace of virgin forest that it was not visible until one had already come upon it, confronting the surprising and picturesque sight of the pond's large, mirror-like surface in its dark frame. Although the sun was still high in the sky, evening seemed already to have descended there. Some sunset rays still glowed on the eastern shore and lent a brilliant, metallic shine to the yellow waterlilies growing so defiantly where the stream flowed out of it. The rest of the pond's surface lay in the deep, blue shadows of the forest that rose up on all sides, seemingly reluctant to let go of the small plot on which *Fish-Anders* had built his hut.

In front of this hut, the party halted and unloaded baskets and travelling equipment.

'How beautiful it is here!' was the first general exclamation.

'Extremely picturesque; most unusual! Oh, how mysteriously secluded and quiet!' individual voices were heard to say.

'Look, children — this is where we'll drink our tea,' said Mrs Ramm. 'That will be lovely.'

'Oh dear,' thought Kold, who had just moved some rare plants from his hat into a pot made of birch bark; 'now we are to eat again. We just came from an enormous meal at the summer farm. But that is the way it is with these pleasure trips: *food* — that is the main business. One doesn't eat in order to be able to stand a little physical exertion; one seeks out exertion in order to eat with an even bigger appetite.... I may as well save myself the trouble of complaining, however.... Who in this company would understand? Not one!' — and at that moment he could not prevent a small grimace from disfiguring his handsome face.

'Are we to eat again, Mother?' Sofie exclaimed. 'I thought we were going to fish; now we ought really to earn our food ourselves.'

Nobody was at home in the hut. Anders and his daughter had probably gone to a nearby pond to fish. It is not unusual for those small ponds and lakes to be so rich in trout that poor people are able to live on them up in the desolate mountains. The hut was inviting; stools and tables had been scoured white for the Midsummer celebration; birch twigs with new green leaves were stuck under the rafters and in the corner near the stove; and in the small window with green panes stood a neckless bottle filled with pasque flowers and wild roses. On the table a *Kingo's Hymn Book* lay open, brown with wear and old age. Its venerable big print emerged like inscriptions on a stone tablet from under a pair of immense, extremely convex eyeglasses marking the place in the book. The only living creature, apart from the buzzing flies, was a half-grown white pig that got up from the ashes in confusion and, horrified by so many unexpected guests, streaked out of the door.

'How nice and cosy it is in here!' said Amalie. 'It will be sweet to drink tea in this little fishing hut by the quiet, shiny lake. Do but look how lovely! . . . Here in this hut I could truly live. . . . There is nothing wanting. . . .'

'But a heart,' mimicked Edvard. 'Isn't that true, Amalie — you were thinking about "a hut and his heart", weren't you?'

'What nonsense,' said Amalie primly. 'What is that supposed to mean? It has nothing to do with this!'

'Not quite,' Kold remarked. 'Didn't that combination ever occur to you, Miss Amalie? Yet it is both attractive and natural. . . . Be honest, just for once.'

'I don't understand a word of all this; please spare me your combinations,' said Amalie, who now was upset in earnest.

'Kold and your brother were referring to a French play by that title, which has enjoyed great success in the theatres,' said Mrs Ramm in a didactic tone. 'In the play, *Scribe* the writer is dreadfully taken with the idea of living in a hut. It may be charming enough, but that sort of love, with dry bread and spring water, appears to better advantage in novels and comedies than in real life.'

Kold looked around as if searching for help. Sofie was not there.

Brandt, who had regained his good humour after a sizable restorative at the summer farm, exclaimed rather clumsily: 'It does not appear that Miss Amalie will need to search long to find a heart for her hut. Perhaps it will be more difficult to find a hut for her heart. What do you think, Curate?'

Amalie fled, blushing, but Brøcher, who for a long time had vainly been seeking a small living of his own, merely glared at him angrily in reply.

'Well, now I have searched every corner, to no avail,' said Sofie, joining them.

'For a heart?'

'No, for a tea kettle. Imagine, there is none. What are we to do now?'

With much laughter, everybody now got up to look for something in which to boil water. Finally, the only cooking pot in the house was located, but it was full of gruel and had to be emptied and thoroughly cleaned before it could be put to the use just mentioned.

They agreed that whoever drew the lot, regardless of who the person might be, was to undertake this unattractive job. The lot fell on Sofie, and she very daintily picked up the pot with the tips of her fingers and, amidst much banter from the others, carried it down to the water's edge, where she commenced her work without further ado. Behind her stood Amalie, who from time to time interrupted her sister's efforts with enthusiastic exclamations about the landscape.

Brandt was continually in motion. Running up and down with boundless energy and anxiousness to be of assistance, he quoted and he declaimed, and in between he made veiled references to the genuine princess in the fairytale, who takes over the work of the maidservant while the maidservant dresses up and pretends she is a princess, etc.

Kold, stretched out on the grass in front of the house, finally realized that all these references were aimed at Sofie, and he did not know whether to be amused or annoyed. He was much too preoccupied with her himself not to find the other's noisy admiration intolerable.

Sofie had never appeared to better advantage than at that moment. The glorious forest seemed the ideal setting for her. Perfect beauty has moments when it is less than perfect, and the more spiritual its nature, the more it is subject to this law of chance. Sofie's beauty was of this kind; it depended very much on the moment. Someone who had seen her when she was bored or depressed, did not recognize her when her face was animated by joy or reflecting some deeper emotion. Her reputation for extraordinary beauty that later spread so far and wide, thanks to the smallness of our country, was therefore in a way undeserved, because her beauty was not the sort that should be judged by the great mass of people. Curiosity, greedily dogging her steps, was therefore not infrequently disappointed.

Sofie's hair was extraordinarily lovely. It was a family inheritance, of which Mrs Ramm was rather proud. Its abundance was already obvious when Sofie was a child, although as a mere pretty detail, whereas it now blended perfectly with the harmony of the whole. Her hair was deep chestnut in colour and hung so glossily, smoothly and softly that it was an adornment even when in disorder. She wore it in several plaits, because it was too heavy to be forced into a single braid. The long tresses in front touched her neck and shoulders. Her complexion was the blooming sort that accompanies a rich growth of hair, but it was as changeable as the expression and colour of her eyes, which most people claimed were brown, while others maintained they were blue. We confide to the reader in all secrecy that Sofie's eyes were blue, but with a brownish tinge. Her mouth and nose were beyond reproach, considering our anti-classical soil, but it never occurred to anyone gazing upon this face that its features might have been more beautiful. In this case, one might in truth say with the poet, 'Wer kann wissen, wo der Mund aufhört und das Lächeln beginnt.'

Sofie's long neck, sloping shoulders and delicate arms and legs suggested that her slender figure would never deteriorate into obesity. In her movements, she was as quick and light as a savage. As she grew older, she tried hard to move more sedately, and it cost her no little trouble to accustom herself to walking instead of running — a tendency she had had since she was a child running around in the open air. That rapid, gliding walk made one think of the wagtail, who barely touches the ground as it makes ready to take off.

Kold felt that the riddle surrounding Sofie was about to be solved, and that her true self would emerge like a chrysalis from its cocoon. The thought made him strangely afraid. Now it could no longer be avoided. The half-dreamed picture must be completed — or ruined. He could not take his eyes off her, but he had a sensation akin to dread every time she opened her mouth to say something. Fortunately, Sofie remained rather silent.

'Why should she be different from the others?' he said to himself, following every one of Sofie's movements with his eyes as he sat there on his hill. 'Why should she escape the *deceit* that perhaps is women's most natural defence against the world? This *deceit*, this ability to dissemble — are they *born* with it? Is it perhaps impressed upon their souls, as an invisible mark of slavery, while they are still in the cradle? How could this poor, neglected child have escaped it? Maybe precisely because she has been neglected. If only they could grow up as wild as the hawthorn; if only they could be kept meticulously away from this vile crippling called upbringing. . . . Sofie is *naive*, and she has lived very much *alone* . . . . Oh, I want to be kind to her; to support her if I can. . . . Oh, but she is sweet. . ! No, no, especially towards her I am going to be mercilessly strict. If she knows no better than the others how to value what is true in her soul; if she has not kept close and implacable guard over it, with infinite pride! . . . If she, as well, trades her soul for an immature infatuation! Do not yield to *anyone, anyone*, Sofie, *before you yourself* love. . . . And if you allow room for this feeling, then *do not deny it, do not hide it, do not lie* . . . . Oh, if she could be true, true, true! How fine and slight she looks when getting up from her stooped position like that! When she looks up, it is as if her eyes have been harbouring a deep and troubling thought, and when she turns those frightened and imploring eyes towards us, it is as if she were saying: "Have I neglected to do something? Oh, don't be angry — " and then she is all attentiveness to everybody. She has black eyes, I think. . . . Oddly enough, her eyes have never met mine. How can she be bothered to talk to this Lorenz! She smiles at him! . . . How can she stand having that drunken lout look at her with eyes like that!'

Poor Sofie was just as unaware of being the object of this long meditation as she was of Lorenz's gallantry being particularly intended for her. He had fallen on the company like a burden, and now she thought it only proper that she should carry her share of the weight. Besides, she felt sorry for him, and by being friendly to him she hoped to make some amends for the others' roughness and poorly disguised contempt.

The tea was ready and was drunk amidst much noise and merriment, but the people in the party were too dissimilar for there to be any sense of real diversion. There was no deep and true harmony. Now and then some minor friction arose between Mrs Ramm and Lorenz, which amused Kold and upset Amalie. Despite the watchfulness of the housekeeper and of the mistress of the house, Lorenz had contrived to imbibe the remains of the alcoholic beverages brought along on the trip — some cold punch and half a bottle of cognac that was intended for old Anders — and the others had some reason to fear the consequences. Brandt, who in his sober state was melancholy and taciturn to the point of timidity as long as nobody teased him, was rude, boastful and extremely personal in his remarks when drunk. To make matters worse, there was always some truth to what he said. His jesting had that desperate humour with which people in his situation seek revenge on more fortunate people and their scorn, and at times his jests came much too close to home. Mrs Ramm in particular feared him like the plague. Even as a boy, Lorenz had cleverly perceived all her weaknesses, and with particular malice he now made some of these his target.

Picnics — so capable of bringing enjoyment to a few people with a lot in common — should never be undertaken in mismatched company. People do not become better or more important just from being moved into the great and glorious outdoors, any more than a mediocre picture appears to better advantage when mounted in a splendid frame. When you have experienced one such poorly composed *partie de plaisir* you have experienced them all; everywhere one finds the same basic ingredients: much eating and drinking, as Kold had already noted; the same talk and squabbles about nothing, only louder and more good-natured than at home in the living room; a strange urge to make a lot of noise; much fake rapture with nature, as unmotivated as applause from the gallery, by which any little bit of *real* sentiment is modestly or angrily silenced. At times, chance may help things along by means of a minor adventure, but seldom an agreeable sort of adventure: a coat soaked through, a twisted foot, and so on — and it all ends in the pleasure of returning home, which is such a genuine pleasure that one might think it had been the sole reason for all the arrangements.

We therefore skip over a few hours, which can easily be filled out by the reader's own reminiscences, before we rejoin our party. Their merriment had passed its peak, and silent intervals were occurring. During one such pause in the conversation, the curate remarked: 'Here we are carrying on with as much noise as if Anders and his family did not exist. It is truly an odd thing, this, to make oneself at home in a stranger's house.'

'Yes, you're so right,' said Amalie. 'When I stop to think about it, it is really shameful. Suppose someone were to do the same to us! — overrun our rooms while we were out; turn the house upside-down — what would we say? Anders has just as much reason to complain.'

This question gave rise to a small argument. While the more sensitive members of the party, including the housekeeper, unconditionally agreed with Amalie, some of the others thought that this occasion could in no way be subjected to such a comparison.

'Well, children, however that may be, it is now too late to change anything. You may be sure I shall satisfy our host, so that he will be grateful for the visit — what do you think of my putting this banknote in his hymnbook? That will be a pious surprise.'

'If only Brandt had not knocked out the window,' Amalie continued. 'Suppose the poor people do not notice it, but go to bed right here in front of the open window. The night air is supposed to be extremely harmful. I think I'll stuff my kerchief into it; that will be my surprise.'

'I think that most of all it's a pity about the flowers,' added Sofie. 'Just look how pitifully downtrodden they are! Wild roses, bluebells and catchfly... perhaps *Kari* has had to fetch them from more than six miles away, and here we are treating them as if they were just grass.'

'It was undeniably the only and the costliest vase in the house, as well,' said Kold, mournfully contemplating the pieces of the neckless bottle. 'The worst of it is that it's a sort that's hard to replace.'

'Brandt will no doubt be able to; he's very knowledgable in all operations involving bottles,' suggested Edvard. 'Hulloa, Brandt — I don't suppose you could break the neck off a bottle?'

'Off ten if you wish, dear boy. Is it Rhine wine?'

'But seeing these eyeglasses in the hymnbook,' said Mrs Ramm, 'it occurs to me to wonder where old *Synneve* might be? I had completely forgotten about her.'

'Yes, old Synneve!' everybody called out.

'Damn me, she surely cannot have gone dancing down in the village,' said Edvard.

'Synneve has not been away from this place for the past twenty years; that was the last time she came to the Lord's table,' the curate assured them in his professional capacity. 'She is probably well into her second childhood. Incomprehensible! We must have instilled such fear and trepidation in her that she has gone off to hide some place, if she has not headed straight for the forest.'

'Out and away to look for her!' was the general cry.

'Hallee, halloo, a hunt for old Synneve!' shouted Edvard. The barking Croesus led the way.

In the tiny cowbarn, old Synneve sat squeezed into the corner of the empty stall. Next to her stood the pig, as if they sought protection in each other's company. The tiny, withered, shrunken figure, with grey hair sticking out from under her black cap, was a strange contrast to the young, healthy, colourfully dressed people surrounding her. She stared at them like a startled animal. It would seem that old Synneve had long since forgotten any memory of such beings — what they looked like; how they behaved and dressed. Their existence had faded from the sphere of her imagination, which in ever narrowing circles revolved around the wild and desolate spot in which she was vegetating, and which would slowly disappear like the ancient, mossgrown firs. In vain, the party tried to prevail upon her to go inside the hut or to get her to talk. The ladies offered her food and sweetmeats, but they could not get her to eat in their presence. As soon as they moved away, however, she ate greedily.

Evening had descended. The lake had sunk completely into the shadows, while the sun glowing on the tops of the tallest firs announced that it had not yet set. The water lilies closed their chalices and settled down on their broad and shiny leaves. There was calling and cooing from the nearby summer farms; bells jingled rhythmically, homeward bound. . . . In the deepest distance, the strains from a shepherd's wooden horn could be heard.

Kold and Edvard were standing on a log raft the size of an ordinary living room door, which was made fast to the shore with a withy chain. They were fishing — Edvard very eagerly; Kold absent-mindedly, lost in his surroundings. Out in the middle of the water, Amalie and Sofie lay in a small punt — a sort of flat-bottomed boat that could be used only in calm water — occupying themselves with catching white water lilies, of which there grew a few. Driven by Brandt's incessant obtrusiveness, the two sisters had at last stolen off towards the boat and pushed away from shore. The entire landscape was reflected with minute clarity in the perfectly calm depths: the dark wall of firs; the glorious ceiling provided by the sky; the house on the moss-covered, rocky shore with a potato field as big as a living room floor; two clusters of currant bushes and one cluster of red poppies, which represented the garden; the white pig just then walking down the path — everything was reflected in the watery mirror with almost ridiculous exactitude.

From up at the house could be heard, by turn, the laughter of Lorenz Brandt and the sharper, unfriendlier voices belonging to Mrs Ramm and the housekeeper.

Kold's glance continually swept out towards deeper water, while he mechanically monitored and pulled in his baited hook or replied in monosyllables to Edvard's shouts of hope or impatience. Not fifty paces away from him lay Sofie, bending over the side of the boat, her long tresses almost touching the surface of the water. He had to admire the spirited grace with which she now pushed back her bothersome mane of hair, now reached for the flowers that, seemingly immobile, yet evaded her teasingly and disappeared sometimes under the boat, sometimes to the side, on their long, swaying stalks. Sofie seemed to belong to the same element on which she was rocking along with the flowers — dreaming, evanescent, enigmatic, a stranger among the others. She appeared to have risen out of the mountain lake, lured by the magic of human voices, while she herself was bewitching the humans. Amalie, lying next to her, seemed to be such a human child who frivolously or unthinkingly had given herself over to Sofie's spell.

When something has just moved us deeply, we may become very angry if another person comments out loud about that which we, as yet, cannot or will not express ourselves. Kold was aroused from his silent contemplation by Brandt's loud perorations behind him.

'Isn't it just what I say! Look at those two sisters! The one calls herself a beauty and struts about and carries on as if she were one; but next to the other she is, God d. . . me, no more than a chambermaid, a starched-up dairy wench. . . . She, on the other hand, has no name yet, but I'll be a poor sort if she is not given one — a name that will resound from Lindesnes to the North Cape and farther still. That is something, I tell you! You have no appreciation of it. . . . You want something glaring and obvious. That is a figure! Those are eyes! That I call a complexion beyond compare! . . . And whoever says differently, I declare to be a philistine; a stockfish I shall say he is. . . .

As narrow as the stem of a lily,
As loaded as, as loaded as . . . as loaded. . . .'

'As a beast,' the annoyed Edvard supplemented while throwing his line out again. 'Just don't shout so damned loudly!'

'I merely state, my dear Edvard, that you ought not thus to let your beautiful sisters fend for themselves out on the treacherous deep. . . . It is our duty to assist them . . . our duty as their champions. . . .

Handsome merman out of the ocean rose
Bedecked with kelp. . .
His eye was loving, his speech was sweet,
Watch out, oh — '

'Stay away from the raft, Brandt, you're scaring the fish — '

'Are you insane, man!' yelled Kold.

But it was too late. To the refrain of 'Watch out, oh child, for the falseness of men,' Brandt had already released the withy chain and with a kick worthy of Wilhelm Tell sent the raft away from the shore. Edvard saved himself with a desperate jump, but Kold was drifting on the pitiful, teetering craft out towards the centre of the lake, in the company of the equally unsteady Brandt.

'Have no fear! There is no cause for alarm,' said Lorenz; 'there is no danger at all. You'll see, it'll all turn out well. Can you see the bottom? There is a devilish depth to these little lakes.'

'But are you completely possessed, Brandt! Give me my pole — away from that side! Can't you see the raft is about to overturn!'

'I see you are afraid. I am sorry for that, extremely sorry. It must cause hellish suffering, that sort of fear. Modern doctors claim it is something physical, having its origin in an organ that is supposed to be located in the back some place, God knows where. Lean on me. . . . If we fall in, we shall both fall in, that is clear; that is crystal clear. . . . And it will be a miracle if we don't fall in. . . . But it doesn't matter; you'll be saved; I give you my word of honour! I should not deserve being called the champion swimmer? I have swum from Vippetangen over to Hovedøen — what do you think of that? . . . I should not deserve the name. . . Ouch — death and damnation! — Oops — there we are; it's all right. . .! I should not deserve being called the champion swimmer, as I say, could I not take it upon myself to bring such a slight, inflated customer onto dry land. You'll be just as useful to me as a blown-up *bladder*. Ha, ha!'

While Lorenz continued this nonsense, Kold called to the ladies in the boat, asking them to come closer. They were now near enough to stretch out an oar, and the raft would soon have been brought up alongside the boat, if Brandt could only have kept still. That happened which Kold had feared would happen.

Brandt cannot wait for the boat; he wants to get into it with a violent leap; but he loses his balance. The raft tips over, and the two unlucky sailors find themselves in the water. What a scene! An enormous splash and spray momentarily enveloped the entire group and screened it from view. In the middle of the golden surface, the group showed up as dark bronze and looked not unlike the famous group of nereïds in the midst of the large pool with the fountains playing. Croesus, who had swum after the raft and had already reached the boat, added to the effect by shaking his dripping fur all over the poor ladies. Kold, an excellent swimmer, immediately surfaced and instinctively caught hold of the boat, but the sisters' shrill cry of 'For God's sake, Brandt is drowning! Help him!' immediately forced him to go back.

As so often happens with inebriated people when they fall in the water, Lorenz had been seized by a kind of paralysis. After thrashing desperately with his arms a few times, he suddenly uttered a heavy oath and sank. Diving under and grasping him by his long hair was the work of a moment for Kold, who then managed, by tremendous effort, to drag Lorenz towards the shore, where Edvard gave him the necessary help.

The panic was gone. On the shore, Brandt was lying unconscious, pitiful to behold. Everybody was busy rubbing, thumping and shaking him to bring him back to life. Amalie found the opportunity for a faint much too rare a thing nowadays to be neglected. With her eyes closed she lay back in Brøcher's arms, and when she opened them at last and saw Sofie and Edvard in the process of pulling off Lorenz's coat, thus exposing his bare shirt to view, she swooned again. Mrs Ramm did not know whom to scold, because the actual cause of the accident was in no condition to hear her. Nobody understood at whom her complaints were aimed — whether at the victims of the accident or at Amalie's new riding habit, which had been thoroughly ruined. A little off to one side, Kold was leaning against a fir tree for support. He was somewhat paler than usual. With water streaming from his dark hair, he looked like the handsome merman in the song. He tried as best he could to defend himself against the housekeeper, who had seized Mrs Ramm's shawl and was using it to rub him dry as best she could.

'That is wasted effort, dear children,' said Mrs Ramm, when Lorenz showed no sign of life. 'Here, human aid is of no avail! What an event! Let us promise one another to remain calm and composed. Just be calm; just be calm! I will inform his mother.'

'There is no need,' said Lorenz suddenly in a weak voice. 'I'll do that myself. . . . Phew!' he said, spouting like a whale as he sat up. 'What a bath! — But I said so. . . . By my soul I expected it to happen! — Where is Kold? Was he rescued? Praise God, there he is! — That hellishly cold swim did so deprive me of my senses that I scarcely know how I was able to get him to shore.'

101

This confusion on Brandt's part was too unexpected. Everyone burst out laughing, unable to stop. Mrs Ramm had to laugh in the midst of her ill humour, and Amalie found herself unable to maintain her swoon and heartily joined in the general merriment. Even old Synneve was lured forth by it. Her grey head could be seen peeking out of the cowbarn door. Jolliness had returned, and it was quickly decided that it was time to return home. Mrs Ramm decided that Edvard that same evening was to accompany Brandt to his mother's farm, which fortunately was in the vicinity. Being somewhat more submissive after his involuntary immersion, Lorenz agreed to everything without protest. Everybody got ready to leave. When the party was about to break up, Sofie pulled Edvard aside and seemed to be asking something of him with great energy.

'How can you ask that, Sofie?' exclaimed her brother. 'Madam Brandt can surely not be angry with us because Lorenz gets himself drunk and falls in the water. She ought sooner to be furious because we pulled him out again. . . .'

'Shame on you, Edvard!'

'What is it your sister is entreating you to do?' Kold asked, seeing from Sophie's face that she was ardently and reluctantly repeating her plea.

'She has taken it into her head that it would upset old Madam Brandt to see Lorenz this evening; therefore she wants me to stop at Krogvold nearby and let him sleep it off there, not bringing him home until tomorrow. Don't you think I have been enough of a madhouse custodian today? Am I now, to top it off, to waste my night at such a nasty little place for the sake of a whim . . . . And Sofie doesn't consider that the fellow is dripping wet. . . . But that is the usual *impracticality* of women,' Edvard added, very pleased to have occasion to use this splendid new word, which had just become fashionable and which served as a sort of battle cry for all writers of stock prose.

Kold requested that the responsibility for seeing Lorenz home might be turned over to him, and he did this in a way that eliminated all protest on Edvard's part. Kold charged Edvard with sending, immediately upon his return home, an express messenger to Krogvold with dry clothes for Brandt and himself. He added something in a low voice.

'No need; he can get a waistcoat from me; and I'll just nab one of Father's shirts,' said Edvard out loud.

This arrangement did not quite set Sofie's mind at rest. She could wrest no promise from Kold concerning what was on her mind, but as she was mounting her horse, she sent him one of those pleading looks that express more than words.

When Brandt woke up at Krogvold the following morning, sober and strengthened in body, he discovered that he was alone. In front of his bed hung a very handsome complete suit of clothing. Kold had found that he had no other part to play than that of the good spirits, who disappear as soon as they have completed their task. After he had put Lorenz to bed in the best available bed and given him something warm to drink, while also impressing upon the farmer a few guidelines for the following morning, he had hurried back home.

When Brandt collected his thoughts the next morning, the memory of the preceding day's events returned with full clarity, and he now succumbed to one of those fits of regret and contrition that are to his kind what so-called 'moments of clarity' are to the insane: ill-timed and full of misery. He wept with self-pity. He finally realized how it all hung together — his rescue by Kold; his own swaggering rudeness; the others' amusement. His feeling of infinite bitterness towards his rescuer did not soften in the least when he saw the clothes and realized that it was from Kold he was forced to accept this fresh sacrifice. He struggled against the remains of a patrician distaste for accepting this contemptuous alms. But was there any other way out? — He was a tender son. Above all, he must make a decent appearance before his own mother, in order not to frighten her too much. He was a tender son, therefore he did not wish to appear as dejected and crushed as he was, either. His next thought, therefore, was of a remedy that could restore to him some of his confidence and good humour.

* * *

SOFIE'S DIARY CONTINUED

Although my stay in Christiania lasted for only ten days, luck would have it that there, too, I was invited to a ball, where I was to see all the better sort of people in the city. I went along with the secret hope that among my fellow countrymen, I might overcome my unpleasant impressions and again come to terms with my beloved dance. But I was wrong. Everything that had offended me obscurely and indistinctly, now emerged in a more defined and decided form. Here individual traits were more pronounced and contrasts sharper.

I happened to be seated in one of the front rows of ladies. On the floor, the gentlemen were partly standing about in groups; partly sauntering up and down along the rows, just like officers reviewing the troops. Just then, the music started up, and the entire front row was engaged to dance, with the exception of one poor, conspicuously fat young lady. A gentleman next to her said only these few words to his neighbour, but loudly enough that the poor creature could surely hear:

'Weighed, but *not* found wanting.'

Why did she expose herself to this kind of humiliation? — Who among us can be proof against it? — Why are we exposed to it? — All these questions overwhelmed and bewildered me, while one row of ladies after another disappeared, and my row was next. An unbearable feeling of shame took hold of me; I wished I were a hundred miles away. I could feel myself turning pale and blushing by turns. 'I do not at all want to dance,' I said to myself. This came over me suddenly. And really, after I had refused a couple of offers, I felt calm again as if risen in my own esteem. I was sitting between a couple of young ladies, both of whom were most attractive. A small, skinny cavalier with a flat, dull face was observing us with all his might through his pince-nez, but he did not seem to be able to make up his mind. My two neighbours ridiculed him with great energy behind my back; I expected no less than that they would refuse him. I therefore felt no little surprise when he bowed to one of them and she stood up with a most obliging smile!

The other sat out the dance. I tried to start a conversation with her, but it was not possible to obtain any real answers, because she had become so depressed and distracted. A lot of ladies were sitting out the dance. There was no lack of gentlemen, but they were just standing about watching, while those who were dancing looked as if they were engaged in heavy labour. None of the partners seemed to take any real pleasure in the business, and I did not know what to think. I wonder if the reason is that the ladies are not allowed to dance with whom they want?

It also made me wonder that the ugliest gentlemen at the ball almost invariably sought out the prettiest ladies, as if they were not conspicuous enough already. If such a gentleman were to consider *why* and with what thoughts such a lady follows him in the dance, I am quite sure it would have a humiliating outcome for him. To me it seems that the least favoured among the gentlemen ought to seek out the ill-favoured ladies. At least then they would be certain of a 'Yes, thank you' being spoken with more heartfelt gratitude. A freely given 'Yes, thank you' — oh, who does not give it! We will dance with anyone, so long as we can dance. We dance with needles in our shoes, just so we may dance.

One gentleman stood out among the others. He was a tall, slender person with a pale, expressive face. He was not quite young, and from the way in which people deferred to him, one could deduce that he was a man of some importance. Most noticeable was the joy, the spiritedness with which he danced. It is impossible to describe the courtly grace, the true nobility with which he would bend over his lady in conversation or lead her in the dance, and the zest for life, the elation that radiated from his countenance with his every move. He looked as if he had won his lady after a thousand dangers, not as if she had fallen to his lot by force. How willingly I should have danced with him! — It was as if I must fly towards him and throw myself with him into the whirling mass, to the sound of the music which at that moment made my heart beat almost painfully. And yet, it would have given me no pleasure had he asked me. I should have had to give him the same 'yes' with the same inclination of the head, the same obligatory smile, that he knew I would have given to the first fool who came along. He seemed to me too good for that. —

My sufferings in the ballroom — are they not in a small way a reflection of life itself? —

Oh, it is as if these words contained the sum of my obscure sorrows! Happy the child whose greatest fear concerned a lost schoolbook; who has known no other sorrows than the loss of a doll! What dark fate made my mind awaken so early to a contemplation of the more serious aspects of life — to a deep despair and a fear of what we call our destiny? — Our destiny is to be *married*, not to be happy. In that respect I have seen both of my sisters fulfilling their destiny. They took their husbands deliberately, voluntarily, and yet they would not themselves under any circumstances have chosen those men. How vividly I still picture those scenes to myself — they made an impression on me that can never be erased. I have only the most unpleasant memories of both of my brothers-in-law, who succeeded each other as tutors in this house. When *Marie* became engaged to Broch, that stiff, insufferable pedant, at whom she herself had laughed many a time, I was yet quite a small child, but I still remember it. When we were all assembled and the engagement was announced, I said to him: 'How can you believe that; she only wants to play a trick on you!' Marie — who was to die so soon — was the first to be sacrificed; she was the eldest. She is supposed to have been so beautiful, but I have no definite impression of that myself. Perhaps her beauty was of that more serious, spiritual nature which a child does not understand.

Louise, however, was fresh and radiant as a spring day when she came home after a two-year stay with Aunt in Copenhagen. Her beauty, the foreign cut of her clothes, her easy and yet elegant manner, made a deep impression on me. It seemed as if everything she touched was made more beautiful. I looked up to this sister with mute admiration. With the perspicacity only children possess, I knew how to penetrate everything that concerned her. But she was a grown-up girl, and only in my childish way dared I reveal my deep interest and devotion. I ran errands for her; guessed every little wish of hers; and tried in every way to please her.

On my tenth birthday, Aunt *Charlotte* had given me a wax doll, and because I thought it bore some resemblance to Louise, I named it after her. But little by little I identified it completely with my sister; I wove into its make-believe existence all that concerned Louise. If Louise got a new dress, the doll was to have one exactly like it. With this other Louise I talked; to her I dared pour out my heart. I advised her; I comforted her in difficult straits; I dreamed the loveliest dreams of the future with her. The doll had her residence in a deep niche in the cave. There it sat, like a tiny, enchanted princess hidden from the world; waiting for the day when luck would come and fetch it away. —

Yes, I took Louise's fate to heart in quite a different way. That she could do this! How I hated this *Caspers*. . . . He was younger and handsomer than Broch; had a so-called 'good head' and a kind of dry wit which he constantly exercised — but these attributes only threw his crudeness and conceit into sharper relief. He always treated my mother and my grown sisters curtly and without respect, and he — he did not blush to impress upon Edvard the tenet that all women are subservient creatures who deserve no better treatment. It bore splendid fruit. A nice boy before, Edvard now became tyrannical and nasty towards us sisters.

Nonetheless, Caspers fell in love with Louise and deigned to desire her hand. I shall never forget that day. He wrote a letter of proposal in the

106

morning. At the table, everybody was silent. Louise looked blushingly down at her plate and did not touch her favourite dishes which — I do not know whether by chance — had been brought to the table that day. Mother looked solemn, and when we got up from the table, Caspers helped her put away her chair. In the afternoon, Mother spoke about a woman's destiny and about what children owe their parents. I then understood what was up. I also knew what Louise would answer; I knew she loved another man. She had never said so, but yet I knew it. I had accompanied her into this silent love so completely that it was as if it had become my own. Like her, I changed colour at the mention of his name, although I had never seen him.

The night after this solemn day, I was awakened by her lying there on her bed, suppressing her sobs. 'Are you awake, Sofie?' she asked. Did she want to open her heart to me, or was she just fearful of revealing her heart to me? I thought the latter and pretended to be asleep. But when all was quiet, I got up and tiptoed over to her bed. She was asleep. I sat there until morning; I dared not leave my post. I had to convince myself that she was sleeping safely, just as if I were able to guard her sleep. The following day it was announced that she was engaged to Caspers. Then I stole out of the living room, ran down across the meadows, and hid myself in the thickest part of the forest. There I cried bitterly. —

When I saw Caspers caressing Louise, it seemed to me that she was being shamed in public. I could not bear it; I was outraged on my sister's behalf. I could not stand being in the house, but would hide in the forest and in the cave. —

Meanwhile, the dreadful day was approaching when Louise was to be married to Caspers. I kept believing that Heaven would allow a miracle to happen in order to prevent the wedding. No miracle occurred — unless Louise's strange composure be considered one. That pained me more than it pleased me. Whether I wanted to or not, I had to be present in church. There, I watched Louise stand in front of the altar with the man she neither loved nor respected, and who later has made her so boundlessly unhappy.

After the ceremony, when nobody was asking about me, I hurried down to the cave. I had scarcely seen my doll Louise since Louise's engagement. I brought her out for the last time. I no longer spoke to her, because she was dead. She should, she must be dead. She could not survive such a degradation. I took the dead little thing and dressed her in her white clothes; laid her in her coffin and placed it in the innermost recess of the niche. Six small candles burned in painted pewter holders, and just like in the olden times, when people buried their dead with all their earthly treasures, I took her clothes and valuables and all my toys and hid them in there. When everything was in order, I kissed her and cried tears as sincere as if she were my sister. Then I closed up the opening completely with clay and rocks. A fresh layer of soil and moss hid the traces entirely. What was hidden there should never, never again see the light of day. I felt that I was walling up my childhood at the same time. Exhausted in body and soul, I managed to get home and steal upstairs to my room.

And it is true — with this my childhood did come to an end, and a new phase of my life began. The emptiness and loneliness that entered our house after both of my sisters had left it, were well suited to encourage the sad direction of my thoughts. It seems that Mother had to fight many serious battles with my sisters before they gave in. She therefore thought it useful to start processing her other daughters betimes, in order to prevent in them, if possible, what she called 'romantic notions'. Thus I was told in straight-forward, clear-cut words what I had fearfully suspected: *it almost never falls to a woman's lot to marry the man she loves; and yet it is her destiny to marry someone*, because the unmarried state is the saddest of all. 'In this respect, you are all princesses,' Mother said.

I felt dizzy under these conditions. . . . To be married off without inclination; to be thus flung, by some sinister force, without volition and yet voluntarily, into quite a different existence without love! And then, suppose you loved someone else? — Poor Louise! — Oh God, do not let me love like her. . . .! Dry up this wellspring in my mind! Let me escape my fate! I want to live alone — alone until the end of my life, never loving, never marrying anyone. This childish prayer was perhaps ridiculous, but I am unable to laugh at it to this day. —

The solitary state began to assume a sacred importance to me. At times, surely, it was the choice of a strong, free spirit. When I was in the company of the old spinsters in the neighbourhood, I would observe them with agitated interest. Alas, they were not very fit to make the unmarried state seem particularly attractive or uplifting. What a desolate life! How fussily narrowminded they were; how ossified their thoughts and opinions about everything! How pathetic their occupations! For the last ten years, old Miss Møllerup has been ceaselessly at work knitting a stocking and unravelling it. Mother says she has taken upon herself this punishment, which so terrifyingly evokes the fate of the Danaïds, because she was so wicked as to refuse some good offers 'for the sake of a whim'! An old *married woman* in her second childhood might, perhaps, fill her life with eternal knitting, but would she unravel it all again? I don't think so . . . I would suppose she has had children. . . . All these lonely, abandoned creatures exude the same sense of . . . I don't know of what . . . of old maid. Oh God, could not such an existence be made more attractive? Teach me such an existence; teach me to suffer it, to fill it! I want to read; I want to learn; I am willing to work night and day.

By that time, I had already done a lot of reading, but in a superficial and indiscriminate manner. I read what relaxed my spirit rather than enriched it. Even if I had been able to choose better, I lacked the chief prerequisites for understanding and retaining what I read: I lacked knowledge. I was seized by a fervent eagerness to learn. Under our previous tutor, Mr Caspers, I had kept step with Edvard — that is to say, I had gone through the first excerpts of the usual schoolbooks. Now my independent studies began. I read early and late, and the more I entered into it, the more my interest grew. Hiding my books in the same alarmed manner that Amalie hid her novels, I secretly kept up with Edvard until I had surpassed him.

One day I asked him so nicely to lend me a botanical work I knew he had on his shelf. I wanted only to look at the pictures, I said. But he merely said contemptuously: 'You need not exert yourself to learn such things; Caspers says that women were created only to keep house for the men, and that all learned ladies should be put in the insane asylum.' This did not strike a blow to my desire to learn, however. 'It is not for the sake of men, but for my own sake that I am learning.' Still, I never again asked Edvard for a book. All the ones I could get hold of, in part from Father's collection and in part by borrowing elsewhere, I brought down to the cave, where I arranged a small library. A rock closed off the opening so artfully that nobody could discover it. How happy I was when I could go down to my treasures! — I always went home very reluctantly, albeit — I thought — richer than before. Everything I experienced during the day, I connected with what I read. History interested me especially. From the rock by the entrance I would see when someone was approaching. If anyone was coming down by the hill, the book immediately went into its hiding place. I had an immense dread of revealing any knowledge, even to

Father, and Edvard and Caspers could have put me on the rack without finding me out.

My joys and sorrows, therefore, were not those of a child. I had my own yardstick for them. They were defined only by their relationship to my own great worry. By contrast, I took little note of physical pain, a disappointed hope, or the loss of something dear. Instinct told me that the best counterweight to such brooding was activity, and no sooner had I conceived the idea but I began to participate with boundless energy in the running of the house. This, however, happened with an irregularity and feverish restlessness that never accomplished anything. —

Caspers left, and now Kold was to arrive. I hated him before I had even seen him. The first time he sat at our table, I was surprised to notice how young and handsome he was, and that he spoke quite a different language from the other tutors. He did not enter the living room whistling; he did not swear when he talked to the servants. I hated him even more because of that. I came to this simple conclusion: the more highly men have reason to value themselves, the lower they esteem us. Mr Caspers always considered my sisters and me good enough to be his housekeepers; to Mr Kold, therefore, we must be worth even less. In all my encounters with him I suffered from this antipathy, which can take such fervent hold in an inexperienced child's mind. How embarrassing I found those classroom lessons with him! I knew that for all my desire to learn, for all my industriousness, in his eyes I must still be but a poor creature he could rightfully look down on. That divine patience he showed — could it be anything but disdain? When I let him sit there for a whole, long hour, struggling to explain the basics of something I had long since gone beyond, I felt the cruelty and ridiculousness of the situation, but it was as if I had become hardened. A criminal must feel the same way. Once in a great while he would scold me, and I would feel strangely crushed and honoured. . . . Any sign of his ill will could make me proud. Oh, I thought I could feel how I offended him. When the lesson was over, I ran off as if I could run away from my own repulsiveness.

Did I do him an injustice? Once, one single time, this thought occurred to me, but it was so fleeting, so unclear — a falling star, not a guiding star. We ran into each other up at the summer farm. He seemed different there from the way he acted among the others, when he would always be so oddly sarcastic and say everything with an expression that

110 of something dear

never let on what he really thought. He spoke words so peculiar.... I doubted I had heard right. He encouraged me to sing. To sing! But when we came home again, he was the same as before, and I saw that I had been mistaken.

Had I been mistaken? I don't know, but still this prejudice is so firmly established in me that I cannot be near him without feeling ill at ease. —

Meanwhile, I had already become a big girl, but to myself I appeared so repulsive that I could never bring myself to look in a mirror. Of course, I liked lovely clothes intended for grown ladies; any such beautiful display could make a deep impression on me. How I admired the suits Louise had — but I never imagined myself in anything like that. Mother said many a time, 'You ought to put up your hair and get a long dress, Sofie; you are soon a grown girl,' but I always begged to keep my childish clothes. 'I'll join the grown-ups soon enough,' I thought.

Singing was never mentioned. Nevertheless, the next time Father returned to the old business about my going down to visit Aunt, I was suddenly willing — whether it was just for the sake of the singing, I don't know. Perhaps the reason was a secret dissatisfaction with myself; perhaps I hoped that life under grander, more refined conditions would bring the answer to many riddles that were bothering me, and would lead me back to myself and my own people in a spirit of reconciliation. I shall say nothing about the experiences I have had in this regard. My pain and disappointment belong to me, and I shall have to try to make my peace with them. But what I can do — and I want to do it — is to make certain that they do not disturb others. —

In other words, my childhood was sad, perhaps sadder than that of many another child who to a lesser extent than I enjoyed the external conditions for happiness. There were shadows, invisible to everyone else. But among those shadows, a ray of hope and solace might occasionally fall. That happened one autumn afternoon, just the day before I was to leave and a few days after my fifteenth birthday. I had bid farewell to the cave and was now sitting on the rock in front of the entrance, feeling melancholy and almost incapable of tearing myself loose from the place. All day long, a nasty, cold fog had lain over the area after a heavy rain. The light background framed by the mountains was closed by a grey curtain; I could just make out the two big spruce trees down by the mill.

With their indistinct silhouettes, they looked huge and almost menacing. They were standing there like sentinels over the mysterious future — this future that was filling me with obscure fear and dread. I thought about my poor sister Louise, whom I recently had seen again — how changed, oh God! — I thought about old Miss Møllerup's Danaïdical stocking, and the hopelessness of life overwhelmed me. I did not notice that a breath of wind was coming up through the mountain region, and that the air in an instant was growing lighter, until I suddenly saw the treetops glittering like church spires. I watched the fog roll itself up into great, grey masses and sink towards the depth of the river. At one stroke, the landscape lay illuminated by the evening sun, and just as quickly, as if called forth by the same law of nature, this warm and bright thought struck me: '*To love and to live for the one you love*!' Simply imagining such happiness overwhelmed me. I sank to my knees and pressed my face against the rock. I went home confused, like the beggar who has dreamed where an enormous treasure lies buried, and who quiveringly wonders if the dream might come true.

* * *

It is an old custom in the country to have a 'grand parlour', which means having one or two unoccupied rooms in the house, so that they may be put to use on grand occasions two, or at most three, times a year. Then the blinds are pulled up; the dustcovers are removed from the furniture and sconces; the floors and furniture are polished and incense is burned — all in a fruitless effort to remove that indescribable, oppressive air of desolation permeating rooms that are not in constant use, and resting over all creation, over all of nature, when it is not graced and pervaded by human influence. In winter, the icy walls mock every attempt at snugness. The oven is smoking and glowing red, but in the grand parlour one is forced to move from one extreme temperature zone to another. In order to have a grand parlour, the family lives in discomfort all the rest of the year.

Bowing to this custom, the District Governor's family had stowed themselves into the small living room, which was absolutely stifling in summer, but now Sofie had exercised the authority accorded a pretty young daughter recently returned home, and she had persuaded her mother to make use of the garden room, which was a large, shaded room.

This concession led to some changes in the furniture and in the general appearance of the room. After a few skirmishes, the two sisters had won the right of sole execution of this important undertaking. In order to comprehend the importance of such a concession, it is necessary to be familiar with the conservatism governing such affairs in the country, where chairs and tables acquire a sort of prescriptive right to be standing where they are, and in no other spot, and where the same pictures on the wall look undisturbedly down upon generation after generation.

For a long time, there was a great deal of activity in the garden room, but it was carried out in secret, behind closed doors that were not to be opened until everything had been completed.

Indeed, when the solemn day arrived, there was good reason to applaud the change. The only wonder was that it had not taken place sooner. It was a revelation. Everything of value, such as the handsome mirror and the curtains, which were Mrs Ramm's pride and joy, had remained. All superfluous articles, on the other hand — everything worthless in the way of knick-knacks and wall decorations, all those hideous slipcovers and crocheted articles that pile up over the years in family residences, had been swept away and made to yield space for a few, but all the more important, pieces from earlier times. The overall impression was one of stateliness and harmony. Everything that could serve this purpose had been dusted out of dark corners and mouldy crates up in the attics. Five old portraits of ancestors in pompous attire now occupied the side walls; the slight decrepitude of their frames did not harm the effect in the least. The most valuable of these portraits was a picture of a pale young beauty with melancholy eyes, to whom family tradition fortunately affixed a somewhat tragic fate — incurable madness on her wedding day — that made it interesting. A huge ebony table that long since had been discarded as absolutely hopeless, and also some rickety old chairs, had been restored by a master in the art of gluing, who had been brought into the neighbourhood for the occasion. From their respective places, all these splendid old things seemed to be staring at each other in surprise, like aristocratic emigrants who suddenly run into each other in an anteroom in their homeland after having been long tried in an undeserved and shameful exile. The door of the cabinet had been replaced by a curtain; the table in front of the sofa had been moved into the centre of the room; and — incredibly — Mrs Ramm had surrendered her precious brocade throw, which had been used only on special occasions. It had been an arduous undertaking, in which the sisters had all but exhausted their eloquence. Amalie had calculated for her mother that when the throw was put to use at their golden wedding anniversary — if the moths spared it that long — it would have done service for only the sixth time in its life. Sofie had capped the matter by assuring her mother that the throw was almost exactly like the one adorning Aunt Charlotte's living room table in Copenhagen, and that this lady always used her best things in her everyday life.

The District Governor's old, faded easychair, with the pipe-rack above it in his place in the corner, was the sole object in the room that had not been touched; the one thing his daughters' frenzied redecorating had spared out of a sense of reverence. As if they wanted to emphasize this, the vase with the first roses from the garden had been placed on the small table with his newspapers when the day of the big surprise arrived. — The one who was really delighted with the change was Kold. He had grown up in a wealthy home and had retained perhaps too great a sensitivity to his surroundings. But who can blame him! Who will dare to deny the peculiar influence of beauty and comfort — especially over solitary souls, the crustaceans among mankind? Kold discovered that not until it was displayed in the redecorated parlour, could Sofie's beauty be fully appreciated. This parlour, with its somewhat sombre magnificence brightened by the view over the flowerbeds in the garden, exactly suited a beauty such as hers.

One morning, Kold came downstairs and found the family assembled. The glass doors to the garden were open, allowing the blissful summer air to flow in.

Mrs Ramm and Sofie were sewing by the open door; Amalie was pouring tea; and on the sofa Edvard was reclining with his feet up on the armrest, sending Amalie back for the third time with a cup that did not quite suit him. When Kold entered, Edvard got up, because he always showed respect for his teacher. Since the event up at the summer farm, Kold had risen considerably in the family's esteem. In particular, such a minor heroic deed could not fail to impress Amalie and the mistress of the house. Sofie remembered how readily and with how much sacrifice of personal comfort he had carried out her wish, and she could not help regarding him with a softened look. Now the District Governor also arrived. He had just sunk into his easychair, and Edvard had lit his pipe and handed it to him, when the conversation turned to Lorenz Brandt.

Mrs Ramm had a new story to tell concerning Brandt, which occasioned much laughter, but the old man shook his head sadly.

'The poor man; then he really is quite beyond hope!'

'How can you pity him, my dear?' said his wife. 'In this case, surely, one can feel sorry only for those whom he causes shame and sorrow and to whom he shows an appalling ingratitude. And, above all, one must feel pity for his old, respectable mother.'

All declared themselves more or less in agreement, being of the opinion that Lorenz Brandt deserved no more compassion. Kold said that as far as he could judge from his knowledge of Brandt, much did not appear to be lost with him; anybody so able to overcome completely any spark of honour could never have possessed it to any great degree.

'My dear Kold,' said the District Governor gently, but yet gravely, 'this is both harsh and unfair judgment. Thank your God that your own nature and a better arrangement of your life has kept temptation away from you. Brandt's student days happened to coincide with a rather notorious period that sent others besides him astray, and that seemed to make the best among them succumb the most easily. At that time, a student was almost entirely left to fend for himself. The homes of the city were not open to him the way they are now; there was scarcely any form of public amusement — where, then, could those young people go who had come to the city full of life and enthusiasm? They sought each other's company, and a tradition from brave, old drinking days made punch and carousing indispensable. To weak characters, pleasure thus became synonymous with drinking. Under these conditions, the most richly endowed were most at risk, because they unconsciously longed for more meaningful lives, and because people preferred their company to that of others. In this manner, Lorenz has been swept along. Alas, what expectations attended that man! We all thought, at one time, that he would become something splendid.'

'Who can deny the extenuating circumstances of the conditions you described! But when you say, sir, that the social conditions of students are so much better now than previously, I must say I doubt it. Public amusements are still lacking, and it is difficult enough to gain entry into private families.'

'You ought to be the last to complain of that,' Mrs Ramm interrupted him. 'You, who have been so extremely popular — people practically killed you with invitations, didn't they?'

'Me, madam?' said Kold with a smile. 'I assure you, I lived in Christiania for two years without a soul being aware of my existence, with the exception of my landlady and my tutors.'

'But then you were discovered, however, and I know for a fact that you were included everywhere.'

'Christiania is supposed to have become such a very social city of late,' remarked Amalie.

'It is true that during the latter part of my stay, I was busy drifting about at balls and parties; yes indeed, that is quite true. All of a sudden, Christiania developed a desire for social life on a grander scale. But people did not have time to wait for this situation to develop naturally; everything was immediately supposed to have a European flavour. For that, useful subjects were needed. A certain talent for being amusing was all that was required. Those select commodities then went into circulation and were subjected to incessant wear — indeed, they were so worn that in the end many of them could no longer recognize themselves. I saved myself in time, as you can see, dear madam . . . . A city may be fond of parties, but it is not thereby said that it is *hospitable*, and it is certainly of very little help to the great mass of people who find themselves on the outside, to see a handful of their former friends constantly being preferred, or to see a few often random and doubtful merits leading to success. No, by God, there is very little evidence of encouragement, and if the general tone is now improved, and dissipation is growing more rare, the cause must be looked for quite elsewhere.'

'Probably,' the District Governor added, 'in a deeper recognition of the value of civilization, in a more scientific struggle — in other words, in the times themselves, which are changing even here. It must be a comforting thought to the young nowadays that the days of darkness are past and the foundation for good has been laid; now it is just a matter of building on it.'

'Alas, yes, this foundation — I would that it existed! Things would not be so bad, had it already been laid, but that is just what we are working on, and we do it in the sweat of our brows. We move the rock; afterwards it is easy to roll. . . Our descendants will be able to judge how badly off we were in our time! — The former generation, which in cynical thoughtlessness trampled under their feet what we are now striving for, should be considered fortunate compared with ours; at least they had unanimity thanks to the crude and unformed situation. Now we are divided among ourselves. . . Those individuals who desire to do right — and — I might almost ask — what is right; how are we to deduce it from this confusion?— they often meet with the greatest resistance from the people closest to them.'

'In truth, this discord and eternal strife is sad to behold; sadder still for those who are affected by it,' remarked the District Governor.

'No, the conditions are not more favourable! The opportunities for dissipation are still there in full measure, but we have had our eyes opened; our time is more *self-conscious*. Therefore we shall resist. We may let ourselves be swept along, but we shall not be so easily led into perdition as Lorenz Brandt.'

Whenever the discourse between the two men took a more serious turn, the two older ladies usually left it gladly, but Kold had noticed that Sofie, who to all appearances was absorbed in her work, was attentively following what was being said. This young girl was accustomed to her own reflections about life being different from those of her surroundings, and this had often confused her and made her disagree with herself. She seldom expressed an opinion save in the most inconsequential matters. Now, however, if often happened that Kold said something that illuminated her own silent reflections. Sometimes when he glanced at her, he was surprised by her expression of excited participation. He then felt a great urge to draw her into the conversation, but it never seemed to be quite the right moment. The reticence he had created between them seemed to him both embarrassing and silly, and now he just watched for an opportunity to do away with that reticence.

The occasion came, but in quite a different way from what Kold had expected. An event that was invisible to the others, but which reached deep into his innermost being, gave his entire relationship with the young girl a colour and significance which it otherwise might not have had.

One day, as they were sitting together in the garden room, the mail was brought in and fell like a bombshell into the loud conversation. One moment later, the deepest silence reigned, interrupted only by the rustle of pages being turned. Mrs Ramm was wont to interrupt this silence at times with a casual exclamation when something in the chronicles of the day stirred her interest. This time, however, she found nothing to remark upon, but she directed a question at Kold. A moment afterwards he left the room.

'What was the matter with Kold?' said the lady. 'He did not reply to my question, and when he left, he was as white as a limewashed wall.'

Without thinking, Sofie reached for the paper Kold had been reading.

'Give it to me,' said her mother and started her search. 'I see absolutely nothing. . . . Among the obituaries there is just something about the octogenarian Mrs A., besides a Miss D. — Neither of those is of concern to him. That two houses have burned in Lillesand can surely not cause him any pain.'

Kold reappeared at the table, somewhat quieter than usual. To the sympathetic inquiries the family could not help making, he gave evasive replies. They were completely mistaken. An invitation to accompany the family on an afternoon outing was refused, however.

When the house had become quiet, he stood by the window up in his room. He was draining the old cup of remorse in which we toast the memory of our dead — the remorse that of course is nothing more than human nature's eternal, fruitless pain at its own inadequacy. If the dead were to return, would we then be capable of something more?

'*Margrethe*!' his thoughts whispered. 'Are you dead, my wise and tender friend? Shall I never again hear your voice that knew so well how to comfort! And you have died alone, unloved, misunderstood, forgotten . . . . Yes, it is cold and barren at such altitudes! — You have also thought yourself unappreciated by me, though God knows how often my thoughts have visited you, admiringly and gratefully. . . It is true, you never saw any sign of it, not a single one. . . You did not even get those meagre pages! — Oh, if you can do so from your Heaven, then comfort me in this; I cannot forgive myself!'

Eight days later, Kold received a sealed parcel, which contained some writings Margrethe had left behind and which, addressed to him, had been found among her personal effects.

With that strange feeling — half sadness, half shiver — with which we contemplate the handwriting of a loved one who is dead, Kold stared long at the familiar writing. Oh, these symbols, by which human life still pulsates in all its grandeur and pettiness and lovable weakness — what a contrast to the inaccessibility and cold, unapproachable nobility of death!

This contrast is the reason why everything that reminds us of their transient life among us — clothes, objects they have used, a word scribbled on a piece of paper in order to test a pen — touches the strings of sorrow much more bitterly and fiercely than the contemplation of their spiritual perfections. At such times, it again seems to us that the dizzying distance is diminished, and we are filled with the sweet, comforting thought that the eternal in us will at some point lead us to where they are. A casual letter shakes us more than a profound one; the mere strokes of the handwriting disturb us more than the contents.

Our friend spent the better part of that luminous summer night reading. The papers consisted mostly of scattered notes written without date and sequence; a few had taken the form of a letter, in which Kold's name appeared more as a random occurrence. Perhaps Margrethe had never intended to send them until death announced its coming and she presumably yielded to that pardonable desire of all mortals that they be understood in the heart of at least one fellow human being.

We shall not burden the reader, who obligingly accompanied us through Sofie's autobiography, with another one of the same sort. Only as a contrast to the young girl's impulsive view of life shall we communicate some aspects of the life-philosophy of a woman who has matured through suffering and experience.

* * *

EXCERPTS FROM MARGRETHE'S PAGES

I certainly thought there was another reason behind it. There is something profoundly deplorable and demeaning in those facts, as I have finally heard them from yourself. Deplorable for you; demeaning for us. The real puzzle is that none of the ladies with whom you fell in love has truly loved you. Yet there was absolutely no reason why you could not have married any one of them. Thank God that did not happen.

Some sort of sentiment they have surely entertained, and they would have been offended, indeed, had that sentiment not been referred to as love — it contained all the proper whims and requirements. They did have a sentiment of sorts, or they would not have been able to welcome you the way they did. But it was not a *genuine* feeling. It was not that spontaneous, uninvited and irresistible force which, like a plant born in the shade, feeds on its own sap, unseen and untended, and which cannot be pulled up except by its tap root.

It was that *artificial* hothouse sentiment, the green fruit of *coincidence*; it was the feeble reflection of masculine desire, which arises from an interplay between flattered vanity, commonsensical calculation, and an inherited habit of submission.

With this a man is satisfied; he demands nothing better. And if he has to struggle a little into the bargain, in order to conquer the lady's sentiments, he is as proud as a deity. —

Whenever possible, the men ought to be kept from doing the selecting. They choose mostly according to sensual whims; they put possession above all else.

Women ought not to choose, either. They are so undeveloped that they cannot even make a sensible choice based on common sense. One would be horrified to see the motives that often move them to accept an offer.

The so-called 'arranged marriages' may, therefore, often carry a greater assurance of mutual happiness than people tend to believe. We ought not to scorn them.

The choice should truly be left to one authority only, and that is to *woman's love*. —

Among all the real and imagined qualities that attract a man to the woman of his choice, he forgets just one small, insignificant one: *her love*.

Should he nevertheless notice that this little something is wanting, he thinks: it will surely come.

All men think of themselves as Pygmalions, who can give life to the statue when the time comes that she must descend from her pedestal.

But marriage is not apt to kindle love. On the contrary, a good measure of that article should be brought into the marriage so that a woman will be able to stand it. Even if a man is not a tender husband, he may well be a good husband. He may tend his calling just as eagerly, just as conscientiously. His duties have very definite limits.

A wife, on the other hand, must be *tender* if she is to be *good*. A wife's calling has no such limits. It consists of a horde of undefined, multifarious, nameless details, as invisible as the falling dew, which derive their only significance from the spirit in which they are done. In this, in love, lies its infinity. Without this, it shrivels to become a burden, a trivial execution of duty, which immediately limits it.

A man may sit all day at his desk without once thinking of *her* for whom he nevertheless works. But he devotes a lot of thought to how the article he is working on is going to look in the newspaper, and to the effect it may have on his next promotion.

The wife who loves, thinks only of him in everything she does. To *him*, for *him*, by *him* — everything. He is her ambition, her public, her government department. . . .

It is strange how one can sense, the minute one steps into a house, whether or not this life-giving spark is present. It is particularly noticeable in the atmosphere of the living room. Where that spirit is in command, everything will show the mark of gentleness and inspired beauty. Where it is lacking, everything is dead, cold and prosaic, even in the wealthiest surroundings. In that case, the wife either tears herself loose from the burden and lets the machinery carry on without her, while she tries to submerge her life outside the home, or she becomes completely absorbed in it — a growling machine one would rather avoid.

The novels of *Madame Dudevant* are causing a stir these days. They are dreadful, it is true — as dreadful as the circumstances that have given rise to them. It will not do to assume the usual attitude of bourgeois criticism or to bring out the ordinary yardstick for what constitutes transgression. We must be able to read these novels calmly, with the awful interest with which one observes, from a safe vantage point, one of those violent eruptions of nature that spread terror and destruction in their wake. These novels are not suitable for our conditions. Our society and the French may be considered two extremes — one is an incipient, undeveloped society, tightly furled in its bud, which is only threatened by cold and the lack of care; and the other is sophisticatedly overcultivated and close to its own dissolution. From the morasses of the latter Mme Dudevant is sending her cries for help over the entire civilized world. She does not allow for circumstances; she wants total liberation and complete equality with men in all aspects of everyday and social life, right up to participating in men's customs, their habits, and even their dress. Now, all this goes way beyond our humble wishes and merely repels us. No — we do not understand it. Until time everlasting, men must remain our natural support and protectors. Mme Dudevant wants the dissolution of marriage, which for our women constitutes their only harbour and sole salvation, although they, just like the French women, have a feeling that they could and ought to be happier.*

---

* In her understanding of *George Sand*, Margrethe here seems to be somewhat led astray by the misunderstanding attending her début as an author — a very commonly held opinion of her works, which was considerably modified by her later productions. [*Author's note in 1879 edition.*]

In France, marriage contracts are usually entered into from financial considerations; *there* with money and without love; *here* without money and . . . without love, but with the great difference that in this country the men are *less corrupt*, which makes the disparity much less noticeable. Indeed, we should not deny that our men try, almost unconsciously, to even out some of the disparities in their and their wives' circumstances by being oddly tender and protective towards their wives. No, with all admiration for that brilliant authoress, and in full acknowledgement of what may have been dictated by social considerations — Georges Sand does not suit our conditions. She has no language for our mute complaints; her writings cause only pain and irritation, like all false comfort. We need only those powers that work unseen and silently within their domain, and which, unnoticed, gnaw off the ropes tying us to the old ballast. It was the poor, unknown Mme *Le Gros* who caused the fall of the Bastille by her quiet fortitude in the *la Tude* case. Our attempts at liberation are still confined to their own invisible domains, and we do not in the least understand conquests being made outside of those domains. God preserve us from competing with the men in their daily business, or wresting from them the pleasure of wearing a uniform and a tall hat. What we want is greater freedom of *thought* and *feeling*; the nullification of all the countless ridiculous considerations and prejudices that inhibit such thoughts and feelings. We want truer, less high-flown concepts of virtue, and a healthier moral sense that by itself would withstand every assault made by an immoral public judgment, against which nobody now is safe. We want greater mental independence from the men, so that we can get closer to them and be more to them than is possible now.

An author who happens to be vigorously opposed to the cry for emancipation that has arisen in France, says: women have only one source of experience — their *love* is their understanding, their faith, their genius, their *emancipation*. Very well, we demand nothing more. But then this love must first be liberated, i.e. freed from barbarism and slavery. Oh humanity, protect this first flower of our lives, because all subsequent blessings must come from it. Take heed of its growth and fruits. . . . Do not frivolously disturb its fragile central leaf in the stupid belief that the coarse leaves succeeding it are good enough. . . . No, they are not good enough. There is just as big a difference as there is between the tea which we ordinary mortals content ourselves with and call tea, and that which only the Emperor of the Celestial Kingdom drinks, and which is the *real* tea; it is harvested first and is so delicate that it must be picked with gloved hands, after the pickers have washed their hands twenty-four times, or so I believe.

Yes, there are many such harsh conditions in our lives that prevent us from fulfilling our duties as we should. Yes, yes, let it be shouted to those thousand deaf ears: there is something askew, something wrong with our situation. Ought there not to be a reason for those bitter complaints from both sides? We do not hear any, you will say. But yet they come, these laments, like those inexplicable wails that seem to arise from the shiny seas or to vibrate in the air; it is just that few ears are capable of hearing them.

Yes, we deserve to be better situated. We are better, much better, than our upbringing, our institutions and popular judgment make us out to be. There are splendid natures who fully know how to obtain their rights in their relationship with another individual. Often, an individual surmounts the faults of the race as a whole. Is it because the men, the married ones, have more respect for our sex than the young, and therefore are more pleasant in their social intercourse with us? At least they honour their wives and their daughters. It is to no woman's advantage to be the topic of conversation in a circle of bachelors, where it is well known that one may excel and be honoured only by not being *mentioned*.

Much is being said about the elevated position American women have in their country. It may well be that this is due to something we do not want to acknowledge. This, however, does not prevent it from being just as weighty in its consequences. I imagine that right from the cradle, the practical way in which American women are reared, the laws that accord them every advantage, the men who with intelligently calculated and exquisite egotism protect their position, make them into those proud, independent creatures whose influence extends from the drawing room to all aspects of public life.

By way of contrast, I shall try to give a sketch, just a rough sketch, of the conditions under which our girls live. Even before they are born into the world, our laws have robbed them.˙ At that point it is already considered necessary that they be provided for by a man who will marry them. Getting

---

˙ In the interest of truth, we must remind the reader that with regard to this point of law to which Margrethe alludes, time has brought a change that is more in keeping with what is right and acceptable. [*Author's note in the 1879 edition.*]

a husband thus becomes a vocational study for them, like the law or officer's training for the sons. Their upbringing is planned accordingly — that is, with much more emphasis upon being admitted to their vocation than upon mastering it. In this manner they grow up, without any real skills or knowledge, without deeper interests, in an idle life full of empty pleasures. It is as if their parents, out of pitying weakness, cannot provide them with enough of those empty pleasures; it is as if they cannot anaesthetize their daughters sufficiently against the grave fate awaiting them. At least they ought to have fun and be pampered for as long as they are living with their parents. To this situation is often added a secret heartache, which ravages the young girl's inner being like those stealthy forest fires that cannot be seen in the clear summer light. Then they find themselves at the dividing line: helplessness on the one side; a wretched marriage based on chance on the other. Such a choice is not the worst thing that can happen. As we know, the silk cord is always more honourable than the hangman's rope. At least they get married. And now it is expected that at least the best among them will attain greater consequence than a few miserable ballroom triumphs have afforded them. No, it means only that at this point they enter into the hopeless night of obscurity and insignificance. A noticeable fading distinguishes this transition. Nothing is known any longer about these creatures who once were referred to as the pretty So-and-So. They are scarcely recognizable any longer when they show their faded selves in public. They are no longer individuals; they are Norwegian housewives. Do you know what a Norwegian housewife is? I am not really sure, either, but I do know that I am not acquainted with a single woman who animates a wider circle, either by her charm or by her spirit, and yet I know many who both could and should have such an effect.

Oh, you sad city where one is forever doomed to drink up the dregs of memory! Have you no potion for hope and oblivion! Whoever has become heartsick at your bosom, can never more be happy. Wherever you go, there are crosses showing where a joy or an illusion lies buried. They haunt you everywhere, those restless ghosts. They meet you at street corners; they wave to you from the windows of this house and that which itself stands like a monument, desolate and petrified. . . .

Oh, you big, small city! What is this cloud of chill and despondency that broods over you! You are big enough, you of the thousand beaks! Big enough slowly to peck to death every person who no longer amuses you, or against whom you harbour a resentment. Yet you are not big enough to provide an unfortunate with a corner to hide in. The man who has got the slightest stain upon his honour and the woman who once has been made ridiculous, may just as well dig a grave and fling themselves into it, if he or she does not prefer to bury themselves in Tromsø or Christiansand. You are big; you already have the passions and devastating longings and demands of a big city — and yet how small, how poor you are, because you do not manage to fulfil a single one of them! You refer us to one another in the friendliest manner. We, your children, are to live upon one another, to consume one another, for as long as we retain the smallest unscrutinized fold in our private lives. But forever having to be on our guard against each other does not make us nice. We become infinitely proper, infinitely correct, and also infinitely unpleasant; to the best of their ability people board up themselves and everything they own. Whoever really has something to protect — a heart or an individuality, for instance, or some other great misfortune; whoever wishes to live honestly by what is his and who has the least need of other people, that person is usually made to pay most dearly. Here no fullness of life and pleasure can intervene; there are no happenings, no earthshaking events, no partings except due to death, no softening light-and-shade. . . . No emotion fed by the fountain of illusion and imagination can endure it; it is bound to exhaust itself. First to wear out are friendship and love, whose progress actually is just one long funeral procession through all the stages of chill, denuding reality. And as for admiration and enthusiasm. . . ! Oh, those unhappy souls who once have caught such an ailment and perhaps are forced to live for ten years more! Not even *resentment* can endure, although it is, as we know, the most tenacious of all emotions — resentment, which year in and year out, perhaps at the same time of day, encounters its adversary at the very same street corner. Resentment, too, tires of honing the looks it gives, and we ourselves become dull and decrepit like those emotions. In the meantime, misfortune has taken such a lot upon itself. Oh yes, you big, small city — we, your children, become so heartily sick of each other, and yet we must suffer each other until we are carried away. And when the bells toll, each one of us knows for whom they toll, and we grow melancholy as we think of how long we have been living off the departed, in the manner of good Christians — and then we discover that we were actually rather fond of that person.

Yet I do know something within your compass that is faithful — something that never grows fatigued; and that is sorrow. Sorrow broods over itself and does not worry about others.

Once I overheard Mother, who did not think that I was nearby, saying to old Aunt *Hanne*: 'Margrethe never talks about it, but it is obvious that she is wasting away. But is it not a mystery that such a girl as she can go off and grieve over that *insignificant* person? . . . . She wants to hear nothing about N.' 'Oh, leave her in peace,' said Aunt Hanne.

Now, it is indeed strangely bitter to hear others, on our behalf, denouncing as poor and despicable *the very thing* which we ourselves would give our lives to obtain. It would be a relief to hear them pronouncing us unworthy of such happiness. Because that is the truth. Any candid person must feel unworthy of such a great, unimaginable happiness. Insignificant, they call him. Do they know him? Furthermore, of what help is it to me what they say or believe? The voice they consider lisping and banal is music to me, indeed the only music I understand, which goes straight to my heart. It has been said that he is cold; that he is empty and affected; that whatever charm he possesses is due to his tailor in Hamburg. All this the ladies say, and yet they talk about him without cease. The men claim he is a man of character. What is that to me? Over me he has exercised that unconditional superiority, that secret power which will keep my feelings fresh and bashful to the last, and which makes me think that nothing would have been difficult or trivial could I but have suffered it for him . . . for *him* — and which makes it so that I must die of grief that it could not be so.

It reached my ear once — *how*, due to *whom*, I do not know — that the reason there was no union between us was that he feared dragging a love such as ours down into the poverty of Norwegian bourgeois domestic life. Were he to marry, it would have to be to a rich woman. Perhaps many may seek comfort in this phrase, but I hear the hollow sound in it. No, and no again, I know better. The only poverty dividing us is the one he shelters in his heart. I was rich enough; I was rich enough for us both.

Oh, we ought not to scorn a faithful spirit! When the cold, crippling days come!

How can a man continually and in cold blood offend a woman by whom he knows himself loved! And yet, even in our country we see men trying their hand at spiritual seduction, misusing the power which chance once granted them over a poor creature as they systematically pursue and wound that creature. Of course, you must keep in mind that the outcome, the implacable outcome, of all such bravura here in our tiny society, is a prosaic *pater familias*, a decent, faithful wife — preferably one who brought with her a fresh and untouched mind — and daughters whom the fathers will defend with life and blood against the misfortune of losing this treasure.

The other day there was talk of a young girl who for several years was subjected to this sort of treatment. In the course of it, her youth had withered and her future been wasted. She had loved and been loved by a person with the mind of a fiend, and in the course of this relationship she had suffered all the privileged maltreatment, every variation and degree of this secret torture at which the whole world is present, like a doctor summoned to count the pulse beats and advise how far it is possible to go. These species — you know them; you know them! This desire to see us suffer; this persecution for as long as we flee; this chilling 'What now?' when we pause, timid and overwhelmed; this untiring ability to egg on our weakness with alluring speech and cold faces, vague words and ardent looks! These people punish us when we are weak, and they punish us when we show strength. Witness their rage when we want to tear ourselves away — their jealousy without tenderness! — Oh God, what am I saying! Of whom were we talking? Of the young woman who was cheated of her life, like myself, like myself . . . like myself. Her gentleness and forgiving nature were praised . . . . I think it was exhaustion; inability to suffer any more! She visited his house; they met as friends; she even helped her friend, who got him, with her sewing. . . . I could not do that.

Am I intransigent? Yet I believe in an inner forgiveness that comes through prayer and penance. I even think that if it involved a talented person, it might be possible to feel joy in the spiritual results of his life. But the *bashfulness* — the *fear* that has become a part of one's nerves! One person must surely turn pale at the sight of the other, and if the offender does not, the person who has been offended against surely must.

Oh God, you do know that I have fought against the resentment and the bitterness! Help me to be victorious in this struggle! You know that there have been hours when I thought Your Heaven could not have room for two such as us, and yet this miserable city must encompass us both.

No, I cannot relinquish my faith in him. A thousand times I condemn him, but then comes a voice that says his hardness was only the consequence of youthful arrogance, of immaturity — our national heritage. Nevertheless, I believe in a diamond behind this crust of arrogance, vanity and worldliness, but this diamond must be polished in its own dust; only something equally strong, equally pure, equally enduring will help bring the diamond into the light. I know what this is; where it is to be found. I know it; nobody, nobody else does.

My birthday! I discovered today that I am still young in years. It seems to me that I have lived for such an infinitely long time. I was only fifteen when I became acquainted with him. For as long as I was under his spell, I was like someone the trolls have bewitched into the mountains. Such victims sense nothing of the outside world; they do not remember it; they have lost the yardstick for what we otherwise call time. When they come out, nobody recognizes them. Thus it has been with me. I was a trusting, bedazzled, naive child; now I have awakened with the wise eyes of age and suffering — eyes that, having been hurt, see through everything. In the interval lies my youth, obliterated. I have known nothing of its joys or harmless pleasures. . . . I have read nothing, learned nothing — not even how to win friends among my own sex. Everything confronts me with unfamiliarity and wonder. Nevertheless, I recognize these faded faces, these figures that have grown old. As if in a dream, I have seen them when they were young and beautiful and radiant with hope. Time has duped everything in its path.

Also him! Of his life, as well, which was so full of expectations, time has made a cruel parody. He is married. Nothing has come to pass of all that I would have sacrificed myself for so willingly. Naturally, his fate was to be more glorious than anything I could have given him! His wife is not rich, at least not in spirit and amiability. His home is administered with anything but beauty and grace. I often heard him say that he did not like children, because they disturb that peace and harmony of life without which adults cannot exist — unless, if necessary, the children come in a matched pair as lovely as Thorvaldsen's marble wonders, which might produce a similar effect in a drawing room. He has six children, but not one of them is pretty. He is said to be a tender father. I can write this down without malice, but also without regret; not indifferently, but still without emotion, as something that does not concern me — is not supposed to concern me — any longer.

When from my corner I watch the young girls moving about in a ballroom, so graceful and light, with the confidence of youth, and so radiant with joy and thoughtlessness, I am filled with melancholy, an almost *motherly* melancholy, if I, with my twenty-six years, dare use such an expression. A host of worries arises in this melancholy; worries to which I can give no name or shape. Our fathers and grandmothers compressed all the innumerable and nameless questions of our time into one single, handy, capacious and easily understood question, the well-known classic: 'Can you cook porridge?' Alas, in our time we have discovered that this is not sufficient; that happiness in a home is not assured just because *she* who enters it brings this science and all its ramifications with her. I would rather say . . . no, I don't know what I would say or where I would begin or end. Suppose I were to say: 'Have you, young girl, just in your mind, made the colossal leap from your present existence to the next one that awaits you, and for which you, in accordance with the law that the Creator laid down in you and which demands your share in life's struggles and joys, are quietly longing? — Have you ever, for the duration of an entire quarter of an hour, seriously compared this future with the life you are still leading? — At the moment, everything breathes for you alone. Parents, older or younger siblings, servants and friends — everybody around seems to exist only for the sake of your pleasure and your comforts, and for the success you are to become. And anyone who sees you finds it so natural, because you are so alluring — those roses and those veils suit you so well that it seems you will never have to take off those airy garments of joy.

Do you know what it means suddenly to have to live for *everybody else* but not to seek reward or gratitude from them? — Have you thought of w at it means to fall from your gauze heaven right down into the most massive reality, whose guardian and responsible head you are to be? — Do you understand, oh priestess of bagatelles, you, the Vesta of daily life — do you know how to watch those thousand small, smoking lamps so that not one of them goes out? Can you gather all the dissonance of nursery and kitchen; can you fight the daily, lonely battle against coarseness and imperfection, without doing violence to the nobility and gentleness of your being? Can you be both the *inspiration* and the *instrument* and so incredibly many contradictory things all at once, often in one breath — so many things that they cannot be counted? — Can you, while divided in yourself and tenfold burdened and fatigued by this cumbersome and obstinate reality, also be the *soul* in your children's upbringing, as well as be your husband's brilliant, restoring friend? And, my young sister, can you bear the disappointment that the world has seen just your beauty and considered it your only worth — and can you afterwards walk past your mirror with a consolation at the ready? — In brief, can you do all this without *giving up* ; can you roll the rock uphill every blessed day and every evening calmly watch it roll down again, because a fairy has whispered to you that each time the rock will, nevertheless, come to rest a few inches higher than the day before? — A few inches closer to the goal every day!

And then, if it should happen that your will and your eagerness have been stronger than your physical constitution, and there appears in that constitution something we call nerves, whose presence and mysterious link with the soul the doctors acknowledge, just so long as you don't ask them in their capacity as husbands and good citizens — if they should become rebellious, those nerves, then Heaven help you! Your entire being would become one suffering, quivering nerve, which would cause you to tremble at the sound of a door being opened, and which would keep sleep away from you at night. . . . Could you then pretend that you have no nerves, because you are yourself the *main nerve* in it all, upon whose calmness and strength everything depends? — I do not ask you, young girl, if you are able to do all this for the man your soul has *chosen*, because then, you favoured member of your sex, I know that you can, and your luminous eyes confirm that you can. But can you also do all this for the man — you get; who falls to your lot when the die of life is cast, no more and no less randomly than the dancer who just now is coming to ask you to dance? You have several weighty reasons not to refuse him, such as that otherwise you might have to sit out the dance; while perhaps you have only one counter-argument — that you actually don't like him. — Are you able to do this — and much else which my thoughts skip over in horror — for this man, and to seek your reward in yourself only, and possibly in the hope of a quiet corner with your children some day — a hope that will sink from fatigue and become a wish for the grave? —

I have detained you long, young girl; much too long. I see your eyes resting on me with disapproval and impatience. . . . I understand you. You kindly return the question: whether I myself could do all this? No, no. Wherever I see one among us mastering this task to the full for the sake of *God*, quietly and bravely and without letting her gentleness and the youth of her heart perish, I am filled with admiration. I bow deeply to this unobserved greatness, this daily heroism — more deeply than to any man's accomplishment, however brilliant it may be — but I could not do it. . . . Heaven have mercy on me! I could not do it *at all*.

One year later.

Yesterday he walked past, but stopped, detained by an acquaintance, outside the window by which I was seated. I had not seen him at such a close distance for a long time, and I watched him from behind the curtain with the quivering, half curious fear with which one observes a fallen beast of prey that once frightened us. He had grown older; that proud and arrogant carriage was stooped, and the elegance that used to distinguish his person was gone. He spoke in a lively manner, but the wind carried the sound away. Yet I thought

I heard the familiar voice. Then he looked up . . . heavenly mercy, was it madness that touched me just then! — That look pierced my soul just as in former days; it pulled me down towards him as if with invisible arms. . . . I could have dissolved in sadness and sorrow at his feet. . . . Yes, it must have been madness. . . . I have always suspected a woman's faithfulness of being some form of insanity. —

No, no, this is against the agreement; I must be left in peace.

I have searched in sacred books and sermons; I have listened in the churches; but I have never found this ailment mentioned by name. Only a few easily understood sorrows of general concern are mentioned there, in such a way that they represent the entire concept. But those sorrows that are not experienced by everybody and that do not advertise themselves by outward signs; sorrows that do not demand other people's attention but, on the contrary, must conceal their woe — all those most silent and dangerous heart-wounds are always ignored, always lumped together with the general concept of suffering or perhaps even of sin. Why is this? When a child is hurt and cries from the pain, it is satisfied only when its mother examines the spot and puts her soothing hand on it. Why do the clergy never mention this pain? Don't they believe in it? Have they forgotten it? Oh, look carefully, you holy men, and you will discover that you have not forgotten it! Look carefully, and perhaps you may find a corner in your soul where this ailment — precisely this ailment — is engraved. Mention it, call it by its name, and a gasp will go through the church — a gasp that is the suppressed sigh of all the thousands who have heard the call. What comfort have you experienced? Tell us. Explain to us why that which is most glorious in us must become a poison; why God laid down this desire in our souls in order that it be destroyed — and we be destroyed along with it! Oh, I hear the answer! It is also in accordance with spiritual economics that he who is hungry should not be given alms, but should be turned over to the public welfare — this huge, invisible, anonymous welfare! — But what if a person is still starving? Can't you do anything to prevent his hunger? Is religion to be merely the last resort of the inconsolable? Would it not be better if religion took preventive measures, such as not only curing the victims, but disarming the executioners and doing away with all the laws that are based on despotism and prejudice? Would it not be better to straighten out the tangles from which the suffering *springs* and to turn the hearts towards each other in love?

Now peace has come. It is the peace of death, I know; therefore it is light and joyful and secure. I know that I shall die, and I imagine death as a journey that lies ahead on a clear and delightful summer morning. There is nothing more for me here. . . . In His mercy, God will forgive me for not having the courage to live except for this one and only thing. Oh, praise be to Him who made the ties weaker! How many lives that seem to progress smoothly and calmly towards their destination, are not just one long struggle with death? He will take me up to His Heaven, so that I may lead a more pure and perfect life, without barbs and bitterness. Maybe there; maybe there!

Something in Dr E's face says that he has thought about people and human sorrow. He may have understood me, because it is already a long time since he confided to me that my condition is hopeless. With the others, it passes for a nervous weakness that may be cured by means of naphtha and valerian. The other day, I asked the doctor to tell me when — with me he does not have to resort to the usual arts. He surmised: 'When the leaves fall from the trees.' Tears came into his eyes when he saw how happy it made me. He had to promise not to worry my family until absolutely necessary. I shall depart as noiselessly as I have lived. When the leaves fall, I shall disappear as quietly and as silently as they. No upheavals, no night nurses, no musk, no inquiries — none of those ceremonies by which death makes itself known in a house and which make it so intolerable for the others.

20 June.

It will make Kold sad to hear that I am dead. He will perhaps think that I believed myself forgotten by him. That, too, will make him sad. My young friend, could I but tell you how calmly and trustingly I accept your silence. And yet, it would have given me a great deal of joy had I heard from you. No, I know that you have not forgotten me. Can a brother forget a dear sister? And I really was a dear sister to you. You know that you never had, and never could have had, any other power over me. I managed to bring out all that was best and sweetest in you. Let us be thankful that we found each other in the midst of all the petrification here, and that our encounter was so beautiful and warm and so brief.

Now hear a last word from your friend. You now believe that your heart is dead and that you are proof against any new attachment. First disappointments always leave behind this belief, until you realize that this, too, was a disappointment. Perhaps you have already experienced this. You will feel yourself captivated again, more deeply and truly than ever before. If she is a young girl who is pure and loveable, oh, then I pray for her! — Treat her with care; do not offend her. Do not rush things and say: I love this young girl, she must be mine; but say: I want to bring this girl to love me — if not, I must relinquish her. Do not take her by surprise so that she, confused by the attack, gives you her hand without being able to think why she is actually doing it. Teach her to *believe in you* ; if you cannot win her trust, then regard all as lost. Let her feelings mature through a deep and heartfelt contemplation of all that is *best* in you. Like the must, her feeling will ferment, and if it is *genuine*, it will overflow from its own sweetness. Then you must take heed and accept it as a gift from her hand. Accept it in the same way it was won — humbly, carefully, chivalrously. For, as truly as people do not appreciate it and miss it bitterly, as truly as it is your intention that she share life's burden with you, *this is the only thing that endures*. Yes, as truly as God exists and will keep by me until my last hour — if you do not get this treasure, nothing else is worth having.

Midsummer Eve.

It is happening faster than I imagined. Last night I thought my last hour had come. Today, however, I got out of bed and tidied my drawers, did some writing, straightened things out, and put fresh flowers everywhere. I shall now seal the part of my earthly testament that is to be sent to Kold; he shall receive my farewell to this world. My thoughts about eternity, about my hope of a continuing personal existence, I have not confided to paper. I have never been able to talk about it with any human being. I am feeling light-hearted and happy. God will not put this feeling to shame, but will have mercy on me, because I have suffered so much. Everything has now been overcome, even the thought of the *black box*, for which I have had an ingrown, childish fear. Are the horrors of destruction to be hermetically preserved by every means! — why cannot a human being be allowed to go to his rest in the earth whence he sprang, without this abominable custodial crate that separates us from the mother who so dearly longs to be reunited with us. How sweet the thought that those maternal arms embraced us firmly and tenderly, that we had already become one with her. . . . But if it cannot be otherwise, then put me in the box; just do it as quickly and with as little fuss as possible. There is nothing left for the doctors to discover about my poor, wasted body. They will just say that the lungs have been too inadequate or the heart a little too capacious. . . . Nobody must touch me save old Aunt

133

Hanne. . . . Aunt Hanne has been kind to me; — she has had a quiet thought for my fate. . . . She is another one who has sat in her lonely room with her knitting, quietly honouring the only thing worth remembering in life. . . . She has not forgotten that youth has a heart — a heart of which it may die. — I want to be put in the box wearing my blue silk dress and the red coral necklace and bracelets. . . . I wore them one evening — one happy evening. . . . Oh, my only one . . . my thought and my dream in this world. . . . It is still worth enduring life for the sake of just one such evening. . . . Thank you for having existed and for having filled my life, making it rich and wonderful. . . . Thank you, thank you, for everything — for the joy you have given me a glimpse of; for the happy presence of dreams; for the overflowing measure of pain . . . everything has been grand and of full value and among those things that you can take with you.

Twelve o'clock. Not a cloud in the sky. . . . The air is glowing and scented. The fjord is one big mirror, catching the burning rays of the sun. . . . Oh, God's earth, you are beautiful. Farewell, you beautiful earth!

* * *

'Poor Margrethe,' said Kold when he had finished these pages. 'Yes, go to your grave, you and those like you, wherever they are. Here we need only tough and busy hands; not a mind and deep feelings. Go to your rest again, poor child! You arose too early. The morning is grey and cold, and the fog lies heavy over the meadows. . . . Sleep sweetly and safely until the sun and the birds come out. . . .'

'But I will take these seeds of pain that I have gathered in your trail, you withered one, and I shall keep them faithfully, planting them — somewhere. Farewell, Margrethe, and thank you for your friendship.'

'Farewell!' he said, pressing the last page against his brow and lips before putting it away. Only then did he notice that the brief summer night had faded, and that the first glow of day was falling red across the scattered papers. The cold breath of death that had hovered around them in the evening was gone. . . . Margrethe herself had gently removed it. Filled with the wonderful calm that often succeeds a violent emotional upheaval, and that communicates itself apathetically to the body as well, Kold pulled down his blind against the first invading rays of the sun and went to bed, immediately falling into the sweetest sleep.

Georg Kold was one of those people of whom it may be said that they have not been brought up — manners and grace were given them in the cradle. He was impressionable, and his warm and easily stirred emotions, coupled with his purity of character, made up for whatever his character might be lacking in strength.

Because he had grown up in the lonely mountain regions where his father owned and operated one of the country's most important mines, his seclusion, which had been enlivened primarily by reading whatever there was of fiction in the house's well-equipped small library, and by the few strangers who visited the house in the summer, had only too successfully imbued him with those ideals about life that are such a blessing for as long as one — is allowed to keep them. A happy family atmosphere, a home in which he experienced only the harmony that prosperity and culture together can produce, was equally ill-suited to disturb the illusions of this quiet life of dreams.

Kold advanced imperceptibly towards the age when it became necessary to plan his life. Because he had no real feeling for his father's profession, Kold's plan was to go to Christiania and study. With regard to the more practical aspects of his curriculum, things were only so-so. A scanty interest produced equally scanty results. He, the dreamer from the forests who had been raised in solitude, was much more strongly attracted by the more idealistic side of life, which was less explicit in its requirements. It asked more of the imagination and produced more elevating results. Now that he had the means to do so, Kold buried himself with double eagerness in the so-called abstract studies, and the living, moving human life in the midst of which he found himself seemed to him the best and surest medium for acquiring what he had read about; for explaining to him what was unclear about it; and for solving its riddles. With a mysterious power, this life pulled him into its vortex and offered him instruction, its own instruction — too willingly, alas. The reader will recall that Kold, in his letter to Müller, had referred to some of the experiences he had encountered in the city — experiences that, given to honest sharing in their own way, had allowed what they robbed from him to help him in getting to know other people.

To a greater extent than others, lonely souls are like a convex lens in their ability to gather and to concentrate; therefore, many of the problems posed by the times passed through the young man's soul as inklings before they assumed real shape in the general consciousness. Kold lived and breathed these thoughts, and in the ardour of his feeling he expressed them on occasions when it would have been better to remain silent or to talk about something else.

While struggling to make it clear to himself how the more idealistic phenomena of life manifested themselves in science, art and poetry, Kold had happily survived that critical point at which one fancies oneself a poet and a writer, and he had succeeded in becoming something of a thinker as well as quite a good stylist.

In the District Governor's house, he had been given plenty of leisure to continue his favourite studies. Anyone who had seen him during the first part of his stay in Christiania, would now have found him completely changed. He had been quite successful in perfecting our young people's instinct to pull an invisible armour over his most vulnerable side. In the art of tempering every natural expression of feeling, and of seeming unconcerned when he was anything but, he was a match for the best. . . . Dangerous and much-too-clever armour, which at times ends by suffocating its owner!

Perhaps more than anyone else, Müller had influenced Kold in this direction. Georg Kold's parents had died almost simultaneously a couple of years after he had moved to Christiania. His home was closed up, and the mines passed into the hands of strangers. During this crisis, Müller sacrificed himself to the care of his young pupil — advising him, managing his practical affairs, and showing a fatherly concern in everything. We must also take into consideration the influence which this honest older man, of strictly sober habits and inclinations, may have had on the younger man's life.

Their personalities were ill suited to each other, however. An iron temperament like Müller's had touched too harshly one so basically different; one that must have been incomprehensible to him. Their friendship had been like the tale of the clay pot keeping company with the china vase — only by fleeing does the latter manage to save itself.

In conversation with others, Kold was polished, courteous, and not without a touch of irony, which to a more careful observer would have revealed Kold's most vulnerable spots. In his present environment, nobody had observed his temperament that closely, with the possible exception of the District Governor. His wife always described Kold as a monster of 'insensitivity', and to the younger people, who were more reluctant to think that someone was so unlike themselves, Kold was at any rate a riddle.

Strong emotions, on the other hand, betrayed themselves in his outward appearance. His physical complexion was also of the delicate sort that easily succumbs to spiritual attacks, and more than once he had been forced to plead illness when he had simply received too strong an emotional shock.

Margrethe's memoirs had shaken him profoundly. He recognized the tentative, but knowing way in which she came forward to meet him. While appearing not to be concerned with him at all, she had managed to tug at the deepest strings in his soul. Nobody else had this ability to divine the silent language of thoughts; to dissolve doubt; and to give comfort when it was least expected. This voice reached him with double insistence now that it sounded from the grave — a voice made clearer still by a pain now silenced.

What Margrethe had written had an immediate effect on Kold's thoughts and feelings about Sofie. The half curious suspicion with which he had so far observed her, at once gave way to tender interest and compassion. Like Margrethe, Sofie was also standing alone in her surroundings, without the support of the other woman's experience. An infinite desire to approach her seized him, but an equally strong shyness held him back. He could not bring himself to draw her into one of those ordinary, everyday discourses, or to address a few words to her in the presence of others. He never succeeded in meeting her alone. Thus their relations assumed a rather forced and strange aspect, which made people take notice. Anyone slightly familiar with life in the country knows how perverse such a situation can be.

Despondent over this and angry with himself, Kold went to bed one evening and had this dream:

The little scene up at the summer farm which he had mentioned in his pages to Margrethe — the ones she did not receive — was repeated. Sofie was sitting on the fence singing, in her childish clothes and with her thick plaits hanging down her back. He clapped his hands and called out a resounding 'Bravo!' Sofie turned towards him a face whose expression of pain and fear almost stunned him — but the face was no longer that of the child Sofie.

He watches her figure glide in front of him among the trees, but he cannot reach her. Every time he believes himself close to her, she disappears. Near the edge of the cliff she is forced to pause — he thinks she is sitting there on a rock. But look! she is not there, either. But from the abyss below the sound of singing reaches him — wild, wailing, fading and melting away, as alluring as the song of a siren. He wants to leap down, and awakens with a scream. He still hears the strains of the song wailing in the depths below. Bewildered, he leaps out of bed and runs over to the window. It is Sofie who is singing. Then her instrument must have arrived! Sofie's person had made him forget completely about her music.

With impatient haste, Kold dressed and hurried downstairs to the garden room. Sofie was alone. He paused for a moment, uncertain. She was sitting with her back turned towards him, wearing a freshly ironed morning gown with pale stripes. Her long tresses, perhaps not meant to be hanging free that day, were forced smoothly to the sides, but in apparent rebellion against this restraint her heavy, undulating locks formed the sort of hairdo seen on antique cameos. When Kold entered, she turned around. Her expression of slight surprise reminded him of his dream.

'Well, there is the piano; then we shall have music in the house — that will be splendid!'

'Just so you don't get too much of a good thing,' said Sofie with a smile. 'What do you think of exercises such as these?' and she went through a couple of chromatic runs. Kold held his ears.

'Enough, enough! Now do play something beautiful after that, or sing something, I beg you. . . . You do sing, don't you?' But as he was saying it, he dreaded hearing again the traditional reply, 'Oh, no! a trifle; it's not worth listening to.' Fortunately she replied:

'Yes, I do sing. Singing is my delight. If only I knew something lovely, I would sing it for you. . . . You, more than anyone else, have a right to it.'

'I?' said Kold, astounded.

'I actually owe my singing to you. It might perhaps never have come to anything. Don't you remember one time when you ran into me at the summer farm? — However, how could you remember such an insignificant occasion. . . . To me it was important.'

Kold understood her, but he let her continue.

'You encouraged me to develop this talent, and you did it in such a way as to allow me to think about it all in a whole new way. . . .'

'Ah, indeed!'

'From that moment on I had such an urgent desire for it, and therefore I accepted avidly the offer I had often refused, of visiting Aunt in Copenhagen. There I worked as industriously as possible, but the time was too short. Now I almost regret having put an end to it.'

'You terminated your stay yourself. Why did you do it?'

'I don't know; I was overcome by such homesickness that I could not bear it any longer.'

'And now you are longing for Denmark again? Have you perhaps not found everything as wonderful up here as you had imagined?'

'No ... yes ... no, actually ... yes, of course,' said Sofie in some confusion, whereupon they both burst out laughing. 'I can't deny, though, that a lot seems different from what I had imagined. Even so, there is so much in Denmark that is pleasant and good, and for which one may yearn.'

'I can certainly understand the homesickness,' said Kold, 'yet I don't think that it would ever get the better of me, supposing that my stay abroad was voluntary.'

'That's because you haven't tried it yet.'

'No, it's because I am convinced beforehand that homesickness would disappoint me were I to yield to it. I would make it confess all the false perfections of home; I would only allow it to make me conscious of the real advantages. Besides, there is a measure of weakness hidden in homesickness, actually — a desire for comfort, or a distaste for new impressions.'

'And yet — and yet I fear that it would steal up on you.'

'Oh, I believe you, I believe you! ...'

'But why does it have such power over us, this feeling, when a voice is telling us that we are wrong to succumb to it?'

'Yes, what can be the reason? It's the secret of nationality. I imagine that in some way, the characteristics of a country's landscape leave traces and imprints on its population, and that a person who has been torn loose from his own soil feels a loss that draws him back with the powerful tug of memory. As far as I can see, in Denmark more than anywhere else, a Norwegian must become conscious of his national idiosyncrasy — and a Dane up here would feel the same in reverse.'

'Perhaps it's due to the low esteem in which the two countries are holding each other these days,' Sofie remarked. 'In Denmark, people have a hard time giving credit to anything Norwegian.'

Kold hesitated in some surprise, and he came close to saying, 'Have you had this profound experience in your aunt's drawing room — although I suppose not from the two "of the first order"?'

'Do you find it comical?' said Sofie, seeing his smile.

'No, not at all; on the contrary, it's sad, of course — but it can still be explained.'

'What do you mean?'

'I mean simply that now that the old bond between us has been severed, while leaving us thrown together and irresistibly drawn together in many ways, this dissimilarity must have a different effect — a less attractive one. It's human nature; it can't be any other way. For good reasons, any national uniqueness in us must offend a Dane more than Danishness offends us. It awakens memories of a situation that once existed and that now, thanks to the force of circumstance, no longer is with us — memories that must be given time to heal. We, on the other hand, have an easier time showing approval, because we have undeniably drawn the lucky number in this lottery of world events. We appreciate quite enthusiastically everything that is good down there; everything in which they are ahead of us. It's certainly not going to prevent me from setting great store by spending more time in Copenhagen. But, unfortunately, I have no Godmother down there.'

After a pause, during which Sofie thought about what he had said and, with apparent lack of self-consciousness, accompanied her thinking with a couple of soft chords, she said:

'Furthermore, you can scarcely have any idea of how different life is down there, compared to here. Life down there seems easier, more carefree, more superficial; people are more content with themselves and with their neighbours, and they take everything less to heart. . . . When they tire of the daily struggle, they reach for amusement with an undiminished appetite. Down there, one wants to do everything; one has time for everything; but here. . . .'

'Here,' Kold supplemented, 'here we treat the disharmonies of life with great thoroughness, and when we are tired from the day's burden, there is no time for amusements — of which there are not many more than those provided by wild nature.'

'But,' he added in greater seriousness, 'this spiritual restraint and these deprivations on which we are nursed do indeed produce strong characters, though exacting ones, and they produce deep natures, however painful and introspective. . . . Yes, our Norway is a severe mother to her children.'

While he spoke, Sofie had fixed her eyes upon him, and her face seemed to reflect anxiety.

When Kold noticed this and asked, with a smile, whether she was homesick for Denmark, she said, 'I almost believe so; I know no better solution than for you to lecture me from time to time about all the disappointments that feeling may cause us.'

'I'll be happy to give you as many lectures as you wish,' he said warmly. 'You know, of course, Sofie, that I have an old right to do so . . . and that I have some catching-up to do,' he added with some emphasis.

'And I,' said Sofie, blushing, 'I'll sing for you in return . . . if it will help soften some of our "disharmonies".'

140

'Good!' he said with a radiant face, 'that is an agreement. I am to lecture to you, and you are to sing for me. We'll begin right away.'

'With what?'

'With the singing! With the lectures. . . . With the singing, the singing!' they called out at the same time.

Sofie bent over to find a sheet of music, but just then her mother entered. Mrs Ramm seemed somewhat surprised at this lively *tête-à-tête*.

'Are you up and about so early, Mr Kold? Then I trust you will give us the pleasure of drinking tea with us? Sofie, do see if you can hurry it along.'

Sofie seized with alacrity this excuse to postpone the singing, for which she had suddenly lost her desire.

The ice had been broken. Kold and Sofie sought each other's company, *not furtively*, but openly and without restraint. They stayed together at the table, on walks, and at parties, having indeed much to say to one another. At first, the others were somewhat surprised, but Mrs Ramm, who took it all in the only way in which such matters ought to be taken, decided to use delicacy.

Happy days! Neither of them thought of giving a name to their relationship. Sofie listened only to Kold; she drank in his words; she believed everything he said. He had again become her teacher, and she was supposed to make up for what she had missed. And he! For the first time in his life he dared give vent to those words that had been restrained in his soul for such a long time.

A new phase of clarification and consciousness had entered Sofie's life. It affected her entire being — she was more certain, more trusting, more eccentric — at times somewhat inconsiderate. She grew amazingly active. She rose with the sun, and when she fell into a sweet and solid sleep after a long day spent in reading, in music, in long talks with Kold and in domestic concerns, she still thought that the day had been too short. Her help in running the house was a source of pleasure to her mother. Mrs Ramm had become accustomed to Amalie's being of no particular use, since the latter spent most of her time in such 'ladylike' pursuits as painting in water colours and strumming her guitar a little from time to time.

In certain respects, Kold found Sofie to be different from what he had expected. It had nothing to do with her beauty and grace, which may have surprised him, but which still had been allowed for as a possibility. Although he soon noticed how her charms wanted to ensnare his mind, he still retained a fresh memory of all the suffering to which a hungry soul may be subjected when it is forced to subsist on beauty alone; therefore those captivating charms had so far kept him at a distance. Nevertheless, he discovered a soul in Sofie; a soul strong enough to meet his own. Her spiritual nature had been a riddle to him. He believed it to be both talented and strong, but he had always thought her nature had something single-minded and eccentric in it — something in many ways misguided. He had dreamed of struggles and resistance. The understanding that suddenly unfolded between them, and that was so lovely and harmonious and enriching for them both, surprised and spellbound him. This was to be his best defence against a blind infatuation that again would spoil everything — or so he imagined at the time. Margrethe had entrusted him with the young girl's happiness. Her last supplication to him had been on behalf of her, the unknown one. And he would not betray Margrethe's trust. He was indeed so eager and so absorbed by this new responsibility that he did not dwell much upon Sofie herself — that is to say, upon her person, her dress, and those thousand occasions

From which the God spins
the strong bands to ensnare the heart —

. . . In enchanting, urgent words, his view of life overflowed into a spirit that was all too willing to receive it. He found not only a willing ear, but often a maturity and an independent thinking that met him on his most daring excursions of fancy, and that often in their feminine intuition soared higher than his own.

Was it possible that Kold now felt his defences were not quite to be trusted? — As if by instinct, he avoided all physical contact, even of that most respectful kind which any gentleman may permit himself towards a lady. On their walks, he never held out his hand to steady her over the rocks by the creek; never offered her his arm at a difficult spot in the mountains. In part, Sofie's agility made that sort of help superfluous. On such a walk, she one day got a thorn in her hand that pained her very much, but she suppressed the pain, and Kold would perhaps rather have counselled some common remedy like patience, than extract the thorn in the manner of a Daphnis.

A few weeks passed. It was already the middle of July — July with its heat, colourful evenings and glorious nights. The sound of scythes could be heard, and a million flowers sent the last of their scent into the houses. Happy days! It was a happiness without name or object, to which the intoxicating breath of summer lent a new and dangerous enchantment. And Sofie's whole person was radiant in the reflection of this happiness. She bloomed like a rose. Everything she did was done with the lightness of a supernatural spirit. Her singing was a rejoicing; her walk a floating flight. She could be observed coming and going like a vision.

'You horrify me with your quickness,' her mother often said. 'You can't possibly have got there and back already!' But Sofie assured her that she had been there, and that she had been walking quite sedately.

It seemed to Kold as if this time could never end. But it did end — too soon! The District Governor suddenly asked him to take a business trip to Christiania. Kold was used to such assignments; the District Governor knew that he was doing Kold a favour with them. This time, it struck him like a clap of thunder. He tore himself loose with a struggle, and undertaking his journey with restless energy, he was already dreaming himself back again. At his departure, he gave Sofie his hand and recommended to her the books she was to read during his absence, and he also promised her some new ones which he would bring back with him.

A relationship between two young people that is based solely on mutual interests and that therefore has no other purpose than a purely spiritual exchange, is an extremely rare thing with us, for good reasons. Such relationships seem to belong to more joyful, free and progressive conditions than our own.

When such relationships nevertheless do evolve, they draw attention to themselves, like all phenomena that do not spring from their native soil. Mothers and guardians cannot abide such friendships. To them, they are too *impractical* and often constitute a hindrance to their daughters' happiness. And the mothers are right. Why this dangerous testing ground? As we know, our children can be happy by taking the usual road, with no questions asked as to whether they possess a mind or a soul. ... A bit of youthful attractiveness coupled with a fair quantity of practical competence — more is not called for, of course. The knot is tied, and the business is done. What can be accomplished by the girl's reaching for something higher? While enriching her mind and clarifying her view of life, she forgets the slights and offenses awaiting her outside as a result of the mistaken interpretation of the outside world. She may perhaps also forget about *good fortune*, which has introduced itself meanwhile in the shape of a 'well-to-do man' or a cousin who may be promoted. She must even count herself fortunate if her platonic friend, for whose sake she is defying all these evils, does not himself become the worst traitor. As I said, the mothers are quite right. In this situation, as in all conflicts between the two sexes, *she* has everything to lose, while *he*, on the other hand, stands to lose nothing. A young girl who with all her fervour nurtures such a relationship in both writing and speech, must either possess extraordinary strength of mind, or else a naïveté that suspects nothing. An unusual combination of both qualities made Sofie submit to such a relationship completely and without reservations.

Therefore, the peculiar pact Sofie and Kold had formed soon gave rise to general comment. Nor did they restrain themselves, that is true. People had encountered them on foot and on horseback. Returning home from parties and excursions, they always managed to sit together.

At a ball shortly before Kold was to leave, he and Sofie hardly talked to anyone else. There was whispering in every corner. 'In front of the entire company like that!' — it surely must mean an *engagement*, but, on the other hand, they were both so strangely cool! Nobody had yet seen him take her hand, and the pose he assumed during their long conversations that, incidentally, were held in the presence of everybody, was as constrained and formal as if he had a queen before him. The worst of it was that when Kold went home after midnight, Sofie, who did not dance, fell asleep and did not wake up until full morning, when the ball was over. Sofie suspected nothing until the next public occasion, when she found herself being congratulated, at which she was extremely surprised and which she denied drily and with finality. Her mother also denied everything, but with that mysterious air that permits everybody their own interpretation. This caused complete confusion while doing nothing to soften the general feeling.

When Sofie had been out among people, they found a hundred things about her to comment upon. One thought her too free; another too stiff; yet another thought she made it much too plain that she was bored — in brief, it was incomprehensible how Mrs Ramm, that amiable, cultivated lady, could have produced a daughter who was so strange, so high-flown, so peculiar, so childish, so — people did not know what. Her 'childishness' consisted in her sometimes breaking out of the ranks of the grown-ups and joining the children in their play, to their great delight. At the parsonage, she was wont to slip upstairs to old Miss *Nandrup*, who, despite being completely bedridden, was full of vitality. It was as if the old woman got a new lease on life the day the young girl stepped into her room, kindly asked how she was, and then listened with much interest to her many sad and funny stories. It was mostly when Sofie was absent that people felt the need to criticize her. When she was present, her personality cast its spell over everybody, and they were impressed by her against their will. Just like ever-growing rings encircling a stone dropped into a puddle, a reputation is always magnified in its more distant reaches. In the neighbouring community, rumour had practically turned Sofie into a mythical beast.

One day, while the District Governor's entire family was away, with the exception of Sofie, a family from a distant community came to visit. Sofie received them alone, and sensing the duty incumbent upon her as hostess, she did everything in her power to please the strangers. A beautiful dinner table, as well as walks around the farm, gave the visitors no opportunity to miss those who were absent. They left full of admiration for Sofie's gracious attentions. In summing up, it is necessary to reveal that Sofie enjoyed her greatest reputation among the elderly gentlemen of the neighbourhood, who were all more or less warm admirers of hers. Men are never as petty in their judgments as women, and since no offended vanity was at play, these older men accepted Sofie's friendship in the spirit in which it was given. Anything outlandish in her demeanour amused them without causing offence; the mere sight of her awakened happy memories. She seemed to them the reflection of an ideal they had dreamed of long, long ago, and which had not been completely buried by unalleviated dullness and thirty years of office dust.

Lorenz Brandt's visits at the District Governor's had lately become much more frequent, because he had settled at his mother's for the immediate future. Unfortunately, on each occasion it was obvious that things were going down-hill with him. The green coat, the home-spun vest, and the wax-cloth cap with its cockade (he had sold the suit of clothing Kold had given him, because his pride did not allow him to wear it), were all visibly taking a turn for the worse, and he himself seemed to be rapidly approaching the last sad stage, that animal-like stupor which is impervious to shame and regret. Towards the others he was louder and more offensive than ever, while towards Sofie he exhibited an equally exaggerated, pathetic admiration.

'God knows who is most to be pitied,' said Amalie to Sofie, 'Mother and I, towards whom he is so nasty, or you, who are the object of his admiration.'

'There is no doubt that I am the most unfortunate,' was Sofie's opinion, 'because I, at any rate, try to tone down his feelings for me, whereas Mother and you do not particularly trouble yourselves to soften those feelings he has for you.'

Actually, his persistence was beginning to bother her a great deal. Whenever possible, she avoided being present during his visits. She was very much frightened by the thought of meeting him alone out-of-doors.

One afternoon, Sofie was upstairs in her room, located beyond the larger room that was Amalie's. She was sitting on the small, low sofa between the windows, reading a book Kold had lent her. Outside, a long-awaited rain splashed refreshingly down on the dry fields. Now and then, when faint lightning flashed in front of her lowered eyelids, Sofie looked up, mechanically following the rolling thunder that as yet was far away. While absorbed in her reading, she heard that someone passed through the outer door, that her own door was opened and closed, and that slow steps were approaching. Thinking it was Amalie, she looked unconcernedly up a short while later. Before her stood Lorenz Brandt, fixing her with staring, almost bewildered eyes.

'Oh, why so afraid?' said he. 'Am I then a monster? I haven't said anything yet.'

'What do you want? Whom are you looking for?'

'You, precisely you — nobody else. I have something to say to you.'

'Then this room is not the proper place for it; how dare you force your way in here?'

She got up to leave, but in vain. With the gnarled stick he used as a walking cane, Brandt had positioned himself in front of the door, in a way that indicated his intention to cut off any attempt at flight. He was in the condition which for people of his kind is the most dreadful one: he was sober. His hair hung wet and unkempt about his sunken cheeks. A dark flame, a desperate resolution, glowed in his otherwise dull eyes with their bloodshot whites.

'Here; I can't speak to you anywhere else. Not down there. Do you think I intend to move a heart of stone like your mother's, or to play a romantic scene in front of your silly, hysterical sister?'

'Be silent!' cried Sofie angrily. 'You dare talk like that about those to whom you owe respect at the very least! People who all your life have shown you nothing but kindness and forbearance . . . .'

'Kindness and forbearance!' said Brandt bitterly. 'There, your mother has treated me with kindness! Oh yes, she and the others petted the boy for as long as he was handsome and promising; for as long as luck smiled upon him — in other words, when that was a thing of the past, he was kicked like a mangy dog. Naturally, your father, the poor, scared old fellow, dares not either. . . .'

Sofie interrupted him again. 'Don't mention Father's name,' she said. 'You don't know what you're saying; how awful it is. . . . Bethink yourself — whose fault is it that Father and Mother have changed their behaviour towards you?'

'You haven't changed yours, Sofie. You, the best, the noblest of your family, you have shown me sympathy and goodness. . . .'

'No,' interrupted Sofie, horrified, 'I have shown you no more goodness than the others. . . .'

'Yes, yes, don't deny it! You haven't treated me like some miserable outcast. In your behaviour there was something *quite different*. That tenderness with which you clung to me as a child and which I, in the manner of all pampered youths, didn't properly appreciate, that tenderness has not yet been extinguished in your heart — oh, don't interrupt me — ! This became quite clear to me the first time I saw you after those many years. From that day, from that unforgettable evening up at the summer farm, I date a new direction in my life. It was as if I had drowned my old self, and you became the hope of my life, my new guiding star; yes, you, Sofie, have been singled out by Heaven for a great, a glorious mission — the salvation of a human being. By your hand he will return to the human society that cast him off.'

'I!' Sofie finally broke out. — 'What do you mean?'

'Yes, you and no other!' Brandt persisted with the same odd mixture of fulsomeness and real feeling, 'You see, I am quite aware that I have sunk deep, and that people have a right — but only a *kind* of right — to turn away from me. Because there still lives in me — I feel it — something good and able which their hardness has not managed to destroy, Yes, woe be to this heartless society! — On it I throw the greatest blame, the bitterest blame. Instead of reaching out its hand to a lost soul, instead of seeking to restore him in his self-esteem, society scornfully pushes him deeper into the pit and treats him like a man without honour, even before he has become one. The dreadful thing about my situation, Sofie, is that it is almost impossible to turn around, because the bridges have everywhere been destroyed. Then your will stands there wringing its hands, desperately pitting its strength against the impossible, until it feels its own impotence again — that poor will. The horrible thing is that you are considered lost while there is still the possibility of salvation. I could tell you details of this that would move you to tears, since you are such a good person, and that ought to be able to move a stone. During those gay, enthusiastic days that became the seed of my downfall and the downfall of so many others, I had a comrade, a friend. He was the spirit in our social gatherings — the evil one, I must add. The wildest and the most extravagant among us, he was the first to arrive and the last to leave at every party. Being also favoured with a certain superiority, he dragged the younger and weaker ones with him to the edge of perdition. He saved his own skin in time and obtained, through powerful patronage, one of the best parsonages in the country. . . . There he has for some years been proclaiming the word of God from his sullied lips. . . . Then I thought of him, of this good friend, who was so much to blame for my misfortune, and in a good hour I decided to go to him. — Now his good example will work on me, I thought; seeing his true piety and honourable way of life will give me strength, — and I prepared myself for this reunion . . . Sofie! For a long time I went hungry in order to get a decent suit of clothing. . . . What it means to starve! But for four months my lips did not taste the drink of damnation, in order that I might appear before him as a worthy person.

And I arrived — and he received me well? Oh yes, I didn't go hungry, and I got a roof over my head, but like a beggar I was tossed food and given shelter in a room off to the side, where they sheltered their workmen and vagrants. And when I appeared, his wife and children hid themselves as if I were a leper. The rumours had preceded me to that far corner as well, where he, honoured and well satisfied, was enjoying the fruits of his hypocrisy. Yes, he was one of the numerous profane clergymen in this country, who use the weakness that comes from dissipation as a pious mask with which to dupe the poor, trusting peasants. But don't think that he let me go without seeing me first — heavens, no! The next morning I stood before him, and His Reverence gave an unctuous admonitory lecture and then dismissed me, while pressing an *entire dollar* into my hand, which I didn't have the presence of mind to throw in his face, that miserable hypocrite! When friends treat me in this way, what do you think I've had to put up with from strangers? — In this house as well, where once I was loved like a son, I am met with this contempt, which is all the more dreadful in that it hides under a smooth, cold demeanour that I can't get a grip on, and that slips out of my hands like an eel. In this way I've been hunted like a wounded, exhausted animal, until I sank before your feet. Sofie, from you I expect life — you have it in your hands — decide!'

Sofie, in whose pitying face could be seen the compassion with which she had followed his story, had almost forgotten his real purpose because of what he said. Perhaps she had not yet understood his purpose properly. His last words suddenly brought her back to reality.

'How?' she cried. 'You surely cannot mean. . .?'

'That you should join your destiny to mine; that you shall become my salvation, my hope, my support. . . . Yes, I do mean that. . . .'

Frightened, Sofie stepped back as far as she could. But when she noticed the wild, almost desperate gesture with which Lorenz followed her unconscious movement, she collected herself with the greatest effort, approached him again, and, placing her trembling hand upon his arm, said gently, 'Bethink yourself, Brandt; you cannot be in earnest. I should dare to take upon myself such a challenge? — I, who am so young, so inexperienced, who don't know the least bit about the world — I should have that power over you which others, much closer to you, have not been able to exercise? — You say that I myself have encouraged you . . . . Oh no, no, it's impossible that you can be so mistaken! — I've been friendly and polite to you, as I would have been to anyone else. . . . And why should I deny it? — Moreover, your fate, which I compared with what we had once imagined for you, affected my heart, and it would not occur to me to hide that. . . . I haven't seen you for many years, and the contrast is therefore bound to seize me painfully! — If I, like the others, had observed you step by step, then I fear I should have reacted in the same manner as they, and you would now be just as angry with me.'

'This long, well-practised and moral speech is most becoming to you,' said Lorenz bitterly. 'It is an inherited talent, I notice. Now I'm only waiting for the chapter about my bent old mother, which your mother knows how to recite so incomparably — continue! I am listening with reverence.'

'I certainly shall not continue. We have talked about this far too long. Let us leave. . . . Let us leave! — But first you must promise me that it will be the last time. . . .'

'And that is all you have to say to me? And you thought you could fob me off with this?' said Lorenz, coming a step closer.

'My God! What, then, do you want? What can I — what should I do?'

'You must be mine. . . . Oh Sofie, do not fail to acknowledge your calling! Why do you think such an angel has been put into this world, if not to save those who are lost? It is a woman's destiny to sacrifice herself.'

'No, it is not a woman's destiny to fling herself into certain disaster without being able to save anyone. . . .'

'Sofie,' he said and fell to his knees while impetuously reaching for her hands. 'Don't pronounce this sentence so harshly, with such finality! I don't demand a promise from you yet; only give me hope, a little bit of hope, that you will hear me when I deserve it. . . . I know that the way I appear now, I must seem merely repulsive to you. . . . Your revulsion is so natural! You are not to see me unless I can appear before you in a way that is worthy of you. . . . But yes, see you I must, in order to gather strength for the new life I am to lead, for my rebirth — just see you in order to find a ray of hope in your eyes. With that, I'll face everything, the world's disdain — yes, even if Hell itself rises up to tempt me.'

'I beg you, I beseech you, Brandt,' said the deathly pale Sofie, 'leave me alone. . . . Forget that you ever spoke of this. For God's sake stand up, Brandt . . . God knows how your misfortune touches my heart! I'll so willingly believe in everything that serves as an excuse for you; in everything that still is good in you and that could be salvaged — but not by me, not by me! I'll always be on friendly terms with you. . . . I'll not forget that you've been like a brother to us. . . . I'll defend you in front of everybody and assist you in word and deed like a sister . . . if you yourself wish it — if you don't force me to avoid you and hate you. . . .'

'In other words, "Ritter, treue Schwesterliebe widmet Euch dies Hertz." Thank you very much. Of advice I have plenty, of action somewhat less, that's true — and are these your last, irrevocable words?'

'Come, come! . . .'

'Aha, I understand,' said Lorenz after a pause, while his eyes rested on her with a sharp look. 'Another has forced himself between you and me. So those were your modest scruples about not being equal to the responsibility! But you can't fool me; just look at how you're blushing! Then he has wormed his way into your heart, this smooth windbag; he seems to have been able to corrupt you with his fashionable, heartless phrases! Be on your guard against this person, Sofie; he will be your misfortune.'

Sofie did not answer, but without thinking she bent over to retrieve the book that had fallen on the floor, while a burning blush covered her face. Brandt anticipated her movement. He tore the book out of her hand, looked at the title page and roared: 'Didn't I think so! There is his name, the d . . .!' And like someone possessed by the furies, he tore the book into many bits and trampled on it. 'Oh,' he muttered, 'if only I knew why I hate this person so!'

'I suppose his greatest wrong was that he leaped into the water and saved your life,' said Sofie scornfully.

'Yes, death and damnation, you're right — that as well; that's just why I hate him,' shouted Brandt in mounting fury. 'Didn't he by that manage to create another triumph for himself and fresh humiliations for me? — Oh, I understand, he has since become twice as interesting and irresistible. . . . But I'm sure his turn will come some time! I wish my troubles would smite him ten thousand times over! Yes, God grant that he be writhing at your feet, desperate and with his prayers ignored, like myself . . . . And you, Sofie, take care! From now on you'll feel what it means to push a man over the precipice.'

He left with one last, dreadful look. In the doorway he gave his dog, which had long been whimpering outside, a brutal kick, so that the poor beast tumbled aside, howling. Amalie, arriving a little later, found Sofie sitting on the sofa, trembling in every limb. She could scarcely indicate what had taken place.

'That dreadful man!' exclaimed Amalie, affectionately trying to calm her sister. 'The things one has to put up with! — Look, there he goes! — And clear across Mother's carnations! — It is indeed frightful!'

Frightened and with some satisfaction, the sisters now watched how Brandt, followed by his baleful dog, ran straight across the flower beds in the garden, climbed over the picket fence, and disappeared in the field. Just then the thunderstorm broke loose, accompanied by violent lightning.

A victim of new thoughts and emotions, Sofie closed her door after Amalie had left. Of Lorenz Brandt she thought no more.

Part Two

The strangers who had once paid a brief visit to the farm while the District Governor and his family were absent, were a Dean *Rein* and his married sister — middle-aged people who were both living farther north in the country. They were on a trip to a township within the District Governor's territory, to which the lady's husband, a member of the country militia, had been transferred. Their route took them practically right past the farm. In his younger days, the Dean had known the District Governor and his wife. It was therefore a matter of great interest to him to see these old friends again after so many years.

The reader will recall that the travellers had found only Sofie at home and will also remember the pleasant impression she had made upon them — an impression contrasting strangely with the baroque, vague and somewhat unkind opinion they had formed about her on the basis of hear-say. Whether this favourable impression was due to a mistake is hard to determine. Prejudice and preconceived notions have great power over us and often play tricks with the best among us.

After the worthy pair, well settled in their comfortable carriage, with some effort had turned around farther down the tree-lined approach and had waved yet a last farewell to their young hostess, the Dean remarked, 'It was certainly unfortunate that we did not find the family at home.'

'Say rather that it was great good luck,' replied his sister, 'that we met the *elder* daughter and not the *younger*. She is supposed to be a real monster — capricious and full of whims. Wild and daring as a Cossack, she evidently exhausts all her father's horses. She would have been quite capable of slamming the door shut in our faces.'

'Dear me! This sister was certainly quite a different sort!'

'Yes, wasn't she! That was a sweet person! I am completely and perfectly captivated by her. . . . And pretty! It's strange that not more has been said about such beauty. In this case, rumour has been too moderate — contrary to its custom.'

'Yet I have heard Miss Ramm spoken of as an attractive girl,' remarked her more taciturn brother.

'And so gracious and pleasant! — And the collation, how tasteful it was! The dishes so plain and yet so delicious; I know what goes into accomplishing such things in the country. . . . And how prettily she served us at the table while entertaining us at the same time. That is no easy task; I should know.'

'She displayed an extraordinary degree of domestic activity,' said the Dean reflectively.

'And it was nothing superficial, I assure you! "Yes indeed, my fine little lady", thought I, "this is certainly all very pretty and nice, but there is more to life than knowing how to set a tasteful table and doing the honours in a pleasant manner. There are other things that cannot be done with gloves on, and I suppose it's not really of any concern to you, for you let your mother take care of such matters. We'll soon discover that, however." Although the time was short, I did make a full sweep of the whole house with her. We were in the attics and in the cellar, in the dairy room and in the weaving room, and I must say I asked her pardon in my heart. She certainly was at home everywhere, and although she assured me that she took only a very modest part in the practical concerns of the house, she showed herself so well informed and spoke so knowledgeably about everything as if she had no other interest in this world but weaving, cheesemaking and churning.'

'I wonder if she is musical?'

'I hardly think so. The younger one, on the other hand, is supposed to be a musical genius. But in her case one clearly has to suffer the disharmony along with the harmony. Such gifted children are never a real joy. . . . Here from the hill the farm really does appear to great advantage. I wonder if the mill belongs to the District Governor? Do look around, Frederik!'

154

'I wonder how old she is?' said the Dean and looked out the other side.

'Who? The eldest? I can tell you exactly. She must just have turned nineteen, twenty or twenty-two, at most twenty-three. When I saw Mrs Ramm seventeen years ago, the youngest of her girls was three or four years old, and she was expecting again.'

'Twenty-two or twenty-three! Then she looks extremely young for her age!'

'Certainly not in her deportment. Quite young girls do not have that confidence; they are more physically awkward; more affected, if you will. . . . Do you know, Frederik — that would be a wife for you!'

'What sort of idea is that!' the Dean exclaimed almost angrily and eased himself up from his comfortable, reclining position. 'A girl so young, so lovely! With her claims!'

'Hm, yes, claims! Why not? A man like yourself, in your prime, not yet fifty, can offer such a pampered lady a position which she might long search for. Mrs Ramm's two eldest daughters are both living in rather modest circumstances.'

'But four stepchildren, Mikaline! . . . A big household in the country!' her brother protested, although he would not take it amiss if he were gainsaid.

'Four children! Oh well, children are a gift from God! . . . Seriously, dear Frederik, the plan is not such a bad one. Be sure to visit the farm on your way back; allow yourself a few days with that hospitable family; and look into the business more closely. . . . Besides, it's not proper to snub them with too short a visit.'

The half facetious turn the conversation had taken reached more deeply into the worthy Dean's quiet thoughts than his sister knew. His visit to the District Governor had not been completely by chance. When he was somewhat along in years, Dean Rein had married a cousin of Mrs Ramm's. After a brief marriage, to which no hint of censure could be attached, his young wife had died, leaving four little ones to his charge. As we all know, there is no better way for a widower to honour his wife's memory than to marry again as soon as possible. Does this not show that he cannot do without that sweetness of domestic life which the dear departed had taught him? The more painful his loss, the sooner he longs for compensation. Usually he embraces the business with more warmth than the first time around.

Rein was in this position. He heartily longed for a new matrimonial connection. He was tired of loneliness, and besides, the management of his house and the rearing of his children created a situation of some urgency. No female in his own neighbourhood could be considered. Rumours had reached him that District Governor Ramm's daughters were unusually well brought-up, domestic and pleasant girls. He knew there was a grown-up daughter as yet unmarried; the other one he imagined to be still in the process of growing up. Therefore, when his sister was about to start her journey to her new home, he surprised her by offering himself as her companion. It could give him pleasure to become acquainted with her new home, and also it would give him the opportunity to renew his old acquaintance with the Ramms, something he long had wished for. That the trip had a hidden mainspring, he would not quite admit to himself.

The mistake concerning the two sisters confused him badly, however. He was not disappointed; far from it! The trouble was that he had found something else — much more than he had expected. Sofie's manner, her youth and her beauty were qualities the modest man no longer counted on finding in the life's companion he was looking for and who was to sweeten his advancing years. Yet he was not insensitive to these advantages; they had made an impression on him which he tried with all his might to overcome.

When he returned after a brief interval, he found the family at home. Everybody hurried out and surrounded him before he had yet descended from his carriage, and there were happy cries of welcome. Rein was rather taken aback by seeing an unfamiliar, somewhat heavy-set, rather handsome young lady next to Mrs Ramm, who was introduced by the latter as the daughter of the house.

'But my amiable hostess?' he asked in surprise, addressing Sofie, who appeared behind the others.

'That is our *youngest* daughter, who has already been so fortunate as to make the Dean's acquaintance.'

'Yes, of course, of course,' said this gentleman, in a confusion which he thought to hide as best he could.

But the good man's struggle was just beginning. It was a matter of forgetting Rachel and turning his mind to Leah. Amalie's friendly, more dainty manner, which suggested a maidenly modesty that was partly true, partly assumed, and her respectable, more sedate appearance, also pleased him. During the two days their guest was with them, it was Amalie's turn to help in the house. She served out the food at the table; she poured tea, and so on, and these occupations became her well; they suited her personality, so to speak, because they also prevented a certain artful, affected side of her from showing. Rein could not deny to himself that this domestic, steadier girl was the most suitable one for him, and he tried to turn all his attention towards her. But, as has been mentioned, this was not done with an untroubled mind. Because Amalie had to see to the serving, the responsibility for entertaining their guest fell more to the lot of the younger sister. The Dean was a man who well knew how to appreciate feminine grace. Sofie possessed the sort of grace that seems to be reborn and liberated by culture — that is to say, in which the outward breeding has reached a felicitous harmony with the inner one. This happy harmony is seldom achieved by our young girls, therefore they are so easily prey to stiffness and affectation as soon as they have crossed the border from unselfconscious childhood. For what we call affectation is surely just a fumbling struggle to give shape to the human being awakening within, accompanied by painful awareness of what has gone wrong. The most richly endowed are as prone to affectation as the rest — often more so. Perhaps Sofie had escaped this shoal only because she had been placed in cultivated surroundings while quite young. In this respect, the two years she had spent in her aunt's house had been a powerful influence.

When Sofie started playing and singing, displaying talents of which the Dean had as yet been unaware, things became truly difficult for the poor man. He had played the violin in his younger days, and he was a passionate lover of music. When Sofie lifted up her glorious voice, he completely forgot the trivial conversation he had been carrying on with Amalie concerning life in the country, the location of the farm, etc., and he answered distractedly and at random when she, undaunted, started again from the beginning.

Alas, the Dean thought; this young girl is one of those chosen beings, one of those scented offshoots of poetry, who have sprung from our hard soil due to some misunderstanding, but who will never take root here. She is not made for reality and for our domestic life. — However mistaken this conclusion might be, he at least sought some comfort in it.

But then again, when they were walking around the fields and their conversation turned to quite practical and rural concerns, this view of Sofie did not fit. She had grown up among these things, and she understood them so thoroughly and talked about them so naturally that it seemed as if this was her proper sphere. His sister's words: 'That would be a wife for you!' echoed most temptingly in the Dean's ears. And then there was the fatal confusion that at first had drawn his thoughts towards the wrong person! — The worthy man returned home in a dejected mood, angry with himself, but accompanied by many invitations to return soon and make it a proper, long visit.

That happened sooner than the Dean had imagined. Shortly afterwards, some family concerns called for another journey up to his sister's, and upon his return, he did not neglect to interrupt his journey at the District Governor's, where he was received with unfeigned pleasure. He had made a favourable impression on Sofie as well. There was something gentle and confidence-inspiring in his manner that in no way detracted from the respect his age and clerical dignity commanded. He had the youthful mind characteristic of so many older men, which contrasts so strangely with the world-weariness and precociously serious view of life displayed by our younger generation. He loved young people. He defended their faults as if they were merely the shortcomings of youth, and he warmly entered into the things that interested them, although without wishing that he were young himself. Nothing in his looks or manner suggested such an urge. Both his manner and his person were vigorous and thoroughly wholesome. Rein had been a very handsome man, and so he still was. His thick, black hair was scarcely touched with grey. Thinking and mental effort had left no ravaging marks on his face, which radiated intelligence and kindness coupled with firmness of spirit. His figure and his glorious voice seemed better suited to a noble military personage than to a man of the Church. Sofie told Amalie she had such a high opinion of Rein that she — did not want to go to church in order to hear him preach. Their own minister had asked Rein to conduct the service for him, because he himself had to be elsewhere.

Sofie's statement, which was intended as and understood to be a jest, nevertheless contained a sad element of truth. Mrs Ramm went to church with her daughters almost every Sunday. For her, the knowledge that she had 'been to church' — that is, that she had been *seen* in church — took the place of devotion, but for those who went there with higher aspirations, this was not sufficient. Sofie shared the fate of thousands of children. Having grown up in sterile times and under the tutelage of an insipid and worldly mother, she had to make do without the blessings of having formed a living bond with the divine at home. Fortunate are those who gain this blessing without effort, and who are provided with this amulet before life's struggle begins so that they are not doomed, like Sofie, to wrest it from those very struggles and sufferings. Sofie's open, religious mind had at an early age sought God in nature and in everything great and beautiful, while she dimly sensed a lack of inner peace in Him. Through the church she should have been able to move closer to the Divine, but it was precisely in her local church that Sofie had been the least able to find such closeness. The entire service in that place disturbed and depressed her. This will hardly surprise anyone familiar with divine service in many of our rural churches — at least with the way it was conducted some twenty or thirty years ago. Imagine the hour-long, uninspired sermon and the quantities of hymns which congregation and sexton performed according to their own separate tempo and key, and add to this the many ceremonies, baptisms, communions and catechizings that were lumped together on one single occasion — all this was bound to deprive the service of everything solemn and to prolong it until fatigue overwhelmed body and soul. Picture all this in a congealing cold or in a stifling summer heat!

On the Sunday Rein was to preach, the weather was lovely, sunny and clear. The entire Ramm family went off to church in order to hear him. The small, dark and narrow house of God was packed with people. Rein had ordered the big choir door to be opened, however, so that the sweet summer breeze could make its way in and keep the air fresh. The sun was shining through the dense foliage outside, which formed a pale green, translucent canopy in front of the entrance. It looked so pretty. Every eye sought this spot, and each according to his own need could find rest in it or longingly lose himself in the great, fragrant, airy, divine hall outside.

The hymns this day were fewer and had been chosen with greater care than usual. Rein then delivered a sermon that probably would not satisfy today's requirements, but that did not fail to make a certain impression, aided as it was by his gentle, dignified personality. The congregation listened as if it were the first time they found themselves addressed in their mother tongue. Vivid attentiveness had taken the place of the usual dead silence. Even the old, whitehaired man who could always be found in his seat under the pulpit, where he invariably indulged in a sweet sleep, today was awake and a couple of times made a futile attempt to see the speaker.

What caused this unaccustomed liveliness among the congregation? There were no sweeping gestures, no great and riveting eloquence, no mounting and resounding pathos! Was it the Gospel itself — the beautiful Gospel telling of *Christ*'s defence of the outcast, sinful woman who was confronting selfrighteousness and despotism? — Was it the way it was delivered, this story of how our Saviour in this scene preached *equal rights to mercy and gentleness*, just as He had proclaimed *equal responsibility on the part of everyone*? It was all this and perhaps more still. This man who so calmly and bravely explained it all to them, gave the impression that this was the conviction of his soul, which he would defend not only in the course of certain ceremonies on the decreed and appointed day, but also on the following day — every day of the week. He gave the impression that he would claim this right of the weak in whatever situation he was placed — in the courtroom; at the next Church Assembly; to his own wife just as much as to those unfortunates who sometimes seek our clergymen in order to plead their despair, and who are living witnesses to how brute strength has long since cancelled this law of equality instituted by Christ, reserving mercy for itself only.

It was this impression of something trustworthy, something truly humane, that the listeners unconsciously absorbed from the clerical stranger when he preached in their church.

In his relationship with the District Governor's two daughters, Rein had taken the position becoming a sensible, aging man. During the days he stayed with the family, he occupied himself exclusively with Amalie, showing her every attention suitable to his age, and Amalie met him in a trusting, friendly manner and was flattered at being thus singled out. She even confided to him that the tranquil, domestic life of a country parsonage was the ideal of all her wishes — words which the listener could not help interpret as favourable to himself.

In the course of a private talk with her parents during his last evening, Rein applied for Amalie's hand. He expressed himself more in terms of this being his wish rather than his desire, and as he dared not address Amalie herself in the manner of an infatuated youth, he put his cause into her parents' hands.

Both the District Governor and his wife were agreeably surprised. The match was a very respectable one. The Dean was in every way a well-regarded man, whose house enjoyed a reputation for order and prosperity.

Without any further ado, the Ramms therefore assured him that their daughter would be extremely honoured by his offer.

Amalie was summoned to her parents. She displayed a resistance, however, for which they had not been prepared in that quarter. Amalie fell to her knees and, sobbing, begged them not to make her unhappy and break two hearts that were made for each other. It came out, at last, that she had already long been secretly engaged to Brøcher.

'Well, there we have it!' said Mrs Ramm.

'In God's name, my girl,' said the District Governor and lifted her to her feet, 'calm yourself! There is no question here of making you unhappy; nobody will force you. We have shown you the prospect of connecting yourself with a good and respectable man, who would be able to surround you with all the good things in life. You have chosen for yourself a lot that is, in the eyes of man, at least, a lesser one.'

'A ne'er-do-well like Brøcher, who may perhaps, ten years from now, have prospects of a living up north in Finnmark,' Mrs Ramm added.

'Oh!' cried Amalie, 'we are both young and don't need so much. Love and contentment can sweeten even the plainest lives. . . '

'But you surely don't expect, in the devil's name, to live on his curate's salary, do you?' said the District Governor.

'Oh, Father,' stammered Amalie with downcast eyes; 'what if we did? . . . You know, that big place under the Bratli Mountain stands empty. Brøcher has hopes of leasing it on favourable terms. . . . It is so sweetly situated by the water!'

'That old tumbledown nest! You're surely dreaming!' cried her mother.

'We'll fix it up. . . . Oh, we'll arrange our lives at Galterud* as if we were in Paradise.'

Her father shook his head, but Mrs Ramm was far from taking it in such a resigned manner.

When Amalie had left the room, her mother exclaimed, 'Did you ever hear such foolishness! How can Amalie find anything to her taste in that pedant? Such an incredibly prosaic person! . . . A girl with her taste and feeling. . .!'

---

* Galterud = 'Pig-Clearing'. [*Trans. note.*]

161

'Oh well, Mariane, unfortunately there is nothing to be done about the matter. We — ' on certain occasions the District Governor always availed himself of the plural form — 'we have ourselves supposed the match to be possible and have been gracious to Brøcher.'

'You express yourself so oddly, my dear. . . . We are supposed to have been gracious to Brøcher! . . . We are supposed to have encouraged him! . . . We have accorded Brøcher the same graciousness that is due to every guest in our house.'

'Yes, yes, my dear Mariane; I simply mean that . . . that we have treated him in a manner that . . . that has not exactly discouraged him. . . . Well, what has passed, has passed. If Amalie supposes herself happy with this — in God's name! — Now it only pains me to know that we have caused Rein a disappointment.'

Rein accepted the refusal with great propriety. He acted as if nothing had happened and expressed himself very feelingly about Brøcher's situation, which he tried to place in a more favourable light. He even promised to use his influence on Brøcher's behalf, and he left the farm — it seemed — in calm and confident spirits.

* * *

Georg Kold knew nothing about all this. He was now expected home any day. The evenings were already growing darker and cooler, and on the farm they had almost finished bringing in the hay. Mrs Ramm seemed to pay more attention to Kold's return than was her wont. She arranged everything in his room with particular care, as if she half regarded him as a son of the house. The reader will recall that when she noticed the mutual interest developing between the two young people after they had treated each other so coolly for a long time, the District Governor's wife had decided that she would act as if she had noticed nothing. She exacted from herself a silence on the subject that she quietly admired in herself. Actually, this silence was only the hunter's stealthy immobility, which is due to his awareness that blinking his eye may cost him his prey.

Mrs Ramm now thought that it was no longer necessary to observe quite so strict a silence and therefore dropped hints that did not fail to awaken the most painful horror in Sofie, who — I suppose it must be said — had lately been fully occupied with controlling herself. Sofie was no longer as calm as she had been earlier. 'God,' she said to herself. 'Mother says so; everybody who sees me alludes to it — and what did that dreadful Lorenz say! . . . Have I deserved it? Have I behaved so badly? . . . Put all regard for propriety aside? . . . At the time, my conscience accused me of nothing. I felt so strong and safe in his presence; I was so glad to hear him talk; to exchange ideas with him all day long; and to ask him about many things, getting the answers even before I had asked. That I sought his company without guise, and he mine; that we preferred to be undisturbed — was there anything bad in that? . . . I did not have time to think about it. Sometimes, when a scruple arose that other people had awakened, he immediately saw it, and he knew so well how to overcome it with his eloquence that I was ashamed at my cowardice. I feared his ridicule more than anything else. . . . I called that fear cowardice, but what am I supposed to call this? I would not dare to do it at all, now . . . no, not at any price. I don't understand how I could have been so brave before. Now I quake at the mere thought of seeing him again. . . . I can never speak to him alone any more. . . . That pleasure, then, is gone!'

Anybody will have sensed that the beautiful teacher-pupil relationship Kold had achieved with his former student was of a suspect kind. With a personality such as his, it would under no circumstances have been possible to continue for long at the point of real or imagined lack of passion on which their relationship had been balancing prior to his departure. Any impulse from the outside is dangerous, but most dangerous of all is a separation. Much too soon had this entered into their relationship. For as long as Sofie was near Kold, their talks, which had opened up new worlds to her, had completely absorbed her. Hardly had he gone away when she felt a sense of emptiness and loss, and his *image* began to preoccupy her more and more. Feature by feature it appeared before her with all its captivating power, in a variety of situations. The smile with which he had said this or that; a strange grimace occasioned by something that had displeased him; or the sound of his voice — only more vivid, more imploring. Before she knew it, her image of Kold had merged with her sense of intellectual loss. She transferred all her longings to it and wove it into all her dreams. Perhaps Sofie might yet have been able to delude herself for a while with the changes taking place within her, had other people left her alone. Nothing is more calculated to egg on the curiosity and attack of the great mass of people than a young girl's growing awareness of life. The purer and deeper this awareness is, and the more fervently it tries to protect its treasure, the more mercilessly do people attack. It is a shame; a great shame! Even so-called innocent teasing is never quite innocent. In such instances everybody, even nice people, are frivolous. People who make much of their sensitivity and who would consider it a dreadful wrong to steal flowers from a grave, are not troubled in their conscience when they rob tranquillity from a young person's breast — when they defile a mystery that makes angels put a finger to their lips and that the poet, poor mortal, tries fearfully and awkwardly to unveil.

One day, when the ladies were sitting together and sewing in the living room, the lady of the house exclaimed: 'Who is that driving up the lane? Do take a look, Amalie, you who have good eyes,'

'It seems to be Kold,' answered the latter; 'I think I recognize his grey hat.'

Sofie's heart stood almost still and then started beating so violently that, in order not to expose her feelings, she had to pretend she had dropped something on the floor.

'Straighten up the living room ... take out those withered flowers. . . . And Sofie, my cap with the blue ribbons!' said Mrs Ramm, adjusting her clothes in front of the mirror.

'Bah,' said Amalie, 'false alarm! It's only old Lieutenant Hanke. . . . It seems he intends to spend the night here.'

'That is not going to happen,' said her mother, ill-humouredly tying her everyday cap back on. 'That silly old fool! You receive him, Amalie; say there is nobody at home. . . . Say whatever you like, just so you get rid of him.'

'Am *I* to. . . .'

'Let Sofie, then. But don't detain him, Sofie!'

But Sofie had long since left the room. The discovery that it was not Kold, but somebody else, had not calmed her. She had run through the garden and down the path with a speed as if she thought it would be possible to flee from her own inner turmoil.

'Have things gone this far!' she said to herself. 'I can no longer control myself. I've imagined his return a hundred times over; I've pictured it to myself in every conceivable situation, at any old time of day, when I was alone and when I was surrounded by others. I've tried to prepare myself, but in vain. Oh, how will this end! . . . The best thing would be if he arrived while we have company — all the people in the neighbourhood, the more, the better! With all those faces around me I would be brave and strong, and once our first reunion was over with and he had noticed nothing, things would go better.... I've heard that young girls may harbour an inclination, and for a long time at that, without being aware of it themselves. I suppose that is very beautiful, but I don't understand it; it seems to me an impossibility.... I can't deceive myself. I know my destiny; I almost knew it ahead of time — it has been hovering above my head like a dark and nameless danger, ever since the time I walled up my doll. Yes, I know that this person has a dangerous power over me — that I shall have to struggle with him about my life, and that I'll sacrifice to him all that is best in me so that he, in turn, may make me boundlessly unhappy. Oh God! Then this misfortune has crashed over me after all! . . . But he is coming! I shall see him again.'

At that moment, infinite joy filled her breast. She let escape one of those wailing sighs that are like the skylark's jubilant upward spiral from the ground; and, as if she had also borrowed the wings of the lark, she flew across the bridge and along the dangerous path towards the cave.

* * *

Kold did not arrive at any of the hours Sofie had imagined. He came in the middle of the night, when everybody was asleep. In him as well, a change had taken place, although it was not so noticeable to himself. Confronted with the spiritual framework he had erected around her, he felt safe. He was so proud and happy about the responsibility he had shouldered that his entire paralysed will was spurred on. Everything that had been lying congealed and neglected in him; the most profound and spiritual thoughts that a man never exchanges with another man, and that in many a life may lie eternally buried — everything swelled and shot into new growth.... And it belonged to her. In humble anticipation, he placed before her image everything that was flowering within him.

Sometimes, in a quiet and dangerous hour, Sofie suddenly stepped out of her frame, and then she was no longer the Sofie who in rapt attention lost herself in his wisdom. On the contrary, she would softly put her finger on his lips and then look him in the eyes as if she were about to burst into laughter. In delicious fear, he always shut such visions up in the depths of his soul, like a miser heaping treasure upon treasure while wanting privacy to count his riches.

165

Kold was able to maintain his innocent self-deception chiefly because he was in undisturbed possession of his secret. With miserly worry he had avoided everything that might have drawn suspicion in that direction. Nevertheless, in so doing, he could not prevent the consciousness of it from radiating out of his entire being. People did not recognize the former unsociable, melancholy Kold; he had again become the man he had been at an earlier stage. People gathered around this happy face in the same way they would seek comfort in a long-awaited glimpse of the sun during persistent grey weather. A man's secret is not as piquant a thing to disturb as that of a young girl. Was that the reason, or did people really have no idea of the reason for the change in him? This much was certain: he himself had never given the smallest hint of it. Not the smallest pebble had dropped onto the smooth surface reflecting his happiness — so comfortable in its victory, so sure in its possession.

It was now the day before his departure for home. It was a Sunday. The August sun, which had been burning hotly during the day, fell behind the jagged Bærum hills, and the fresh air outside tempted people into the streets. Christiania was not as lively then as it is now. The full weight of a Sunday afternoon lay upon the quiet city. A few people were promenading back and forth in the streets. Here and there one might see a man in his shirt sleeves, resignedly smoking a pipe by his open window.

Kold also wandered aimlessly about for a while before deciding to try the road leading into the countryside. The dust immediately forced him to turn back, however. The outskirts of town are really just for those who own horses and country places; for them this beauty existed of which Christiania was so proud. For the remainder of the people, the dust from the carriages of the rich, and the city with its summer lassitude, represented reality. Up at the fortress, things were a little more lively, but in this liveliness there was something self-limiting and philistine that was far from producing a gayer mood. Here the good city burghers, dressed in their Sunday best and walking several abreast, took their calm turns about the ramparts, pausing only to watch for the smoke of the steamship they were awaiting. On such days, when the weather was beautiful, the harbour sometimes presented a lively spectacle in which the people waiting could indulge themselves by observing the countless number of sailing boats floating about, bound for the islands in the fjord. On this day, however, the sea was absolutely calm, and the quiet was broken only by the occasional sound of an oar splashing in the water before disap-

166

pearing below the ramparts, or by the sentry's monotonous 'Change guard!'

Kold stood for a long time on the parapet of Tritschler's Bastion, looking thoughtfully out over the water. Now and then he cast a fleeting glance at the passers-by. He could find scarcely any young people among them. 'Where is the youth of Christiania on such a day as this?' he almost said out loud.

Our capital has no places of amusement, the way other major cities do, where one may sit in a shady glade and enjoy refreshments for very little money and be revived by music and by the sight of a motley, moving mass of people. Such a release for wholesome, unspoilt *joie-de-vivre*, available to every social class, does not exist here. One is forced to walk in the dust along a good stretch of sunbaked road in order to reach green solitude. But the student, who all week long has been worrying over his books, has the least need of anybody for such Werther-like dreaming out in nature. He wants society, life, reality. Few of them have families to turn to; most of these poor young people are left completely to themselves. How Quakerly quiet the city is on such a day, while our Hydra, crudeness, lies luxuriously sunning itself! On just such a Sunday, many a young and lonely soul has taken his first steps on the slippery road to perdition. Oh, hospitable Christiania, in whose praise so much has been said and written by visiting dignitaries and artists — if you could just open your many doors and give your *own* children a place by your hearth!

It is not certain that Georg Kold made all these reflections; at least he had no reason to apply them to himself. He was just debating with himself which of his many invitations for the evening he would accept, without feeling any particular desire for any of them. His sociable mood suddenly failed him on this last evening. Longing was tugging at him, and in his mind he was already back home. Such was his frame of mind when he was addressed by an old acquaintance who was sauntering by; a student who was not among those fortunates who are frequently invited out. Kold took a couple of turns around the ramparts with him.

It just so happened that nobody had yet mentioned Sofie's name to Kold. It never occurred to him that this star might have been discovered by others besides himself. His companion now innocently chanced to inquire whether there were daughters in the family with whom Georg was living. When the latter had answered this question with some circumspection, the other asked just as innocently whether it was one of those Miss Ramms who, during a brief stay in the city, had caused such a stir with her beauty that nothing else had been talked about for some time, etc., only there had been general regret about her presumed *lameness*, since she never danced. In his driest and most emphatic manner, Kold denied knowing a lame Miss Ramm.

The pebble had been tossed into the pool. Those few words left behind a restlessness and strange dissatisfaction that forced Kold straight home to his lodgings, where he started packing and then ordered horses. 'It is certainly strange that this did not occur to me sooner!' he said. 'It's obviously much better to travel by night, by which means I'll avoid the heat and the dust.' — He was hard on his horses and allowed himself no rest, again due to his utter loathing for the highway.

At two o'clock the following night, he stopped outside the gate, wandered down the tree-lined approach to the house, and quietly entered the farm on tip-toe. He was just about to knock, but then thought the better of it and walked slowly through the little picket gate into the garden, where he sought a bench underneath the lilac tree.

It was a beautiful night in August — a time when the moon regains its supremacy over Earth. The cool freshness of the night immediately washed like a bath over his tired limbs. Against the last strip of light on the horizon, forest and mountains were sharply silhouetted in dark, bronze-coloured lines, while the gentle light of the moon, which was ascending above the trees in the garden, already illuminated the tops of the nearest objects. It tried to penetrate the foliage that was quivering in weird, elongated shadows against the walls of the house. Like a sentry, a slender young poplar stretched its shadow in front of an upstairs window to the right, which was the first thing Kold sought with his eyes. Down below, everything lay in semi-darkness. A single ray stole up the path towards the flower bed in front of the steps, but it struck only a cluster of straight, white hollyhocks stretching like ghosts out of the darkness. No sound could be heard from the house; only a cricket was singing in the wall. The thunder of the waterfall down in the valley and the rhythmic strokes of a corncrake were so monotonous that they blended with the stillness of the night.

Kold was in a strange mood. Deeply and uneasily, he inhaled the fragrance filling the air — a peculiar mixture of roses and freshly mown hay. He wished he had a hundred senses with which to enjoy fully the glories of this night, which at this moment reflected his own soul. What was happening in his soul just then was as different from anything he had hitherto felt and experienced as this night, with its bewitching dark, its changing, enchanting lights and its intoxicating scents, was from a foggy day in March. Pale and strangely unfamiliar, every image from his past paraded past against this backdrop. How colourless and meaningless was the happiness of which he had dreamed before, compared with the new joys swelling his heart!

While Kold was pursuing these reveries, fatigue enveloped him, and he dozed off, leaning against a tree trunk. When he awoke, the shadows of the night were gone. Dawn was casting its first faint light upon the windows, turning all the colours into flames. A fresh morning breeze shook the leaves and disturbed the fine veil of beads which the dew had spread over the flowering rose bushes. A shudder went through the man who was just awakening. Almost paralysed with fatigue, he got up and walked towards the house. There he stopped, as if touched by an electric shock that then resumed pumping blood and life through his veins. Lifting his eyes towards Sofie's windows, he thought he had seen a white arm that seemed to wave at him! — Upon closer inspection, however, he discovered that it was Sofie's white cat, which she had the bad habit of keeping with her at night, and which was now performing its morning ablutions on the window sill.

* * *

At last they had put it behind them, this first blushing reunion. Mutely, unable to speak a word, they confronted one another. Each was so overcome by emotion that he or she failed to notice a similar reaction in the other. Sofie had undergone an outward change as well — it was hard to say in what it consisted. In a short span of time, the summer with its happiness and longing had unfurled her. She had become more soulful; more interesting. This also confused Kold. Each impressed the other, while each suffered a private sense of dispiritedness.

Things went on in this manner for some time. Kold would bring Sofie a new song or a book. When she had finished with it, she would return it with an ordinary word or two of thanks, but they found no words with which to enter more fully into the subject. In her singing, however, Sofie was more eloquent. In this, in art, she had her own defence against the

169

terrible timidity from which she suffered. Music carried her irresistibly along. Her voice, her entire being, became one with the spirit of her songs. More than once she sought refuge behind this shelter that was so comforting to her — and so dangerous for him.

After such a scene one evening, he stormed across the meadows. 'It's over,' he said; 'all is lost. I've become a completely spineless creature in front of her; she has completely overpowered me. This evening, after we had left the table, how she did sing! She has never sung like that before.... The looks she sent me across the sheet of music were so absentminded — she was scarcely aware of my presence, while I saw and heard only her.... When I finally collected myself to say something, she was gone.... What must she be thinking — I, who left so boldly and so satisfied with myself, as if I had given her the whole world! ... I might just as well throw myself at her feet at once, but I dare not. As yet I have won nothing, nothing! ... Alas, those cheerful conversations during which I talked so instructively and played the part of her mentor — now they seem to me so terribly silly, and yet I'd like to return to them. Why can't they be revived? ... They must!'

Those cheerful conversations would not come about, however. Kold wandered about in the fields; every day he went down to the cave; but he never encountered the one he was seeking. Once he summoned up his courage and asked straight out if they might take a walk. He thought that when they were thus walking those familiar paths together, the old feelings and the old ambience would return by themselves. Sofie was willing, and he waited for her by the stairs, happy and uneasy. Sofie arrived! but Amalie was with her. This happened repeatedly when he had hoped for a *tête-à-tête*. At such times, he either shifted into a mood in which it was suitable for a sensible person to talk nonsense, or else he dried up and became taciturn. This made poor Amalie suffer, because she was the butt of his sarcasm. He would even be bitter towards Sofie, which she, in turn, could not understand. 'All kindness, all interest in me is gone; he even mocks me,' she said to herself. But he was the one who felt hurt and withdrew. For days he would work in his room, while she walked about quietly and watchfully, with an uneasy heart.

When they had tormented each other in this fashion for some time, Sofie could bear it no longer. One day she walked up to Kold and said, 'I don't know how to tell you about a mishap I have had with your book.

I am quite in despair over it, especially because I know how fond of it you are.'

She handed him the volume of Paludan-Müller's *Psyche* which Brandt had ripped up.

'Oh, there's no great harm done!' said Kold, no less confused than she. 'Those things can so easily happen, and if it gave you any pleasure — to read it, I mean — then it gives me pleasure.'

'I certainly didn't do it myself,' answered Sofie, conquering a smile. 'I might just as well tell you how it happened. Lorenz Brandt was here one time while you were away. . . . He was in a terrible state. . . .'

'He ripped up the book! . . . But what, then, made poor Lorenz fly into such a rage?'

'I almost think it was your *name* ' — but at that moment the whole scene with Lorenz was vividly before her. She stopped, and a violent blush spread over her face. There was a pause, during which Kold observed her inquiringly. Immediately sensing the slight advantage given him by Sofie, he said gaily and with his customary ease:

'Is that possible; is Lorenz that furious with me? I had thought we were the best of friends since that day when he so bravely pulled me out of the water! . . . But you really must not mind about the damage. I'm about to propose a trade — you may give me one of your books instead.'

'Oh, more than gladly, if only I had one that was a worthy substitute for this one.'

'Oh, the first one you come across will be good enough; haven't you got *Elisa, Or A Model for Wives?*'

'No, I have not,' said Sofie drily.

'But then you surely have Robinson — Platou's geography — Balle's textbook?'

'Well,' said Sofie in the same tone of voice; 'you certainly have wonderful notions about my library! Then I shall give you *Thieme's First Nourishment.*'

'. . . *For the Healthy Human Mind.* . . . That is simply marvellous! You certainly know how to pick what is best for me!'

'But then I may keep your book?'

'That's only reasonable. You keep the *remains* of my *Psyche*, and I get *The Healthy Human Mind* in its stead. God grant that I may keep it unblemished,' he suddenly added in a serious tone of voice.

Somebody was approaching. Instead of pursuing their theme undisturbedly as in former days, they confusedly cut their conversation short with some remarks about the weather.

It is claimed that true feelings are always full of doubt. With regard to Sofie, however, not even this much could be safely said. Doubt presupposes hope, which it accompanies as the shadow follows the light. But Sofie's feelings had been reared on hopelessness. She had never thought of or dreamed of such a happiness as having her feelings reciprocated. Within her experience, such a possibility had not yet arisen. This certainty gave her manner a firmness and a quiet, but determined reticence that confused Kold and made him uneasy. At times, her reticence contained a touch of sullenness that reminded him horribly of her old childhood antipathy.

But a day would surely have to come when hope was to enter her soul. Poor Sofie, how do things look within the dark and quiet chambers of your heart? Is there also room for this splendid new guest, and how will it get along with the dark, joyless spirits who at one time established their right of occupancy there? . . . Badly enough, we fear; there will be tumult and exodus and desperate fights. Poor Sofie; God grant that all the light and happy spirits may be victorious! . . . In the meantime, farewell peace; farewell resignation!

Kind, forgiving nature finally intervened to dissolve the oppressive mood and allowed Sofie and Kold to forget for a while the distress caused by living under the same roof. On a pleasure trip which the whole family, including Kold, made to a farm in a lovely part of the country, a rapprochement took place, and there evolved one of these conversations without content, without continuity, of which not a word can be recalled later, and whose whole charm lies in that which must remain unsaid. Sofie and Kold played around each other like children. If they were apart for a moment, it was only in order to have the pleasure of seeking each other anew. They were so engrossed that they did not notice the others' polite efforts to leave them alone. There is a way of protecting such a couple lost in each other that is more offensive than crude and unsuspecting interruption. But, as already noted, Sofie and Kold observed neither the one nor the other; they were happy, so happy that when they broke up to start the homeward journey, it seemed to them that this day had rewarded them for all the preceding weeks' sufferings. Unfortunately, they were not able to carry this happiness home with them unscathed. And besides, how can there be talk of happiness in a condition consisting of nothing but uneasiness; in an eternal mutual hunting and fleeing; in a breathless teetering between all sorts of conflicting emotions; in this state which one never finishes describing, but which Goethe alone has managed to sum up in four lines:

Freudvoll und leidvoll, gedankenvoll sein,
Hangen und Bangen in schwebender Pein,
Himmelhoch jauchzend, zum Tode betrübt,
Glücklich allein ist die Seele, die liebt.

Himmelhoch jauchzend for a trifle; *zum Tode betrübt* for a trifle. Such trifles were what so often plunged Sofie from her heaven back into reality.

As it happened, she had the day before been singing a Swedish romance, every word of which Kold thought had been written for him. Suddenly her mother had asked him whether he did not think it was lovely. He might easily have escaped with a general assent, but he was far too moved. After praising the music, he had declared the words to be tasteless nonsense.

In the farmyard, the carriages were ready for the return trip. Was her denying herself his company here dictated by a need to be alone so she could let her full heart overflow into the fresh autumn evening, or was it a voluntary penance she had taken upon herself? At any rate, Sofie had no desire to sit inside the carriage; she got up on the driver's seat. Kold, who had gone inside to light his cigar, was just arriving when Mrs Ramm called,

'Is that where you want to sit, Sofie? Well, as you wish. . . . But then Per will have to stand in the back . . . and do watch the reins well, dear Kold, and don't overturn us too often,' she added teasingly.

Sofie, quite horrified by this arrangement, which he might think was in part her doing, quickly leaped down, but thereby made matters worse, because he was just drily declaring his intention of walking home.

'Walking?' said Mrs Ramm; 'there is certainly room in the carriage.' The hapless Sofie had just taken her seat inside.

'Thank you; I prefer to walk. I have enjoyed the company of the ladies at such length today that it would be to misuse my good fortune,' he said with an expression that turned his gallantry into an insult.

He was already on his way down the road.

'Well,' said Mrs Ramm to Amalie, 'you and I cannot pride ourselves on having had too much of his company.'

Kold walked home, radiantly happy, without the least suspicion of having hurt Sofie's feelings. She, however, sat in silence all the way home, angry with him, with her mother and with herself. 'That is the punishment,' she said to herself, 'for believing the — impossible, for just one moment.'

When they reached home, she ran past her mother and sister without saying good night and hurried upstairs to her room, where she gave vent to her sadness in a flood of tears.

The next day, Sofie was strict with herself and as reserved as ever. However, her behaviour did not give the impression of anxious flight. Her demeanour was modest and sure, but she also kept her distance. Kold had not expected this, and his impatience was carried to the highest pitch. But matters were to get worse. At the dinner table, the maid entered with a letter which she handed to Sofie, who in obvious confusion put it away on her person.

'Who brought it?' her mother asked. The maid had been given it by the housekeeper, who had got it from one of the workmen, who in turn had received it from Ole the idiot — a pauper receiving poor relief on the farm. But here all inquiry came to an end, because Ole had but one answer to all inquiries, no matter what form they took, and that was 'I dunno.'

'Those are certainly mysterious letters you are receiving, Sofie,' said her mother. 'They are always brought by invisible hands.'

'Bah,' said the District Governor, 'a note from the Breiens asking the loan of a new waltz or for a collar pattern. That is no doubt the whole of the secret.'

'The Breiens? No, my dear, it's not from them; I'm familiar with their chicken scratches.'

'I d-don't know whom the letter is from,' Sofie stammered.

But this was too much for Kold. In the agony of his soul he strode up and down the floor of his room.

'Do not love too soon, Sofie! Do not throw away the priceless treasure of your own self! Didn't I say so at one time! . . . What ironic devil is just now reminding me of those words? . . . Do not love. . . . Oh, there's no danger, have no fear! . . . Yet I did believe. . . . Yes, I have dared dream of it! But I believe it no longer. This calmness, this cool friendliness. . . . A young girl doesn't have that kind of self-control. . . . And why should she? Hasn't she understood that I am no admirer of affectation and artificiality? . . . I don't understand her! . . . After a day like yesterday, when we seemed to understand each other so thoroughly that the word which had been hovering constrainingly between us seemed to me superfluous, an empty formality — after such a day, when I thought we must silently fall upon each other's breasts, she is suddenly distant, like a stranger.... What, then, is this? ... And yet she is hiding a deep emotion. I have seen a hundred signs of it.... Suppose it may be for another! ... It is incomprehensible that this possibility hasn't struck me until now.... This secret exchange of letters and her confusion. Is it possible that another might.... But who is it? ... Where is he? She stayed long enough in Christiania.... Perhaps even in Denmark....'

Here he stopped to listen, tore open the window, and stood for a while holding his breath. Soft tunes were floating up to him from the garden room. Sofie was singing one of those melodies by *Kjerulf* in which suddenly, from behind the grey wall of northern melancholy and self-denial, a southern zest for life stretches out its hand after us and sends us melting looks. But the window is so high up! When we look closely, the princess turns out to be our dear nanny, humming the old, familiar children's songs to us and asking us so nicely to stay close to the house.

Kold walked downstairs, made a detour through the garden, and took up an unobserved position by the garden stairs. It was a cloudy, but mild, September afternoon. The door was open, and through it he saw Sofie sitting by the piano. The light from the lamp fell on her face. What a contrast to her expression earlier in the day! Her eyes were aflame, and they seemed bigger and darker than usual. She seemed to have sung her pain awake. She was singing as a woman dares to sing only when she is alone. She sang as if her heart were breaking. Now he could also hear the words, but those words, with longing in every breath, were not calculated to soothe his restlessness. As she was singing

> My thought I sent you,
> I sent you my look.

she happened to raise her eyes to where he was standing. He was trembling. 'Oh, why can't I run over to her? ... What is keeping me back? A word, just one small word, that hides a certainty I cannot bear.... *Oh, Sofie, give me your hand across this abyss! ... Give me a sign!*'

He made a forward movement, then suddenly turned around and hurried down into the darkest part of the garden.... But Sofie's voice still followed him like a tortured call:

175

Alas, how my heart was burning
Because its call found no response.

The following afternoon, Kold was returning from a walk in the fields when he found the ladies sitting on the garden steps. Mrs Ramm and Sofie were sewing, and Amalie was knitting, interrupting her work now and again in order to sniff an enormous bouquet of stocks and mignonettes of which she had just robbed the large flower bed. This bed was Mrs Ramm's pride, and it had indeed produced an extraordinary display of colours this autumn.

'This weather is so lovely,' Mrs Ramm remarked to Kold, 'that we cannot bring ourselves to go inside. Such warm weather for this time of year!'

'That is true; I also dread going inside to stuffy rooms. One ought to close up the houses and move out-of-doors for as long as our brief glory lasts.'

They talked awhile about the wind and the weather, about the autumn and about their neighbours. On the latter subject, Mrs Ramm was particularly in her element. She really had a gift for storytelling. She knew other people's private histories down to the last detail; even about those of whom one would least expect it, she was able to relate some peculiarity, to which she was always happy to add some instructive reflection. Their discourse was suddenly interrupted by Edvard.

That young person was just at the unfortunate transition between school and a freedom not yet mastered, in which one becomes interested in all sorts of trends without sticking to a single one, and in which one is interested in everything without knowing how to become occupied with anything. Edvard wrote verse; he played the piano; he sketched — everything equally erratically and usually disturbing to the others. Because of all these talents, his mother, whose pet he was, saw in him a true marvel. Sofie was the only one perspicacious enough to see that this was leading nowhere. She sometimes called Edvard's attention to this and asked him to busy himself with these occupations in earnest, which the young gentleman naturally took in bad grace, since in his own opinion he was now an adult.

He had just been heard fantasizing on the piano; thereafter disciplining his dog and causing it to howl dreadfully; and finally running in and out of various doors. Now he suddenly presented himself to the company in a disguise consisting of one of those ladies' hats that were fashionable some thirty or forty years ago, and which are of a size and shape so fantastic that we now can scarcely comprehend that they were used in public. The reader may perhaps recall a kind made of black, felted fur, adorned with an ostrich plume that stuck straight up in the air, in sharp contrast to the usual arrangement of this form of decoration. A long, red stole and an immense sewing bag completed Edvard's costume. Greeted by the others' laughter, he approached curtsying, while in his walk and deportment he was aping an old spinster living in their neighbourhood.

'Ah! Miss *Møllerup* ! Please do sit down, dear Miss Møllerup. . . .'

Edvard opened his huge bag, looked pensively into it, sighed deeply and shook his head. When Amalie was sniffing her bouquet for a moment, he seized the opportunity and grabbed her knitting, took out the needles and started unravelling the piece, but at this point his dog came rushing after him and made him lose track of the part he was playing. . . . '*Chasseur, aporte!*' The sewing bag flew over the hedge, and the old spinster and the dog took off after it like a whirlwind.

'Oh yes, we are laughing, children,' said Mrs Ramm, 'but there was a time when Miss Møllerup was not an object of derision, but, on the contrary, brought many a man to tears. At that time, she was the handsomest and most sought-after girl for miles around.'

'Miss Møllerup? . . . That's impossible. It's incredible! . . . That awful Miss Møllerup! She's weak in the head, too, poor thing!'

'Miss Møllerup was the handsomest and most celebrated girl of her day,' Mrs Ramm repeated with emphasis. 'I know the story of her life. An aunt of mine, who was her intimate friend, has told me all the circumstances regarding it. It is very sad, but it is instructive — it might serve as a warning to many a young girl.'

'How is that, Mother — in what respect?' asked her daughters.

'That will be interesting!' said Kold and sat down on the steps. 'You simply must tell us the whole story, madam, so that your daughters may really benefit from it.'

'Oh dear, yes!' begged Amalie. 'It surprises me that you haven't told it to us sooner, since there is something extraordinary about it.'

'If I have not done so, my girl, you may be sure I've had my reasons,' said her mother, sewing with greater industry than ever.

'Not at all because it contains anything offensive,' she continued, when nobody was interrupting her. 'There's nothing in it to which a young girl may not listen without blushing. But the story of the unfortunate Miss Møllerup does contain elements of those mistakes of passion, of those extremes to which a mind may be driven when it doesn't know how to regulate itself; and it's my opinion that young and innocent minds should not have their thoughts disturbed by those kinds of things. Such were my reasons, if I had any. . . .'

'All this can only serve to pique our curiosity to the utmost,' said Kold, who was far too well acquainted with the lady's delight in storytelling not to be aware that one did her no favour by respecting her reasons for demurring. 'As there doesn't seem to be any direct danger to our young and innocent minds, you will not get away. . . . Thus: Karoline Møllerup was the handsomest and most celebrated girl of her day.'

'So she was. She was handsome; yet there was something in her personality that was even more overwhelming than her beauty. She was very unrestrained in her merriment, but when the fancy took her, she could also be very cold and stand-offish. She was what one calls 'out of the ordinary.' The Christmas holidays and other occasions were wont to draw a number of young people up to the gay and hospitable part of the country where her father lived. That was in the good old days, when people knew how to have fun; when Christmas meant twelve to fourteen balls and when people only got up in order to dress for another ball. Miss Møllerup was the centre of all the young men's enthusiastic attentions, and before they left she had usually succeeded in making half a dozen of them miserable. When anyone castigated her for this and thought that she had been too hard on this or that person, she replied, "How can I help it? I have not encouraged him!" And well she might say so. She was not really coquettish, although she was accused of being so. However, I suppose people were at a loss for a better word to describe her behaviour.

'Whatever position Karoline Møllerup held in her own circle, Cavalry Captain *von Heinen* was said to hold in his — irresistible to and proof against the other sex. The rumour of her had just reached him. He was at that time garrisoned in her neighbourhood with a number of other officers — I suppose it was during the years 1780-1781. It was therefore an easy matter for him to arrange an invitation to spend Christmas at the Møllerups. Bending a mind like Karoline Møllerup's seemed to him a challenge designed uniquely for him. Indeed, it was said that he had made a bet with his friends that within a certain date, he would be able to show them a written confession of her love. He was already savouring his triumph ahead of time, and certainly, all that a man can do to win a girl, he put into motion. He was her constant escort on every occasion. In the theatrical comedies that were so fashionable in those days, he always played the lover and she the mistress, but that was as far as it went — it was only on stage, that is. Karoline was her usual self — gay, delighting in life, never at a loss in assisting him to invent new sources of fun, always the gracious hostess — but when he began to act tender towards her, she dismissed him brusquely and coldly, just as she had done with all the others. He began to feel uneasy. Everybody had at once marked him out as the one who would be victorious. Now there began to be general talk of a probable refusal, and many of those to whom he had expressed rather too great a certainty about his victory, could scarcely conceal their malicious pleasure. He doubled his advances — in vain. The fatal day arrived when the Captain had to return to his squadron. It is said that his face was lemon yellow when he took his departure, and that he sent Karoline one last look! — a look that is supposed to be that *certain thing* which the old spinster says she can never forget.'

'Wasn't he in earnest, then?' asked Sofie, quite pale with emotion. 'Did he really not love her?'

'That has nothing to do with the story, my girl. . . . Don't interrupt me! . . . After that day, an odd change came over Karoline. One might suppose that this look had bewitched her. She grew very quiet and in the course of a short time conspicuously lost her looks. A year passed. Then she confided to my aunt that she had loved von Heinen from the first moment, but — she offered as her excuse — she had not been able to get the better of her own behaviour. She would act very differently towards him when next he came, however — she had waited and waited, but in vain. Finally — ' here Mrs Ramm's voice fell to almost a whisper — 'fear and longing drove her to write a letter to him, where she in the most passionate terms confesses her love for him and implores him to return — because she cannot live without him!'

Amalie let her knitting drop and hid her face in her bouquet.

'Dreadful!' breathed Sofie, with genuine horror written all over her face.

'Ghastly! Horrifying!' Kold agreed.

'The poor girl! Let us not judge her too harshly,' continued Mrs Ramm. 'Our mistakes carry their own punishment with them. Here it followed close behind. My aunt, a virtuous, well-brought-up girl, was simply aghast, as you may well imagine. She finally persuaded Karoline to write another letter in which she, in more appropriate terms, begged him to return the letter, the fateful letter, to her. It arrived — far too soon — together with one from von Heinen that — just imagine! — in a few lines contained the assurance — '

Mrs Ramm's lips closed against the dreadful thing she had to relate. Nobody dared ask a question.

'It contained an assurance that he never again would have been able to part with this precious document, had he not fortunately arranged to have several copies made thereof, which were circulated among his friends as an innocent diversion in leisure hours and as a consolation for those who had been made fools of by a wily flirt.

'She never recovered from this blow. She fell ill for a long time, and when she got up again, she was out of her mind. She was incessantly writing letters, which naturally were prevented from going in the post. I suppose her madness passed, but she was and is feebleminded. Since then, writing letters and tearing them up, knitting and unravelling, have become her sole occupations.'

After this story, there was a long pause. Finally Kold said, 'And the moral, dear lady?'

'I don't know what you mean by "moral", but if you are referring to the warning and instruction others may receive from such a story, then I think it is obvious enough. Any transgression of the limits to decent behaviour carries its own dreadful punishment.'

'That's probably true, but still I must confess that I don't quite understand. It seems to me that in this case, it was the Captain who offended against decency, but you have not told us that he was punished. The poor old maid, on the other hand, was punished with dishonour and madness and all sorts of terrible things, but in what way had she actually transgressed?'

'You cannot have been paying sufficient attention, or else I must have expressed myself very badly. It was *she, the maiden herself,* who wrote to him, without his having declared himself properly.'

'Yes, I certainly did understand that, but even so, the offence doesn't seem quite obvious to me. She wrote to him because *she* thought she had some amends to make; because she, as we know, had been the one to turn a deaf ear. She naturally assumed that the Captain was a decent man and not a rogue. . . .'

'But dear God! You surely won't defend such an insane action — such an obvious breach of feminine conduct! . . . Is it perhaps your opinion that the ladies are to do the proposing and the gentlemen to hand out bashful refusals?'

'Heavens, no! That's not at all what I mean; that would certainly be to deprive the ladies of their most precious privilege. I merely thought that any *true, deep* attachment on their part as well — since they are also human beings — has the right to express itself, so long as it stays within the limits of what is allowable — from the point of view of *elegance and good taste*, that is; and I also think that the circumstances and the people involved were rather out of the ordinary. It was not in itself unfeminine that Miss Møllerup wrote such a letter, driven by her passion and blinded by her faith that she was loved by the person she herself had driven away. *How* it was written seems to me the only thing in question. Oh, such a confession could be as fragile and scented as a lily-of-the-valley, so truly feminine, in other words!'

'Yes, my dear Kold,' said the lady with an arch smile, 'it is as I say — you always have such odd notions, and you and I are always going to disagree. It's just that your theories can't be put into practice in real life. As is well known, you gentlemen cannot tolerate declarations even if an honest-to-goodness angel of God took the trouble, and I fear our brave knight himself would be the least able to weather the test.'

'That would simply depend, madam.'

'Suppose you had been in the Captain's place, and you had received such a letter — what would you have done then?'

'Show me the letter, and I'll tell you what I would have done.'

'Well, I suppose it was written by an otherwise lovable girl, and that it was as fragrant with lilies and roses and everything as you might wish. . . .'

'Had it been an *honest* and truly feminine letter, then I should have been on my way that very moment. . . . and I should not have stopped to rest or eat until . . . until I had thrown myself at her feet; until I had . . . oh, until I had — '

'Yes, certainly! . . . But suppose you did not love her. . .?'

'If I did not love her? . . . Then I'd . . . . Oh, I'd. . .! Well, I really don't know. . . . then I'd feel the deepest respect, gratitude. . . .'

'Thank you very much, indeed! Respect and gratitude — that will certainly help her wounded pride!'

'Pride, pride and always pride! Why must it be offended? Is it then a greater shame for a woman than for a man not to have affection returned, when it has the same common human root?'

Here he encountered a look from Sofie; a look whose peculiar expression he knew so well: wonder, pain and joy were mingled in it. Electrified, he continued:

'Why may not this emotion meet ours and guide it? Yes, guide it, because woman's love has a much surer and deeper instinct for spiritual harmony than ours. It leads to happiness, while ours does not. I cannot admire the sort of femininity that sees its ideal in passivity and silence, which will reduce them all to puppets and automatons.'

'But, as it happens, this is what the world requires of women, and the law of the world is something a woman must heed.'

'But surely not when her life's happiness is at stake?'

'Especially then; especially then! To submit is her only salvation. Therefore, a young girl cannot be too strongly admonished to control her emotions and, if possible, get rid of them while there is still time.'

'Get rid of them! God have mercy, what an expression! . . . If you were right in this, madam, surely every young girl would have cause to bemoan to God that she was ever born.'

'Mr Kold,' said the lady in a solemn tone, 'this is not a subject to be treated in front of young girls. Fortunately, the sort of principles you express cannot be of any danger to my girls. I have brought them up to be virtuous in accordance with tenets that are better suited to life. I taught them very early to distinguish between a real and an imagined world. In the novels, these beautiful, tender feelings are always reciprocated, always crowned, and faithfulness is eternal. In life it doesn't happen that way. It's pure luck if a girl's affection is returned, and eternal faithfulness is of no use at all, if they don't all want to go around as old maids. It's their destiny to become wives and mothers, not to waste their lives brooding over empty infatuations. The sooner they can put those behind them, the better for them! . . . Because, you see, not even in the ballroom does the quiet wish of a young girl draw forth *the one* she particularly wants to dance with. She dances with anyone at all, and she has fun just the same.

I have lived according to this tenet. I married my husband without passion, and our marriage has nevertheless been a happy one. I found my happiness in resignation and in the fulfilment of my duties. Nor did my eldest daughters marry from inclination, but they have yet become happy wives. . . .'

Here Sofie made a violent movement as if she wanted to say something, but she merely lowered her head.

' — And my daughters,' said Mrs Ramm in conclusion, 'will thank me for it some time; thank me because I have taught them that self-denial is a woman's most exquisite virtue.' She got up majestically.

'Oh, you shouldn't have done that!' cried Kold impetuously, likewise getting up. 'Forgive me! But you cannot mean what you say there. It is indeed a shocking sin. . . . It is suicide! . . . It is to destroy the most wonderful thing a human being possesses — faith, hope and love all at once. . . . And what, then, remains on which to sustain life? . . . Self-denial! This anaemic endeavour of the soul, this disguise for being tired of living — is that supposed to be a substitute for the living emotion that would have suffered everything with ease and joy? . . . Is that any way of husbanding the most precious powers that God has destined for the blessing of future generations? . . . The mothers themselves enjoin their children to deny these feelings as if they were something shameful; to eradicate them as if they were sinful — they are to be cried out through tears and protracted suffering, and then, when such a soul has been sufficiently martyred and emptied, it is to be offered to some man. . . . It is upon the ruins of the temple that he is to build his house!'

'Indeed, you are exaggerating far too much. On such a flight of fancy I can no longer follow you. . . . My dear Kold, do let it be the last time we discuss this subject. In this matter we don't understand each other at all! . . . Lord, it's already eight o'clock! Come, children! It's high time we broke up. While I'm sitting here lecturing on the duties of woman, I'm forgetting to feed my husband.' She laughed as she walked inside.

During Kold's last remarks, Sofie had left her seat and walked down towards the flowers in the garden. She was bending over a bush when Kold approached.

'You have expressed no opinion during our feud, Miss Sofie; you haven't said a word.' His lips were still quivering with emotion, and his burning eyes were resting upon her.

'Look at this rose,' said Sofie, blushing, 'how lovely it is, scarcely out, and it is the middle of September! I'm debating with myself whether or not to break it off.'

'Just take it, otherwise the night frost will do it for you. . . . But that was no answer to my question! . . . Sofie. . . . Look, there is another one, an absolutely beautiful one!' He put his hand deep down among the thorns and got the rose after some struggle. 'This one is even more beautiful!'

'Really?' said Sofie with an exquisite smile. She held the two roses up next to each other. 'Do take a good look at them! I wonder if it isn't because you tore your hand, whereas mine was obtained so easily?'

'That may be,' he said in confusion, 'but you still haven't answered my question. Was I right or wrong?'

'I have answered it.'

'Give me this rose,' he said, 'that is just the one I want.' He threw his own rose far away.

'No, you may not have it,' said Sofie and held it up in the air. When he wanted to reach for it, she quickly ran along the flower beds, up the stairs, and disappeared behind the glass door.

Kold took after her like a shot, and when the young girl saw that she was being pursued indoors as well, she let out one of those piercing screams into which children who are taken by surprise while playing can put such a mixture of both joy and fear. This scream stopped him; he remained standing, full of thought, with his eyes fixed on the door through which she had disappeared.

Breathless, Sofie reached her own room, where she yielded to her long-suppressed emotions. Like all deeply sensitive people who are forced to keep up a façade much of the time, she was given to violent outbursts. A hitherto unknown and intoxicating joy was coursing through her. For a long time she stood there, drawing deep breaths in order to collect herself. She tore open the window; it was as if the air in the room would suffocate her. 'What did he say that's making me so happy and lighthearted! Indeed, what was it? Was it a dream? I felt so small, so humble in my love, but now it is no longer a poor, small thing — it is something; it has worth in his eyes; I dare to be proud of it! Oh God,' she cried, stretching out her hands towards the twinkling stars, 'Thank you, thank you, because you allow me to live for the one I love! . . . But no, I cannot believe it. Something will and must happen to upset it! Why should I deserve to be so happy over and above my sisters — above thousands of my sisters!'

* * *

Equipped for hunting, Edvard was standing out in the yard with some friends the following afternoon. A couple of farmers who were good shots were to lead their party. The hounds were tearing impatiently at their leads. They were still waiting for Kold, who had promised to join them. When he was ready and about to rush downstairs, he stopped without thinking by a door he was accustomed to walking past every day. It was wide open, because the maid had just finished cleaning before the holiday, and this allowed him to look into a room he had never seen, although he had been on the farm for three years. It belonged to the young daughters of the house. The room was unoccupied and filled with a profusion of objects. The walls were covered with drawings and paintings of every size and description, without any attempt at discrimination. *Madonna della Sedia* had to be content with having a *Cleopatra* with dying, upturned eyes by her side; 'The Conflagration of Copenhagen' divided an *Abélard of Grevedon* from his *Héloise*. Kold's eyes searched in vain for some sign of Sofie's presence. They travelled from a secretary festooned with those thousands of useless objects called knick-knacks, which he loathed, past a cornucopia made of wool yarn and filled with dusty flowers, and finally came to rest upon a harp over in the corner, against which the maid had propped a long broom as if it were a plecter. The sight of the harp removed any doubt Kold might have had as to whose room he was in. A door immediately opposite stood ajar. Without knowing how he got there, he was standing on the threshold. Here, here was the sanctum. The old great-grandmother on the wall seemed to be its stern guardian. She looked at him grimly, as if she wanted to say: 'Back, you rash fellow, what do you seek here? You are one of those snakes that bring misfortune upon families; who poison the hearts of the daughters with the madness they call love. . . . Back!'

Yes, this was where she lived. The air and the light in this room were different. It naturally seemed so to him, but it is doubtful that it will excite any interest in the reader. Here was none of the artistic clutter that appears to such great effect in novels, but that, translated into our merciless reality, signifies only that the woman or maiden in question is an untidy woman or maiden. Both of Sofie's slippers were present, standing harmoniously side by side on the flowered carpet. On the floor there were neither musical instruments, a riding hat, gloves, or other equally tantalizing articles scattered about. No snippets of letters, no revealing portrait on the table. Finally, we are forced to confess the absence of a 'snow-white, narrow little bed.' A dark red, full curtain hid all of one side of the room from view. Everything breathed peace, simplicity, and yet an elusive elegance. The window to the garden was open; the shadows were dancing on the floor; a chaffinch was twittering its evensong in one of the poplars; and on the windowsill sat the white cat with glittering eyes, seemingly listening with mixed emotions.

Kold felt an urge to get down on his knees; he could not move his feet. Then his eyes fell upon the rose, which had been put in a glass of water on the table. It was standing there so lovely and so fresh. Supporting itself on its green leaves it was bending over the edge of the vase so that the shiny table-surface reflected its blushing image. Before he realized what he was doing, Kold had taken the rose and placed it on his breast. In another minute he was down in the yard, and the party set gaily off for the forest.

Georg Kold was nearsighted. He seldom bagged anything on his trips, which did not cool his hunting fervour. As so often happens, however, luck came his way when he was least expecting it. Two rabbits ran right into the absent-minded hunter's firing range practically at the outset, and a poor stock dove was lying at his feet before he quite knew how it had come to pass. Almost horrified, he looked at the small, beautiful, blue creature as it lay warm and bleeding in his hand, and to Edvard's joking congratulations he replied that it had happened out of sheer carelessness.

The morning hunt was over, and the tired hunters gathered to take counsel among themselves. First they were to rest, and then they were to go up to a field higher up in the mountains, where there were supposed to be plenty of game birds. Kold wanted neither to rest nor to keep on hunting, however, and since they were quite accustomed to his going his own way, this did not bother the party. For Kold the hunt was over — or perhaps had not yet begun. The game proudly shouldered was just a visible trophy of a lucky day's work. His buoyancy of spirit had returned to him. He was aware of suddenly having thrown off the burden of doubt and indecision that had been weighing upon him for so long, and a brave resolution filled his heart. He would declare himself to Sofie. This little distancing from her had finally loosened the ties that for so long had bound his willpower in her presence, and, as if he feared anything that might weaken his resolution, he would allow himself no rest until he found the one he sought. The bow was tightened — now the arrow was to find its target without any obstacle.

At first his walk down progressed rapidly. While humming a tune from 'The Hunter's Bride' which he had heard Sofie sing, he had already put behind him the most difficult part of the mountains. But soon his less sure, less energetic steps along the mountain path told him that his strength was beginning to fail him somewhat.

He was standing before the stile leading into the forest. In front of him, below the meagre field of rye, he could see the smoke rising from the first small farm. His eyes wandered along the hillside towards the distant fields, where a bluish shadow of deciduous trees broke up the dark mass of spruce. It would take him several more hours to get over there, but he did not want to rest until. . . . Just a quick break over there where the hillside was sheltered so deliciously by the overhanging rock, and where the September sun was shining so gently and softly through the birch trees! . . . And he stretched out on the moss.

It was so quiet. Only the many bells from the fields were playing their soft melody for him. . . . The spruce trees were soughing slowly and soporifically above his head. Now and then a movement of air would sweep across him, like the beating of mighty wings. He got up, but only in his mind — the ground was holding his limbs like a magnet. He had not yet crossed the magic border, but his imagination was being rocked along the airy paths leading to it. These imaginings now took on fantastic shapes, mingling strangely with reality. He is still in the forest; the same melody is humming in his ear. All of Sofie's family is present; only she is absent. Again he is shooting the stock dove down and then has a feeling that it is *Sofie* he has hit. But there the dove is lying in the grass next to him, and the birch tree by the stile is swaying its long branches in a secretive manner.

He is dreaming:

On the narrow ledge in the steep rock, Sofie is standing in happy unconcern, as if sensing no hint of danger. Light is radiating out from her figure. She looks lovingly at him and waves with the rose in her hand. He rushes up to her and seizes her, and quivering with joy he brings her down to safe ground. But as she twists herself out of his embrace, look —

it is no longer Sofie, but Mrs Ramm's dainty little person. She is looking at him with those cold, blue, enamelled eyes and says, curtsying: 'Many thanks for your trouble! You have saved me from being broken to bits. . . . I am a very valuable mechanism, I'll have you know. Everything inside me is perfect and complete, except that I have no *heart* . . . Nor is one called for, *because self-denial is a woman's most precious virtue* . . . .'

It sometimes happens that we wake up in a panic that is all out of proportion to the content of the dream. Kold awoke with a scream, his brow covered with beads of cold sweat. For a long time he was unable to overcome his sense of terror, but in the end he had to laugh. The bit of rest he had taken and the glorious air soon gave him back his strength, and he was walking as if he had wings. 'It is a strange day, this,' he said; 'everything must and will succeed for me. I feel the courage to challenge the gods.'

He reached the farm by mid-afternoon. As he crossed the path leading into the garden, he learned from the farmhands busy loading grain that Miss Sofie had been out with them, but that she had just recently walked down towards the river. Kold then got rid of his game and headed in the direction indicated, just as he was — dusty and flushed with exertion. No sooner had he crossed the stile and arrived at the path following the river, but he stopped to listen. Through the noise of the waterfall he heard voices and the barking of a dog. In between, he thought he distinguished Sofie's voice, which had a piercing sound to it, as if of fear. Like an arrow he was off and reached the ford, where he found to his surprise that the log that served as a kind of bridge had been thrown aside. Fortunately, there was not much water at this point. He got successfully across with a couple of daring leaps, forced his way through the bushes, and immediately found himself confronting a scene that both surprised and angered him.

Since that last meeting between Brandt and Sofie, she had not seen him at all, but he pursued her all the more impetuously with letters that grew increasingly importunate. This is a form of maltreatment against which a young girl living under our primitive conditions has no protection. In the countryside, it is difficult to get daughters married off suitably, while at the same time an all-encompassing hospitality allows any passing stranger admittance into the family with no questions asked. This, of course, entails no risk at all. In our virtuous country, passion dares only show itself in its legalized form. But these high-minded intentions notwithstanding, many a thing is thriving which those of more refined sensitivity might consider immoral. It happens not infrequently that in the name of this virtuous intention, those misalliances are formed that call upon our fear and our pity. In the name of this good intention, the most miserable among the lords of creation have the right to besiege a girl; persecute her; drive her to the utmost despair. Of course, their intentions are none but the most honourable — meaning that they are ever so willing to share their misery with her.

Still, poor Lorenz was not among the worst. Sofie replied to one of his letters, in the way it is possible to answer such letters — evasively and as soothingly as possible; then she let it go at that. In his writing, however, Lorenz had now changed from supplications to threats and virtual denunciations. He would waylay her, he wrote, and then she would have good reason to regret her behaviour. He had now nothing more to lose. He was selling his life for a shilling. If she would not live with him, she was to die with him, and so forth.

The poor girl was really caught between the frying pan and the fire. Her last encounter with him had, despite his ferocity, left her with a deep and painful pity for him, which always made her take his side and, whenever possible, try to maintain his good reputation. To involve her parents in this affair would be to extinguish the last spark of sympathy for him. Nevertheless, the position in which she thus placed herself, of having to bear her fear alone, drove her to the breaking point. She scarcely dared go out into the fields or to walk along the road by herself. She started every time there was a rustling in a bush.

That afternoon, while Sofie was out in the grainfield, the little orphan boy who was living on sufferance at the farm brought word from her mother that she must immediately go down to her in the cave. As she had recently been talking to her mother about an improvement to be made down there, she entertained no suspicion, but flew down there like a bird, as if carried by the joyful dream that filled her. No sooner had she arrived by the entrance to the cave, but Lorenz Brandt stepped out from inside the cave in order to meet her. He was staggering, and triumphant joy suffused his dull features.

'Where is Mother? . . . Have you tricked me into coming down here? . . . It is abominable!'

'I only wanted to assure you, my precious friend, that you are dear to me . . . infinitely dear . . . .' said Brandt with a lolling tongue. 'I have chosen this charming, romantic spot to explain to you the state and condition of my heart. . . . A condition that is of the sort. . . .'

'Let me go; just let me go!' said the horrified Sofie, seeking to get past Lorenz, who was now blocking her way.

'Why such fear, my darling! . . . What is there to fear? . . . You are beautiful, extremely beautiful. . . . But nobody is going to have the temerity to offend these divine charms with so much as a look or a syllable. . . . Yes, if I offended them, I would not be a man of honour . . . but a scoundrel, a low, God-forsaken rascal, with no breeding and totally lacking in manners. . . . Yes, if I have offended you. . . .'

'Oh no, no, I certainly know you haven't! But let us just leave; we may talk about it at home. . . .'

'Still fear in these beauteous features? . . . Young girl, you don't know Lorenz Brandt. No, you don't know him. He's not one of those tricksters, those sheep in wolves' clothing, who go sneaking around defenceless innocence in order to ensnare it and seduce it by means of dangerous arts. He's a Norwegian of the good old sort. . . . Every drop of blood in him is genuine, you see! . . . He's made of a different fibre from that Troopist, that fancy weakling, who goes around turning your head. I'm acting in good faith, I am! . . . Whatever I say, I'm saying out of the conviction of my heart . . . out of the conviction of my heart I say: You I choose among all the girls on earth. . . . To you alone I offer my hand and my heart! . . . The devil take all the rest. . . . Oh, girl! Do you remember the tranquil days of our childhood!

> Two plants in Hilding's garden grew,
> Never before in the North were seen
> Such lovely plants, in the heav'nly green
> Waxing wondrously. . . .'

Here Sofie made a desperate attempt to get past him, but Lorenz, stronger than she, with a single kick pushed aside the log across the creek. This manoeuvre made him lose his balance somewhat, and he reached for Sofie, whom fear now overwhelmed to such a degree that she completely lost her head. A little more experience would have taught here that the danger was more imagined than real. A calm, fearless demeanour would have kept him within bounds. Indeed, the mere sight of her had made him forget his cowardly threats. But the fear of an eighteen-year-old does not reason; it is instinctive, uncontrollable and boundless; it does not weigh the chances, but only quakes in the presence of brutishness.

With a scream, Sofie dashed back towards the entrance to the cave, but since the cave formed a closed vault and thus could offer her no refuge, she climbed up the steep cliffs with the agility born of fear. She succeeded in reaching the middle of the steep bluff, and there she was hanging, without sufficient support for her feet and clutching a fragile bush that threatened to give way at any moment, and she called for help with all her might. Down below, Lorenz delivered himself of the most piteous entreaties and laments, and the grey poodle joined in by howling at the top of its lungs.

But do not say that reality lacks its inspired moments. No winged god of old, no hero out of the stories of Lafontaine or Clauren could, under similar circumstances, have arrived at a more perfect moment than Kold did just then. In no time he had pushed Lorenz aside and with a powerful leap reached the frightened girl, who with a shout of joy threw herself into his arms.

History has nothing reliable to say about how he got across the river with her, but it does tell that he did not stop until he reached the stile by the two spruce trees, and that there he slowly let his burden slide down onto the moss.

But Sofie opened her eyes and threw herself violently around his neck again. 'Oh, don't let me go; don't let me go!' she begged. 'Haven't we suffered enough?'

'What are you saying, Sofie! . . . It is I; it is I! . . . Sofie. . . . And you confess it! . . . Oh, say it once more!'

'Yes, yes, I confess it,' she said and raised her shining eyes towards him. 'I have said it; I could not do otherwise. . . . Now repudiate me, if you can! . . . You cannot!'

How many words were the lovers able to say? . . . Perhaps not a single one. They kissed each other; they clung to each other in such a passionate fear that it seemed as if they sensed the bittersweet significance of this moment for all the rest of their lives. . . .

Was it a matter of minutes, or 'was it seconds, nothing more/Bliss can't last for evermore,' as the poet tells us? . . . Alas that it must be so; alas that it must be so! The Norn, the dark, peevish Norn, does not take much account of an hour or a day when suffering is involved, but if she notices a human joy about to unfold, she miserly counts the grains of sand!

Sofie let out a soft cry of fear. Close behind them, up on the fence, a hideous, small, gnome-like figure stood staring at them with dreadfully wide open eyes. In its hand was a long hazelbush stick, which it stretched out towards them with a peculiar grimace. The vision appeared so suddenly that it looked as if it literally had shot up out of the ground.

But the waterfall was grumbling nearby, and therefore it was only natural that little Ole — for it was none other than he — could sneak up on them unnoticed in his bare feet.

'What do you want!' Kold exclaimed angrily, himself shaken with fear for a moment.

A special talent, an initiation in the art, which Kold fortunately possessed, was necessary in order to get out of Ole what errand he had been sent upon, when this was not limited to the job of a carrier pigeon, but consisted in something requiring human thought or speech. And then this particular errand was of such an extraordinarily complicated nature. Not only had Ole been charged with finding Kold in order to tell him that a stranger who wanted to visit him had arrived at the farm, but also that the stranger as well as the mistress had set out to meet him.

'Did you hear who it was?' asked Kold.

'I dunno!'

'Have you ever seen him before? Has he ever been to the farm before?'

'I dunno!'

'Is it the gentleman who was here this spring, and who gave you one mark for holding his horse?'

A smile, a grimace, lit up Ole's face, and he accompanied this with an expressive pointing of his finger towards the farm.

'Müller!' whispered Kold with a black expression. He could already discern a couple of ladies, accompanied by a gentleman, moving down the path along the hill.

Kold turned towards Sofie who, shivering from all the excitement, was supporting herself against the spruce tree.

'Collect yourself,' he said; 'walk towards them. . . . I'll stay here! . . . Oh, be clever! . . . You can do it better than I. . . . But tomorrow! . . . Oh, Sofie, Sofie!'

'Müller!' muttered Kold. 'What devil takes him up here just at this moment? But he shall know nothing. I am going to keep that satyr's glance out of my sanctuary.'

From his hiding place he could see Sofie joining the party, which was moving slowly down the path among the thicket of nut bushes; only then did he dare to come forward. On the bridge he stopped to collect himself more fully. He leaned towards the steep waterfall as if he wished to confide his young happiness to the depths.

The night, the shining summer night, was already well advanced when the company parted to go to bed. Sofie had been walking about as if in a dream the whole evening. Her blushing cheeks and the special, peculiarly absent-minded look in her eyes might easily have told a sharp observer that something out of the ordinary had happened. Fortunately, her mother and her sister had been too occupied with the guest to pay much attention to her. By means of an uncharacteristic talkativeness and gaiety, Kold had tried to draw attention away from Sofie. To her he did not dare speak at all, but he had found occasion to put into her hand a note in which he asked her to meet him at six o'clock the following morning. The meeting was to take place beneath the two spruce trees, those silent witnesses to their pact, and he suggested that hour as the most convenient one for a brief encounter, while the whole household was still asleep. Sofie was carrying this note about with her. Every other moment she put her hand around it in disbelief, as if to convince herself that it was there, and that this also was really true.

It was twelve o'clock. The two friends had said good night and withdrawn to Kold's room.

At last it had come, the moment when Sofie dared to be alone with her thoughts. She had only one more task, which her mother had asked her to do.

Yes, reality has its inspired moments — significant, poetic, artistically perfect moments, in which life, in the midst of its everyday slumber, suddenly opens out into full bloom and fragrance. But it also has moments, collisions, combinations of events, that occur in such a fatal, such an ominous way, and with such cutting irony, that one must try hard to maintain one's faith that these events as well constitute a part of the all-loving, omniscient Providence, because they look more like a fragment of a poem conceived in the fertile mind of a demon.

And this demon! We all know it by name. It has such a prosaic ring to it, as if it were nothing to worry about. We call it *chance*. In the life of a male, it is a sort of house-elf, a bothersome mischief-maker, against which he may nevertheless be bravely on his guard, and which he may subdue as circumstances permit. In the life of a woman, chance is a terrible power to which she must surrender herself unconditionally, mutely and passively.

Adjoining Kold's room, separated by only a thin plank wall, there was an enclosure with access from the corridor, which served as a clothes-closet for the household.

To this clothes-closet Sofie had been sent in order to fetch some linen. As she slowly opened the door, she heard Kold and Müller talking together on the other side of the partition. The two voices sounded so clear and strong in the stillness of the evening that she might have believed herself in the same room, had she not known better. For a moment she was lost in listening to the beloved voice. Then she heard her name being mentioned. Terrified, she found what she had come for, and she wanted to hurry away, but before she had managed to do so, she had against her will heard so much that she could not leave. She stood there as if nailed to the floor, unconscious of everything around her. Her soul lay in her ears.

In the room where the two gentlemen were sitting, we find Müller in his old seat on the sofa; Kold is sitting on the sill by the open window, apparently concentrating his attention on the treetops and the shiny night sky. The first few introductory remarks he had probably answered in a somewhat perfunctory and absent-minded manner.

'Yet it does seem to me,' Müller continued, 'that you must by now have acquired a broad knowledge of the duties and privileges of a District Governor, and that the auxiliary part you have played as a tutor has also come to an end, now that the young gentleman has been accepted at the University. Or perhaps you have other auxiliary parts to play here in the house?'

'The District Governor has no more sons.'

'No, but daughters.'

'But none of whom needs my instruction. The eldest is almost as old as I, and the other has just returned from an institute in Copenhagen.'

'Well, you might play other supporting parts. Anyway, then you have nothing more to accomplish here at all? Well listen then. That position in Stockholm, which once you desired so much, is now open to you.'

'In Stockholm, you say?' cried Kold, turning around.

'Well yes, in Stockholm, in Stockholm — is that so incomprehensible?'

'Alas, dear Müller, do you still have those kinds of plans for me? I thought you had given them up by now.'

'Do I still have such plans? Yes, may the devil take me, I still do, and a bad thing it would be if I did not have them for you. While you are taking your ease up here, with idyllic notions about life, and thinking of nothing, or what is worse than nothing, we have been active on your behalf. As is customary with the bad sort, luck is with you. Now listen. N. has been given a year's leave of absence from Petersburg, and our clever S. there takes over his position, which it is assumed he will keep permanently, because it is said that N. is going to marry a wealthy merchant's widow in Gothenburg and probably will not return to the diplomatic service. Therefore, S.'s position will be vacant and is to be filled by a Norwegian.'

'And that position might be mine! I don't imagine that is entirely to be relied upon.'

'You may have it. I immediately went up to see His Excellency *Due*, who fortunately had not left yet. He gave me every hope for you. You have only to submit your application, and before next spring you must be in Stockholm. Your uncle was simply delighted. "That is just the position for Georg; he is ill-suited for the philistine conditions of ordinary life," he said. Now, my boy, run around, sing and dance — only don't fall upon my neck.'

'I thank you, Müller. . . . How good you are, taking such pains over me. . . . But. . . .'

'Well, but. . .?'

'Frankly, I have quite lost my desire for this position.'

'Ah, you have lost your desire for it; I see. . . . that is strange. Yet once you yourself thought. . . .'

'Oh, that was a whim, a passing fancy. I suppose that to a young, immature person such a career might be somewhat tempting. Actually, it is just a make-believe life. I no longer believe myself suited for anything like that; I feel myself drawn towards a purer, more independent position in life, even if it is nothing remarkable.'

'Well, that is praiseworthy; that is beautiful. It shows a solid discernment, a discernment that is rare in one of your years. However, I should like just to hear about those pure plans. Perhaps you might like to become a clerk in the Auditing Department!'

'Yes, why not!'

'Yes, why not! . . . It is a solid and honourable position, a position in which one may at times experience the most pleasant surprises, such as that *A.*, having wagered that at precisely the end of his tenth year, he would become an Administrative Assistant, reaches that cherished goal a year ahead of schedule. Luck is on your side; within twelve years you might become the head of that office.'

'That's not impossible.'

'Or you might wish to become a country attorney? What a delightful little game of 'Polish Pass' you might have with the peasants on Sundays! That would be just the thing for you! Or do you rate the post of country bailiff more highly?'

'That's a good thing as well. Then you are as good as a Member of Parliament already! . . . No, my dear friend, at the moment I am really not thinking of anything in particular. Right now, my life is so pleasant that I cannot be bothered to torment myself about the future. At New Year's my time here is up, and sufficient unto the day is the evil thereof, I think.'

There was a pause, during which Müller exhaled large clouds of smoke and Kold amused himself with molesting his riding crop. Finally Müller said,

'She is handsome; your taste is not bad.'

'Who? To whom are you referring?'

'I merely stated,' Müller calmly persisted, 'that she is attractive, and that your taste is not bad. Indeed, in a way that has scarcely ever happened to me before, she has really struck me. We met her on the path when we were going out to find you.'

'Ah, are you referring to Miss Sofie?'

'Quite right, Miss Sofie, that is what you called her at one time. As I said, she met us on the path, where we were also so fortunate as to run into you. So that is she, I thought, who has cost poor Kold so much trouble and time, and whom you last time described as a frightening, hysterical person. She seemed to be in an excited state; her voice was unsteady; and her lovely hair, the like of which I have never seen, was in very artistic disarray. It was certainly a pity to waste such a vision on a fossilized heart like mine. Her mother asked her what she had done with her hat, to which she replied that she had been too daring in going up the mountain and had slipped and lost it up there. Mama scolded her for her wildness, but with a look towards me as if to say, "Have you ever seen anything more charming?" Me she greeted with a certain coolness of manner, and I have in vain attempted to approach her this evening. There is something unusual about her. But she is pretty and lovely as the Devil's own invention. Are you perhaps not of the same opinion?'

'Yes, undeniably, so she is. Miss Ramm is a very pretty girl,' said Kold and broke his riding crop in two. Sofie's smile, the special one with which she had announced her happiness to him, just then appeared treacherously in his memory, and in alarm he added, 'But there is something unattractive about her mouth. You said, I think, that S. has already arrived in Petersburg; can that be possible?'

'In Petersburg. That something unattractive about her mouth has completely escaped my attention. Her face is, I believe, the sort that ought not to be analyzed. Altogether it makes a striking impression.'

'What a success he has become in so short a time! And N., what was it you were telling me, that he. . .?'

'N. is retiring in order to get married.'

'Yes, yes, quite right, to a rich widow. . . . But he is supposed to be Baron Manderström's successor in the Cabinet; who, then, will get that position?'

'The diplomatic service is suddenly beginning to interest you, Georg! . . . I'll tell you all about that later. . . . About anything you like, Georg. . . . Just put aside your riding crop. I'll mend it for you later. . . . Listen, Georg, I have nothing but good intentions as far as you are concerned,' said Müller, with a movement as if he intended to put his pipe aside, while slowly guiding it back towards his mouth again — a manoeuvre with which Kold was very familiar, and which spelled unusual seriousness.

'You see, I wanted so much to make something great of you, and it would be possible, too, were it not for the obstacles you put in your own way. These eternal infatuations are, for someone of your constitution, pure misfortune. They are forever unbalancing you, disturbing your mood and hindering your development. And regardless of your assurances to the contrary, you will in the end be caught in earnest. I am not saying it will end thus with your present attachment; very possibly it may end like all the others. But whether it is serious or not, it comes at a damned awkward time. Listen, Georg, tear yourself away. . . . Immediately, if you can. . . . Go to Stockholm and save your soul! When ten years have gone by; when you have become a mature, prosperous man, then, in God's name, fall in love as much as you like. . .'

'But Müller! Do listen! . . . There is no talk of — '

'A damned business! Tell me, how far have you advanced with her? Perhaps the evil may yet be avoided. In a pinch, perhaps I could talk to the young lady and get it settled in a decorous manner.'

'Are you mad! For God's sake! Indeed, I am telling you, this matter does not concern Miss Ramm. She has not the least influence on my plans for the future.'

'That would give me joy, if I were able to convince myself of it.'

'Convince yourself that this does not concern her!' said Kold, agitated in the extreme. 'Do try to understand! I do not love her. There is nothing, nothing between us.'

Poor Kold! Dear lady reader! If you are above *twenty* years old — if you are under twenty, it cannot be done — but if you are more than twenty, we wish to put in a kind word for Kold, right here, before you completely break your stick over him. Indeed, it is bad of him, very bad, and, allowing for personal taste, anyone can imagine a better and more graceful escape. Kold, when being thus slowly put on the rack, might perhaps have slammed his fist on the table and said, 'Yes, damn it, it is true, every bit of it, just leave me alone!' But then he would not have been Kold, our Kold, and he might perhaps not have loved so warmly and anxiously and been so protective of his treasure as was the case. And let us be honest. Who among us has not been thus irritated and finally driven to the point of no return and become a Jesuit without willing it, almost without *knowing* it? Anyone who dares to say, hand on heart, that this has never happened to him or her; that he or she has never said anything about a most dear friend that this friend might not hear; and that he or she has the courage to read in black-and-white everything this dearest friend has said about him or her — well, whoever can do that, may cast the first stone. And, finally, we wish to remind the reader that every one of these unfortunate words falls upon a soul which is *least able* to understand them, and that with every one of these words, which a malicious spirit seemed to place upon his tongue, Kold was renouncing his greatest joy in life.

'You do not love her! Oh well, that's another matter,' said Müller, and the glow from his freshly packed pipe cast an almost demonic light over his unattractive features. 'However, you cannot deny that it sounds damned incredible that you could live under the same roof with an eighteen-year-old beauty and not be affected by it.'

'You ought to have a higher opinion of me, Müller,' said Kold, taking his refuge in offended gravity. 'I, who recently confessed to you, in black-and-white, all my adversity, all my bad luck in this department. After all, such experiences do tend to make most people more sensible. I willingly confess the power of beauty — but is it not possible to imagine qualities that outweigh it, and especially the kind of qualities that repel me?'

'Those must be cursed qualities that could have such a discouraging effect on you. As you do not care for the little lady, I expect you can confide to me what those qualities are that spoil her. Is she perhaps just as lazy and obstinate as when she was your pupil?'

'Lazy and obstinate!... A lazy and obstinate young lady!' cried Kold, scarcely able to control himself. 'What does that mean? It is surely quite meaningless!'

'Is she then simpleminded ... stupid? ... You thought so at one point. . . .'

'I thought nothing. She was stupid as a child, but she may have acquired intelligence since then. I believe she now has as much as she needs of that article.'

'Just as I thought. When all is said and done, she is a model of a young lady. The devil — surely there is something! Is she flirtatious, frivolous, scheming, malicious?'

'The things that occur to you! I think Miss Sofie's heart is the best possible. She is a girl of strong character, with a lively, forceful spirit. But there is something original, not to say *eccentric*, in her views. . . . What do you think of her sister?'

'Ah! *Eccentric* ! I understand. . . . She is romantic, hysterical, *emancipated* ?'

'Exactly; you hit it on the head,' said Kold and burst out laughing at the ridiculous turn the embarrassing interrogation had taken.

'Really! No, seriously. . . . Is she that sort? Yes, she did look as if she might be. A Norwegian *femme emancipée*! That is funny; that is something quite novel! How does it manifest itself? Does she smoke cigars? Does she wear spurs? Does she ride a horse in the manner of the blessed Queen Caroline Mathilde?'

Kold turned red with indignation. He could have murdered Müller.

'Now, don't take offence. Then she does not smoke tobacco. . . . She does not wear spurs. She is a spiritual Amazon, a hyperborean Georges

Sand, exuding a red-hot hatred against the entire male sex and its baseness and despotism?'

'Exactly.'

'Which, however, does not prevent those ladies from having their little private inclinations?'

'Naturally.'

'And I suppose you do what you can to feed the flames?'

'Of course. Have I anything better to do?'

'And without catching on fire yourself?'

'Have no fear. It is but another flower to be braided into my triumphal wreath. Besides, emancipated ladies are the least dangerous.'

'So I have heard say. I have had no experience in the matter myself. My poor Bolette was not in that category.... Has she already declared herself?'

'Hm ... not quite, but I expect it to happen very soon. I have my refusal ready, you may be sure.'

Müller fixed him with his eyes for a long time. 'Is that so? Really!... That is impressive!'

A pause occurred, during which Müller appeared to have become lost in thought. 'Listen, Georg, do you know — it's best not to carry this game too far. If you will listen to my advice, let the whole thing drop. Actually, I feel sorry for the poor girl. Behave decently towards her and prepare her for the inevitable ... not too *suddenly*.... That will not do. Not too suddenly.'

Kold looked at him in some surprise. Only then did he notice from Müller's expression, which had quite changed, that the latter was considering all this in deep seriousness. It had never occurred to him that intelligent and wise, but somewhat unemotional people may sometimes appear extraordinarily simpleminded. He was almost horrified at having succeeded, by means of a broad jest, in doing what he had been completely unable to achieve with all his dissimulation — he had disappointed Müller. This jest burnt upon his lips like a sacrilege, and yet he dared not take it back. Was he to have his precious secret pried out of him, a secret that scarcely was his own and in which he himself almost dared not believe — by a man who might perhaps put it to indelicate use?

Some people insist that there is commonly implanted in the female spirit a happy talent — nay, urge — for renunciation.

We are not going to enter into a subtle discussion of the nature of this special talent, but will leave it to the psychologists. We indisputably encounter it in so many gently resigned physiognomies, but also, we must regretfully add, in so many lined, almost petrified ones. Such faces tell us that this 'natural' taste for suffering has not been entirely sufficient, and that renunciation has been a struggle for them.

It is true that this renunciation may, like a sad omen, veil the face of a child playing with its doll. This renunciation could be heard in the answer which the small six-year-old girl, invited to a children's ball for the first time, gave her mother, who was wondering why she stood there so quiet and mournful when she had just obtained her dearest wish: 'Alas, Mother, if it were only a *small pleasure*, I'm sure I would be happy, but such a *great happiness* will probably come to nothing.'

As long as this renunciation is the reflection of the humbleness which God placed in a woman's soul, it is beautiful, moving and rich in blessings. It is her best support against the capriciousness of fate; it is what makes her happiness more radiant, her devotion and endurance in adversity greater than a man's can ever be. He speaks and acts; she *suffers* and *remains silent*. Yes, it is beautiful, this willingness to suffer and to remain silent; this muteness of God and nature in woman. It is made to be victorious in its quiet power.

But people discovered that gross advantage might be taken of such a capacity for quiet renunciation. In the interest of society, it was not enough that a woman was able to sacrifice and remain silent; she was also supposed to be able to *suffer degradation and remain silent*. And people changed this humbleness of God and nature in her and turned it into cowardice and timidity; they robbed it of the spirit of love and freedom. Coarseness no longer bowed down before it, but misused it. And people invented a host of embarrassing and despotic laws and fenced her in with them in order to keep her forever in a state of fear. In a word: they suffocated woman's entire faith in *great happiness* and gave her *small pleasures* as compensation.

Sofie had grown up in this spirit of thraldom. With her mother's milk she had absorbed the rules governing this thraldom, and never, in the narrow sphere of her native rural society, had she experienced any transgression against them. She had watched her sisters mutely submit and bring their lives as their sacrificial offerings. But in Sofie there had nevertheless been an early stirring of a notion about a femininity that was purer and truer to the divine intention than the monster people call femininity. We have seen how this idea struggled unobserved against its surroundings, until she herself gave it up as a delusion. Then she got to know Kold. He had himself been taught to abhor the enslaved and subservient mind and to recognize something nobler and more elevated in Margrethe. His youthful faith imagined that resurrected in Sofie — resurrected to happiness and to life. He wanted only to add his faith and his young and courageous confidence. During the brief span of time between Sofie's homecoming and Kold's departure for Christiania, he had exerted an astounding influence over the young girl. Through him, the chimera became reality. He opened to her perspectives on life of which she had never dreamed in her wildest fantasies. In his ardour, he saw neither the obstacles he had to overcome, nor the dangers to which he was exposing his pupil. Sofie thought just as little of dangers, but the moment did arrive when she, forcibly removed from her safe, familiar ground, saw herself as one with him, high above the rest of the whole world. She probably then felt with some trepidation that *he* must also give her shelter; that the only thing that could save her was his *love*. Thus it is possible to understand how she must have felt when this support suddenly failed, and to what depths of despair she fell when she thought herself betrayed by him.

As if turned into stone, she remained standing in the same position in which she had caught every word of that dreadful conversation. Outside, she mechanically handed the maid, who was just arriving, the linen she held in her hands. She tip-toed through Amalie's room into her own, where the small night lamp on her bureau had been lit. Its faint light hurt her eyes, and the room seemed to her frighteningly large and empty. Behind the curtain, she shrank down on a footstool, quivering. No corner seemed to her narrow enough and dark enough to hide her and her pain and humiliation. How it had all happened, what those terrible words were that she had heard, she could not quite put together in her mind. She knew only that her brief dream was over; that it was lying in the dust. Betrayed, derided, her love thrown to the mercy of a stranger, debased to serve as entertainment!. . . It never occurred to her that it might all have its roots in her own interpretation. Anyone who has followed Sofie's development with any kind of understanding will not be surprised by this. Sofie reacted strongly and impulsively to all impressions. Irony was incomprehensible to her when the most important things in life were at stake. She had not yet acquired the present day's facility in denying emotions and, when necessary, in wearing a mask of derision before that which is most profound and sacred. Every word she had overheard had struck lethally at a soul which training had made uncertain and fearful. She was devastated. She was overwhelmed by an oppressive fear, as if she were conscious of a wrongdoing. And her wrongdoing was that she had believed in happiness; that she had dreamed of it and reached for it with a brave hand. In what low esteem had she not in her arrogance held Amalie's lot; how ridiculous had she not many a time considered the latter's true, feminine attempts at making her bad luck appear in a more advantageous light! Just that very day she had been unable to keep from teasing her sister in a way that had hurt her. Oh, she could have fallen on her knees to beg her forgiveness. She could have asked forgiveness of everybody, even of the lowliest, had she been able to give a name to her trespass.

In the midst of this urge of her soul to find something with which to blame herself, she had begun to undress. One or another burdensome task would at this moment have given her relief. Then she remembered that her mother had asked her to have carried in from the garden a plant that could not endure the night air. This she had forgotten, but it must not be forgotten. As the maid was already asleep, Sofie wanted to and was obliged to do it herself. She walked softly downstairs and opened the glass door to the garden. . . . How happy she had been just a few hours ago when stepping through this very door! The night wind struck her with its cold breath and chilled her thinly clad body to the bone. Guided by the indistinct light falling on the shrubbery through the windows, she found what she was looking for. Only by mustering all her strength did she succeed in lifting the heavy stoneware pot and moving it into the living room. At the door, she remembered that the table on which the pot was standing might be damaged by the moisture, and with an eagerness that would have done honour to those ancients who induced their own martyrdom, she went back, lifted the pot over to the window, and carefully wiped off the table with a cloth. Having returned to her room, she completed her preparations for the night with greater care than usual. She braided and smoothed her hair, guiding each strand of hair into place. Then, and only then, did she stretch out in her small, narrow, cold bed. Clad in pure white from top to toe, she looked like a sacrificial offering. Dare we leave her at this point with the last, silent wish with which one screws the lid to a coffin: 'Sleep in peace!' No, the grave has its privileges. Stay awake, poor living soul; stay awake, struggle and bleed to death, and may Heaven help you!

It is sweet to be awakened by joy! How softly, how gently it touches our eyelids, giving the soul time to swell so that it will not burst from such an overflow of happiness. It touches our eyelids so sweetly and tenderly that we sometimes doze off again as if under the care of an indulgent mother. But sorrow is more to be trusted. If you have ordered the services of this hardfisted awakener, you may be sure of being awakened with a vengeance, and you would not easily go back to sleep. In Sofie, as well, it knocked just at the hour she carried in her thoughts. Her pain awakened fresh and lively with her. It was no longer dull, stony and worrying, the way it had been in the evening; it needed air and movement. She rushed out into the garden, which, still unvisited by anyone or anything in the grey dawn, must give her restless mind a place to hide that was less insufferable than her tiny room. We see her there, now immovable on a bench, now hurrying through the garden walks, then again standing still in order to brood in front of a flower, as if she wished to study each vein in its petals. But it was only her unhappiness she was brooding over. She was trying hard to gather all the fine threads of which it was spun. She wanted to become fully aware of her situation.

She recalled Kold's behaviour during all the time that had recently passed — how peculiar it had been; how it had continually allowed her to dangle between hope and dread. Then the scene from the day before, intoxicating with its joy of certainty . . . a certainty that had not seemed to need words. They had been interrupted. Had his behaviour *subsequent to* this moment also showed that the same consciousness filled them both? She had hurried off ahead of him; he had joined the party somewhat later. It did not occur to her until now with what pleased surprise he had greeted Müller! It was not the manner in which one received an unwelcome intruder. . . . How high-spirited he had been the whole evening! How sharply this gaiety had contrasted with her own quiet bliss! She finally weighed with painful care every word from the conversation she had overheard. . . . Alas, he did not love her! It did not matter whether or not he had meant the ridiculous accusations against her — he had been able to *express* them!

She was not concerned with what had prompted his behaviour towards her; with whether this was the result of calculated duplicity or just of frivolity, a permissible form of male flirtatiousness. . . . He did not love her! Was she then supposed to worry about whether he was *wicked* as well! As late as yesterday — just a few hours ago — how rich, how strong, how entitled she had felt! During one overflowing moment, in the arrogance of her happiness she had transgressed against the form which society imposes upon such a scrupulously important matter. She had said the word *before he did* — not consciously and as a result of her own will, but as naturally as a flower unfolding when its time has come; as easily as a fruit drops from the branch by its own weight. . . . And she had been right then; right before God and man! . . . Because even mankind sometimes forgives a breach against its laws, so long as it is *successful*; just as people may also close their eyes against a real transgression, so long as the person involved does not become desolate or unhappy. Yesterday she had had the right; today she had lost this right — today she was wrong. He did not love her! That involuntary abandonment of herself which a few hours ago had been her pride, had become an offence. She would gladly have bought it back with her heart's blood. 'Alas, if only I had not done it; if only I had not done it!' was the incessant refrain of her lengthy contemplations. Regardless of what train of thought she started, it always ended with the same 'Oh, if only I had not done it!'

Meanwhile, the day is dawning. The grey twilight is taking flight; the shadows are darkening and beginning to assume shapes. The thin sliver of a moon is completely disappearing on the smooth and shiny sky, while the ridged layer of clouds to the east is reddening. Sofie appears suddenly to collect herself. Towards the east, where the red light is streaming in, the garden ends in a lane whose double rows of linden trees form a solid vault above. It is intersected in the middle by a path which is separated only by a gate from the road across the fields down to the mill.

In the dark shadows of this path Sofie has sought refuge. She is no longer brooding; she is listening. Hidden behind a tree, she quiveringly catches every sound that reaches her from the house. Twice she had been mistaken. But now! . . . Yes, that was definitely the sound of the glass door being opened and closed. Those are human footsteps crunching on the sand. They are approaching; they pass close by her and disappear through the gate. She could not see from her hiding place, but she knew this light, firm tread; she felt the movement of air it caused wafting right towards her. Her heart lifted as if it wanted to follow; her will held it in check. With an almost cramplike movement she flung her arms around the tree in order to hold tight. . . . Thus the caged bird sits in front of the opened door . . . . It hears the tempting song outside; it feels the summer pouring in; but it dares not leave. Imprisonment has broken the bird's courage. Suddenly Sofie ran forward — ran with the speed of an arrow towards the green canopy, then back again, and yet again forwards. Was it only the bird's desperate fluttering in its cage, or was perhaps a brave resolution struggling within her? God knows. . . . But when she turned back a second time, she stood face to face with a person who meanwhile had passed unnoticed down the main walk. This person was Müller.

'Ah, my dear little lady! Are you admiring nature so early in the day? I shall take advantage of that. I have also come out for the same purpose, so we may as well join forces. . . . But I seem to have frightened you?'

Sofie had from the first felt repelled by this man. There was something prying in his piercing eyes that made her feel both fear and dislike; in addition, she already felt that automatic revulsion one cannot repress when confronting someone who has been instrumental in destroying an illusion. His voice awakened a shocking memory in her. She stared at him without being able to speak a word.

He continued, 'I have not yet seen anything at all of the landscape around here, although I have several times had the pleasure of visiting the farm. That is not right, is it? . . . But therefore you are now to show me around.'

'G-gladly,' stammered Sofie, 'but I fear . . . you must not expect much. . . . Here are no remarkable features to satisfy a visitor.'

'But I have heard about the cave. It is supposed to be extremely picturesque. We did not get to it yesterday. How say you, if we were to take a trip there first?'

'To the cave! . . . No, no. . . . That I cannot do. . .'

'Gracious me! Perhaps the mountain trolls still live there? Yet surely not after the sun is up?'

'Perhaps,' said Sofie with a forced smile. 'Actually, I just mean that I dare not go so far from the house, because my presence will soon be required inside. If you wish, I'll show you the garden. Here is a rise from which one gets a good view.'

They gained the top of the little hill. Under the dense shrubbery there were some benches, from which one could see far across the valley. The entire landscape — the rock gorge with the mill roof and the foaming river that later undulated peacefully among the fields — was softly illuminated by the red morning sky. The horizon was in flames, and to the dazzled eye, the shape of the most distant hills was obliterated against this background. First a few rays, fragile and glittering as the threads of a cobweb, shot out towards them, then more and more in ceaseless haste, and finally the entire web of glowing rays was spread over the landscape. The sun was up. At such a moment, it is as if all creation is holding its breath, shivering in devotion. Man stands mute, and the birds are silent in order to strike up all the more fully afterwards. Sofie was lost in this inspiring scene. It is especially the beauty in nature, just as in art, that awakens our pain, this guardian of our soul that is such a light sleeper. . . . And Sofie's longing, which had been forced back for a moment, was now awakened with double strength. She forgot where she was and with whom. Standing on the edge of the hill with one hand shading her eyes, her looks sought only a single point in the shimmering sunlight: the top of two spruce trees behind the mill. It seemed to her that they were bending towards her with beckoning hands. . . . The waterfall was soughing her name softly and alluringly.

'Miss, I should like to tell you something,' an unfamiliar voice was saying next to her.

'It is not quite by chance,' Müller began, after he had, with a wave of his hand, indicated to the girl, so violently pulled out of her reverie, that he wanted her to take a seat next to him, '. . . not quite by chance that we have happened to admire the sunrise together. I was watching you from my window; seeing how you were wandering about the garden, apparently the victim of a disturbed state of mind, and I think it was a good spirit that gave me the idea of seizing the opportunity of a talk with you. You see, my dearest little lady, I really do think it would be the salvation of many an injury, if one could receive medical help in time and not shy away from it in the manner of a woman.'

During this introduction, Sofie's feelings were very much those one experiences during preparations for dental surgery. There one sits in the chair of martyrdom. One watches the dentist approach with a joke, hiding the dreaded tongs in his hand. One's heart contracts.

'A different person from *myself*,' Müller persisted, 'would probably have let it pass; perhaps, faced with someone other than *yourself*, I might likewise have let it go. However, I think you have enough fortitude of spirit to bear something out of the ordinary.'

'The fortitude of my spirit has so far not been put much to the test,' said Sofie, 'yet I think that whatever Dr. Müller wants to say to me will not overtax it.' Her teeth were chattering.

'Very well, without further ado: I know your relationship with my friend Kold. Will you forgive me for giving you my frank opinion, and will you think highly enough of me to believe that it is not base curiosity that drives me to meddle in this matter? There are plenty of those who, on such occasions, hide behind a false delicacy that actually is only cowardice. I do not. I want to give you some information that may be useful to you. I have known Kold from his earliest years. I have been his teacher. We were both alone in the world, and we associated closely with one another, despite differences in age and in everything else. Every one of his thoughts and actions has been clear to me. Therefore, nobody knows his weaker sides better than I. He is a dreamer; he lacks strength of character. Easily fired, he puts everything else aside in order to reach a goal, but as soon as he reaches it, it loses its appeal for him. Scarcely had he been turned loose in the world, but he committed a whole string of such follies — one infatuation followed upon the other, all ending the same way, in coldness and distaste. A couple of engagements he entered into fared no better. He is one of those unfortunate *idealists*, in other words, who can never be satisfied. It was these foolishnesses of his that made him dream away some of his best years up here. And now I want to ask something of you. At last, there is turning up what I — considering our circumstances — may call a brilliant prospect of dragging him out of this inactivity and bringing him into a sphere that will occupy his time and abilities in a worthy manner and — I hope — have a strengthening effect upon his character. This is the occasion for my coming up here. It seems to me that it is my duty to prepare you for this, dear young lady. It will be sufficient for you when I say that it is an unconditional necessity for him to be free and unfettered by any ties. . . . He is leaving. In a short time he will have left the farm. Within a couple of months he will be in Stockholm.'

'I d-don't understand,' stammered Sofie, 'what there would be to prevent him. . . . There is nothing here, as far as I know, that might keep him back.'

'But I understood it very well, when I saw you for the first time yesterday.'

'I think I understand what you are referring to, but I assure you that you are wrong. There is no relationship between your friend and myself; nothing, absolutely nothing that could stand in the way of his fortune. . . . He does not love me!' she added bitterly.

'That is not exactly what I am saying. If I thought that was the case; if I thought anything *serious* was involved, I would certainly not meddle. . . .'

'When you are so certain of that,' Sofie interrupted him in a quivering voice, 'then I do not see what you have to fear from me. . . .'

'But now he is enjoying the undeservedly good fortune that a young, charming girl like yourself is interested in him. . . .'

'Oh, Mr Müller, you have no right to suppose so. . .'

'I don't suppose it, Miss; I *know* it.'

'You know it? . . . He has said so! . . . Has he really? . . . And to *you* ! It is impossible!' cried Sofie and clapped her hands to her face. When she let them fall, the sun illuminated a face made unrecognizable by suffering. 'Oh God,' she whispered to herself, 'then it was true. . . . I was not mistaken. . . . Then it was true!'

'What is true, my dear girl; how can you be so upset about it?' said Müller and pulled her gently back on the seat. 'Suppose you really had this little weakness; even if you confessed it to him in a frail moment — so what? Do you suppose I would judge that so harshly? I know I am an old bear, but I am neither a pedant nor a philistine. It's so easy for a poor woman to break some rule or other! A lively temperament; a mind that feels sufficiently independent to rise above the limitations and pettinesses of its sex. . . .'

'No, oh no! By all that is sacred,' Sofie interrupted him, 'you are doing me an injustice! I am not one of those strong spirits wanting to rise above the limitations and pettinesses of its sex. . . . That is a dreadful defamation! . . .I am not brave; I am not independent. . . . It is not true! . . . I am a poor girl who can let herself be mistreated in silence as well as anyone — who could let herself be hurt to the point of death without anyone knowing.'

Müller felt strangely ill at ease. 'My God, this pains me. . . . I am so far from wishing you any harm. . . . It is you who are doing me an injustice . . . a great injustice. You must believe me, that if I have said these things to you out of interest in Kold, I have also, in truth, had your well-being at heart. Calm yourself, my dear girl! After all, I am not saying that Kold

209

is quite insensible to you. . . . How could he be! . . . Your mere interest cannot but flatter. . . . It occupies him vividly; it will continue to occupy him for as long as he is in your presence. But I fear that for him it was only a game that might have unpleasant consequences for yourself. I did not want you too *suddenly* to. . . . I wished to warn . . . to inform you. . . .'

During this speech, all trace of emotion had disappeared from Sofie's face. 'In other words, for *my* sake you have done this,' she said, deathly pale, but calm. 'Although I do not know how I have come to deserve this interest which you, Mr Müller, are showing in me, I thank you just the same. If your intention was to enlighten *me*, you have succeeded. You have enlightened me perfectly. Do you have anything else to say to me, before we go inside?'

'Nothing at all. . . . Nothing at all. I would just — ask you one more time to . . . to. . . .'

'Oh, you wish to ask me to leave him alone from now on? Not to plead for a feeling he does not possess? . . . Not to ruin this beautiful future of his which you have so much at heart? . . . Was not that what you wanted to ask of me? . . . I can promise you that with *absolute, absolute certainty.*'

'You misunderstand me totally and completely!' Müller cried. 'Miss, I assure you. . .!'

But Sofie had disappeared.

'The devil of a conversation!' said Müller to himself. 'Phew! I can recall having felt this way only twice — when I read that letter from Bolette's mother, and that *first time* at the National Hospital. And who can understand these creatures anyway! She tells me herself that Kold does not care for her; she is quite calm and sensible; but scarcely have I, as gingerly as possible — God knows where I got those delicate phrases from — turned the conversation to herself, but she becomes desperate. She was shaking like the leaves of an aspen! When she left, she wanted to appear calm, but she was beside herself, by God. I must speak with her again before I leave; I must try to calm her down.'

Müller found himself in a difficult and unfamiliar position. Certainly, he had started out wishing to do Kold a good turn, but on seeing Sofie's suffering, he felt strangely sorry for her. In Müller's soul there was only one single sentimental string, and that was the thought of Bolette. He fancied he was seeing Sofie in a similar situation to the one that had hastened Bolette's death. He had suffered the same fate as the bear that wanted to swat a fly and managed to kill his friend at the same time.

Feeling very ill at ease, he sneaked back upstairs to his room, glad that he had not encountered anybody else. As he had taken the precaution of taking his key with him, nobody had noticed his absence. The maid who had come to ask him down to breakfast was therefore convinced that he had been asleep, and she regretted that he had not been given early morning coffee. Müller feared, not unreasonably, that Sofie's suffering condition might be noticed by the family and perhaps give rise to a scene. He was all the more surprised, therefore, to find her at the breakfast table in full command of herself. Very graciously she showed him his seat and appeared so eager in those extra little attentions incumbent upon a hostess that it was just as if nothing had happened. The young girl's self-control imbued Müller with an unfamiliar feeling of something like respect, and it made him wish anew that he might say what he considered a soothing word to her. This was no easy matter, however. He was to leave within an hour, and Kold, who had arrived in the meantime, complicated matters even further.

Müller's discomfort grew, and he gave absentminded replies to questions the others directed at him, while he kept close watch on all of Sofie's movements. Whether she was aware of this or did not want to be aware of it, she foiled all his attempts at a *tête-à-tête*. After breakfast, she took her seat by the window and started sewing, and she kept stubbornly at it until his carriage was at the door. At the moment of departure, the strong, hard man stood irresolute and almost comically confused before the young girl, who succeeded in hiding her hurt behind such a disappointing calm.

Kold had noticed nothing at all. Only when the maid came running in to fetch Müller's pipe that had been left behind, did he look somewhat perplexed, and then he laughingly told the messenger to hurry.

Sofie's absence from their assignation had caused him no real worry while he was waiting. There were a thousand reasons why she might have been prevented from showing up. This would soon be cleared up. When the eagerly awaited breakfast hour arrived at last, he had hurried downstairs into the living room, where he had found Müller and all the rest of the family assembled. Sofie's change of colour when he entered escaped his notice; nor did it strike him as odd that her eyes did not once meet his own. He dared scarcely look at her for fear of revealing his emotions. When Müller finally was well on his way. . .! But when the latter had left, Sofie disappeared into the house. Oh well, it was her week to assist in the house.

Thus the day went by. Evening came, but as yet no sign, not even the faintest hint discernible only to his watchful eye, had revealed the understanding between them. This finally began to seem strange to him. Still, he saw in it only a sharpened admonition to be careful, although he was beginning to find it unbearable. He felt an immense urge to assure Sofie that he could stand it no longer. His only comfort, then, was to pour out on paper, in the stillness of the night, all his impatience and longing.

Müller had walked up to greet Sofie in the garden at a very unfortunate moment. She was quivering between two alternatives, with no other guidance than the contending voices in her breast. For — we must say it — hope had also stirred in her at the sound of Kold's footsteps! Its gentle voice, and perhaps also the ever-present call for happiness we carry in our hearts, had for an instance overpowered all the impulses born of doubt, timidity and thraldom. At such moments, everything surrounding a poor girl constitutes fate — a breath, an atom, may tip the scales to one side or the other. Her conversation with Müller became the rock depressing the scales on the side of evil. It was the final blow to her heart. Her feelings for Kold had been replaced by a deep fear. Now it was just a matter of erecting the wall that was to separate them, and to make it truly strong, truly impenetrable, so that no lament, no escaping sigh of pain could force its way through. By thus unrelentingly excluding any hint of what had passed between them, she would in the end make him doubt that it had actually happened and thus forget what it was her greatest humiliation to recall.

While Sofie was preparing her rock-like behaviour and gathering all her strength to bring this sacrifice on the altar of femininity, whose cruel god she imagined she had offended, she thought only of the obstacles she might encounter in her own mind. In her unhappiness, she no longer thought of attacks from his side. We may therefore imagine her fear the following morning when, after the tea at which Kold had not been present, she encountered him at the door, and he, with an expression that plainly showed his impatience, handed her the letter he had written during the night. Then it was true what Müller had said — he still intended in all seriousness to continue this cruel game with her? Hot, elemental wrath flared up inside her. She took a step back, as if doubting what she saw.

Alas, had she but allowed this wrath to be put into words; had she but spoken at this moment, then all might have been put right again! But her tongue was paralysed. She remained silent, silent, the way a woman must who is not loved. This moment decided the entire course of her life. Like an evil omen, her mother's penetrating, high-pitched voice was calling her at just this instant.

Sofie heeded the call and left Kold standing there, stiff with astonishment and chilled to his innermost being by the icy stare Sofie had fixed on him. The letter had dropped to the floor, and the maid, who just then happened to pass by, picked it up and handed it to him, while staring after her young mistress in the manner peculiar to that sort of people when they think they have made a discovery.

His mood was one of astonishment; as yet there was no trace of worry mingled with it. A man feels confidence in fortune; he is not easily scared by phantoms. Kold therefore feared nothing bad, but thought it all a misunderstanding — one of those knots that would undo itself. In his heart, he felt a triumphant conviction that Sofie loved him. When she abandoned herself to him, she had done it with such impulsive force and in a manner that vanquished any possible doubts forever. But why was she suddenly distancing herself from him? His suspicion fell upon Müller. Yes, he thought; it is he; it can be nobody else. He has carried out his threat of addressing her, and he has treated the tenderest concerns of her heart in as brutally businesslike a manner as if it were a question of amputating a leg. So that was the reason for her absence yesterday! . . . While he was waiting, Müller had detained Sofie and used that hour, which was to have sealed their young love, to disturb it. In his anger, he had already seized pen and paper in order to write to this meddlesome friend, when it occurred to him that he ought perhaps to be certain in the matter. Through some subterfuge or another, he could easily get the maid to tell him how Müller had spent the morning. The maid's explanation, however, made it clear that such a conversation could not have taken place. Then Müller could not have been exerting his influence over Sofie. Therefore, her coldness must be owing to some other, perhaps more profound, cause. This only increased his astonishment. He was and remained very, very astonished.

The trees were turning yellow and the evenings were growing longer and darker in the course of the struggle that now developed between Sofie and Kold. We do not want to fatigue the reader with a description of it. It is painful to follow so many aborted attempts on the one side, so many indefatigable assaults — and, on the other, an equally nimble tirelessness in repelling them. For, believe it or not, Kold did not succeed. It is easier to catch the fleeing squirrel that swings from treetop to treetop, than it is to confront a woman when she does not wish to be confronted. In this case, luck came to Sofie's aid.

All the powerful agitation to which she had lately been subjected, had been too much for her. She fell ill and was forced to remain in bed for some days, and before she recovered, Kold had to go on one of his usual business trips for the District Governor. He had, meanwhile, had some time to calm himself, and he eagerly seized upon this trip as a welcome break in the unbearable tension. Away from Sofie he would, moreover, be better able to consider calmly what was suitable and what means would most easily carry him to his goal.

He returned one lovely autumn afternoon. The sky was a bowl of the purest, deepest blue, and the setting sun was hidden behind a cloud that, shaped like a gigantic crocodile with jaws agape and a golden belly, was settling over the mountains in the west. A sweet, colourful twilight rested over the fields, and the distant hills were glowing red. His trip had restored him. He was bolder; he had worked out a fresh plan of attack. From now on, he would calmly await the opportune moment that was bound to occur of itself, once Sofie felt herself safer. But the closer he got to home, the more he could feel his resolution waver, and when, after a bend in the road, he could discern the house that sheltered his darling, he had but one eager wish: to throw himself at her feet and not cease to lay siege to her until she had heard him out.

He was reluctant to meet anyone else in his present agitated state, and he therefore sneaked upstairs to his room like a thief. He slowly opened the window to the garden and let the fresh air, so long kept out, pour into the room. The autumn that year had been unusually beautiful, touching the entire landscape with a gentle hand. Although it was the middle of October, asters were still in full bloom, and a few dahlias were standing in their full glory, nodding their proud heads above the flower beds where the dainty flowers of summer had faded. The treetops were still employing only those bright colours that constitute the gorgeous motif beloved by painters. Just as Kold was opening the window, the sun broke through the dark belt of clouds on the horizon and cast a glowing light over the entire view. In this light, all the colours glowed more strongly and played in thousands of nuances of copper, gold and purple. . . . The flowers were glittering like jewels.

At that moment, our friend had little feeling for the indescribable beauty of nature. His eyes were searching all visible parts of the garden, while he listened intently to catch a sound of the one he was seeking. Then he thought he saw a pale figure moving in the low shrubbery on the hill; muted tunes reached him from below. . . . His heart told him that it was Sofie. He was downstairs that same instant, but as he was about to step into the shrubbery by the pavilion, the pale figure darted forward in the twilight suddenly produced by the sunset, and with a cry of 'Lord! There you are at last!' she threw herself into his arms. Another shrill cry made the error clear. The figure disappeared behind the hedge, and poor Kold was left standing with his arms spread open, nailed to the spot. Thus the beloved river-god must have looked the instant Arethusa dissolved into water in his arms.

It was Brøcher's birthday. For a long time, Amalie had been preparing to celebrate this occasion in a manner commensurate with its importance. She had been practising a new song on her guitar, a German song starting with 'In dieser heil'gen Runde', which was actually a Freemasons' song but which, like all Freemasons' songs, was vague enough to fit all sorts of occasions. For a long time she had been occupied in producing a water colour depicting the aforementioned Galterud that was to become her and Brøcher's earthly paradise. Her family and acquaintances had pronounced it very successful, and if one disregarded the fact that the original dirty wood colour of the houses had been exchanged for a glorious yellow one, and that the houses were surrounded by a profusion of emerald green trees, it was indeed very faithful and exact. A person given to ridicule and with a desire to find fault with the picture, might conceivably make the petty calculation that the happy couple sitting under the weeping birch by the door would, when they got up, tower above the chimney — but this little fault in technique certainly did not mar the total effect.

Brøcher was to have been surprised with this and several other presents when he, according to promise, arrived in order to spend the entire day with them. In the early part of the day, the family was supposed to have made a lovely excursion. The curate's favourite dishes — Savoy cabbage with meatballs, and marrow pudding for dessert — to which the District Governor was to add a bottle of champagne, were awaiting him for dinner. The day wore on, but the hero of the day remained absent. Amalie was already beginning to find the white dress she was wearing somewhat cold for outdoors, and the bouquet of flowers at her bosom was fading. Countless times she had been looking out over the fields from the top of the little hill, in the manner of the 'white-bosomed Colma from the mountains of the storm.' When Brøcher still had not arrived by five o'clock, she could endure it no longer. She ran to her desk and gave vent to her martyred uncertainty in the following lines (Amalie was reading *Ossian* at the time):

'The day is fading, and yet you have not come. Where are you, my beloved; alas, where are you? Why do you not come? For eight endless hours I have been waiting in growing fear; in every quivering leaf I have thought to hear your footsteps; — but no Brøcher! Now I can scarcely endure it any longer. I am calm; dreadfully calm. It is as if Nature understands and suffers with me. The day was so gay before; all at once my soul has become surrounded by darkness. All the little gifts with which I had hoped to give you some small pleasure on this day, are looking at me so mournfully, as if to say, 'He is not coming!' Everything is whispering to me, 'He is not coming!' . . . If only you are not ill! You have not had one of your attacks again? . . . I say I am calm; oh, do not believe it! You are perhaps ill, and I am sitting here in useless complaint instead of hurrying to you. . . . Forgive, my darling, but hasten to ease the mind of your
Amalie.'

With many admonitions to be quick, the errand boy Ole had been sent off with this letter, and it was during this interval that the incident in the garden took place.

When Kold later went downstairs and presented himself to the family, he hesitated in the little anteroom to the sitting room. Through the half open door he could hear raised voices. The subject seemed to be Brøcher. Ever since the day when he had come in the way of Amalie's union with the Dean, Mrs Ramm had taken a dislike to him. Although she did not mention the reason for this dislike, she gave vent to it at every opportunity. Through the loud and lamenting voices of Mrs Ramm and Amalie, Kold could discern the District Governor's soothing and somewhat reproachful voice. The room was in some disorder. A quantity of travelling clothes lay piled on chairs and sofas. A little to the side, by the lamp, he noticed Sofie busily sewing. The calm unconcern of her face was in strange contrast to the vehemence of the others. Kold had a great horror of family scenes. He was already about to turn back, when a general exclamation, followed by a solemn pause, made him halt his step without thinking.

'There we are,' said the District Governor; 'now that trouble has come to an end. Well, Amalie, what does he write?'

'You read it, Father; I can't. It is as if the letters were spinning around in front of me.'

Her father read:

'I greatly regret that circumstances have prevented me from coming; the more because I have thereby caused you several anxious hours, my dear Amalie. With regard to my health, I can put your mind completely at rest. My attacks have appeared only at considerable intervals, God be praised! and every time to a noticeably lesser degree. Therefore, my sweet girl may rest quite easy.'

'But Lord, where is he, then?' Amalie burst out.

'I am at Fjerdingstad, at the country bailiff's, where I have been attending a meeting of the Poor Relief Commission since nine o'clock sharp. The business would probably have ended at the usual time, had not the reorganization of the districts been brought up and kept us warm until seven o'clock. It is inconceivable that anything like that can be a matter for discussion, because it must be quite obvious to any impartial observer with the barest knowledge of the matter that the new division into only eight groups of farms is much more cumbersome and much less calculated to serve the needs of the county than the old division into twice that number — sixteen, because the latter — at least according to my personal conviction — in quite a different and more satisfactory manner encompasses *all* the interests, to wit, of poor relief and of schooling, and especially of the *latter*, when one bethinks oneself of the considerable amount of time the perambulating school master has to spend on the road. Later I shall, in a more satisfactory manner, describe to you the full importance of the suggestion I made in that direction; no more about it now, because I know that my Amalie is waiting. Thus, I wish only to repeat how sincerely I regret not having been able to spend this day in your midst. But as our departure is arranged for twelve o'clock, I shall yet be able to make up for lost time and come all the earlier tomorrow, by which we shall gain a couple of extra hours to dedicate to our love. Therefore, at nine o'clock I shall be yours! My regards to all your dear ones, but reserve for yourself, my darling girl, the most loving greetings from your

    Adolf.'

'That was a letter, indeed,' her mother exclaimed, looking towards the ceiling.

'Hm, hmm, there we are,' said the District Governor with a peculiar expression, handing Amalie the letter. 'It was just as I thought, that something like this had happened to prevent him from coming. Well, Amalie, it must be a comfort to you that he is in good health.'

Amalie, however, did not appear to find this comforting reason as sufficient as he had expected. Without saying a word, she ripped the bouquet from her bosom with a tragic gesture and fled weeping from the room.

'What can be the matter now?' said the District Governor. 'I thought everything had now been settled satisfactorily.'

'How can you ask such a question?' his wife exploded. 'First he lets the poor girl spend the whole long day in a state of anxiety for his sake, without sending her so much as a message, ruining all her pleasure and disappointing her longing! Here we have been waiting until four o'clock with the meal. . . .'

'But he did write,' her husband protested.

'Is that any sort of letter for a lover to write! . . . However, that is beyond your comprehension, my dear friend. . . . Did you ever hear such a thing! And on top of it all to torment her with his district divisions! . . . Isn't it what I have been saying! He is no proper match for a girl like Amalie, with her sensitive and overflowing heart.'

'But, my dear Mariane,' said the District Governor, now seriously impatient, 'Amalie will really have to get used to putting up with the fact — despite her overflowing heart — that the man is a member of the Poor Relief Commission; in other words, that he is discharging his duties.'

'Oh,' his wife called out scornfully as she walked out the door, 'that is not necessary. Once Amalie becomes his wife, she will soon enough become very familiar with *poor relief*, I can guarantee you.'

The old man shook his head as he looked after her retreating figure. Then he said,

'It is a good thing we are leaving. This day has made us all distracted.' After a pause, he added in quite a different tone of voice, 'And my little Sofie, how are things with you? Your indisposition has taken its toll on you. You look quite pale and worn.'

'Do I, Father?' said Sofie, quite alarmed. 'You are wrong. . . . I feel fine; perfectly fine.'

'Nor have I heard your blessed voice for such a long time. . . . However, dare I not ask you this evening. . .?'

'Unfortunately, Father dear, I have to finish Mother's travelling cloak.'

'I did not think of that. But you really look as if you are suffering, to the extent that I fear it might indeed make you ill. . . . And yet, especially this evening, it would have done me so much good to listen to you.'

Sofie got up and walked slowly over to the piano, but as she passed her father, their eyes met. She threw her arms around his neck and burst into tears. Again Kold wanted to leave, but he could not make himself move. With growing perturbation he had been listening, from his hiding place, to those references to an impending journey. He dared not enter until Sofie, after a couple of affectionate words from her father, had collected herself and had finally sat down at the piano.

His arrival visibly cheered the District Governor. After cordially welcoming him back, he said,

'We did not expect you back until some time next week, because I thought you might have travelled by way of A., and I was already beginning to get scruples that you might come home and find the cage empty. We have all fallen victim to travel fever, you see. After much discussion back and forth, we have finally decided to visit our old friend, Dean Rein, and spend a few days at his lovely place. We intend to decamp in the middle of the day tomorrow. . . . I suppose you know him from his visit here this summer?'

'Rein! Dean Rein?'

'I had forgotten. You were in Christiania at the time. That is too bad; you would have made the acquaintance of a very nice man. But, do you know, you may just as well come along; there is yet time. Can you imagine, Sofie, why it did not occur to us sooner? Do come along, my dear Kold; there is just room enough in the carriage. I can guarantee you a most friendly reception.'

Kold stood there for a moment, full of doubt. He was like a shipwrecked man whom a playful wave had been washing back and forth on the shore; now he had to find something and grab onto it.

'You can see how reluctant Kold is, Father dear. . . . And he must indeed be so tired of travelling that it is almost a pity to ask him to set out again right away.'

Sofie's expression completely contradicted the innocuousness of her words. Her entire face expressed the anxious tension with which we await a disaster.

He could not be mistaken. Sofie was fleeing from him; the mere thought that he might accompany them made her afraid.

An indescribable pain shot through him. At this moment, he thought Sofie did not love him.

In few, but determined words he declined the invitation to accompany them, and he seized the very first excuse to hurry upstairs to his room.

No, he could not believe it; no, he could not. He would make one final attempt before she left. He would write. He spent the first hours of the night in carrying out his resolution. In this letter, he summoned all that might move her; he begged her to do away with what to him was a dreadful riddle, and to do so before she left, and not to leave him behind desperate.

Sofie got the letter in the morning. Hour after hour Kold waited for her reply. The hour of departure came; the horses had already been put before the carriage. At twelve o'clock sharp, Brøcher had completed his hours of pastoral bliss in the garden glades and had put on his leather coat with the multi-coloured scarf that Amalie had given him. The ladies had wedged themselves into the carriage, which was tightly packed with travelling clothes, and while the District Governor and his lady were occupied in judging how a suitcase could best be strapped on, and Amalie had her eyes fastened on the cariole behind, Kold stood by the carriage step watching all of Sofie's movements, like a man sentenced to death who up to the last moment hopes to see the white flag of a pardon. He blessed every fresh occurrence delaying their departure by yet a few minutes, and it almost seemed like a mockery to him when the District Governor cordially shook him by the hand, saying, 'Well, at long last! . . . Finally, my dear friend, you will be rid of us. I see you have quite lost your patience. . . . Then in God's name, children, we are ready! But, my good Mariane, have you let the hatbox be placed there? It will surely fall off.' While this was being seen to, Kold bent towards Sofie and said, 'Sofie, have you nothing to say to me?'

'Farewell,' said Sofie, so tonelessly; so brokenly!

A sealed piece of paper, which Kold found in his room, contained only his own unopened letter. For a while he stood staring at the empty sheet, as if his eyes might be able to bring forth invisible words.

'Not a line!' he cried and clutched the letter in his hand.

* * *

The part of . . . parish in which Dean Rein's farm is located, is justly renowned for its beauty. Who can ever forget these blessed parts once he has lived among them, and who does not forget all other places the first time he sets eyes on that particular region! Our travellers had put behind them the winding road along the lake and were now trying to ease the climb up the long, cumbersome sand banks by constantly looking back to the scene below, which was unfolding ever more gloriously before them. When they had reached the top, a different scene claimed their fascination. Quite close by, dominating the entire fertile plain, lay the parsonage and the church. The large farm looked like a manor, encircled as it was by trees in all the many hues of autumn, above which rose the slender spire of the church. The long row of windows was shining softly and alluringly in the evening sun — a sight calculated to awaken the happy sensations we have when unexpectedly finding ourselves close to a pleasant goal, with a capacity for enjoyment that has not been weakened by exertion. The distance proved deceptive, however. The road still continued in a long, wide loop before reaching the tree-lined approach to the farm. What wonderful trees! In their strength and luxuriant growth one could immediately see the effects of the southern soil. Why is the

221

Norwegian landscape always represented with its spruce trees? . . .
Forgotten is the birch, the weeping birch, this truly national tree.
Denmark prides herself on her oaks and beeches, but they are
monotonous — they do not possess the beauty of contrast! How lovely
our pale weeping birch trees are! . . . Their gracefulness is almost feminine,
but it is the femininity of a queen.

The tree-lined lane leading up to the house was irregular and might
more properly be called a kind of green vault. It was a mixture of weeping
birches and darker varieties of trees, and along its lower part a dense
hedgerow sparingly let the last of the flickering sunrays through. The
carriage was rolling soundlessly along the firm sand, and the travellers'
conversation ceased in anticipation of their immediate arrival.

At the far end of the lane, the trees spread out in a semi-circle around
the farmyard, behind the stately main building. In a way that was rare
among parsonages, this one was encircled both upstairs and downstairs by
those long, open galleries that sometimes, but unfortunately not often,
may be found on farms of some importance, and that afford such a
welcome change from the monotonous, box-shaped style. The Dean was
already standing on the stairs, receiving his guests with undisguised delight
in seeing them, for which he was rewarded with a kiss by Mrs Ramm,
while he more gallantly kissed the two younger ladies on the hand.

In the sitting room, in front of the waiting tea table with the hissing
machine and the blue Copenhagen cups, they were received by an elderly
woman. Her whole dress and manner suggested that she belonged to the
servant class, or, rather, among those creatures who cannot be put into
any particular category in a household. She was dressed in a black moreen
skirt and jacket, cut to fall a good way down her hips, and she had on a
large, white muslin apron, while her angular, but well-shaped face was
framed by a cap with curled ribbons. A little girl, some eight or nine years
old, not pretty, but with a pleasant and gentle expression, was standing
next to her.

'This is my eldest daughter *Lina*; my two boys are in Christiania,' said
the Dean, 'and may I here present to you our *Dorthe*, who is my
housekeeper for the time being. She was my dear, late wife's nurse and
stayed faithfully by her side to the last. Old Dorthe is somewhat shy
about meeting such important people, but I hope you will put a little
courage into her.'

Mrs Ramm interrupted him with a stream of charming assurances, so that the older woman, made quite bashful by the pretty, strange lady's friendliness, did not know how to express her thanks. Still, this did not prevent her from scrutinizing the ladies with a sharp, probing look when given the opportunity to do so unobserved. Only at this point did the visitors discover that there was somebody else in the room — a small girl of about three or four, who had been hiding behind Dorthe's skirts. A closer look confronted them with a pair of big, frightened, darkly veiled eyes — a true Mignon physiognomy.

'What is your name, my sweet child?' asked Mrs Ramm.

'Her name is *Adamine*, after her mother, but we call her *Ada*,' said Dorthe. 'Do answer, then, Ada, and look at the ladies!'

But just then, the little girl's attention was caught by something else, and that was Sofie, who, occupied in arranging their clothes, came and went through the open sitting room door with the lightness of a fairy. With a peculiar expression — one might call it total absorption — the little one was following every one of Sofie's movements, and, as if she wanted to share her wonder with her old foster mother, she tugged impetuously at the latter's skirt.

Certainly, this vision might have fascinated other eyes besides Ada's. A high-necked, grey dress of merino cloth accentuated in a singular way the young girl's delicate figure and the grace of her quick movements. The fresh air had loosened her hair and restored to her cheeks some of their fresh bloom. At this moment, she looked like the radiant Sofie of old. Only the look in her eyes carried that unmistakable something which betrays that our thoughts are far removed from our busy hands.

To guests staying in the country, the unfamiliar house, its furnishings, situation, etc., are of great importance and demand a not inconsiderable share of the guests' interest and attention. It is not like in the cities, where the levelling effect of culture makes the surroundings grow increasingly featureless, serving only as more or less fanciful and ornate settings for the inhabitants. In the country, the houses in which people live do more than simply set them off; they are an integral part of people — of their customs, their way of thinking, and their idiosyncrasies. It is therefore safe to say that a visit is to the place just as much as to the people who live there. The first refreshment is always enjoyed somewhat distractedly, while the visitors are cheering themselves with thoughts of the moment when curiosity may be given free reins. So this is the sitting room! . . . Whom might those portraits represent? . . . That is really an intriguing old cupboard over there! . . . The visitors' eyes dart quickly through every opened door in order to snatch the secrets beyond it.

This initial crisis of curiosity was eased considerably for our present guests by the double doors' having been left open, affording the visitors an untrammelled view of everything. But the visitors' sense of ease was due even more to the open and casual ambience evident from the start. They freely confessed their impatience to get on with the business of 'having a look around,' and their kind host met their wish most readily.

The farm had originally been built by and been the principal seat of a Danish gentleman, but it had later been turned into a parsonage, for which it was very well suited because of its close proximity to the church. It had already been the home of a couple of generations of parsons. The house was a perfect example of the type of architecture one may see in manors of a more recent period. Nowhere was there anything narrow, low or confining. There were wide, tall windows and vaulted ceilings. The room in which they were sitting was somewhat dark, because the outside gallery and some enormous potted plants cast a great deal of shadow, but precisely this dimness gave the room its peculiar atmosphere of melancholy comfort. The room opened into a larger corner room with windows facing the garden. A certain elegance in its furnishings showed it to be the indispensable rural grand parlour. The arched, rigidly ornamented stucco ceilings and door mantels still survived as reminders of former aristocratic days. Otherwise, things were arranged in the usual manner. At that time, they knew nothing of our modern disorder. The furniture was sedately lined up along the walls, and the pictures — several good, handsome copperplates — were quietly hanging in place. Several smaller rooms adjoined this big room: two handsome guest rooms, the Dean's bedroom and study, and a small library, which had the rare quality of being accessible to everyone, whereas such studies are ordinarily for the exclusive use of the master of the house. Everything the visitors saw bore the mark of solid, unostentatious prosperity, combined with a sense of beauty and comfort. Where it is still possible to find such homes in our country, they represent either the last, dwindling remains of a foreign, imported culture, or the happy beginnings of an emerging native one.

The visitors scarcely noticed that a couple of hours went by. Supper was announced. In the sitting room, the carefully laid table stood awaiting them; Dorthe's dazzling damask cloth, the glittering crystal, and an abundance of heavy silver, appeared to great advantage by the light of two massive, many-armed candlesticks. There was no great profusion of dishes, but everything was excellently prepared. Fresh trout from the lake, marvellous game, good wine — everything gave proof that their host was a man who knew how to live well *in the right way*; a man who knew that all true enjoyment is dependent upon beauty and moderation. Mrs Ramm was inexhaustible in her flattering comments. These comments, however, hid many a sigh produced by her recollection that Amalie *might have been* mistress of all this magnificence. Whether it was because Brøcher really was more stiff and wooden than usual, or whether he only seemed so next to their courteous host, his mother-in-law had never found him more insufferable, nor felt a more vivid urge to tell him so, than she did just this evening.

The Dean himself brought the animated evening to a close and made his guests retire to their rest. While he saw the District Governor and Mrs Ramm, as well as Brøcher, to their rooms, Dorthe proceeded slowly up the stairs, with a large candlestick in her hand, leading the two sisters to their room. She had promised first to show them the entire upstairs, however.

'This door leads to the nursery,' she whispered, 'but we had better not go in there, because then Ada will wake up, and God have mercy on us then — it's not easy to get her to go back to sleep.'

They first entered a large room with several smaller ones adjoining, all of them quite empty except for a few household articles. 'Here,' Dorthe remarked with a melancholy look up at the solitary chandelier in the ceiling, 'was the ballroom, when my mistress was alive; but since that time, Father has had no inclination for such things.'

'A pity,' said Sofie, 'that such attractive, spacious rooms are standing unused. . . .'

'And that such a magnificent, smooth floor is not taken advantage of,' Amalie added, taking a few thundering gallopade steps along it.

'Alas, how are we to use them! We have rooms enough, more than enough, but it seems that happiness and gaiety are a thing of the past in this house.'

'And this?' the sisters called out in astonishment as Dorthe was opening the door to a smaller, completely furnished room. 'How lovely this is!'

'This is His Grace's room.'

'Is this the Dean's! Surely that was downstairs!'

'The Dean's! Bless me, no, this is the Bishop's room.'

The parson's room, and in this case also the Dean's room, is always sacred in a parsonage, but it is not the real *sanctum sanctorum*, because that is the Bishop's room. And truly, the present one seemed completely worthy of its exalted purpose. In contrast to the other room, the walls of which were made of wood only, this one had wallpaper, which in a good state of preservation depicted pastoral scenes in the manner of Boucher. How fresh the colours still were! Those shepherdesses still smiled just as sweetly and the radiant azure of the sky could not fade; time could only leave a few clouds on it. A long, narrow, mahogany mirror looked as if it felt in inferior company. It looked askance and twisted its pale, greenish glass into a hideous distortion of the happy pastoral world directly opposite. There was no better agreement between the ancient, magnificently carved easychair and the new table with its mirror-like finish. As if mediating among the factions, a Chinese Mandarin was sitting on a pedestal over in a corner, nodding and twisting his hideous head every time somebody walked across the floor. One must allow for such minor anachronisms in the way people in the country decorate their houses. The total effect was nevertheless quite pompous. It was also with a certain amount of pride that Dorthe pulled the bed curtains aside so that they could properly admire the fine, Dutch sheets with seams half an ell wide, and the quilted silk bedspread that perhaps had occupied some great-grandmother or other for half a lifetime.

From this room, the old woman led the way to one with a locked door. How different this one was from all the preceding ones! Here and there could be seen signs of a female occupant. Nevertheless, there was something desolate about this room. The air was oppressive, uninhabited. At the foot of a white bed stood an empty cradle covered with an embroidered spread, and below the ceiling a bird cage was hanging, likewise empty. The whole room exuded a sense of departed life, and the sisters felt some of the secret fear that takes hold of us when we are looking at portraits of dead people.... They looked inquiringly at Dorthe.

'This is the room that belonged to my dear, departed mistress,' she whispered. 'Here she died four years ago, having given birth to little Ada. No living being has occupied it since. All these things are just reminders of her — her sewing box and her work basket, and her Bible over there, and her portrait there. Everything was brought up here, because Father could not bear to look at any of it downstairs. This coverlet she embroidered herself; just you look at those stitches, it is really a labour of patience.'

'And the spinning wheel over there in the corner — did that also belong to the Dean's wife?'

'Alas, yes, you may be sure; that in particular was the apple of her eye. She was very fond of spinning. Every morning, at five o'clock in summer and at six o'clock in winter, she was up and spinning for two hours before she went to the coffee table. Dear Lord, how often have I not said to Mother, "Dear child," I said — because child I called her, although she was my mistress — ". . . dear child, why all this spinning? You have God's own blessing of what is spun and woven," I said; "however much you have given away, there will always be plenty left-over," I said, "it's better you should enjoy the peace of your mornings in sweet sleep." "Alas," she said, "you don't know what you're saying. She who is happy can never get up too early," she said; "she really should not sleep at all, in order to savour every minute of her life and to praise God. When I wake up thus with the birds on a clear summer morning," she said, "what better thing can I do, then, than add my voice to theirs? So then I sit down by the window with my spinning wheel," she said, "and I am never happier than when I mingle my voice with the wheel's gay twirling and the twittering of the birds outside!" Alas, she was no doubt right, that one ought to make use of one's time and spin busily. . . . Her life's thread was soon enough spun to an end!'

'Then poor Ada was motherless from the very beginning?'

'From the start, alas; far too soon. Scarcely had she seen the light of this world for eight days. Never shall I forget that moment! It was just four o'clock in the morning. At that time of year, the sun always comes in through the windows at precisely four o'clock, and then she would always wake up. "There is the sun; I am coming!" she said, as she always did, and then she took my hand and placed it on the cradle as if to say, "look after her!" . . . And at that moment, the whole room glowed in the red light, which fell on her as well, and she was lying there looking so beautiful and happy that it was impossible to think of her as dead. But her hand was still lying across the little one. Look after her! Yes, that was what she meant, and that is what I have done and shall continue doing, for as long as I have life and health! But there is something about this child which I can do nothing about — may the Everlasting add His strength to mine! Only God our Father knows where she got that violent temper! Father may be hasty, but he will be his kind self in the next moment, and Mother was as good as an angel from Heaven.'

These details from the life of the clergyman's pious wife moved the sisters deeply. It had made them pale, or perhaps their pallor was due to fatigue. They were clinging to each other while they followed Dorthe, who led the way down to the end of the long corridor, after first carefully locking the door behind them.

'And this is where the gracious young ladies are to sleep. I hope it will please you.'

An exclamation of approval interrupted Dorthe. All anxiety seemed to have been swept away when they crossed the threshold. This room could have served as a model of its kind. Such indescribable comfort can be found only in a country guest room. One cannot say that such a room does not possess a soul of its own.

'And what a mirror! Never was there one like it!' the sisters both cried, their eyes immediately falling upon a rococo mirror that was extremely rare of its kind, and that probably would have robbed a true antique-hunter of both sleep and appetite.

'It would have been just the thing for Princess *Sheherazade*'s chamber! It is almost out of place here! . . . What a pity that the angel has lost its wing!'

'Dear me, yes, wasn't that just what I said!' muttered Dorthe with a mournful expression, shaking her head. 'Didn't I say just that to Father!'

'And what was that, Dorthe dear?'

'That this old piece of trash spoiled the room, and that it was not a thing to offer such young ladies. I myself would have chosen the mirror in the Bishop's room. . . . But Father just laughed and said, "Just leave it be, Dorthe. Lovely ladies are better off looking at themselves in this old mirror than in the Bishop's." Indeed, I did tell him!'

'No, dear Dorthe, you misunderstood us,' Sofie assured her, when she was finally able to put in a word. 'We are enchanted with precisely this old mirror; we wouldn't be without it for anything! It's so beautiful, beautiful, and you'll see — a time will come when people will recognize it for what it is, and the old things will be honoured again. But in a way you're right; this mirror ought to be moved into the Bishop's room, because that is exactly where it belongs, among the shepherds and shepherdesses.'

Dorthe, however, was still shaking her head in disbelief, as if she were thinking, 'they are kind enough to put up with anything — it all comes of being well brought-up.' She carefully blew a withered leaf away from the marble-topped table, cast a glance at the towels on the wall to see if they were still fresh and glossy, and finally left with interminable wishes for a sweet sleep, pleasant dreams, and so forth.

'I must say, there is a widower who understands how to arrange his life!' Amalie exclaimed. 'This house is an absolute paradise. Do look around, Sofie, and don't just stand there as if you're lost. The whole floor carpeted! The most splendid stocks and asters in the vase, and what a bed!' At this point, she fell quite silent at the sight of the red silk damask guest bed, which in size could easily compare with the world famous bed belonging to the knight *von Gleichen*.

'There are two things about this room I suppose I would have changed,' Amalie continued when she was beginning to recover from the first ecstasy of admiration. 'Otherwise it's perfect. First of all, I would paper the walls, because I don't share your taste, Sofie, of finding so much poetry in those bare, wooden walls. . . Secondly, the curtains. These faded calico curtains are quite unsuitable in all this. If I were in charge, I would immediately take them down and put up white, embroidered ones and fasten them with golden arrows instead. . . . How I long for it to be morning so that I can see the view from those windows! I wonder what those two portraits might be. . .? *Goethe* and B.Y.R.O.N. Biron!'

'Byron, I suppose,' said Sofie absentmindedly.

'Oh, but whom does he resemble! . . . There, I see it plainly! The very image of Kold!' Sofie started violently. 'Only look,' Amalie persisted, 'that brow, the smooth cheek, the structure of the neck; it's striking, particularly if you put your hand over the lower part of the face.'

'Yes, it does look like him,' said Sofie indistinctly, and she fastened her eyes on the picture for a moment. It was the 1814 copperplate done from Philips' famous painting.

Sofie lowered her head further and grasped the marble-topped table with trembling hands. A look from Amalie, encountering her own in the mirror, recalled her from her painful agitation, and she vigorously started to unfasten her hair.

In her good-natured chattiness, Amalie had noticed nothing amiss. 'The Dean is really right, when he says that this mirror is more worthy of beauty than any other,' she went on. 'Look at this glass, how deep, how ethereally pure! Isn't it as if your body were inside that gorgeous frame! One might be tempted to reach for the flowers. How charming you look in those clothes, Sofie! When you raise your hands like that to unfasten your braids, you look like the picture downstairs in the sitting room, which is supposed to show the beloved of one or another of those old painters. I'm sure she could have been no more beautiful than you. . . . I must stand aside, otherwise I disturb the effect.'

'No, no,' said Sofie, and seized with uncontrollable pain, she pulled her sister closer. . . . What did she mean by her sudden flood of tears!

'Lord, sweet Sofie, what is the matter with you?'

'Nothing, nothing. . . . I was just thinking. . . . I was thinking, now that you are also leaving soon, I'll be so completely lonely.'

'Don't talk about it, Sofie dear; we'll never, never be parted. My cottage will never be so small that there won't be room for you as well. . . . You, *he* and I — what a delightful three-leaved clover! But alas, poor Adolf, not even *Justedalen*! . . . We may have to wait a long time before he gets anything!'

There are names and notions that have the same effect on certain moods as a cold shower has when one is hot. Sofie straightened up; every trace of her momentary emotion was as if spirited away.

The light was turned off; only the night-light was burning on the small table. The gigantic bed had closed its downy billows over the two sisters, but not before Amalie had carefully counted the window panes and made a cross above the door. As we no doubt all remember, this is the unfailing magic formula by which, when sleeping for the first time under a strange roof, one conjures up dreams that will *come true*.

'I don't know how it is,' Amalie whispered after a while, 'but one does feel so anxious the first night in a strange place. All the things that may have happened on such an old farm! . . . This room is so friendly and cosy — and yet, I wouldn't dare sleep in here by myself for anything in the world — not even for half an hour. Sofie, Sofie, where are you going? For God's sake, don't leave me!'

'I'm just moving the night lamp. . . . I don't like those kinds of portraits in a bedroom; they stare at you every time you open your eyes.'

'Oh, there is no danger with these portraits. I once read about one —
a lifesize oil painting that suddenly started moving its eyes when the lady
was getting undressed in front of the mirror. . . . Ugh. . . . I don't dare talk
about that now. . . . Good night!'

'Good night, Amalie, now not another word.' A long pause followed.
'Are you asleep, Sofie?'

'No.'

'Didn't you hear something? A distant sound, as if of someone
moaning?'

'I've been hearing it for quite a while, but I didn't want to worry
you. . . . Perhaps it's just the wind.'

'The wind? As you can see, not a leaf is stirring. There it is again! It
sounds like wailing or crying. It's coming from the direction of the room
that used to belong to the Dean's wife. Don't you hear something like the
sound of steps dragging down the corridor? They are getting closer. . . .
Listen!'

Suddenly the door opened, and a white figure, with one hand shading
a candle that cast a sharp light on a pale, gaunt face, stepped noiselessly
into the room. Amalie screamed and quickly disappeared under the
covers.

'Is that you, Dorthe dear?' said Sofie. 'What is the matter? I hope
nobody is ill?'

'No, no, bless me, nothing like that!' the old woman said. 'It's
nothing, really nothing. Oh dear, I don't quite know how to ask this
favour of you. I was standing outside your door for a long time, because
I thought you were asleep, but then, when I heard you were awake. . .!
You see, Ada has woken up and is howling like one possessed; she
absolutely wants to have the prettiest of the strange ladies come in to see
her. I imagine she is referring to one of the young misses,' she added,
diplomatically addressing herself to both of them. 'I've reasoned with her
and promised her gold and green forests — but what good is that! When
she takes something into her head, we must all do as she says. . . . And
yet. . . . Were it not for the fact that our worthy guests are sleeping
directly below! Oh dear, I can't tell you how ashamed I am! . . . I'll never
get over it.'

'Don't take it to heart, Dorthe dear; I'll be happy to go in and see
little Ada!' both sisters called out as one. Neither of them wanted to be
left alone, and it all ended with their both going, led by the inconsolable

Dorthe, who kept assuring them that this was the first time she had ever been guilty of such barbarity as disturbing the peace of sleeping guests. She appeared to be feeling much like a person who has been caught robbing a church.

When they entered the nursery, the little girl was sitting up in bed with her radiant eyes fastened on the arrivals. When Sofie and Amalie approached, she disappeared under her covers. In vain did Amalie address her with friendly words; the wilful little one remained obstinately hidden. But no sooner did Sofie bend over her than she slowly sat up, and before the other knew what was happening, Ada had flung her little arms around her neck with passionate violence and kissed her. Then she lay down and closed her eyes. Sofie was standing there, uncertain what to do.

'You may leave now,' Dorthe whispered; 'she'll be asleep in a moment.'

Only now, when she saw Ada lying there immobile as a marble image, did Sofie realize the wonderful beauty of this child. Ada had practically none of the usual soft and dimpled plumpness of a child. She looked like a wraith — frail and delicate. There were still tears on her cheeks, but over her chiselled features a blissful, satisfied smile was playing, in which there was also a trace of roguishness, revealing that she was not in any way asleep yet.

In the morning, the two sisters were enjoying their coffee and tiny, homemade rusks in bed, in keeping with old, established custom. Amalie was reluctant to tell what she had dreamed during the night. It was clear that she had counted on a more significant, poetic dream. It all boiled down to her having been occupied in replacing the faded curtains with new ones; it was not even certain whether the golden arrows had been included. She had also seen Sofie taking down the two portraits and putting up the old picture of their great-grandmother instead.

'And you, did you dream anything?' she asked Sofie.

'I dreamed about Ada.'

When, on a visit in the country, one has finished looking around inside the house, comes the turn of what is no less interesting, namely the outdoors. That is usually assigned to the following day. Until one has become thoroughly oriented, there can be no thought of quietly enjoying the life of a guest. Our visitors had been to the stables and to the cowbarn, to the chicken-coop and to the rabbit-hutches, to the dairy room and to the weaving room, and they had surveyed the various arrangements for threshing and rolling. However common in themselves, all of these things were something out of the ordinary in the Dean's establishment. Praise was given; comparisons were made; quiet plans were laid. Quite extraordinary, however, was the arrangement made for a school on the farm. A formerly empty machine shop (the Dean's foreman had been an unsuccessful inventor) had been turned into a school house for the poor children of the community. Here, from their eighth to their fourteenth year, the boys received instruction every morning from the school master and from the resident student teacher. The other section was set aside for the girls and was, since the death of the Dean's wife, under the supervision of old Dorthe. The sexton's daughter taught them all the plain and useful handicrafts. In addition, the girls were given instruction in other housekeeping arts, in the course of which they took turns doing whatever work was suited to their age and strength. Now the housemaid might require them to iron and mangle clothes, now the cook would need someone for scouring, polishing, cleaning garden produce, and so forth. The entire morning was spent in this manner; in the afternoons the children belonged to their own homes. It was a truly pleasant thing to see the many clean children, with their happy faces. When the ladies entered the room, curiosity caused a momentary halt in their humming activity, before it was all the more eagerly resumed. The looms were resounding and the spinning wheels were buzzing, and needles were flying so that it was a pleasure to watch.

There was nothing oppressive or institutional about all this activity. All the windows were open, and outside, on the green slope leading all the way down to the pond, there was also a great deal of activity. Here the laundry was spread out to dry, and all summer long dazzling cloths could be seen put out to bleach. A few young girls were rinsing clothes; others were wringing them out and hanging them up. A small, silvery blonde thing of about six was busy making sure that a late hatch of chickens stayed nicely on the other side of the pond, so that they would not get in the way of the clothes. Sofie, the quiet, introspective Sofie, seemed to find more to interest her here than in anything else she had seen. She followed the activity with a certain pensive attention, as if she might be trying to connect it with points in her own memory. She sought information about everything from Dorthe, and she talked with the children in a friendly manner.

The Dean, who had spent a long time with the District governor and Brøcher over in the boys' school, now joined the ladies to ask their pardon for having to leave them, for it was the time he had set aside for visits from the farmers. The other gentlemen went inside with him, while the ladies, led by Dorthe, were to visit the garden and the children, and to take a trip down into the Tyri Valley, where several industrial enterprises were located. A considerable tile works, a nail factory, and two mills (the latter belonging to the Dean) — provided work for a number of people. The entire valley was therefore heavily populated. The tenant farmers under the Dean's farm had since time immemorial had their own little farms there, and all sorts of artisans had decided to make their living by joining the small colony whose lively activity increased with every passing year. This was where one became fully acquainted with the fruits of the humanitarian clergyman's labours. The tenant farmers' cottages here were entirely different from the dirty hovels generally seen in rural areas. From every house, prosperity and cleanliness shone through the polished windows. Many of the cottages were nicely painted, and even the poorest one had its own little garden, sometimes even adorned with apple trees and cherry trees. The visitors were nowhere confronted with the hideous sight of ragged children, who ordinarily gather in such places in order to help each other while away the day.

'Yes, my dear ladies,' said an old, half blind woman, who was sitting outside her house warming herself in the October sun, 'it didn't look like this in Tyri Valley in my youth. Then there was nothing but want and poverty and drunkenness and fights. Everybody scrambled for his daily bread as best he could, and whoever couldn't get it lawfully, got it outside the law. At that time, everybody was glad to see them starving children leave the nest, so the day they had been through confirmation and was let loose on the world, that was a happy day for their folks. Now there's nobody as thinks they have too many children; there be no hand so small it can't be put to use. Yes, indeed, they can count themselves blessed in Tyri Valley now, compared with before. Such a clergyman I don't suppose is to be found anywhere else — may the Lord Everlasting bless him and give joy to that pious angel of the Lord up there in Heaven, because she, you see, his wife, she's been ever so good to us. With permission — might the ladies be family?'

When the ladies returned to the house, their host had not yet finished his negotiations with the farmers. A couple of them were still waiting in the anteroom to his study. Everybody came to 'Father himself' for advice and encouragement; one in spiritual matters, another in temporal ones. Dorthe had already for the fifth time peeked through the door to see if the last one might have left, so that she could serve the meal. Finally, the Dean came. A shadow of discouragement or fatigue could be seen on his face, but it soon gave way at the sight of his guests and at being confronted with the magic inevitably exercised by a freshly laid and waiting table.

At the table, the conversation turned to the things that had so thoroughly won his visitors' approval. Each person had some little thing to relate, and everybody wanted to express admiration.

'A splendid task, well executed!' said the District Governor.

'Extremely worthy of imitation,' Brøcher assured him. 'What do you think, my Amalie,' he aid to her half audibly, 'for us, who are about to *begin*, this was a beautiful example.'

'Easy, easy; let us first get something for *ourselves* before we start thinking about making others happy,' his mother-in-law whispered on the other side. The District Governor gave her an imploring look, but Brøcher, who was well accustomed to that sort of pill, swallowed it in patience.

'Yes, I have been admiring you, Dean,' said Mrs Ramm with her most gracious smile. 'When seeing the blessing you have bestowed upon those around you, one is well aware that just ordinary good intentions are not sufficient to accomplish what you have done.'

'No, in truth,' said Rein, 'one doesn't get very far with good intentions. If I dare say so, what is called for is an almost stubborn eagerness and an equally strong and constantly renewed endurance. In the beginning, I encountered a great deal of difficulty. The common man has an aversion to change. He has no faith in anything of which he cannot calculate the consequences exactly and tangibly, the way he can with the couple of pecks of oats he sows on the ground. When I took over this living fifteen years ago, I found the congregation here sadly neglected. Everything was mired in poverty, ignorance and vice of every description. An old and obstinate curmudgeon was the leader of the tenant farmers. For as long as he was alive, it was impossible to accomplish anything. The children were lazy and resisted having to go to school; the mothers complained loudly that their children were taken away from them and that they were more in need of help than of seeing it diminished at home.

Not until the old fellow was dead and his son had taken his place, was it possible for me to lay the foundation of what I have been able to build later, with God's help.'

'Indeed, my good friend,' the District Governor said, 'the rest of us have good intentions; you *carry them out* — therein lies the difference, you see! Who has not had philanthropic notions at one point or another. . . . I have also had ideas in that direction. When I assumed my position on the farm, I fantasized about the ease with which one may make improvements. But I don't know how it happened — it never came to anything. The nature of my business was so very different from yours. Besides, clergymen are so much better able to do these things than the rest of us. They alone are in a position to combine so beautifully the spiritual care of their flock with the temporal, so that they may be called their shepherd in a double sense of the word. I thus contented myself with giving, when want stretched out its hand towards me, and I comforted myself with the thought that what I did not give them, they helped themselves to. Ha, ha!'

'One may calculate,' Brøcher remarked, 'that every year in our parish, out of twenty legal actions, two-thirds will be concerned with encroachments upon property rights. In consequence, our poor-tax is enormous.'

'Theft is almost unknown here,' said the Dean, 'and I never give alms.'

'For the good reason that in your fortunate region, it is no longer needed,' said Mrs Ramm.

'Formerly, there was great need here, but even then I didn't offer hand-outs. You had better believe me a hard-hearted man.'

'Ah, Dean, you'll make us believe no such thing! With your humanitarianism. . . .!'

'Permit me, dear madam. . . .'

But the lady was not easily to be deprived of an opportunity to give one of her unctuous little lectures.

'You should not give praise to philanthropy? You should not know the sweet satisfaction of easing the need of others? I regard it as one of the principal Christian duties, and most especially as a woman's most essential adornment. Therefore, I have also awakened this urge in my daughters from their earliest age. You cannot conceive how happy it made them to give things away. Finally, I was hard put to control their enthusiasm. And many a time I had to punish them when they had gone too far. Which one of you was it, girls, who tore a hole in her dress so that it might look worn enough to give away?'

'It must have been Amalie,' said Sofie, with a somewhat impatient expression.

'No, it really was Sofie,' the other assured her.

'Yes, yes, you're right; it was Sofie who had that curious idea.'

'I also remember,' Amalie continued, 'that when she gave her dresses away to the tenant farmers' daughters, they had to give her their solemn promise that they would mend them again.'

'Yes, but despite those solemn promises, that never did happen,' Sofie contributed, 'because every time we saw them, the holes were bigger and bigger, and that was how it always was. One blamed it on not having a needle; another on the lack of thread; a third person didn't know how to sew. And before you could count to three, the whole thing was a rag.'

'And then you got the idea of starting a sewing school on the farm,' her mother added. 'But your mama would have none of that. In those days, you had so many notions in your little head.'

'Alas, yes; it may well be that I had some notions. But do you think, Mother, that this was one of the crazier ones? I really felt that something different was called for. . . . One may easily lose the desire to give. . . .'

'Lose the desire to give!' said her mother. '. . . No, God be praised, there is no danger of that. You're generous enough; it would be quite wrong to say otherwise.'

'Forgive me, madam,' Rein interrupted her, 'but I can easily believe it. I am convinced that Miss Sofie is right. In fact, she has answered perfectly what you said to me just now. Far be it from me to deny the beauty of giving. It is the natural desire of every generous heart. My Adamine was so easily guided, but in this matter I could tell her nothing. She never stopped to reflect, but just followed the dictates of her nature. Thousands do the same. For as long as conditions are no better, there really is nothing else one can do. Besides, there are instances when generosity provides real satisfaction. Those are the times when the gift becomes just what it ought to be, a form of support — that is, when one assumes with fair certainty that the recipient is engaged in a struggle for improved circumstances. But in this case we are not talking about this type of needy people, but of the lowest class. We are talking about that animal-like, unreasoning, helpless poverty, the sort of misery that is handed down from generation to generation and that does not even raise its consciousness towards something better; we are talking about those whose wretched hovels congregate around every farm of any size, the way insects gather around dropped fruit. Towards these people I consider any form of instant generosity to be useless, indeed harmful. Anyone who has indulged in this kind of generosity is forced to admit in all honesty that they derive more trouble than pleasure from it. It is like tossing one's gift into a bottomless pit, which is exactly the case. One might as well toss half of everything one owns into the same pit, for all the good it would do; the pit is apt to expand — it's like the holes in Miss Sofie's dresses. This type of poor people must be accustomed not to *receiving*, but to *earning*. They will only maintain and add to that which they have earned. One must try to instill in them a concept of better conditions; to sharpen their quest for them; to show them the means of achieving them; and to get them to realize that each one of them, even the poorest person, is master of his or her own destiny. A desire to work, virtuousness, enlightenment — those are the pillars upon which everything else rests, and when these are lacking, all effort is futile.

'If one has earnestly set oneself this task, one soon notices that it is not an easy one. A lot more is called for here than just hand-me-down clothes or a few crumbs that will not be missed from your own abundance. You must give them of your time, of your soul, of your best energy. The gifts then follow, as a reward and as an encouragement. It then goes without saying that it is the young people to whom one must devote oneself — not to say take possession of! — There is nothing to be done with the old ones. One must let them die along with the old vice. It is a slowly growing seed, but one must not tire of pulling away the choking weeds, or become discouraged if for a long time there is no sign of fruit. Thus, everyone ought to do the best he can according to his own situation in life, and one's efforts cannot fail to be blessed in the end. I have had the pleasure of seeing several instances of imitation here in the parish, and farmers and property owners come daily to get advice and information — sometimes people come out of sheer curiosity. My little colony has gained a reputation which I hope it will in time grow to deserve.'

'I suppose we had better declare ourselves beaten, Dean. You have developed your system so interestingly that there is nothing in it for us to object to. And, at the same time, my little Sofie was thoroughly absolved of her sin.'

'If an involuntary cooling-off of something that previously gave me pleasure can be called a sin,' Sofie said, 'I really do feel comforted. The Dean has shown me that the reason is not to be found in myself so much as in the general conditions. But why do these conditions have to be such that one cannot do good even if one wants to? Surely it's different in other countries, isn't it?'

'You mustn't think any such thing,' her mother put in; ' — such dreadful descriptions of poverty as we get from precisely those places!'

'Yes,' Sofie replied, 'in the cities I'm sure it's terrible, but in the countryside, where there are more manors and farmers just as there are here, the situation seems to be different. As a child, when I read about life in the castles and on the great estates, it was precisely the relationship between the masters and their subjects that impressed me the most. It was so beautiful, so touching! Truly noble masters regarded their peasants almost as children, whose well-being concerned them personally. The mistress would go from house to house, now praising, now criticizing, comforting the sick, and everywhere she was greeted like a mother. Oh, those feasts, in which the master and the mistress themselves would take part — how beautiful they were! When I read about all this, I thought how wonderful it would be to be like that, if only in a small way. But here in our country I never see anything of this. On the big farms, they know very little about the miserable creatures that live nearby. We scarcely see them, except when they do the work they are supposed to do for us, or when we toss them a bit of alms. Nothing is done to instruct or improve them — they are just punished when they do wrong.'

'Well, I must say, that was a beautiful description, indeed! This is how your own home appears to you, while all of us, including your parents, are the sort of heartless beings you just described?' said Sofie's mother in the sort of voice that swings like a pendulum between seriousness and jest.

'Sofie is exaggerating somewhat,' the District Governor observed, 'but I am afraid there is a lot of truth in it. We care far too little about those below us.'

'Oh, Mother mustn't take it so seriously. I really have nothing particular in mind. I was just describing an old impression, and I have, in truth, not given much thought to the matter lately. I was so forcefully reminded of it today, however. All my philanthropic childhood fantasies again came out in full force. With every step I took today, the old wish came alive in me — to live and to work in such a place! To be involved in creating this happiness all around. How wonderful it must be!'

Sofie was naively addressing herself to the Dean. Her cheeks were flushed; she was not accustomed to speaking at such length. But the Dean did not look up at all. He was balancing an apple on the point of his silver knife and staring at it as intently as if he really wanted to form an impression of what it looked like, this small, round, smooth, reddish object that had brought so much misfortune into the world, and as if he pondered how on earth it could have been so irresistible to poor Adam. . . . For, when all was said and done, perhaps Adam was at least as weak as Eve. He was tempted only by someone who was his equal, while she had to defend herself against the Devil himself.

After a pause, the Dean said in a voice of suppressed emotion: 'May God grant you, my dear young lady, a sphere of activity that is commensurate with your noble heart.' After which, he turned to the District Governor with some remark about the administration of poor relief.

'Speaking of poor relief,' Brøcher interjected with a slightly arch smile; 'the Dean, who is a man of reform, has no doubt already introduced new district divisions into his parish?'

But Mrs Ramm raised her glass, and her 'Should we not thank our gracious host?' immediately intercepted the direction the conversation threatened to take.

'That person,' she said as she was giving her husband his after-the-meal kiss, 'will surely bore Amalie and us all to death, before he gets some miserable living off in a remote corner of the country, where we'll never see her again. The poor, misguided girl! . . . Were I in her place, I certainly know what I would have done.'

'Let us hope for the best, my Mariane; things may turn out better than we think.'

* * *

Rein really was an excellent host; excellent in a different sense from what is usually understood by this word. He knew how to please his guests by simple means. His visitors were never aware of any efforts to entertain them. Once in a great while, they made an excursion to the surrounding countryside. Visitors were more infrequent still. On this latter point, Rein had his own definite opinions. He had formed notions about the inviolability of domestic life that were rather at odds with our native ideas in this area. He was considered eccentric because he had chosen his own circle of friends, and because he had not turned his house into an inn, where any passing stranger was at liberty to knock the residents awake in the middle of the night. But whoever did find himself a guest in that house, felt the security and the quiet comfort that only *true* hospitality can produce. Everything was so quietly and so smoothly done. There was no sense of the household routine's having been disturbed due to the presence of guests, but everybody felt gently obliged to conform to the customs of the house, without suffering inconvenience themselves. After dinner, everybody withdrew to his own corner to enjoy a rest in whatever manner suited him best, and then everybody gathered again for tea.

Following such a siesta, we find the family gathered in the corner parlour. Sofie was singing to her own piano accompaniment. She sang a couple of modern arias clearly, beautifully, artistically, but without emotion. Everybody was listening and declaring her to be in exceptional voice. The Dean alone was not as attentive a listener as he normally was. He was absentminded, and he frequently glanced out of the window as if looking for someone. Finally — it was just during an interval in the music — old Dorthe appeared in the doorway with the mail pouch. The rapidity with which the Dean seized it struck the old woman as unusual — still more striking was the deprecating gesture with which he warded off the question she was just then asking him. Not even to want to hear whether the two browns were to be tethered or let out to pasture! This had to be something important. She was hesitantly preparing to leave when she fortunately discovered that the children had brought the curtains into some disorder, right next to the Dean. From her vantage point she watched him put aside no fewer than five letters with big, official seals, all of them marked 'Important', before he with a momentary look of disappointment searched the pouch again with greater care. He was successful — he pulled forth a smaller letter, which he proceeded to open. As soon as he had read the first few lines, his face lit up. 'God be praised! It's something good, I could see that; it's probably from the little boys — Kristian has perhaps finished his preparations for the University. Yes, indeed, they are my clever little boys!'

A moment later, the Dean took the District Governor and Mrs Ramm, as well as Brøcher, into his study and closed the door behind them. The sisters were wondering what it was all about, when Mrs Ramm stuck her head out and called for Amalie. Sofie was left alone, but only for a moment. Amalie came storming out and threw herself around Sofie's neck with shouts of joy. The Dean, that blessed Dean, had just taken Brøcher on as his chaplain! The Bishop's announcement had just arrived. Adolf was to take office already by the New Year. It was so advantageous, so very advantageous! They were to live in the Dean's house, and the whole row of empty rooms upstairs was to be renovated and furnished for their use.

The older people returned. Brøcher was pale and moved — this good fortune had caught him completely unprepared. He looked as if he wanted to cry, but could not. He cleared his throat and blew his nose incessantly. The old father's joy was plain and without words. He kissed Amalie on her lips and on her brow, and he grasped Brøcher's and the Dean's hands in both of his and shook them cordially. Mrs Ramm was the only one who was not at a loss for words. When others were moved, she felt solemn, and she never lectured so splendidly as when others were unable to say a word.

'God bless you, my children,' she said. 'A rare, most unexpected happiness has fallen to your lot. Make yourselves worthy of it! Never forget to thank this noble man for what he has done. You, Amalie, must remember that he above all has a claim to your grateful heart. Be to him a source of solace, cheerfulness and comfort; be an ornament to his house, a mother to his children. . . .'

At this point, Brøcher automatically stepped closer, as if to remind them of his existence.

'My daughter,' the lady continued, 'you may in a double sense praise your fortune and feel grateful to Providence. You have made the choice of your heart, and now luck enters into the bargain. Brøcher's is not an ambitious, romantic nature. Alas, that is not what counts; it is not the dazzling gifts of genius that assure the quiet bliss of domesticity. Brøcher is a man of common sense and sufficient intelligence; an honourable man, diligent in his chosen calling; a man I appreciate. He will provide just the right support to my Amalie's more gentle, romantic temperament. He will make her happy.'

This was too much for Brøcher's modesty. The restraint that had kept his emotions in check was cut, and he ran out of the room with his handkerchief before his eyes.

There was another person in the room who had not added her voice to the general chorus of joy. That was Ada. The little girl had conceived a passion for Sofie; she followed her about like a shadow, keeping watch on her every movement. None of the others could claim to enjoy any special favour with her. She could just tolerate Amalie, but Mrs Ramm not at all, although the latter courted her favour in every way. Brøcher she loathed. He had once had the temerity to want to kiss her and had called her his little darling, and this she did not forget. As it happened, Ada had been out in the kitchen and had heard snatches of what was taking place in the parlour — such things seep through the keyholes. Whether she had misunderstood what she heard, or whether one of the maids, knowing her passion for Sofie, had been heartless enough to tease her, Ada had somehow got the idea that it was Sofie and not Amalie who was going to come and live in her house. For Sofie's sake the empty rooms were to be done up and furnished. With every sign of violent joy, Ada had run in to Sofie. The latter had been hard put to explain to Ada that she was mistaken, and when Ada had finally understood, she just stared at Sofie with her big dark eyes and left the room without saying a word. When Dorthe wanted to put her to bed an hour later, she was nowhere to be found. The sisters came along to help look for her. Ada was in their room. She was lying on the sofa with her head buried in the pillows, sobbing. Tenderly, Amalie and old Dorthe tried to calm her, promising her a thousand wonderful things if only she would stop crying and accept her fate, but the little one persisted. '*Sofie* is to live with us; nobody else.'

'Then do you think I should become Brøcher's wife?' Sofie inquired.

A vivid grimace suggested how inexpressibly unworthy Ada found him.

'Well, there you are! Brøcher doesn't want me with him, just his wife.'

'But I don't want Brøcher. Papa didn't ask me about it; I don't want Brøcher to come and be chaplain. You are to come. Anne cook said that Papa had said that you were going to live in the big ballroom, which is to be painted yellow, and I am going to live in the little room next-door, and that is going to be painted pink.'

'Am I not going to be allowed to live in the yellow ballroom at all, then?' Amalie asked.

'No.'

'Then I'll be so sad, and then I'll cry, boo-hoo-hoo.'

'Yes, but you don't use real tears when you cry; I saw that in church yesterday. You just do like that with your handkerchief.'

'Shame on you,' said old Dorthe, 'now you are being very naughty. Should you not be glad that the pretty young lady is coming to stay with you — she who is so nice to you; who has given you a heart made of amber; and who has cut out so many pretty horses for you?'

'Do you call that horses? Lina said they were camels, and those with two humps were dromedaries, and those with three humps were — what were they?'

'Listen, I want to tell you something, little Ada,' said Sofie. 'If you had been nice and behaved yourself, I would have come to visit you and Brøcher and Amalie, but now I am not coming at all.'

The little girl sent her a knowing look. 'How long would you stay if you came?'

'I don't know; perhaps for a whole month; perhaps for two, if you were good.'

'Won't you come at all, then, unless *she* is living here?'

'No, then I won't come at all.'

'I'll let you, then,' she said to Amalie, with the manner of a queen.

'But I don't want to, unless Brøcher is also living here.'

'I'll let him as well,' Ada said, after a somewhat longer reflection.

'You angel!' Amalie cried.

'There's a dear girl, my own treasure!' said Dorthe. 'There you see, she's really a good girl at heart, but one must be serious when dealing with her.'

'Yes, that certainly seems called for!' said Sofie with a smile.

They were late getting to bed that night. Conversation had received an infusion of fresh, new material. Even Ada had repeatedly begged for a postponement of her bedtime, until she had fallen asleep on the bare floor by Sofie's side, with her brown locks resting on Sofie's dress. Everybody was happy or appeared to be happy. Mrs Ramm was cordiality incarnate towards everybody. She had already given Amalie the most splendid hints regarding her furnishings. For the first time in half a year, she asked Brøcher about the condition from which he was suffering.

It was almost midnight before the sisters were alone in their bedroom. Amalie entered dancing and singing. Scarcely had she crossed the threshold, however, but she stopped and made a gesture as solemn as if she wanted to conjure up spirits.

'Sofie, Sofie! There are dark and mysterious powers governing a person's life, which no human intelligence can fathom. Do you remember my dream?'

'Your dream?' said Sofie, somewhat absentmindedly.

'Then Fate did want me to be mistress of these unfamiliar rooms! — Then it was written in the stars, after all, that my hand was to take down these old curtains; that my hand was to . . . '

'Is it to be calico or muslin?'

'Now I stop to think about it, neither one nor the other,' said Amalie, who always could be pulled down from her soaring flights of fancy as easily as a paper kite. 'There's a sort of embroidered linen that is supposed to be sweet. . . . But Sofie, seriously, isn't it strange how my dream is coming true? Now I'm wondering whether the other part of it, the one concerning you, will also come literally true.'

'What, then, did you dream about me?'

'Don't you remember? — I told you that I saw you standing over there, busily occupied in taking down the portraits and putting Great-Grandmother back up. I've already decided that you are to come with me when I come here to stay, and then you can help me arrange this and that; you have such good taste.'

'That might be.'

'When I come to think of it, I prefer not to have the pictures changed about; I prefer my poets. I have discovered that there's something about Goethe's eyes that reminds me of Adolf, and also the profile, especially when you look at it from a certain angle. Do look! Don't you think so?'

'No, not in any way!' said Sofie, almost angrily. 'Neither from the one angle nor the other.'

'Well, of course it's not really sufficiently youthful — but what I wanted to say is that I don't want them changed. I never could understand your enthusiasm for that grim old face, nor why you didn't seize the chance to get rid of it when the garden room was being redone. The minute I go anywhere near that picture, I feel as if I am about to be scolded.'

'Have no fear. You are not about to get it, either, for that matter. Great-Grandmother and I belong together; my cradle was directly under her eyes; I grew up under her scrutiny. . . .'

'No, Sofie, you're really mistaken there; it was not beneath Great-Grandmother's portrait, but on the other side, behind a screen. I can still remember it so clearly.'

* * *

A family event such as had just occurred, must necessarily give the social intercourse between the two families a different flavour and direction. Regardless of how much the event had brought the people closer together, making them all focus on the same point, it nevertheless had an outwardly disturbing effect. The calm and quiet comfort of the first few days was gone. The gentlemen were now spending a great deal of their day with the Dean in his office. Mrs Ramm and Amalie were continually in motion. Every nook and cranny of the house was inspected. The most thorough deliberations were entered into as to how things might be arranged to best advantage. The sitting room was almost always empty. Sofie began to feel very much alone. There was nothing she dreaded more in her present frame of mind.

It is possible to nurse one's memory of a love affair in various ways. One way is to return to this memory as to a comfort, a triumph; another way is to do the opposite and shun it like the plague. It is easy to guess which of these alternatives most often falls to a woman's lot. Only very rarely does a man find something humiliating in a disappointed love when he thinks back on it. When he knows that he has done everything in his power to impress his beloved; that he has left no stone unturned in his effort to conquer the unrelenting one; then he may rest easy. He has nothing with which to reproach himself. He has done his best. He may rest safely in the contemplation of his sufferings and celebrate them in song if he can, thus moving himself and others, while the hope of a new struggle, a new love, is sweetly sprouting among the stubble. When *she*, on the other hand, knows that she has done everything in her power to — *conceal herself* from her beloved, and that she has killed her longing, carefully pulling up every timid seedling of hope, and when she has been able to complete this work of self-mortification, then *she*, indeed, has also done her best — but it is not therefore said that she may rest easy. Regret and self-recrimination with its cruel sophistry are yet to be added to the bitterness of renunciation. A look, a quickened pulse, a sudden blush, a ray of happiness quelled by tears, a hope that faded with his footsteps, in her may become so many poisonous drops, falling one by one on her wound and making it impossible for it to heal.

Sofie had one of those female fakir natures that had to comply with this law of self-destruction and self-mortification governing womanhood, exactly as this law had been instilled in her, totally and completely. Her proud, pure spirit dared not allow the smallest indulgence. Her ideas about a truer, more natural femininity had been destroyed along with her trust in him who had been the first to give some shape to those quiet dreams. Her lack of faith in herself, in happiness, in everything, had returned with double force. It had given her this almost supernatural ability to resist, right up to the last, bitter farewell. She could do no more. For her, this brief dream of happiness had ended in too painful, too humiliating a manner. She could not bear to think of what had passed. She had desperately seized the opportunity for escape this trip had afforded her, and in despair she grasped at every new impression.

Therefore, we ought not to wonder at Sofie's redoubled concern for the welfare of others. It was not dissimulation that made her talkative — excited, even. She wanted to and was compelled to flee from herself. Still, this hard-won calm was ever in danger of being shattered. No more was required than the mention of a certain name, or for the poor girl to enter the upstairs room at night in a carefree mood and then chance to look at that picture whose treacherous resemblance was even more compelling in the twilight. At such moments, she exercised tremendous restraint over herself. She dared not as yet release the pent-up pain. That must be done by a hand stronger, more experienced than her own. She longed for her sister, the sister she had loved so well and who appeared so gentle and real to her in the rosy light of childhood memory. She, the good Louise, would help her interpret everything that seemed to her so hideously inexplicable. She knew what suffering was; she would know how to comfort. In her arms she would cry herself empty.... Oh, how she would cry!... It was best not to think about it, however.... Just not to think about it!

And then again she might, like a child frightened of the dark and scared of its own shadow, go and look for the others, staying close to them, singing to them and chattering and playing with the children.

247

But on this particular day even the house seemed almost dead. Sofie found the sitting room empty. She looked all over the garden, but nobody was there, either. Sad and uneasy she walked off down the tree-lined lane, out of the gate, and, with no particular destination in mind, took the forest road that led down into the valley. There she saw a figure approaching, who had to be one of those she was looking for. But who it was, she could not see, because she was not farsighted. Nor did it diminish her pleasure when she finally recognized Rein. With an exclamation of delight, she walked towards him with outstretched hands. It was just like the response of a child fearing the dark, when it sees its mother arriving with a candle. Rein did not answer immediately. He had stopped and was standing with his arms pressed to his chest, while he heaved deeply for breath. Sofie scolded him for having walked up the hill too fast.

'The best cure for that,' he remarked, 'is for me to walk down again with you. You were going for a walk, weren't you?'

Sofie immediately declared herself willing, and it is not certain whether it was at his or her instigation, but when they started down the hill, her arm was resting in his.

On the way, Rein told her that he had been down at the old mill in order to check on some damage that turned out to be more significant than he had anticipated. Due to unpardonable neglect on the part of the miller, the best millstone had been broken and various other kinds of damage done. When Sofie expressed her wonder at his talking of this as if it were a jest, as if it were nothing, he assured her that he was accustomed never to take mishaps to heart. After all, they were as inseparable from human endeavour as shadow is from the light. The only thing to do was to offer to spite them and immediately try to eradicate their effect. If we did not control them, they would control us and end by turning us into pitiful fatalists, devoid of courage and resting our hands in our laps.

Sofie thought this was an excellent attitude towards life. 'I'll try very hard to make it my own,' she assured him.

'Do try it some time in earnest,' said Rein. 'Consider what we call mishaps as part of a *whole*, and you will see that they show up as small, harmless, barely visible spots. Very often some actual good may come of them, even if it's not immediately obvious. At least, that is what almost always happens to me.'

'Well,' said Sofie, 'when next I return here, I want to know what good fortune this mishap has left in its wake. You are to give a complete account of the glorious things the millstone and the damaged lock equipment have brought you.'

'I can tell you one advantage right now. I've long been dissatisfied with the miller without having sufficient reason for firing him. I might have waited long for an opportunity to equal this one, unless it be that he burned down the house for me. Secondly, had it not been for that blessed millstone, I should not have run into you,' he added gallantly, 'taking this lovely walk with you in this enchanting moonlight. . . . There is the full moon, just at the edge of the hill!'

In this manner they walked through the valley to its farthest end and back, now and then stopping in front of a house to exchange a friendly word with its inhabitants. Not until they had passed the last of the houses, and the forest enveloped them in its lonely darkness, did their conversation regain continuity. Sofie, who was quite taciturn in the presence of others, particularly of her mother, now became lively and talkative. Rein completely forgot that it was to a girl of eighteen he was talking. Among our people, an eighteen-year-old girl tends to be a kind of *misfit*, or at least a ridiculous mixture of someone who is a big child, but not yet a lady, with whom it would never occur to a sensible man to carry on a serious conversation, and for whose benefit a special blend of nonsense and flattery has been invented. Before Rein knew it, he had grown loquacious. His best and long-since buried thoughts were again put into words. It even seemed to him as if they had been enriched when they came back to him. An older man's admiration is always warmer than that of a younger one — it is less egotistical. Rein took pleasure in listening to Sofie's fine, sensible answers, which reached him in her childlike, harmonious voice. He was especially pleased with the freshness and originality her words revealed. A young girl who had the courage to be truthful; who every moment ran headlong against what was considered proper and customary! Propriety and custom, those idols of her sex into whose mysteries women are initiated from the cradle, and to which they offer up a worship of dishonesty, cowardice, pettiness, deception — deep, thorough dishonesty. Oh, how this dishonesty had slowly quelled his youthful enthusiasm until, tired and realistic — yet too gentle to feel scorn — he had made up his mind to live alone. Indeed, he was already a confirmed bachelor when concern for others made him decide to get married. His had been a model marriage. When people wanted to cite an example of a happy wife, they talked of Mrs Rein. Whether *he* had been equally happy in his innermost being, no doubting tongue had ever queried.

By this time, the moon had risen all the way. It was playing over the shiny, tiled farm roof and outlining the whole row of trees in the lane in a most picturesque way. Now and then a light glinted among the shadows. But how had it happened that they already were so close to the farm! It must have come out to meet them, because it was not natural for it to be there already. The Dean walked that way a couple of times a week, and then — he was rather a heavy man — it sometimes seemed more than far enough. Neither was he aware that his steps had grown as elastic as those of a young man. He did not himself see how his dark eyes were shining. Nor did he hear the sound of his own voice. Nobody saw or heard these things. Rein was in the middle of a dream, one of those pleasant dreams one has towards morning and in which one is strangely aware that it is only a dream, so that mingled with our joy there is a certain melancholy fear of waking. . . . Indeed, he was dreaming that he had found *her* whom he had sought for so long; that it was she who was now walking by his side with those light, floating steps; that it was his young wife whom he, young and happy, had brought home to his house the day before. . . . They had been out for a walk in the moonlight in order to look at their surroundings, of which, however, they had taken no notice; and they were now approaching their home, their own home, which awaited them with fresh and redoubled pleasures.

But alas, he had only to step back inside among the others, and it was over. The mirage vanished, and reality inexorably resumed its rightful place. He saw Sofie again by the light of the lamp. . . . Oh, she was indeed desperately young and beautiful! 'How anyone can still want to play tag after such a walk,' he said to himself, while from his comfortable place he was watching Sofie dart like an arrow around the table with little Ada. . . . 'It can make you quite dizzy to watch!'

This evening the Dean was, for the first time, rather quiet and taciturn. His guests were certainly well aware of his despondency, but out of delicacy every one of them avoided touching upon what they assumed to be the reason for his mood. Only when they said good night was Mrs Ramm unable to resist — she laid her still beautiful, heavily be-ringed hand upon the Dean's and said in her softest voice:

'How are we to bring back the good mood of our dear host? . . . And who could have known, when we parted so merrily last night, that this

250

terrible accident was to befall you! . . . What figure do you place upon your loss, my dear Dean?'

'I suppose the loss itself is the least of it,' the District Governor added; 'the worst part of it is that once things start going wrong with old equipment, there is simply nothing to be done. One must let it go to the Devil. . . . Repairs and efforts are usually to no avail.'

'Curiously enough,' Brøcher remarked, 'I dreamed last night that that very mill was in flames.'

'Yes, in truth,' the Dean said with a good-natured smile, 'dreams are curious, indeed.'

Rein spent a restless night, during which he did not once think about his broken millstone, but throughout which his heart was so heavy that both halves of the millstone might have been resting on his chest. How had this come about! After all, he had fought against the temptation honestly and like a man, and now he was confronting the monster all over again! When he had left Sofie at her parents' house, he had been full of noble resignation. He had been perfectly calm when he saw her again. In a fatherly way he had taken pleasure in her graciousness; he suspected no evil. Then he suddenly saw himself — like those poor people who are lost in the desert and who think they are progressing, when they are actually just walking around in circles — about to step in the footprints they themselves had left behind. One thing eased his mind, however: this misfortune was not so much his fault as *Sofie*'s. She had conjured forth temptation. She came towards him in such a challenging way; towards nobody else, scarcely even towards her own father, did she show so cordial a manner. Sometimes, when something in this new place had struck her, it was as if she put words into his mouth, while, to top it all, she looked him boldly in the eye. The other day he had overheard her saying to Ada, 'If I were your mother, now,' or, 'now I am your mother. . . .' That was exactly what she had said one time while lifting Ada up on her arm! . . . He had joined them just then, and the little girl had flung her arm around his neck as well, pulling them together. . . . Alarmed, he had snatched the child to him. . . . What was she thinking of when she said things like that? . . . 'Oh, you old fool,' a mocking voice whispered to him again, 'she's thinking of nothing at all. Doesn't this straight-forward manner precisely go to show that the thought is so alien to her that it doesn't even occur to her! She would not act this way towards a younger man.'

When dawn came, he was still pacing up and down in his chamber. But the good man had succeeded in regaining his equanimity. 'No,' he said, as he extinguished his lamp and stood staring into the foggy autumn morning, 'it is not going to happen. I might ask for her. . . . Her parents would give her to me — with pleasure, I think. She herself might comply, inexperienced child that she is. . . . She is still untouched by the influence of passion. . . . At least, I haven't heard of anything! . . . But that is precisely why it must not be. I despise such assaults. I don't want to be a robber. This beauty, this touching grace, this — ' here followed the whole list of Sofie's attributes — 'must belong to someone younger and more fortunate than myself. If only she were my daughter! If only Ada would grow up to be like her! Tomorrow they are leaving. Therefore, it's only for this one day that I have to be or *appear* to be calm. I hope to *be* calm.'

Heaven had no doubt heard this worthy man's resolution and found pleasure in it. Meanwhile, the Norn quietly and unconcernedly is spinning those threads that link people's fates, while laughing at their calculations and resolutions.

* * *

Dorthe, decent old Dorthe! Who does not know old Dorthe; who does not have such a Dorthe in their own family! It was she who told you so many pretty tales, until you fell asleep before you had heard the end of the story. It was she who interceded for you when you had knocked out window panes, and who every day, with incomparable tirelessness, undid whatever the least bit of sensible strictness had accomplished. . . . It was she who cried so bitterly when, brave and bold, you left home for the first time, and who could not sleep for joy the week you were expected back. . . . Alas, you returned with your first jarring experiences with the world! . . . And then, when everybody was gone, even the very youngest, and there was nobody left to 'spoil', old Dorthe sat left behind and sad. And while she was sitting there dejectedly, she suddenly remembered that she had had suitors, and she married someone from her own class, which is to say, she married poverty and misery.

Thus she has got a home of her own, but with all the roots of her heart she remains attached to yours. There she lives her real life. It has become the fairy-world she opens to her children. If anything of importance occurs in your family, Dorthe has had significant dreams and visions which she comes to tell you about. She writes verses for festive occasions which the person to be confirmed or married has to write down from dictation, because for all that Dorthe has the gift of speech and is well-read, she has never reached the point of communicating her inspirations through a pen. Dorthe is waiting only to become a widow. Then she closes up her cottage, and if the old home fires no longer exist, she will seek yours, and with all the pent-up tenderness of her faithful heart, she will fall upon your children.

As a young girl, our old Dorthe had been a servant in the childhood home of Rein's wife. She had nursed and raised her, because Rein's wife had also lost her mother very early in life. Later, after a brief marriage, Dorthe had gone to live with her foster daughter. The fruits of Dorthe's child-rearing methods were not uniformly good, however. Little Ada had not at all inherited her mother's serene, equable and gentle temperament. Dorthe's blind love and boundless indulgence had developed in the little girl all those dangerous talents which may turn into something great and glorious, but equally into something most unfortunate.

Little Ada controlled the entire household. When she was playing with Lina, who was three years her senior, this sister submitted to her unconditionally, as if it were the most natural thing in the world. Even Ada's father could not resist Dorthe's intercessions on those rare occasions when he decided to be strict. If anyone had accused him of treating his children unequally, he would have found such accusations odd, not to say unfair. Was he not just as gentle, just as indulgent with them both? Certainly, but he did not stop to reflect that one daughter was as pious and well behaved a child as the other was wild and wilful. And yet the father's eyes rested on Ada with quite a different expression from that with which he regarded his other daughter. Who would not have done the same! Beauty has a miraculous, tantalizing power that nobody can claim to be able to resist. Added to this was the worry that such a child must ever cause a father's heart. She was uncontrollable in joy and in sorrow; she was ingratiating when she wanted to obtain something; and she was endowed with strong likes and dislikes. The former of these two qualities was rarely displayed, but when someone was fortunate enough to gain her favour, there was no end or moderation to her love. This was the case with the devotion she had conceived for Sofie. In its intensity, it was more apt to scare Sofie off than to move her. Among all the adults, however, this young girl was the only one who exerted any sort of influence over Ada.

* * *

One day Ada had been naughty. The student teacher living in the house had given Brøcher a trained bullfinch in a cage. Brøcher took great pleasure in feeding the little creature and in coaxing it to sing. Suddenly, the bird disappeared, and it was easy to prove that Ada was the culprit. Yet it was impossible to get out of her whether she had just let the bird out, or had done something else with it.

Consequently, an example was to be made of her. Ada was to stay at home while the others went for a drive along the lake to a farm that, due both to its splendid location and to a certain architectural interest, was a favourite place of pilgrimage for people who lived even farther away than Rein. Dorthe begged and pleaded. . . . She claimed the bird had managed to make its own escape; she even assured them that she had seen it, easily recognizable because of a crooked tail-feather, sitting hale and hearty in a tree in the garden. But neither Dorthe's splendid arguments nor Ada's despair helped. This time her father was adamant. Touched by her tears and supplications, the goodnatured Amalie promised she would stay home with her, but that did not interest the little girl at all. She looked over at Sofie, as if she expected a similar offer from her, but Sofie said gravely, 'I don't at all want to stay home with you, Ada, and I'll not come back until you are a good girl and have made everything right again.'

Ada fell suddenly silent, walked over to the stairs and sat down, and calmly watched them drive off.

Sofie had used an unfortunate expression in asking Ada 'to make everything right again.' The little girl, just as precipitate in her remorse as in her other emotions, had a certain exalted way of making amends that often was worse than the original offence.

Scarcely had the carriage disappeared from view, but Ada jumped up and ran into her father's study. Here, by means of chairs and a footstool, she succeeded in reaching a glassfronted corner cabinet in which the Dean had made a small display of objects from nature. Nobody disturbed her during her secret employment, because it did not occur to anyone to look for her in the study. That she herself was well pleased with the results, was evident by the radiant face with which she received the others when they returned. Little Ada was so sweet and ingratiating that evening that they almost regretted having been so strict with her.

The lamp had just been lit when Brøcher put his head in the door and motioned with his hand. Everybody had to follow him. He led them on tip-toe, with a secretive expression on his face. In the middle of the table in his room stood a covered object, which he roguishly revealed. There sat the bullfinch with his red, glossy breast, balancing on his perch.

'It seems to be moping; I hope it's not ill,' said Amalie, when the bird still did not stir, despite the loud exclamations all around. 'Whistle to it, Adolf!'

Adolf whistled and held out some sugar. But the Dean's keen eyes were not fooled. He took out the stuffed bird and showed them the swindle, and at that point little Ada burst into such boundless, deafening transports of joy that they all had to join in, whether they wanted to or not. Sofie was standing deep in thought over by the window. She was wondering whether this noisy happiness really stemmed from childish, naive pleasure at an offence made good, or whether there was something of a little devil behind it. When she looked up, her eyes met Rein's, which were fastened upon her with a peculiar, sad expression.

Ada loved splendour — her clothes were never beautiful enough. She loathed all that was plain, shabby or ugly. Unlike other children, she did not like to frolic among the servants and to entertain herself with their occupations. The haughty little girl never spoke to the poor children who daily received instruction at the farm. It was impossible to predict how this aspect of her character would develop in time, but for the moment, in this daughter the Dean was not promised any particular support for his philanthropic endeavours.

When Ada was not allowed to be inside with the grown-ups, whose conversation she monitored far too closely, she played outside in the most secluded part of the garden. Her favourite spot was underneath a row of nut bushes, where she looked for nuts among the fallen leaves. Solitary ramblers might, for a long time, hear a mysterious rustling, and then an elf suddenly shot out from under the bush, so dainty and frail and ethereal that fright would give way to admiration.

On the last evening before their departure, just at sunset, the Dean and his guests were returning from a walk. On the green slope behind the house, they met the little goose girl, who was crying bitterly because Ada had chased all the chickens away and refused to tell where they were.

Right then and there, Ada was sentenced to ask little Stine's pardon and not to come inside until she had restored the fugitives. Everybody had already, half in jest and half in earnest, fallen into the habit of turning to Sofie, who now suddenly had the idea that they should take little Stine inside and dress her in Ada's clothes, and then Ada could mind the geese in her place. This threat, so well calculated on the basis of little Ada's vanity, was carried out in jest. A moment later, Lina came rushing inside and shouted that Ada had pulled off her shoes and stockings and was standing out in the middle of the pond.

Ada had taken too literally the punishment that had been meted out to her. With her dress hitched up and her sleeves rolled, she had wandered, just as she had seen Stine do, a little distance into the pond, which fortunately was not deep. There she stood, laughing, with the food bowl under her arm, tossing the grain about. All around her, the entire screaming flock of poultry were fighting, in no way appearing to disdain what was being offered them in such an unaccustomed manner. Ada's cheeks were aglow, and her hair was blowing in the wind. The last slanted rays of sunshine were just then gliding across the pond, illuminating the scene. The whole thing looked like something taken from a fantastic fairytale. But now the calling and cajoling began — scolding mingled with endearments in the oddest way. Ada laughed and took another step farther into the pond. Not until Stine appeared in her usual clothes did she run ashore, where Dorthe swept her up in her arms and carried her inside.

Ada was immediately put to bed, and Sofie helped rub her cold little feet warm again. She reproached herself in a thousand ways for having, by her jest, driven the excitable child to such a game. Her uneasiness forced her to look in on the little girl yet one more time. Ada was asleep with bright red cheeks, laughing in her sleep and moving her lips. Relieved, Sofie went upstairs to her bedroom, where she still had a lot to do before their departure the next day.

At five o'clock in the morning, there was already much commotion in the house. Little Ada had been taken ill. Around midnight she had awakened, burning hot and thirsty, and now she was lying there with chattering teeth. The doctor had been sent for, but he could not be expected to arrive until well into the morning.

The doctor arrived and assured them that the little girl's illness was a fever that would soon pass. Reassured, the Dean again turned his attention to his guests, who were just about to leave him. The carriage had been taken out. But now a critical moment arrived to which nobody had given any thought — Sofie's farewell to Ada. The doctor, forbidding everything that might upset his patient, wanted Sofie to leave without saying goodbye. Everybody was dressed and ready for departure when the doctor came hurrying back with a concerned expression. His little patient had been crying and demanding to see Sofie, and he, who had not been familiar with the child's tempestuous temperament, had thought that he could calm her down by saying that she had already left. But then Ada had burst into such violent sorrow that he had finally been forced to concede the truth. He now asked Sofie to go inside and comfort her little friend — Ada's present excited state might have the gravest consequences. A silence followed those words. Everybody stood about not knowing what to do. When Sofie looked up, her eyes again met Rein's, which were resting on her with an indescribable expression, as if he were begging her for his child's life. She hesitated no longer. With a swift movement, she pulled her parents aside, and they soon came to an agreement.

The two sisters were to stay behind until the patient was strong enough to tolerate the separation.

The elder Ramms and Brøcher left. The sisters stayed. Towards evening, the child's condition worsened. The doctor looked concerned, and Sofie thanked God that she had not gone away.

A melancholy period now ensued on the farm that had recently witnessed so much joy. For six days, little Ada was hovering on the brink of death. As if nature empathized with the conditions inside, inclement autumn weather succeeded the glorious days they had enjoyed before. A piercing wind from the south was incessantly lashing the rain against the windows.

To Sofie, these were strange, urgent, sobering days, during which she suddenly glimpsed the true countenance of life behind its mask. Almost unnoticeably, her own grief assumed second place; she dared not measure it against the father's pale, mute dread. She began to have an inkling that there might be something to live for besides the fulfilment of selfish happiness — and by selfish happiness she meant the courage to suffer the pains and vagaries of life with and for one's beloved.

Perhaps this happiness has to be crushed in us in order to teach us that outside this little circle, as well, there are suffering people for whom one might live. How dry and forbidding this tenet had appeared to Sofie up

257

to this time! For the first time, this thought struck her in a gentle, almost comforting manner. She accepted it as a sign from Heaven that, young and inexperienced though she was, she had been asked to play the part of a mother, and she entered into the challenge with virginal eagerness; with all that was deep and intense in her soul. If she had not sufficiently reciprocated little Ada's love before, because it had seemed too fierce, she now felt as if she could gladly lay down her life for the child. Alas, when she saw Ada lying there so weak; not looking at her, just with a supplicating stare of pain; insensitive to her caresses; scarcely recognizing her — oh, then it seemed to her that she had always loved this child, and that she could never cease loving it. Tirelessly she stayed by Ada's bedside, and she finally succeeded in taking upon herself all the daily care that had ordinarily fallen on Dorthe. The old woman was not aware of the change, because Sofie had a way of accomplishing it that let Dorthe believe the young girl was merely acting according to her instructions.

Plain, ordinary people are no good at nursing the sick. They lack something for which the best and most affectionate willingness is no substitute, and that is culture. They see the sick person merely as a disturbed machine, which by certain mechanical means can be brought to function normally again. They know neither common sense nor moderation. The concept of 'not too much' does not exist for them, and any demand for such moderation by the patient is, in their eyes, merely the sort of whim one might expect from a sick person; to be borne with condescending patience. Therefore, since they are not guided by any spiritual knowledge of the sufferer, and they rarely have any concept of the nature of the illness, any assistance they give is apt to turn into as many mistakes.

Oh, if you have ever been lying helplessly at the mercy of that sort of care, you will remember how these splendid creatures can torment you and torture you; how they seem to possess an almost diabolical ability to divine your wishes just so they can act exactly contrary to them. Can you remember how they would always wake you up just when sleep had finally taken pity on you and embraced you, and how they would always seem to fall asleep just when fear was keeping you awake? How they would bring something to a full boil when it was supposed to be heated only a little; or how, in attempting to cool a drink, they would return it to you ice-cold? Do you remember how jarring their voices could be; how intolerable their every touch!

Only a refined and tender spirit knows how to nurse the sick. Inspiration is what is called for. No man, and no uneducated woman — even if she be a mother — can do it *properly*, by entering into the life and thoughts of the sick person in such a way that they become almost the embodiment of the patient's will. Such a nurse seems only to live for the patient's caprices, while she nevertheless serves only common sense. In short, she knows how to treat the body through the soul.

Old Dorthe tormented Ada with loving questions. She wanted to force her to recognize her, to understand her. She exhausted Ada with desperate and vain attempts at getting her to take her medicine. Sofie had another inspiration. When her pleading was to no avail, she herself took the full spoon, and the patient automatically copied her. Every time Ada was to take her medicine, Sofie would also swallow the obnoxious drink. Sofie felt that she was indispensable, and so did the old doctor. With no actual, spoken agreement between them, these two took turns, so that one or the other was always present in the sickroom. In vain did Amalie beg her sister to allow herself some rest and to let Amalie keep watch for the night instead.

In this manner, the morning of the sixth day arrived. Ada was very poorly. The doctor had prepared her father for the possibility that there might be no further hope. It seemed unlikely that she would survive another night. Everybody stood gathered around the child's bed, silent and pale. The sinister quiet of hopelessness had taken the place of former activity.

Evening came, and the symptoms changed. The doctor told only Sofie about this, however, because he wanted to be certain before raising what might be false hopes.

It was so quiet in the sickroom. Midnight had come and gone. Only two people were watching over the small child — the doctor and Sofie. Silently, scarcely breathing, they kept close watch over every one of the sick child's movements. The light from the lamp fell upon this group, while by the opposite wall, the table with its multitude of objects formed a strange shadow-kingdom of its own. The large flower pot in the middle stretched its giant tree towards the ceiling, and in its shadow were a whole monk's choir of squat bottles and medicine glasses. Lina's doll desperately stretched both arms towards the sky. Now and then, a sound escaped this world of shadows like a groan, a feeble human cry. It came from old Dorthe, who was sitting in the big reclining chair over in the corner, rocking her head and emitting heartbreaking sighs. A couple of times her head fell helplessly down in a nodding movement, which showed that fatigue was battling sorrow for supremacy over the good old soul. A muffled cry did not disturb her. The cry had come from Sofie when Ada reached out her hand and smiled at her.

Meanwhile, the poor father was pacing up and down in his lonely room, trying to prepare himself for the painful blow that he thought was inevitable. 'Oh Lord, it is all over!' he sighed. 'Give me strength, oh Lord, so that I will be able to say: "Thy will be done!" . . . Oh, I cannot yet. . . .' He was wringing his hands.

Then he heard the doctor's footsteps outside, but he did not see the doctor's radiant face.

Rein entered the nursery scarcely an hour later. The sight that met him there made him pause for a moment. By the light of the lamp, he saw Sofie in a half-kneeling position before the bed. On her right arm, which was stretched out across the bed, the sick child was resting her head, apparently deep in a sweet sleep.

Sofie's immobility despite her cramped and painful position would have appeared stranger still to any spectator who was colder and less moved by the moment than Rein. Even the look that Sofie fastened on him was staring and immobile. In her white nightdress, she looked like one of those marble spirits a benign symbolism of death may show at the point of carrying off a victim.

The young girl had arrived at the critical point in which fatigue finally gains the upper hand as the spiritual tension suddenly relaxes. She was in that strange, ambiguous state in which conscious thought has already torn itself loose and is floating around on its own, while the senses still remain fixed in reality and distinguish everything in the surroundings with almost painful clarity. Sofie watched Rein approaching. She saw his mute look of thanks towards Heaven. She heard the slow, easy breathing of the sick child, but everything gave rise to the oddest associations. It seemed to her that her own life had escaped to the child, so that if she now stirred or even blinked an eye, the little one must die.

It was so quiet in the sickroom. Dorthe was sleeping heavily over in the corner. The wind was beating with tired wings against the window panes; it, too, was exhausted.

For how long she had remained like this, whether a minute or an hour, Sofie did not know. Then she heard as if from far away the distinct words spoken by an unsteady, resonant, familiar voice: 'Sofie, can you leave this child? . . . No, no, you cannot. . . . Oh, stay with us . . . forever.'

The young girl was listening.

'Do you understand what I mean?' the voice said, nearer to her. 'Sofie, be this child's mother. . . . Be my wife . . . my wife, everything, everything to us.'

Sofie had jumped up. With open eyes she stared about the room. She was alone.

It was so quiet in the sickroom. Dorthe was sound asleep in her corner, while the child was slumbering calmly on her pillow as before.

'Was it a dream?' she whispered.

Eight days later, there was another departure from the parsonage. Two vehicles were standing before the door. One was a trap, which had been sent in order to convey Amalie home. The other was the Dean's small, one-horse carriage, which was to take Sofie in the opposite direction, to her sister Louise, who lived at a distance of yet another day's journey to the south. Dressed in her travelling clothes, Sofie stepped into the nursery for the last time in order to say goodbye to Ada. She found the little convalescent sitting up in bed, surrounded by all her old toys, which all of a sudden were back in favour and which had never given her as much pleasure as they now did. Her illness had subdued the impetuousness of this child. She was gentle and quite resigned to the impending separation. Sofie just had to promise her for the tenth time that she would stop and spend a few days with them on her return journey.

Wistfully, Sofie looked around the room that was so brightly lit by sunshine — the room that once had been so dark, so laden with anxiety. She thought back on those hours she had spent there, right up to the last, strange — dream? — Yes, it must have been a dream. . . . Nothing that had happened subsequently had undone her conviction that the voice in the night had been just a trick played on her by her imagination. The following days had gone by with their usual smoothness. She had allowed herself to be cosseted in every way by Dorthe; she had slept late in the mornings, read and gone for walks — when she was not with Ada, talking with her, singing to her, or telling her fairytales.

In the long corridor outside the nursery, she encountered Rein. He took her by the hand and led her through the empty rooms into one of the innermost chambers, where all sound was muffled by a soft carpet.

She had not even had time to be surprised when she found herself seated in the big easy-chair in the Bishop's room. She watched the Dean take a stool and sit down facing her.

'Before you leave, I owe you an explanation,' the Dean said. 'You must not leave us with an uncertain impression. Sofie . . . the night when Ada recovered, I spoke words to you that I should like to take back . . . if possible. I made a confession to you. . . .'

There are situations in daily life, peaceful, sunny situations, in which the bravest may feel courage ebbing away, and in which it would be infinitely welcome if the walls would collapse or lightning would strike the roof. The worthy man who now sat facing Sofie, was in just such a situation. He coughed in order to hide the deep sigh designed to unburden his bosom; he glanced towards the door as if he expected an interruption. But no interruption came. The room was so quiet, so blissfully quiet — it was just made for a confidential, undisturbed announcement. The low autumn sun was peeping through the green curtains, its rays making the pastoral scenes on the wall seem alive. The only audible sound came from a big fly that, having already once succumbed to the suspension of life for the winter, had woken up again and was buzzing against the windows as if drunk with the heat of the sun.

Rein had jumped up and was pacing up and down the room with the liveliness of a young man. This put the Mandarin on his pedestal into motion, and it seemed as if he were mockingly trying to nod the Dean into fresh courage.

The Dean sat down and pulled his seat closer to Sofie's. In a voice that had gradually recovered its composure, he then went on, 'You see, Sofie, I was so carried away at that moment when God gave my child back to me. Joy made me weak, and I revealed something which — you must believe me — I had been determined not to say. Have I frightened you? Will you forgive me? . . . Will you forgive me when I tell you that it was not a fleeting emotion, produced by the exaltation of the moment, but a long-suppressed, serious feeling, against which I have had to pit all my mental powers! Please listen to what I have to say in my defence. My visit to your parents this summer was not entirely without design. I was looking for a wife, the way a man my age would go about it, calmly and deliberately. I knew that my old and never-forgotten friends from youth had a grown daughter still at home, somewhat past her first youth. Perhaps, I thought, she might have some qualities that suit me; perhaps I might succeed in winning her! A quirk of fate arranged it so that you, Sofie, were the only person at home. Because I had it fixed in my mind that the youngest daughter was still a child, I took you to be the eldest. This was already bad enough. However, I took the consequences of my mistake. You know that I was refused by Amalie. But what you do not know is that I was thinking of you and continued to be haunted by those thoughts when I returned home to my solitude. I was thinking of you without hope, without desire, without a sense of loss, I may say — much as one thinks about some beautiful experience. With the greatest pleasure did I see you again. Oh, who can say how temptation nevertheless managed to steal its way in! . . . The quiet admiration you awakened in me, and the seriousness that is so evident in everything you say and do, many a time allowed me to forget the difference in our ages. Then, at such moments . . . however, we will not speak of that! . . . My mind always managed to subdue such notions. In this way, the last day arrived; my decision was absolute. Tell me yourself whether I didn't remain true to it, until the moment came when you were about to leave!

'But you did not leave. You remained, and temptation was to be revived under a different guise. I saw you so faithful, so tender, so completely forgetful of yourself while nursing a sick child — *my* child. At such a moment, I forgot all my good intentions. Heaven be my witness that I did not see in you the beautiful young girl, but the person who was closest to me of anyone; who was joined with me in one hope, one sorrow; and who was at that moment sharing my joy. My words were an exclamation of happiness.

'And now, my young friend, I have made you my confession. It has given me relief, because I know that henceforth my feelings for you will flow along calmly and naturally, as becomes a fatherly friend. Don't forget, Sofie, that I am your friend, and that I don't desire anything else. I'll follow your progress through life with the most heartfelt interest. Pray God that happiness be your companion! But if that, which I so ardently desire, turns out not to be the case; if the world should turn against you, then you know, Sofie, that you have a home here that will also be your sister's. Come to us if you are sad. If we cannot offer you happiness, you will at least find peace here. And now, God bless you!' he said, getting up. 'I cannot thank you enough for what you have been to my child! . . . Come now, don't torment yourself with an answer. Is it not so, Sofie, that you will remember that I am your *friend*, and that you will come and visit us as before?'

Admonishing Sofie not to reply was quite superfluous. What could she say? Surprise, shyness and confusion tied her tongue, but her tearful eyes were speaking for her. She made a movement as if she wanted to throw herself around his neck, but he seized both her hands and kissed her on the brow.

'Come now, come; I have detained you far too long. . . Have you said goodbye to Ada? Has your suitcase been carried down? . . . Farewell, farewell!'

* * *

Several days have passed. In a small, extremely drab living room we find two young ladies. It is just the twilight hour, when the trivialities of the day slow their creaking windmill arms and hearts unfold — the only proper illumination for confessions: just dark enough so that one may hide one's own fearfulness and blushing, and just light enough to conjure up in the other's countenance exactly the expression one needs.

Such a confession must already have taken place. One of the two women, the young girl, looked exhausted with crying. She was sagging against the corner of the sofa in such a slumped-over position that it seemed she had difficulty in keeping herself upright.

It is impossible to say whether the other woman, who was sitting on the chair in front of the young girl with her back against the window, had ever been pretty. She certainly was not so any longer; she did not wish to be. Her dress and her bearing were in every way reminiscent of those women who have forgotten that they have an exterior. Like one of those ugly slipcovers with which domestic economy insists on hiding a beautiful piece of furniture, a cap of a most unbecoming style and of rather doubtful whiteness covered a profusion of glossy, brown hair. Her apron, that most tasteless of all feminine ornaments — one with red stripes, at that, the motley-coloured silk kerchief pinned across her chest, and a rumpled calico dress completed the impression. Compared with the elegant creature sitting across from her — elegant despite her simplicity — the older woman looked like a servant girl. It was possible to make this mistake only for as long as she remained silent, however. A pause had just occurred, during which they both seemed to be contemplating the subject of their discussion. Whoever heard Mrs Caspers, the former Louise Ramm, speak, would willingly ask her pardon for having mistaken her for a servant. Her voice was melodious, although occasionally sharp, and its rapidly fluctuating modulation was further underscored by the lively gestures of her small, extremely well-shaped hand, which appeared to have seen better days. Furthermore, her language was cultivated and confident, without the least trace of dialect. As for her manner of expressing herself, it is best left to speak for itself. Such expressions from the lips of a lady may either proclaim mental superiority or warn us of an deep and nameless inner misery.

'So he was cruel to you, my poor little sister,' she said, as if speaking to herself. 'How did it happen, did you say? I suppose he found out about it too soon. You didn't know, did you, that *coldness* is the glue with which one captures that sort of birds.'

'Louise!'

'No, no, I am far from wanting to say anything bad about you. Rather I ought to berate nature for not teaching us that trick right away. You haven't been able to dissimulate, that's the trouble.'

'And you really believe, Louise, that I've been weak and incautious? How can I convince you that that is unjust? I assure you that I have not been what you call incautious. I'm not claiming any credit for that; as you know, it's part of my nature. I have rather good command of myself.'

'Oh well, I believe you; I believe you. You were on your guard right from the first moment. You knew how to find the difficult middle ground between a too-obvious coldness and an emotion that threatens to run away with us at any moment. I'd be very glad to believe all that, but there are still a lot of points in this story that need explanation, as far as I am concerned. You, who are so shy and suspicious, could really allow yourself to be caught by his glib and pretty phrases about showing *courage* and meeting him half-way; about feminine cowardice, etc.! And you really believed that?'

'Oh no, no, Louise,' Sofie interrupted her somewhat more impetuously than before, 'those were not glib phrases! You are mistaken in that as well! Oh, if only I could explain it to you in the right way? . . . He really *meant* it. Nothing can deprive me of that conviction; he meant it. During our long conversations earlier this summer, while we were still quite calm in our relationship with each other, I heard him express himself about these things without disguise and with such conviction! He was excited about a new concept of femininity that would make everybody happier, and he tried to make me understand it as well. Alas, he touched strings that were all too familiar. I felt so brave; I thought that if I ever found myself in such a position, I would act in accordance with this concept; I would be more honest and natural than all the others. But when all was said and done, I was nevertheless so cowardly, so cowardly. . . .'

'And yet this passionate outburst by the cave?' Louise interjected, in a sharp tone of voice.

Sofie silently lowered her head.

'Oh dear, that's just what I'm saying,' the elder sister continued. 'Honesty and naturalness! A blissful new concept of femininity! Bah! Big words! It won't be in *our* time that such things become reality! A lot of evil, a lot of old misery must be sweated out before that can happen. Having some swelled, immature head fantasizing about it doesn't lead to anything. He *meant* it, you say? That may well be, but that doesn't excuse him in my eyes. You are too good to serve as a guinea pig for new ideas. After all, he has taken advantage of your weakness and pushed you past your limits. For, believe, me, a marten that kills three times as much as it can eat, lusts no more for blood than a man's vanity lusts for such victories. You have just been a very ordinary victim of the latter. He has loved his own pretty theories, not *you*, poor Sofie.'

Sofie, who a couple of times had opened her lips as if to protest, was silenced by those last words. In their naked clarity, they certainly expressed the very essence of her deepest suffering. Her sister was quite aware of the impression her words had made, and she repeated, with an attempt at softening her voice,

'Forget it all. God bless you, don't brood over it any longer. This whole story is nothing more than a simple and, unfortunately, quite common introduction to your life, which only now is about to start. We will not talk about it any more, do you hear? From now on, you are to have other thoughts, other interests. I'm sure we'll think of some remedy. Marry Dean Rein!'

Sofie looked at her doubtfully, as if uncertain that she had heard right.

'I seriously advise you to accept the Dean's offer.'

'Do you really mean that! You advise me to do that, you who. . . .'

'You who — just say it — you who yourself suffered an attachment that had to be discarded before you bowed to the yoke. Wasn't that what you meant? Listen, sister, I'm going to tell you something. Mark my words well. As young girls, we all construe for ourselves some strange, extremely onesided notions about happiness. There is only one happiness: to be married to the one we love. There is only one misfortune, and that is, naturally, not to get him. There is something quite touching about this. Our hearts are still so delicate and pure, so romantic, so full of heavenly imprudence, so absolutely unfit for any worldly calculation. No wonder, therefore, that our hearts flinch at the thought of a union — and, merciful Heaven, what a union! — with anyone else but *him*, the *one and only*. It seems like sacrilege or suicide, doesn't it? . . . Yes, it is a strange business, this first love of ours. One really might suppose that God had intended it for some use when he sealed it, strong and warm, in our bosom, and that it was put there to accomplish something great and good and not to be torn off, like some unseasonal fruit, from our tree of life. It never suffers any other fate. . . . To be married to the one we love! — What luxury! What heaven-defying demands! No, my girl, we never were intended to have this kind of advance on celestial bliss; to possess it, ripe and ready, here below. This has been seen to. Men rightly consider it an invasion of their rights. Therefore, it has long since been arranged differently. If we were to get the one we like, where would those men who are ugly and unprepossessing get their wives? Now, as you know, there is nobody so miserable of body and soul that he cannot get a wife, and a rather passable one at that. No, it simply cannot be otherwise. That would disturb the cosmic order. Just draw a line through this entire first, sensitive chapter of your life. Happiness for us is that the man who desires us does not *repel* us too much; that he is a good man, just an ordinary, *decent* man, do you hear, and that he can protect us from want. And if you want to know what *misfortune* is,' she said, suddenly lowering her voice and bending towards Sofie's ear, 'I'll certainly tell you a little about that on occasion.'

Sofie shuddered.

'You see, Sofie dear, if your are reasonable in your demands, a simple little calculation will make you realize that an offer from such a man as Dean Rein is not only good luck, but abnormally good luck.'

'Rein! No, you cannot mean it. And you forget that he has given up all thought of me. He has assured me that from now on, he regards me the way he did before, . . . as. . . .'

'A father, a friend, I suppose?'

'You don't believe it, Louise?'

'I believe,' said Louise, forcing back a smile that was playing around her sunken eyes, 'that he is a very modest man, a wise man. He did not want to frighten you, and in that he has acted well. However, as far as his friendship and paternal feelings are concerned, just leave those to me. I can guarantee you that they will constitute no obstacle at all, should you on some suitable occasion let him understand that you are a sensible girl who has considered the matter and found that so many real advantages could easily make up for a trifling difference in age.'

'What? I myself should — ?'

'Tell me one thing. What do you think of the Dean? Say it without any beating around the bush.'

'Of course you know I think well of him, *extremely* well. As you know, I already wrote and told you so this summer. Since that time, I've been to his house. It was so pleasant to be there; everything was so attractive and well-ordered. There was just the sort of peace that we to some degree lack at home. I thought Amalie was lucky because she was to live there and see this gentle, friendly man every day. Now *that* is a thing of the past; I don't think I'll ever go there again.'

'You think extremely well of him; you envy Amalie the luck of living in his house! But in Heaven's name, what more do you want, you ungrateful child!'

'Nothing, Louise. I want nothing more in this world. Why should I! My instinct rebels against it; there are no external circumstances that make it necessary. Why do I have to be married?'

'Because it's something that has to happen sooner or later. Certainly I have explained to you that there can be no question of choice in accordance with our own minds, and after this day you'll be less able than ever to make such a choice. For God's sake, put it entirely out of your head. Mothers are right in this matter; it's just that they preach too much about it. They make us see the business as worse than it really is, or else they try to coat the pill; they help us imagine that a real inclination exists. I don't want to do that, Sofie; I'm merely appealing to your understanding. Believe me, our situation in life is purely a matter of luck; a game of chance. However, in those games where the biggest prizes are set out as bait, the prizes are never handed out. Don't go after them with the greed of a fortune hunter. If fate offers you a reasonably decent chance, then grab it — grab it while there is still time. There's something safe about such a chance that the mourned-over happiness doesn't have, because it bases its calculation upon one thing only: love. Love is supposed to make you happy and good; in spite of everything, it's supposed to smooth out all roughness, clear the way for everything, suffer all deprivation — dear God, it's supposed to do so much, that poor love, just given the opportunity! . . . But where the heart is not engaged, you make your calculations with greater certainty. You may weigh all the advantages carefully on the scale. Take his position, his good income, the reputation he enjoys, his tolerable family connections. . . . Don't think that any of this is unimportant. Call this happiness! Fresh courage, my girl! Youth soon passes, and with it these anxieties of the heart. . . . Once you've got the better of them, you've won the game; then you'll have all those tangible advantages when old age comes! . . . Do you know what *unhappiness* is?' she asked with such suddenness that Sofie almost felt as if she had been struck. 'Look at me. Do you remember what I was like when I was living at home, Sofie? You think, perhaps, that I've changed?'

A pained, almost shy glance at her sister's hard, sharp features was the reply. Perhaps this look stirred a memory. The bitter irony that had been quivering over Louise's face vanished, and she repeated sorrowfully:

'You were fond of me then. Isn't it true that I was gentle and good? I had the sort of gentleness that seems sufficient for a lifetime. Sofie, have you ever noticed a field of wheat, with heads newly formed, rippling in a soft wind? Each single head is so delicate and silky and glistening. The blue cornflowers are scattered among them as if the wheat were not sufficiently beautiful without this extra adornment. My soul was like that once. Have you seen that same wheat field when it has been mowed down in the autumn and the sharp stubble is left? Do you know what it means to have a husband *unworthy of respect*, and what it's like to suffer deprivation with him? . . . Oh, you young girls, you think it's so easy. You always think of misfortune as something romantic; you fancy yourselves so resigned and so elevated by it. But I can tell you that the most dreadful aspect of misfortune is the destruction it causes to our innermost being. The woman who can neither love nor respect the man she is tied to, little by little loses her self-respect. I don't mean that she becomes scum herself — it's possible for her to remain a respectable person. But that which is best and finest in us, that which constitutes — what shall I call it! — the *perfume* and *sweetness* of our being, its *graciousness*, that goes under. May all the powers of Mercy protect you from this misfortune! Choose whatever else you want in life; live alone and

269

abandoned; live as a thrall; beg for your sustenance—but don't let anyone force disgrace upon you.'

'Force!' Sofie's lips scarcely breathed the word. She was paralysed by what she had just heard. 'Oh, you were not forced . . . .'

'If by "forced" you mean that I was threatened, no, then I was not forced. I wasn't maltreated, nor dragged to the altar like that unhappy Great Aunt Regina whom Mother told us about, who then played them the trick of going mad afterwards and ending in an asylum. No, that wasn't quite what happened to me. However, you can have no idea of the imperceptible, but steady erosion the daily droplet of persuasion causes in a young and impressionable understanding and in a mind still soft as wax, or of how cleverly every little circumstance can be made to serve the purpose. I remember, for example, that in order to overcome a certain unpleasant impression on my part, Mother always expounded to me on how neatness and propriety were of no great significance in a man — indeed, they might even indicate great inner shortcomings. . . . My spouse was a slob then, just as he is now, and I assume you remember that I very much wanted to be neat and attractive.'

Here Sofie blushed; she recalled that whenever the conversation turned to Kold, her mother had singled out precisely the opposite quality as an advantage.

'In the end, I really did think that a gentleman who was concerned with his appearance must be either a pedant or a fool. And so it was with many other things as well. My aversion was disarmed before I could rally to my own defence. When a poor girl then gives her consent, she's said to have done it of her own free will and to have caused her own misfortune, if it comes. Those who counselled her are not responsible. Oh, my parents will have to account before God for this!'

'Louise, don't say these things! . . . Don't speak so harshly! Oh dear, dear Louise! . . . Surely Mother meant well, and if she knew, if she had any idea of how unhappy you are now. . . . Oh, it would break her heart!'

'Do you think so?'

'And Father, he surely took no part in all this, did he? He didn't advise you to do it, or try in any way to bring it about?'

'He didn't prevent it, he *allowed* it,' said Louise darkly. 'Can you tell me, then, what kind of madness it is that so often possesses parents when they are about to marry off their daughters? It's as if even the best among them lose all reason. They are worse than those savages who can hardly wait to exchange their gold and sandalwood for European Nürenberger trash. Even if they have only one daughter, who is their comfort and joy, they gladly send her to Tranquebar; they submit to every kind of deprivation, to never seeing her again, just for the pleasure of knowing that she's sitting around somewhere on the Coromandel Coast . . . under the name of "my daughter, Mrs So-and-So"! . . . Sofie, there are aspects of our lives it will not do to dwell upon too long. It's a good thing that so few people do. We, who are born the equals of men in the list of God's creatures; who are just as noble and just as well endowed; and who are untouched by men's vices — we are nevertheless held in peculiarly low esteem for as long as we are subjected to their scrutiny and rejection. It's possible that elsewhere money balances this unequal relationship, but in this country, where the daughters as a general rule have no property of their own, they are not much better off than merchandise that can't be sold fast enough, which is pushed to the front and tagged and handled and which the merchant would rather sell at half price than retain on his shelves. . . . In keeping with this system, I was sacrificed after Maria. I suppose you hardly remember Maria?'

'She was tall and slender; she looked like Amalie. . .'

'Amalie! The lovely, quiet, serious Maria! Yes, as much as a genuine pearl looks like one made of wax. I was still so young that there was no hurry about me. . . . But Maria had reached the age of twenty-five — a terrible calamity! — without any prospect of an engagement. And then she, who was worthy of a king, was wasted on *Broch*, that dry old stick — such a boundlessly, hopelessly narrow-minded Peter Nitpicker. Unfortunately, he obtained a small living in Nordfjord, and, feeling self-important because of this appointment, he embarked upon a ridiculous courtship, which ended with poor Maria's assenting to the bargain. Once in Nordfjord, Broch took it into his head to become a Pietist, and, since no pleasures existed that he could forbid his wife, he forbade her to read a good book on Sunday, unless it was godly. Maria wasn't able to endure it for long. She had no children, and within three years she was bored to death — or, as it said in her obituary: "She expired in devotion to her God after a debilitation of long duration." She withered like a plant in a botanist's case, that's what she did. Maria had Father's pious, patient spirit. . . . But I, Sofie, I am more like Mother. I cannot die that easily. . . . I can only. . . .'

She fell silent, and with an indescribable expression of grief — grief for herself — she buried her face in her hands.

Sofie was unable to say a word. She moved closer and flung her arms around her sister. At this movement, Louise looked up and exclaimed as if frightened: 'Oh, what have I said! How did I come to tell you all this! . . . Those aren't proper things for you to hear! . . . Believe me, it was not my intention. It was *your* destiny we were talking about. You were standing at the same crossroads where I had once stood, and then . . . and then. . . .'

'Just talk, talk, if that can ease your mind,' said Sofie. 'Oh, Louise, that is precisely your great wrong, that you didn't speak up sooner. You have sinned against yourself, against your parents and your siblings, by never confiding in us. You didn't want to write; you didn't come to visit us. . . .'

'And whatever for? What business had I at home? To whimper and complain? I was to go home and place this terrible grief upon you all?'

'Oh, you wouldn't have needed to complain. Should we not have been able to share your grief regardless? You would have noticed it in everything, in our tenderness towards you, in our efforts to cheer you up. Oh, we should have been so good, so good to you!'

'Poor sister. You would, certainly. I did go home once, as you know. It was three years later, and I was neither happy nor pretty any more. Sofie, only the attractive, happy children are welcomed home. Wherever I went, I noticed that this was no longer the case with me. That is just the way things are. The same world that sacrifices us in cold blood, later asks us with wondering criticism why we aren't happy. Neither Father nor Mother would have the strength to bear my unhappiness in all its nakedness. Mother, above all, needs to fancy me happy. That's why I write brief and dry letters — I would rather be considered an unloving daughter than have to dissemble. I have done even more than that. When Father was here for a visit, I pretended that I was pleased and contented. I had only one aim, and that was to shield his eyes from this vale of tears. . . . Do you think I am not homesick? Many a time, when I just step outside to draw a breath of fresh air, I find myself walking down the road as eagerly as a pilgrim, bareheaded in the cold and dark — it makes no difference. And then it seems to me that I must keep walking and walking until I come to my father's farm, to the place where I used to sing and laugh, and where I never had a bitter thought. . . . How is Father, Sofie?

You haven't told me enough about him! Oh, tell me more! Does he still come down the stairs so softly and open the door so quietly that people scarcely notice his entrance? Is he growing bald, or does he still have his handsome grey locks? Do you know what I dream of so often? That I am sitting on his knee, like in the old days, and that I'm kissing his hands and his grey hair, and his eyes are looking at me so lovingly! If only I could . . . I could . . . I could just once. . . .'

Her voice failed her, and she burst into spasms of crying.

Poor Sofie again found herself on the spot. Scarcely had she escaped from one difficult situation, but she found herself in another. She had sought refuge with her sister, hoping to find comfort, and she found herself confronting someone inconsolable. Indeed, their parts had been reversed so thoroughly that she forgot how their conversation had started. She had been listening to Louise's almost involuntary outbursts with the most conflicting emotions. Painful sympathy, aversion and fear mingled with surprise at the metamorphosis that had taken place in Louise. In her memory, Louise remained a gentle, joyful creature who with happy unconcern and innocent coquetry enjoyed the homage paid her wherever she went. In those days, there was no evidence of any particular tendencies of spirit or character. She had been lovely and captivating; more was not known about her, nor do people ask more where a young girl is concerned. She is supposed to be a *mystery*, otherwise she is not a young girl. Oh, how dreadfully life may provide the answer to this mystery! What possibilities may lie hidden underneath this beautiful veil of youth? What demonic tendencies, what superb talents for being unhappy or for making others unhappy? Look at that young girl! She is so bashful, so silent, so sweet. Perhaps too *silent*, you may say. Alas! Rejoice in it, but do not be angry with her, or surprised, if you see her again a few years later as an importunate gossip or a bitter, malicious old Sibyl. Do not ask of any young girl what she wants to become; ask that of her destiny, of those hands into which she is about to fall.

Was this the Louise of those days speaking? What notions! What a language! Yet, in the midst of its ruthless, energetic bitterness, this language had the force of truth, affecting the younger sister against her will. There was not time for her to notice words and to take umbrage at them. She looked in horror through each one of those words, down to the bottom of a soul that seemed devoid of all poetry, all hope, all faith. But Sofie was so young. She did not comprehend a misfortune that could produce such devastating effects, and in the consciousness of her own inability to help, she remained silent, almost unsympathetic.

But now Louise was crying. At the sight of her tears, the young girl suddenly regained her power of speech. She fell to her knees in front of her sister, letting her heart overflow with affectionate words. Louise listened for a while in the dreamy silence with which one hears the twittering of birds. She lost herself in the contemplation of that lovely face, which in the indistinct light seemed to belong to a merciful angel that had descended in order to hear her distress. Her tears were flowing more gently. Suddenly, she pushed Sofie away and remained seated for a few seconds more, listening in tense anxiety. Sofie's ear had as yet caught no sound when Louise exclaimed: 'Leave, leave! It's *him* !'

The sound of a cart rolling across the yard, followed by a whistle and the sharp crack of a whip, announced that the attorney was returning from one of his trips around the district.

* * *

In a few words, to the extent demanded by our story, we shall describe the conditions in the attorney's home. People who hinted that things were 'not all they ought to be,' agreed pretty well in one respect: they put the blame on Louise and pitied the attorney. Louise had not made herself loved in the neighbourhood. From the start, she had not found it worth her while to please anyone. He, on the other hand, was well liked. His unfailing good humour, his inexhaustible fund of jolly ideas, and his readiness to spearhead every sort of enterprise, whether for the purpose of pleasure or of something serious, made him one of those persons who are indispensable in the countryside. In addition, he was generous, and his personality might be called attractive, although he himself protested against any such description. In short, he possessed several of those qualities that are so pleasant *outside* the home, but for which a wife at home pays with a thousand-fold bitterness in her heart. This was the aspect of the man people addressed when they talked about him; this was the one thing they could explain without awkwardness. As far as his reputation was concerned, it was clear that great circumspection must be exercised. People seldom touched upon this side of him, but when it did happen, it was usually to tell about some *honest* feature or other. His reputation was neither better nor worse than that of so many others in similar situations, who share the fate attached to certain transactions: it is hard for those involved to keep their hands quite clean. It was not good; it was not bad; it was like game left hanging a little too long — one is better off not seeing it in the kitchen, but waiting until it appears on the table. Nobody could give proof of any particularly nasty streak in the attorney; indeed, by means of some clever twist it might even be possible to bring out some features that might be called noble and good.

Only one fact could not so lightly be reasoned away. People knew very well that Louise's husband squandered a large part of his irregular income on certain low connections outside the home, while he let his child, a boy of ten, look after himself without education or discipline. When this matter had been sufficiently criticized, as was only right and proper, people believed themselves all the more called upon to add, subsequent to this sacrifice on the altar of truth and morality, 'Actually it's not surprising that the poor man looks for some consolation elsewhere; who could stand seeing such a chilly, sour face around him all the time!' People needed to think as well of him as possible, because they needed him.

Only one person judged him more harshly than all the others. That was the being who in such cases either really is or wants to be the most blind, but who is the most mercilessly clearsighted when the blindfold of love is lacking.

Regardless of the experiences this one person might have had involving what most deeply concerns the soul of a proud wife, *his* uprightness and unstained character, she no longer touched this string in front of her sister. To him she *never* expressed any hint or doubt, but her bonechilling silence spoke more loudly than any criticism or complaint. Louise despised her husband.

When talking about cultivated people, 'respectability' is such a negative concept that using the word leads to an almost awkward situation. It is the given; it is the air we breathe; we only think about it when it is *lacking*. It is the imperceptible background against which graciousness shows to great advantage and captivates us, but if it wants to stop being a *background*, if it wants to be something in itself, it becomes obtrusive and unpleasant and puts graciousness to flight. Louise had all she could handle in being *respectable*. After all, she was supposed to be respectable for *two*. But gracious she was not, poor Louise. She was gloomy and dissatisfied; never was there a smile to be seen on her face.

Alas, Sofie was reminded far too often of her sister's simile about the mown field of wheat! Then she might often sigh from the bottom of her heart, 'Oh God, make me unhappy, if it be Your will, but not bitter, not like — ' she had not the heart to complete the thought.

Nor was Louise liked by her servants. They hated her for the strict industry and economy she was forced to exact from everyone, which they could not reconcile with their master's extravagant mode of living. Louise herself was completely absorbed in that restless diligence which can be so uncomfortable in a home. She was always to be seen in the attic, in the kitchen or in the weaving room. In her house, the living room was always empty and cold.

He did not seem to mind much, just so long as on the evenings he was home — and they were real exceptions — he could have his game of cards and his grog with his two indispensable friends. He did not at all seem to miss the domestic comfort which Louise took so little trouble to provide for him. One of these friends — a farmer's son, a half-educated scoundrel, crafty and of somewhat doubtful reputation — was the attorney's confidant and jack-of-all-trades. The third member of the party, an old major who was living on his pension and who was a passionate card-player, had some money. He was always the butt of the other two's jokes, if not of even worse things. The truth is that the major almost always lost — at times not inconsiderable sums. But he had the weakness that he was fond of bragging about his luck at cards, and after one of those thoroughly unlucky evenings, his friends were always made to promise that they would not give him away — a promise which they not only gave, but kept with exquisite care.

These card-playing evenings were the most insufferable of all. Louise fled as far away as she could, in order not to hear their laughter and loud witticisms, and Sofie usually found herself exiled to her own little room, where she had recourse to a little handiwork by the light of a single tallow-candle.

This was the gentle, sheltered haven to which the young girl had turned in order to find a cure for her disappointed heart. Early every morning, at four o'clock, Sofie was awakened by the clanking of a loom in a room not far from her own. This in itself would scarcely have sufficed to interrupt her sleep, because at her age people sleep wonderfully well despite sorrows, but it was Louise, her restless, unhappy sister, who was making those sounds. It was for her child Louise was working. Not even in this child, her only son, did the future seem to promise her joy. In his character, this boy was already showing a great deal of similarity to his father. Because he was left completely to his own devices, as we have already mentioned, Louise had realized with growing concern that staying at home much longer would completely ruin the boy. On her own she then made an agreement with a merchant in a small town nearby, that the boy was to live in the merchant's house and be raised as one of his own children. Louise was a very competent weaver, and since she was unable to pay the merchant in cash, she had persuaded him to accept products of her own domestic industry instead. Alas, how many thousands and thousands of times had not her fragile hands set the shuttle flying, before she reached the sum that equalled perhaps only half of what her husband had squandered the previous day or lost in a heedless transaction! How harsh, how hurried those strokes sounded, as if the poor woman gave vent through them to her bitter, impatient heart. . . . Sofie never slept from the moment the loom started up. The first few days, she had got up and gone in to see her sister, but the latter had almost roughly made her go back and forced her to lie down again as if nothing were amiss. Anyone may imagine the impression all this must make upon the young girl.

Louise, the once so graceful, beauty-loving Louise, who had seemed made for an elegant and harmonious existence — now in an environment such as this! What a bitter parody of herself she was, when she sat at her loom, dressed like a servant girl, or when a stranger entered and with an uncertain, measuring look asked for her mistress! The blame lay not only in Louise's strained financial circumstances, because contentment can imbue such circumstances with a measure of charm that lends to everything something touching that might be lacking with more *ample* means. In this, perhaps, lies the secret of what we call *cheerful comfort*. In Louise's case, straightened circumstances rejected such mellowing influences while taking pleasure in their own barren nakedness. It was an unhappiness that denied itself nothing. Sofie once took the opportunity of telling Louise, half in jest, that she ought to be more vain and dress more becomingly. 'For whom?' was the laconic answer. 'For your own sake,' Sofie wanted to say, but she sadly held her tongue when she recalled that Louise's better self no longer existed. She tried to make her own dress as plain as possible, however, in order not to contrast too sharply with her sister.

Sofie had been staying at her brother-in-law's house for about two weeks when Amalie told her in a letter that Kold had already left them. Actually, his time was not up until the end of the year — indeed, there had been an agreement of long standing that he was to spend Christmas with them. He had left right after Amalie's return home, however, due to some preparations in his plans for the future which would brook no delay. Their father had been very sorry about this. Mama as well was in a bad mood and wanted Sofie to return home.

Sofie did not feel moved to prolong her unpleasant stay at her sister's when there was no need for it. She therefore armed herself with these reasons when she told her sister, as gently as possible, that she wanted to leave before the time originally agreed upon.

'You do right in that,' Louise said, not looking up from her work.

The talk between the two sisters which we told about earlier, during which they had poured out their hearts to each other in a confidence inspired by the first warmth of their reunion, was, in a way, their last as well. After that almost involuntary outburst, Louise's mind lay dark and silent, like a volcano that had been closed off after an eruption.

One time only did their conversation again touch upon confidential subjects, but Louise remained as cold and unmoved as if their talk concerned anyone but herself.

It was again the twilight hour. Sofie had laid aside her work, but Louise had a stack of linen on the floor in front of her, from which she was busily cutting and sewing. Fearfully, Sofie spoke her tender childhood reproach that although Louise's thoughts had been with someone else, she had nevertheless been able to turn herself over to her fate so quickly and with such seeming heedlessness. She asked Louise a question about this lover from her youth.

Almost tonelessly, and without letting go of her work, Louise began, 'He was well regarded and important in his own circle, but I don't think he was actually *popular*. I was not acquainted with his real character; possibly it had great defects. . . . That is not what matters. It's not *he* who has to be examined; it's *ourselves* . It's of ourselves we must ask the question, and I have answered it for my own part: for him I *could* have lived, *would* have lived, with all my soul. We do not choose a man because *he* is the best, but because he is the one who'll bring out the best in *us*.'

'And he — did he return your affection?'

278

'He gave me every reason to think so. But I only *believed* it; I didn't *know* it. In this respect, the men are more certain than we are, because all our tinsel of lies and dissimulation actually does us very little good. It is more difficult for us to judge when affection doesn't have to play hide-and-seek, as is the case among the men. We dissimulate in order to hide affection, and they dissimulate in order to parade it, and then it's not easy to tell true from false. In other words, he was certain of me; much too certain. I returned home. . . .'

Here she paused, while she carefully measured out the linen.

'You returned home. . .?'

'Sixty-five yards — what do you get if you divide that by four?'

'Louise, you said you returned home; what then, what then?'

'Yes, I returned home, without an understanding having been reached between us. Still, I was so certain that the first letter to come into my hands would be from him. No letter came. With every week, my courage sank, and in the midst of this despair my fate crashed in over me. . . . Don't ask how such things happen. . . . Do you have the scissors?'

'Oh God, did he know anything about it?' said Sofie, mechanically handing Louise what she had in her hand. 'Could he not have been informed?'

'Oh yes, I suppose he could have, if somebody had told him. You know that I was engaged for a short time only. In a desperate moment, I wrote him a letter, but I burned it. I wrote another, but I dared not send it. I was in his power, but I didn't have the sort of omnipotent trust in him that would allow a woman to throw herself at the magnanimity of a man. Where in the world would one get such trust, anyway? He *might* have rewarded me with joy and happiness, but he might just as easily have added another humiliation to my misfortune. I didn't dare. . . Afterwards, when it was too late. . .'

'Oh God, what then?'

'Afterwards, when it was too late, I got a letter from him. — There, now I'm done.' At this, she made a cut with her scissors and ripped the linen in two with a deafening sound. Sofie inquired no more, but the hideous sound grated on her ear for a long time afterwards.

Sofie spoke no more to her sister about her own concerns. Once, the latter came upon Sofie in a state of extremely low spirits. She was crying and saying she wanted to die. 'Bah,' Louise had said with her bitter smile, 'don't expect it; one doesn't die of grief, otherwise I'd have been first served. Those first sorrows of one's youth are like the first contractions in childbirth. From the very start, you are convinced you cannot endure them, but the midwife sits there calmly in front of you with folded arms, saying "That's nothing; that's nothing; there's worse to come!" '

Such statements made Sofie unable to speak; it was as if a burning hand had wiped away her tears. Her sister either did not or would not really understand her grief. She looked down on it with aristocratic condescension from the glacial height of her own unhappiness. Both resisted any touching of their deepest wounds.

Even so, this did not prevent Louise from preaching her pragmatic approach to life and impressing upon her younger sister, whenever possible, some useful rules for living. She thus devised her own method of dealing with Sofie's closest concerns — she just treated them as if they did not exist.

This did not fail to have an effect, although Sofie herself was the least aware of it. She had progressed much further than she herself knew or would have thought possible; nor would it have been possible if Louise, like a tender sister, had pampered her pain. Quiveringly, Sofie had looked into an abyss, and from that moment she no longer dared look up towards the radiant, sunlit peak of love. There are moments when one is grateful to have firm ground under one's feet.

* * *

On a clear afternoon in November, as the sun had already begun its descent into a colourful halo of vapour, the young girl finally came to a halt outside the gate to the tree-lined drive leading up to the Dean's farm. She was supposed to have arrived the evening before, but she had preferred to stay the night at a nearby relay station. The closer she came to her destination, the more anxiously her heart was beating. When she had left the Dean's farm, she had certainly been surprised at what had happened to her there, but she had yet been as calm as if the Dean's application had not concerned her. He might just as well have been reading a chapter from a novel aloud to her. With the same feeling of calm, she had been determined to keep her promise and stop at the farm on her way home. Now she was at the gate, but here she was so overwhelmed by anxiety that she brought the horse to a halt.

What a peaceful picture lay before her! What a pleasant, quiet place to be!

An echo of autumnal beauty still lingered over the region. Along fences and shrubs, a light cover of white frost indicated where the sun's rays had not been able to penetrate. But the fields were green, changing into ever softer shades of colour as they disappeared towards the purple rim of the forest. The birch trees looked majestic even in their leafless state. A couple of rowan trees farther down the row tossed their flamboyant red crowns arrogantly, as if to say that now it was their turn. Thousands of thrushes were giving their strange concert, consisting of a single uninterrupted, but not unmelodious sound of whirring, whistling, fluting, calling, raucous voices.

With a feeling of melancholy, Sofie let her eyes wander towards the farm, which, along with the church spire, was outlined in a bluish shadow against the red afternoon sky. Her ears were straining to catch a familiar sound. She imagined with what tremendous joy little Ada would rush towards her to fling her arms around her neck when she suddenly stepped into the sitting room, but then she heard again in her anxious mind: 'Poor Ada! Oh, shall I ever again come into this sitting room?' As if the little girl had heard this thought and responded to it, Sofie heard, from down by the farm, a long and persistent, then slowly fading, mournful cry. Perhaps it was a distant woodpecker; perhaps it was only the tame ducks protesting against having been confined to their winter prison too soon, but Sofie's thoughts of her little friend and of the disappointment she would have to cause her, had been so thoroughly aroused that her uncertainty about what to do came to a head. She ended by hoping that chance would decide for her, and scarcely had this prayer escaped her, but her horse, tempted by a couple of green blades of grass which the frost had overlooked, suddenly took a few steps through the gate.

This movement jolted Sofie's slumbering willpower awake. With all the spontaneous strength of instinct, she seized the reins in both hands, restrained the horse, and with a speed that resembled flight, she set off in the opposite direction.

* * *

During all these events, Georg Kold had spent a quiet, but industrious period. We rejoin him at his work table in his lodgings in Christiania. He has just stood up after spending several hours writing. Is he ill, or is his face just reflecting the fading March light in the rather dreary room? His face no longer has the contented expression we know from his days at the District Governor's. He takes a few rapid turns up and down the room, now and then stopping by the window to cast a disinterested glance down at the dirty street. It is not without pleasure that he sees Müller coming around the corner and setting course for his place.

They still saw each other with some frequency. On Kold's part, however, every vestige of frankness had disappeared. He had finally entered upon the right course: he had curtly and firmly refused every intrusion into private areas where he knew that Müller would never understand him. Müller respected this and did not attempt to overcome Kold's reserve, and it is to his credit that he did so without any diminution of interest in his young friend. Kold, for his part, needed Müller as a diversion. He was, after all, a very interesting person. His distinctive, somewhat crass view of things amused Kold, just as it surprised him many times to see the surgical confidence with which Müller swiftly went over every phenomenon of life where there might be some illusion to excise. He could sit there in silence for half an hour at an end, listening to Müller's whimsical and often baroque volleys. Since Müller, like all lively, talkative people, regarded a silent listener as a good one and transferred some of his own superfluity of words to Kold, when the need arose, he was hardly aware of the latter's taciturnity and often left Kold after such a monologue with the impression that his Georg was really an unusually entertaining person — a person with whom one could talk.

Kold had placed a tin of tobacco in the centre of the table and lit a row of wax tapers; preparations which Müller rewarded with a nod of satisfaction and an inquiry about Kold's health, because he had not been quite well lately.

'You ought not to go outside,' Müller continued with a searching look at Kold's features, which, just then illuminated by the flame he was using to light his cigar, seemed to him strikingly gaunt and suffering. 'The air is horribly treacherous; enough so that even healthy people ought to take care. Give me your hand!'

'Oh, nonsense,' said Kold deprecatingly. 'You're making too much of a fuss.'

After Müller's unfortunate operations at the District Governor's, he avoided everything that might lead their thoughts in the direction of those scenes. Kold scarcely ever mentioned his own stay there. Perhaps they both felt that it was a point that could bear no explanation between them.

With Müller's usual agility in these matters, their conversation had already embraced various subjects, when he suddenly exclaimed,

'What do you say to the news from the District Governor?'

Kold looked sideways, like a man who has lit a fuse and is about to blow up himself and all the rest of the world. . . . 'What news?'

'Then you haven't heard it yet? Little Sofie is engaged. She's to be married to Dean Rein, a very worthy man of fifty, who has his own house, chattels, children — everything all set and ready. Mama will not need to be concerned about her trousseau. Well, that's what I call a quick decision. Indeed, by God, there was something quite unusual about that little one; she did look determined.'

'It's not true.'

'Perhaps, but it's at least certain. Edvard Ramm just finished telling me. The wedding is to be very soon, and both of the sisters, both the lovely little Sofie and the romantic Amalie, are to be married at the same time. I can even tell you the date as accurately as any gossip. Let me see — the first of June, Mrs Ramm's birthday. It's to be a big affair, and, as an old acquaintance, you're sure to be invited.'

'That might be.'

'They're really ridiculous, these weddings,' Müller went on. 'Dear Lord, such a to-do, so much fuss and carrying-on just for the sake of a formality. Because, when all is said and done, it's the scrawniness of formality that's supposed to be covered up by all this. Just remove the tinsel, and we shall see. The bridal gown, the entire well-trained wailing chorus of dressed-up ladies and maidens, certain groupings and manoeuvres such as that the bride is to walk up towards the altar on the right and then be pushed over to the left, which I suppose, is a symbolic suggestion that the man changes from being her protector to being her master . . . . Take away the singing, the bell-ringing, and that apple of mama's eye, the bridal chamber. . . . Oh me, oh my, I can just picture Mrs Ramm on that day! . . . Finally, take away the sermon, which surely we most of all could do without, and then the naked formula remains — but who in the world would find that sufficient? No young lady would consider herself properly married by the clerical act alone. If ever I become so undeservedly fortunate as to have a wedding, it will take place without any riots. Most of all, I would prefer to fetch the bride without any ceremony. I'd make just as good a husband and make my payments just as readily to the Widows' Fund, and I'm sure we'd agree just as properly and just as faithfully to plague one another throughout life, as if the minister had joined our hands.'

Kold listened to this speech with about the same emotion as that of Lord Nigel*, when on the eve of his execution he heard his humorous friend, Sir Mungo, describe the various executions he had witnessed.

Even after Müller had left, Kold remained standing as if paralysed. 'Impossible! Impossible!' was the only thought of which his mind was capable, and which incessantly rose to his lips.

He went to look for Edvard in the latter's lodgings. He left him with the knowledge of certainty and of hopelessness. Edvard was surprised at the agitation this piece of information caused in his usually calm and sober-minded teacher. He stared after him in astonishment.

No — it was impossible to go home. Kold knew he would suffocate within doors. He later explained to Müller that while running through the streets, he had had the sensation that the houses were moving to block his path, threatening at any moment to tumble down on him. Finding himself beyond the city limit, he felt relieved, and he was driven forward in the direction taken by his thoughts, along the northern road.

It was towards the end of March, that doleful season in our climate, when nature is just getting ready for the long and arduous task of casting off winter's yoke, which this year had been unusually harsh, following a too beautiful summer. This is the season in our country when nature looks almost hideous. The brown fields with their scattered, glaring patches of snow disturb all the contours and deprive the landscape of all perspective. The whimpering cries of the spring birds and the hollow, subterranean roar of the creeks, imbue our minds with a restlessness, a spasm of longing, that cannot be described. One feels the urgency of having to reconcile the demand for an imminent end to winter with the knowledge that this is bound to end in disappointment, and that the worst is actually yet to come. The air is mild, but the ground gives off that chilling damp which is more noticeable than the harshest cold of winter.

Kold had passed the Botanical Gardens and was rushing headlong up the steep hills ahead of him. God knows how far his inner turmoil would

*See Walter Scott's novel. [*Author's Note to 1879 edition.*]

have driven him — because he sensed only the relief of constant movement through a searing pain — if some half-completed roadwork had not forced him to a halt. He turned around. Below him lay Christiania in its ever-present veil of fog. Seen from this angle, the valley in which our capital is situated appears somewhat uncultivated and disjointed, very much disturbing the picturesque effect that is restored only at a greater distance. This is less noticeable when summer spreads its soft, delicate tints over the landscape, but at this particular moment it reflected the beholder's feeling of destruction. With its dark, irregular mass of houses in the deforested valley, he thought the city looked collapsed, like an immense gravel pile that had left bits and pieces randomly about, while the fjord struggled to hide the destruction with its white shroud. A bone-chilling wind was blowing against Kold on his hurried way down. He was without an overcoat, but he did not notice, because fever was already pulsating in his veins. The following day, his landlady sent for Müller, but unfortunately he was out of town, and when he unsuspectingly ascended the stairs to his young friend's room two days later, he found Kold delirious with fever.

* * *

Sofie was engaged. She was engaged to the good, amiable Dean. 'Impossible!' everyone will exclaim, just like Kold. 'Impossible!' A young girl, endowed with more self-awareness, more resistance than most, and with a heart still bleeding from a freshly torn-out inclination, willingly consenting to marry a man who was old enough to be her father, and whom she surely had no more intention of marrying than the Grand Mogul.

Not impossible, sensitive friends! . . . Often, very often, life confronts us with such disparities, indeed worse ones, and then they make nobody wonder. This is due to habit. A momentary pause of surprise is overcome with the assurance that *this* is possible, and *that* is possible. This is precisely society's secret, a mystery which a humble storyteller dares scarcely reveal except in shy reverence. We therefore bypass whatever struggles Sofie may have had with herself, while we attempt to point out some of the external forces that co-operated in luring her inside that circle from which there is no further escape.

One might readily believe it is true, as people maintain, that all women want to be, and have a talent for being, matchmakers. It is certain that men are not endowed with any such talents. No, Heaven be praised, they pollute only their own affairs, while appearing to lack both the desire and the ability to busy themselves with the affairs of others. This is indeed a strange sort of malice on nature's part! Is it not as if it were secretly trying to restore some of the balance by endowing the half of humanity that is forbidden to make its own arrangements in matters where feelings — and nothing but feelings — should decide, with this brilliant ability to meddle in other people's business? It is remarkable that those alliances in which such an invisible small hand has played a part, often turn out well, and yet again, it is not so remarkable if we note that a feminine predilection is the point of departure.

Louise, who wrote such infrequent and brief letters home, found occasion to tell her mother in one of those letters — in all confidence, of course — what had taken place between the Dean and Sofie. In so doing, she left the business in the most capable hands. After her initial surprise, Mrs Ramm felt that this was a difficult, extremely difficult, assignment, even to a person of more than common ability. This concerned an offer that was not an offer, a refusal that was not a refusal; it was an offer that had been rescinded, a refusal that had never been given. She was sufficiently well acquainted with her daughter to know that she was not likely to get anywhere by the usual means, such as persuasion, etc. In brief, this was a matter requiring the greatest delicacy.

The first thing she must do was to affect complete ignorance of the business. From this hiding place, she began her artillery emplacements, in which Amalie's relationship with the Dean and his home was of most welcome assistance.

When Mrs Ramm and her daughters were sitting with their sewing in the sitting room during the long winter evenings, this was the most frequent topic of conversation. After all, it was to be Amalie's home. What, then, could be more natural for a mother than to dwell upon and emphasize all the comforts and advantages of the Dean's home! And all those comforts and advantages originated in one single person. She now recalled many details that all were calculated to place this person in the most favourable light. Mrs Ramm was very eloquent, and winter evenings in the country are very long. When alone with Sofie, Mrs Ramm's effusions became more elegiac. In a sisterly, confidential voice she might exclaim, 'Alas, Sofie, you may believe how hard it is many a time to contemplate how Amalie has forfeited her own good fortune! When I think of what she *has* and of what she *might have had*! But we parents can do nothing in such matters; we can only wish. Your father is old and feeble; we may lose him at any moment. It must be hard for him to realize that he is not to see one of his daughters really happily married. . . . I am stronger and can bear it more easily! . . . What a joy it would have been for him to see Amalie united to Rein! . . . Yes, those parents who know their child to be in such hands could peacefully close their eyes!'

Weeks passed. Then came a day when Mrs Ramm was silent and withdrawn, with a sad, pensive expression on her face. There were more such days. When Sofie one evening found her mother lying on the sofa with eyes that looked as if she had been crying, she felt concerned and asked whether she was ill. 'No, I am not ill,' her mother said, 'but I have heard something that has shaken me profoundly. Sofie, I know that Dean Rein has made you a proposal of marriage, and that *you as yet have given him no answer!'*

'Be not afraid, my dear child,' Mrs Ramm continued, when she saw the fear suffusing Sofie's face upon finding that a secret that was scarcely hers had been misused — a fear that might perhaps also have something to do with a realization that she had as yet given him no answer. 'Be not afraid! . . . You well know what your parents' wishes might be in this matter, but that must not put you under the slightest obligation. Your poor old father is not even to hear of it, and I myself shall suppress the wish upon my lips.'

With a tenacity that was truly unequalled, Mrs Ramm kept her promise. If the conversation turned to Amalie's future home, she became taciturn where formerly she had been so eloquent. She often interrupted her speech with a suppressed sigh, an expression of pained resignation on her face. This maternal resignation affected Sofie all the more because she knew that it had not been exercised in similar situations involving her sisters. For her sake alone did her mother suffer this self-abnegation.

Mrs Ramm had no intention of abandoning a favourable position without having an alternative force in reserve, however. She took Amalie into her confidence. The two sisters were devoted to each other. Their impending separation was often a melancholy subject of conversation between them. The possibility that fate would not part them after all, but would allow them to live together in such a delightful fashion, sounded to Amalie more like a fairytale than anything to which she dared attach any real expectations. For that reason, and possibly because of an innate shyness in front of Sofie, it did not occur to her to attempt dissimulation. She merely embellished the fairytale; in all the loveliest colours at her disposal she tried to embroider the delight of being able to live together in this manner. It is not unlikely that these artless, sisterly effusions made a greater impression on Sofie than any other form of persuasion, whether in the form of passionate supplication or cloaked in false resignation, and that they, more than anything else, contributed to Sofie's becoming familiar with the idea and to removing its sting.

For this idea was not *unfamiliar* to her. It is impossible to say exactly when it first began to take shape, whether it was as early as during her visit to Louise. That sort of herb does not grow from *happy* soil; it requires neither care nor shelter. It is the seed of bitterness and disappointment; it shoots up in the course of a single night, like Bab-el-Baba's sword in the fairytale — sharp and ready to wound its owner. The young girl who has been betrayed and catapulted from her happiness will be able to perceive such an idea, while the young girl whose dreams are still intact will scarcely be capable of it.

Nevertheless, how many such desperate decisions might still be conquered or allowed to die quietly by themselves! But the peculiar position in which a young girl is placed relative to the outside world will only rarely allow such a quiet act of self-examination. She will be allowed neither the time nor the peace. Once the faintest suspicion of a possibility is present, the world will have a thousand conjuring tricks ready, and then she had better take care — the air is pregnant with them. From every side she will hear mysterious words that separately are harmless, but that together constitute the complete magic formula. She will hear them in her mother's sighs, in her father's silence, in the innocent chatter of her brothers and sisters. . . . And then there are her friends and rumours and gossip!

We have talked about the coercion to which Sofie was subjected by those closest to her. There was also another figure who passed by her as a warning; a figure who is familiar to us: the unhappy Lorenz Brandt.

* * *

On the farm, nothing had been seen or heard of Brandt all autumn long. Two potted plants — a geranium and a myrtle that promptly withered — had at various times been mysteriously placed in Sofie's room.

She did not want to inquire, but she suspected they were greetings from Lorenz.

On a dreary morning in February, she was busy in her room when she heard the padding of a dog's feet in the anteroom. Croesus ran towards her, wagging his tail, and before the frightened girl could close the door, Lorenz Brandt was standing on her threshold.

It was he, and it was not he. His clothes and his posture were different from what the Ramms had grown accustomed to seeing, and this change encompassed his entire figure, which seemed smaller and thinner than usual. He had obtained another cast-off tailcoat, which was carefully brushed, but which still did not seem to demand attention for its own sake, seeking only to hide as much as possible. He had a similar, motley-coloured waistcoat, also new boots that squeaked horribly, and a fairly clean shirt collar. The total impression was of a certain pathetic respectability that required more care and greater expenditure of time and skill than the most opulent toilet.

Sofie involuntarily took a step backwards, but a glance at Lorenz told her that he had not come to frighten her, but possibly just to conquer any vestige of such a sensation on her part.

He had modestly taken a seat on a chair by the door. While he was sitting there like that, with his elbows resting on his knees and his head in his cupped hands, the change in his features also became more striking.

The unnatural puffiness had disappeared, leaving his features hollow and gaunt, the way a stream, long swollen, may often sink too low, disturbing the subtle harmony between the stream and its bank. The leaden colour of Lorenz's face had given way to a dull, terracotta yellowness, which further emphasized the almost classical purity his features had originally possessed. An impartial observer left to contemplate him as he was sitting there with a fixed stare, almost as if bewitched, would have said that here was a glorious human shape gone to ruin, but remarkable to behold even in its destruction.

We shall not repeat every word of the painful conversation — or monologue, rather — that now ensued. Reader! Have you ever dreamed that you were about to give a speech upon which your own and the entire world's well-being depended, before an anxious public, and that you suddenly could not remember a single word! Lorenz must have felt just that way when he began his first stumbling introduction. He talked about his improvement — his *real* improvement — and about the sacrifices he had made to this improvement. He spoke of some expectation he had of entering into a respectable position. But perhaps he did not believe it himself. He talked a lot of nonsense back and forth; he stuttered as if he were about to confess some wrong-doing. His witticism, his bragging and his confident rudeness had all left him, and while he praised the self-conquest that had driven those demons away, he might perhaps at that moment have given his life to have one of those demons come to his assistance. The waters of his spirit had also sunk below the level where they ceased to flow and were scarcely able to cover the traces of death and destruction concealed at the bottom.

Sofie had as yet said nothing. Since she had last seen him, she had herself experienced so much suffering; she had heard words that pierced her like a dagger; she had learned how every word may have the power to hurt. She remained immobile, steadying her hand on the table, while her quiet, thoughtful, unblinking eyes were riveted upon Lorenz. Whither floated her thoughts just then? . . . Far, far away from him. She was thinking of Ada in her illness. She scarcely heard half of what he was saying, and for a moment it was as if she again saw the eyes of the suffering child directed at herself in supplication.

Emboldened by the fact that Sofie gave no sign of either fear or disgust — perhaps he even fancied hearing a reply through that gentle, sorrowful expression — Lorenz became increasingly self-assured and calm in his explanations. He told her how he had felt more desolate and outcast than ever since the change that had come over him — a change that dated from the day he had frightened her so. The victories he had won over himself seemed to him so colossal, so superhuman, that all creation would surely marvel at them. . . . His dog had been twice as meek towards him, twice as devoted. Only people, those wise people, would not believe in them. They only met him with coldness and scornful doubts. His mother's reproaches now found a defenceless target in him. The fierce need for a single encouraging human look had lately begun to consume him. He had reached the point where it seemed to him that one more harsh word would push him back into the abyss without any hope of salvation. And then, in his discouragement and prostration, he had come to her, who surely must despise him the most. . . . And she had not said that harsh word, but had let her gentle eyes rest upon him.

'Now I feel strengthened and brave and rich after all,' he concluded, 'although I have but four shillings in my pocket, and they are destined for a bullet for poor Croesus, who is getting old and who is beginning to have a hard life with me.'

Croesus lifted his head from his paws and looked up at his master, wagging his tail as if he understood what Lorenz had said and was grateful for this proof of his tenderness.

'Yes, old boy, poor old boy, they are for you! . . . And now I want to say goodbye to you, Sofie,' said Lorenz, moving closer. 'I don't want to abuse your goodness. I have seen you; you have listened to me in patience; I don't ask more of you this time. God bless you for it. May life be good to you!'

He was already over by the door, but paused in embarrassment. 'Look here, Sofie,' he said, diffidently extracting a parcel from under his tailcoat. After layers of careful wrapping had been removed — a yellow cotton handkerchief, then some grey paper, and finally a piece of delicate tissue paper — the parcel turned out to be a small box made of polished wood; the sort that can be bought in the markets for a trifle. . . . 'Don't take it in bad part, Sofie,' he said, 'but I wanted so much to give you this to remember me by. . . . Because it will be a long, very long time before you see me again. . . . Not until that has happened which I have told you about. Let it stand on your table up *here*, but not *downstairs* . . . . Whenever you look at it, then remember me and send up a prayer for me. . . . Look, here are scissors and a thimble and this little mirror, in which I have imagined seeing your reflection, just as now — -'

A sharp voice interrupted them. Mrs Ramm was standing in the doorway, her dark brows drawn up in a threatening manner, and her colour a more vivid shade of brick red than usual. Sofie immediately understood from the way in which her mother was trying to assume an expression of unconcern and wonder, that she had been in the anteroom listening to everything.

'What in the world! Is that you, Brandt? I could not imagine whose those squeaking boots up here might be! Are you still so unfamiliar with this house that you can thus mistake the doors? It's your own fault, Sofie, for leaving the doors open. If you would like some breakfast, Brandt, it is now ready downstairs. But I want to tell you beforehand that there will be only *coffee* to drink and *nothing else*.'

'N-no, thank you, madam,' Lorenz stammered, pale as death.

'As you wish. We never press anyone.'

She opened the door wide and chased the dog out with her hands. 'Out with you. . . . Lorenz . . . what am I saying! . . . Caro, Croesus, out!'

The dog and its master crept out the open door.

'Wait a moment. Is not this your box? Were I in your place, Brandt, I should try to locate its owner. I should advertise. However, do whatever you like; I make no inquiries as to how you came to possess it.'

'Oh, Mother!' Sofie cried out in anguish.

When she was alone, she cast a look around her, one of those looks with which one searches for a lifesaving remedy, something with which to stop a haemorrhage. In such a situation, one does not hesitate to tear up whatever comes to hand, regardless of how costly it might be. Yes, Sofie was now contemplating one of those wounds that no person can heal or even soothe. At Sofie's age, one is still so unaccustomed to seeing those wounds. Habit has not yet dulled one's perception of them. One would gladly give a piece of oneself in order to allay the suffering, and yet all one has to give is alms, always alms! One wants so much to give a blessing, a 'God give you strength!' over the wretched head that is trying to raise itself, but it merely becomes an insult. While wanting to give restitution, one ends by adding yet another humiliation. The young girl felt this all the more painfully because, having become an instrument in this unhappy man's life herself, she feared that her failure to pull him up might make him sink deeper still.

Distractedly, she opened and shut all her drawers. Twice already she had taken all the money she owned into her hand and tossed it away again in disgust. Nevertheless, she did take this money, and she emptied out all of Amalie's, and she was already over by the stairs. . . . No! the money burned her hand. At least he must not see it. Again she rushed back inside, wrapped an envelope around the money, sealed it, and ran off.

The weather was mild and still. There was a slight thaw, and water was dripping from the rooftops, on which a transient layer of snow was still visible. A few large, wet snowflakes were fluttering in the still air, as if teasingly enjoying their existence before perishing on the wet and dirty ground. One could hear the dull, thumping sound made by the flail falling on the full bundles of grain. It was just the right kind of weather for the sparrows, great flocks of which were flying around on the farm, twittering and enjoying the good life.

Sofie had reached the tree-lined lane. She could see a figure, whom she assumed was Lorenz, moving far in the distance, but suddenly it disappeared, and she feared that his head start might have been too great. She winged her steps — then she heard her name spoken with joyful surprise.

Lorenz was sitting by the edge of the ditch, employed in cutting off some slices of bread for his dog with his folding knife. When he saw Sofie, he tossed the whole loaf to the dog.

The young girl was breathless from the turmoil of her emotions and from her running, and Lorenz, who had not counted on the happiness of seeing her once more, stared at her speechlessly.

'I came,' she finally said, 'I only wanted. . . . Lorenz, why did you go so fast! . . . I was supposed to give you this from Father.'

A blush flitted across his cheeks. This was the first time she had addressed him with the sisterly 'du' from the old days. From her overflowing heart she gave him *that*, when she had nothing else. He listened entranced.

'I am supposed to give you this from Father,' she repeated in the same manner as before. 'It's for a service you rendered him.'

'Yes, of course, a service,' said Lorenz, smiling. 'For six months I have not visited him; that certainly is a great service, that.'

'Who says so! You know yourself what it is. You have done some writing for him.'

'Yes, yes, of course, some writing. . . . some not insignificant writing,' said Lorenz, with a touch of his old humour and a twinkle in his eye.

He read the writing on the envelope, looked at Sofie with a smile, and then again at the letter.

'Sofie, if I were drunk now — don't be afraid! I'm just saying, *if* I were. . . . After all, it's better to talk about being drunk than actually being so — it's a step, isn't it; a step forward? Now, if I were drunk, I should give you a rip-roaring speech about pride and human worth; I should finish by throwing this money disdainfully at your feet . . . before putting it in my pocket. And even now, something is bubbling up from the depths of my soul which is protesting against this money. But it is bubbles, Sofie! They don't rise far enough, and I can no longer find the old words for them. Instead, what I do remember very clearly is that these boots have not been paid for, and that I have had no dinner for two days. Thank you for this money. . . . it comes at a very opportune time. . . .'

Tears were streaming down Sofie's cheeks. 'Oh Lorenz, don't make me feel ashamed; don't talk about it! Put it away! . . . Lorenz, go to your mother, tell her all the good and promising things you have been telling me, and she will believe you; she must believe you. Or, if you are unable to do even that, tell them to yourself; tell them to your deepest, innermost soul. One will hear you, who will give you more than people are able to give you. Alas, Lorenz, people can give each other nothing, no, nothing, nothing. They can only hurt and harm one another.'

'Have you already discovered that, Sofie?' said Lorenz, with a searching look at the face that had used to glow with health, and where sorrow now had left its first, faint mark. 'It's too soon to have had that sort of experiences. What have you been through?'

'Much, much. Farewell!'

'Farewell,' he said sadly, clasping her hand. 'Farewell, you angel of mercy. . . . You sunray on the prison wall, farewell!'

She was already several steps distant; then she turned around once more.

'Lorenz,' she said with a smile, 'you wanted to give me that little box. Am I not to have it?'

'Oh God. . . . Sofie! . . . How can I reward you? You will never see me again, *never*.'

'That is in the hands of God; be strong and have faith in Him.' She put the box under her shawl and walked slowly home.

Her thoughts were again directed towards Ada's home. She felt some of that balm, that strange peace, which had come over her during her anxious nursing of the sick child, and she lost herself in a succession of possibilities and images.

Lorenz stared after her for as long as there was the smallest speck left of her to be seen.

* * *

Rumours and gossip! Of all the frightening images in a woman's existence, these are the most illusory, the most horrible chimerae. Nothing has a greater power to cow and subdue a woman into obedience. Nothing affects her life more demoniacally than these ownerless and irresponsible attacks which we are accustomed to calling rumours and gossip. Everything else has merely prepared the soil; rumours and gossip will bring forth the bitter growth. What is being said does not have to be nasty or defamatory, indeed no. Thanks to our society's deep commitment to approval, which has placed the fragile crystal of femininity in the centre of society's own impurity, admonishing the crystal always to remain *crystal clear*, no stain is needed in order to obscure its pure lustre; only a breath. All that is necessary is for people to *talk*. It is impossible to describe the strange fear which this miserable tohubohu can exercise over a young mind.

A young girl is suffering from a heartache. Mimosa-like, her mind has closed over it, perhaps for a long, long time, until the lovely insect, love, is dead. Then she slowly, painfully, unfolds her mind again to the world and the light. Naively she believes herself unnoticed by others; she believes it in the consciousness of the nobility and impregnability of her suffering. She has given away nothing; she owns her secret. Poor mimosa! Your secret is in everybody's possession; you may read it in anybody's eyes. From every side, you will hear it interpreted, embellished, twisted, soiled — here an object of sympathy, there of derision. If it is very interesting, it may perhaps be offered for sale on the book stalls. The young girl then is seized by dread; she wants to flee back to her own internal contemplation. But the sanctuary has been violated; the treasure is gone; and she then throws herself into the arms of some misfortune or other, which never fails to be at hand.

Our poor Sofie was just as unable to protect herself against this process as anyone else. Her mother had watched her turn pale at the slightest mention of her relationship with Kold. It was worth trying an attack on that flank, and her mother decided to risk that attack.

One day, Mrs Ramm returned home from a visit to the same Mrs Breien who has been mentioned before in these pages. With the zeal of motherly indignation, she related to her daughters a scene that had taken place between her and that lady. Mrs Breien had, with hypocritical sympathy, inquired about Sofie's health, and at last, after suitable circumlocutions, she had delivered herself of the opinion that the girl's ailing look was due to jilted love for the tutor who had left them. Indeed, it was not just her own opinion, but everybody else's, she had added when she saw Mrs Ramm's piqued expression. A maid who had been in service at the District Governor's and who had subsequently changed employer, had related seeing with her own eyes that the young Miss, in an extremely emotional state, had handed Kold a letter he would not accept; that it had fallen to the floor; and that he had been forced to take it when the maid handed it to him. The reader will be able to recall the scene in which Sofie returned Kold's letter to him, unread. The postman had several times brought letters from Sofie to the post office, and she had been in a hurry to return from her visit to her sister's just to see Kold, but she had nevertheless arrived too late — the bird had flown.

'Oh,' cried her mother, who seemed unwilling to let herself be calmed down, 'are we still going to be made to suffer because of that person! Is it not enough, Sofie, that he has been playing games with you — on top of it all, the neighbourhood gossips are now to get hold of this story and talk it to death for a year or two. It would be better by far if you could be away for a while, until they are done talking. . . . Yes indeed, as hard as it would be for me to do without you, now that Amalie is also leaving — still, it would be the best thing for you. If it were not such an impossibility, I would suggest that you leave when Amalie does and stay with her for a while.'

'It is not an impossibility,' Sofie mumbled, her face white as a sheet.

'Yes, my girl, with *your* sense of delicacy I would certainly hesitate to do such a thing. . . . Well, I don't know. . . . *My* feelings would dictate against it.'

'As his wife, I both can and will,' Sofie said coldly and calmly, but audibly.

With a shout of joy, Amalie flung herself around Sofie's neck.

That evening, Sofie wrote a letter to the Dean, and two weeks later his answer had arrived in the most proper form.

Not until then was Sofie's father made a party to the secret. The old man refused to believe it. It came upon him too unexpectedly.

'What, Sofie! The Dean! Sofie, you say! . . . Mariane,' he added, almost as if frightened, 'we are not in any way to blame . . .?'

'To blame? . . . What on earth are you thinking of? Not with one syllable has Sofie been influenced; not with one syllable. I myself felt as if I had fallen out of the sky when the child told me.'

'Sofie! The Dean! My little Sofie. . . . Well, did you ever! . . . My poor girl! . . . It is, of course, a great happiness!' he said, and sat staring straight ahead.

* * *

With almost maternal care, Müller had kept watch at Kold's sickbed. Silent, powerless, astonished, cold reason was now confronted with

296

undisguised passion. Müller had accustomed himself to treating passion as a disease requiring a particular treatment, just like typhus and typhoid; as a disease that is no longer harmful when its crisis, *proximity*, is past. The unfamiliar turn taken by Kold's illness disconcerted Müller somewhat. Half surprised, half curious, he stayed at Kold's bedside listening to outbursts that more or less confusedly always involved one name; that were always addressed to one person, whom he implored and accused by turn. It was both pathetic and heartbreaking to hear the sick man, who at such great cost had guarded his secret from Müller, incessantly going over the whole unhappy tale, with the detail of repetition and urgency of suffering of somebody unburdening his heart to a tender mother. When Kold was conscious, his manner towards Müller was cold and suspicious and full of bitterness. Müller, however, must be given credit for deserving the sort of praise reserved for an inexhaustible, ever-patient mother. With stoical fortitude he put up with the sick man's moods. Perhaps he had not understood a word of the whole thing, but it had imbued him with a very uncomfortable feeling, and he asked himself whether he indeed was partly to blame for his friend's suffering.

The May sun was shining into the sickroom with greater power. Kold was able to sit up. Friends came to visit him, and there was talking and card-playing. In the usual manner of convalescents, Kold was lively and participated in all the entertainment. Still, Müller's suspicions had now been aroused. He did not like this liveliness, and Kold's preoccupied manner of staring fixedly ahead in the midst of such animated scenes told him that the young man was obsessed with some thought or other. He could hardly be contemplating a journey or some other impetuous step — the day, the fateful day when Sofie was to be united with Rein, was already too near. If Müller might only see his patient successfully past that day, he would be saved. Perhaps Kold had not paid particularly close attention to the date, 1 June — it had not been mentioned between them at all since that first time.

A young and brilliant Swede, whom they both knew, was visiting Christiania just then. Müller wanted to ask him and some other friends to get together on that particular day and celebrate Kold's first permission to attend an al fresco evening party. Half a barrel of oysters and a crate of good wine, sent to Müller by a grateful patient in one of the small towns on the West Coast, had just arrived, as if especially ordered for the party.

It was the next-to-last day of May. Thoroughly pleased with his clever plan, Müller parted from Kold in the morning. He spent the evening finding a good place for the party and making some further arrangements. He was not able to look in on Kold again until the middle of the following day.

Scarcely had he entered the house, but Kold's landlady came out to meet him with a rather worried expression. 'Oh dear, is that you, Doctor! And he is not with you, either?'

'Whom do you mean?'

'Why, Mr Kold, of course. No sooner had you left him yesterday, when he went out, and he hasn't been back since. If he wasn't such a nice and proper sort of person, you might almost think he had gone and done harm to himself! God's truth, I haven't been able to sleep a wink all night.'

Müller heard no more. He was already upstairs. In Kold's room, everything gave the appearance of a hurried departure. On the table was a note.

'Don't be angry, dear Müller, not angry. — You would not have been able to restrain me. A struggle with you would just have deprived me of the little strength I have, which I need so badly. When I see you again, I shall be calmer. Believe me, I am not ungrateful.

Please ask my landlady to open all the windows and to leave them open until I return.'

'After him!' was Müller's first thought. 'That madman!' he said, collecting himself; 'he's already up there!'

The journey up to the District Governor's farm ordinarily took two days. By travelling all day and the following night, and by ordering ahead for his horses, Kold succeeded in reaching the last relay station by dawn, and from the station it was but a short walk to the farm. He allowed himself only a brief rest at the relay station in order to bring some order to his rather rumpled appearance, and then he set off to cover the last stretch on foot.

It was about seven o'clock in the morning when he reached the entrance to the tree-lined lane. He walked a few steps down the lane, then leaped the fence and followed a narrow footpath that made a detour and allowed him to enter the garden unnoticed. From the dense shrubbery, he could observe the house and anyone leaving it.

It was a truly beautiful spring morning, so clear and warm! Nature was unfurling the first fresh splendour of spring. Every tree, every bush seemed to be showing off the young, glistening foliage that no burning sun had yet darkened and no speck of dust defiled. The garden was freshly groomed and ready. Narcissus and primrose encircled every flower bed. No human footprint had yet disturbed the freshly raked gravel walks, but the apple tree and the chokecherry had scattered their petals down over them. But Kold noticed nothing of this. His eyes remained intently fixed on the house, from which he could already hear signs of life and activity. There was the sound of kitchen equipment and of many buzzing voices — through them all, Mrs Ramm's high-pitched voice could be heard issuing curt and dictatorial orders in the manner of a general penetrating the din of battle. Through the open window, the canary was mingling its strident voice with those of the chaffinches outside. . . . A maid was polishing the windows of the verandah doors; they were flashing in the morning sun. But Sofie's window upstairs was open. A white curtain was waving in and out like a greeting — or a farewell. 'She is already downstairs,' he said. That was what he wanted to know. He left his post and found his way through the most secluded garden paths down to the familiar gate leading into the fields. From there, he set off in the direction of the mill.

There were still beads of dew on the grass lining the path; this path where he had so often followed Sofie's trail. Not until he had got this far did he slow his steps and let his eyes take in his surroundings. Every bush greeted him like an old friend. He recognized each little family of flowers. Such a rockstrewn meadow tends to develop a rather varied flora, which is missing in richer pastures. The yellow wild primrose was already there, and that rosy ornament of the forest, the wood sorrel, was in full bloom. . . . The last of the red-tipped anemones were spreading their carpet over the brownish, mossy hillocks. Lilies-of-the-valley revealed plump buds behind their broad leaves, but they had not unfurled a single one of their fragile buds as yet — perhaps they were reluctant to make any sacrifice to the feast. Everywhere there was fluttering and stirring, buzzing and whispering — the rustling of a thousand tiny, invisible lives. Poor Kold, who had just escaped his winter prison, had given no thought to spring. He was not prepared for this new and powerful impression. A soft and melancholy tune was playing over the meadow; it was Ole the idiot who was sitting on a hillock blowing his willow whistle. No sign of surprise or recognition stirred in the sleepy blue eyes when Kold walked past him. . . . The whistle fluted on undisturbed; the soft, dreamy sound of spring seized him with fresh memories and made him acutely aware of the difference between before and now. How boldly he had greeted spring on this same path! And just the last time — just when Sofie was expected home — with what longing and swelling anticipation! . . . Now he was sneaking along like a stranger, ill, unappreciated, tortured by fear and uncertainty — overwhelmed by everything. The sweet, intoxicating scent of the ground shook his nerves and caused him unspeakable pain. He threw himself down on the ground and burst into a flood of tears. For a moment he was enraged at himself for this involuntary outburst, and he looked menacingly around, as if to see whether some small bird had noticed.

The tears made him feel stronger. They left him with a feeling of anger, anger with her, with himself. . . . The mere thought of what he had suffered and of how the sight of her might perhaps make him soften, was enough to make him furious. No, no — no softness, no weakness was to ruin this encounter, this dearly bought encounter, upon which life and death seemed to depend.

From the mill, he sent Sofie a note with a passer-by. After that, he would wait for her in the cave.

With rapid steps, he hurried upwards along the familiar, sheltered walk. If only the note would reach her hands safely. . . . How would she react . . . would she come — *immediately* — *passively* — the way one heeds the request of a dying person? All this occupied him to such an extent that he sensed nothing before he was at the entrance to the cave. He was standing face to face with Sofie.

She was sitting on the wide stone bench in the cliff wall. The white shawl she had wrapped around herself seemed, in the overhead light, to merge with her white throat and pale face, producing somewhat the effect of a marble bust. For a moment, Kold thought that his imagination was playing him a trick by making him think he saw the figure that constantly occupied his thoughts. But the figure stirred; it half rose and then sank back, regarding him fixedly. For a while, they were staring at one another.

'You don't seem to recognize me, Miss Ramm?' Kold finally said in an uncertain voice, as if he feared the apparition might vanish.

'I recognized you at once . . . although. . .!' A wondering look at his altered appearance completed her thought. 'Have you already seen Father? Shall we go and find him?' She again wanted to get up.

'I have not come to see your Father. I have come to talk to you. Now that we are face to face, perhaps I may at last be able to. . . .'

'I didn't know that this was such an important wish of yours. This is the first time I have been aware of it.'

'That is true; you have not read my letters. You have denied me all access. After all, even a criminal is allowed to plead his cause.'

'Because I was convinced that you, Mr Kold, had nothing, no, *nothing*, to say to me that I ought to hear.'

'Nothing, Miss Sofie, really nothing? Do you then think that I would have stormed up here straight from my sickbed; that I would expose myself to the humiliation of being seen here on such a day as this . . . that I would willingly serve as a decoration at your wedding celebration? . . . And, finally, do you think that I would have confronted the worst obstacle of all, that of inconveniencing you, if what I have to say is not precisely something you *ought* to hear? And now, will you listen to me. . .? Have you the time?'

All colour had left Sofie's cheeks. She got up and sank back again. A look full of supplication and saying more than words, fell on him.

'I don't want to frighten you. Let us talk calmly. . . . You see how calm I am. . . . Sofie, tell me the truth. . . . There is something between us, a point, something obscure that I cannot understand. . . . Explain it to me! . . . Why have you treated me so badly?'

'Have *I* treated *you* badly?' said Sofie, looking at him with a smile that plainly told him she had suffered.

'Do you remember the day when you, as if driven by a divine inspiration, confided to me the most precious secret of your life? . . . You threw yourself around my neck and said that you loved me.'

'Must I be reminded of it!' Sofie exclaimed, hiding her face in her hands.

'Don't blush because of that. In that hour, you were natural and truthful; something your sex never dares to be. Do you know how it affected me? I was intoxicated with happiness; I could scarcely believe it. When I saw you next, you were cold and distant. I still thought it was the sort of restraint your surroundings forced upon you, and I waited patiently . . . no, not patiently at all, but I waited. Such an unrestrained moment did not come, and it was you who avoided it. You were and remained inaccessible and displayed an incomparable ability to avoid every opportunity for an explanation. Tell me yourself whether I have left undone anything with which I could have moved you! Don't you believe that I have *suffered*! Nothing can torture a man more than the *incomprehensible*, that which he cannot fathom, and against which he is forever striking his head, as if against an invisible wall. I would have thanked you, had you told me in a straight-forward, cut-and-dried way why you treated me that way. Tell me now! Tell me the worst of all, that it was all a mistake; that you that one time spoke words of which you were unaware because you were so frightened. Isn't that true; that was how it was?'

'No,' said Sofie, who had been listening to his words with strange looks, 'that was not how it was. I spoke the truth, and I knew exactly what I was saying.'

'You knew it? The happiness I felt — you shared it?'

'Yes, I, too, was happy.'

He thought for a moment. 'Has anybody spoken ill of me behind my back?'

Sofie shook her head.

'Oh, if that was all! Nobody could have told you such things better than I. Yes, I have been weak; I have made mistakes. Like most people, I have stains of regret on my soul that I wish I knew how to erase! But yet you must believe that I abhor all that is low and impure. I have no person's unhappiness on my conscience. Demand it, and I'll spread out my entire life before you.'

'I have thought of you, but I have never thought of your *virtues* or of your *shortcomings*,' said Sofie with a touch of disdain. 'Whatever you might have had to confess to me, I should never — that much I know — have demanded to know. . . .'

'Yes, that's true, love knows all; it tolerates all; it forgives all!' said Kold bitterly. 'And this feeling, which was so sublime, so unconditional, it survived for one whole, long day, and then it expired by itself, like a nightlight one forgets to put out before going to sleep, and which one does not even recall in the morning. . .?'

'Because it had to go out. You put it out yourself, as you ought to know. Not I, not anyone else, is to blame. . . You yourself brought forth a confession just to mock it and to deride it most cruelly afterwards!'

'I? In what way?'

'Now I shall tell you everything. Just that evening, a friend of yours came to visit you.'

'Dr. Müller! Hm, yes. . . . It was that very evening. He certainly arrived at a most inopportune time.'

'To him you confided all that was going on in your soul, which I was too simpleminded to see through. I overheard that conversation, at first unintentionally, then because I must and wanted to hear the rest. To this stranger, whom I knew to be your most intimate friend, you revealed pretty much all that had passed between us. You denied your own affection and made a laughing stock of mine. . . .'

Kold had been listening breathlessly. An indescribable mixture of surprise, inquiring unease, uncertainty and hope were fighting in his expression. 'Sofie,' he said after a moment's silence, 'is that conversation which you overheard the only thing that has separated us?'

'Yes, the only thing.'

'Is it true? . . . Swear to me, is there nothing else that has turned your heart away from me?'

'No, nothing else! Nothing else!' she repeated to herself in distress. 'Well, no, there is nothing *else* . . . .'

'Oh, God be praised!' Kold exclaimed jubilantly. 'Then everything can still be mended! What did I say? . . . I no longer know! . . . Did I repudiate you? . . . It is certainly possible. At that moment, I would have committed murder rather than betray any part of our secret. . . . And to *him*, my friend, you say. He would have been the last person on earth to whom I would have confided it. Oh, you don't know what one may take into one's head to say at such a time! . . . There are people in whose presence one wants to turn everything inside-out; to talk derogatorily about that which is most dear. . . . But you don't understand that. Oh, everything will be well — but we must have courage! There is not a minute to lose.'

She sat immobile, staring at him. The hand he had seized was as heavy and cold as marble.

And he implored her. All the eloquence of which soaring anxiety can make the human tongue capable; all that true tenderness can contribute to the effort of moving and stirring another heart, he did try.

'Sofie,' he said. 'You have been dear to me ever since you were a child. Rejected and misunderstood by the others, you could always count on my silent defence. I bowed to that willpower, that young independence, which the others called childish obstinacy. Perhaps my own character needed this support from someone else. When you left, I remained . . . to wait for you, I think. . . . Oh, everything that I had thought and dreamed I found surpassed when you stepped towards me after your return home. My selfish fear of finding myself disappointed turned into a much more terrible fear. I wanted either that which was greater than everything, or nothing at all. Your love had to be tried and true, and I swore to myself that I would gain it in a noble manner. You were to have a regard for me first. You had to become so trusting that you could throw yourself around my neck and tell me on your own. Have I not shielded my fragile flower? But I remained on my guard against myself. All the crudeness, all the shameful games men so often permit themselves in such relationships, those intoxications based on the suffering of another person, they were never to touch you. You were too naive to understand such things; too proud to tolerate them. . . . Oh God, and now the misunderstanding of one moment, just one moment, is to. . . .'

'Misunderstanding! No, no, not a misunderstanding. How could I doubt what I heard? . . . And if for one moment I had been too weak to doubt it, you should know that. . . I did not want to tell you at first. . . .'

'What, what?'

'That your friend, that Dr. Müller, later confirmed everything I had overheard. Your feeling for me was but a passing inclination; one of those that had so often caused disappointment in yourself previously. . . . You were just about to assume a position, a splendid position, but in order to be able to do so, you must be free of all ties. . . . He begged me to let you go.'

'Really? . . . He begged you to do that? . . . Ha, ha! . . . Müller? But he did not talk to you?'

'He sought me out in the morning in order to tell me.'

'Then it was Müller! . . . And all this he told you so drily and caimly . . . oh, so thoroughly! Poor Sofie, yes, you have also suffered. But don't blame me or this *friend*, as you call him. Your limitless lack of trust is to blame. Me you should have trusted, not my words. Oh, I understand everything! . . . My mistake, my monstrous mistake, was not to be able to gain that trust. I wasn't able to make you understand what I am like; I wasn't able to lift you up to where you could have learned it! . . . But my *love* I did have. For I have loved you, Sofie, yes I *have*! — And precisely because I wanted to hide it from everybody else, because I knew that not one among all these people who have forgotten what love is — not one of them would have understood the way I felt. Precisely because I cherished my feelings for you above everything else, things had to go the way they did! . . . But how could you have doubted my feelings as well! How could you have allowed such a dreadful misunderstanding of me, of yourself. . . . Sofie! . . . And if this was possible, and you really were able to believe that I was the sort of outrageous scoundrel as you must believe, as you did believe I was . . . why did you not then call me to account? Why didn't you crush me with your scorn! . . . Oh Sofie, Sofie, why didn't you *speak*!'

The poor girl only gave him a look like that of a fettered deer being made to suffer.

'Come, come,' he said violently and grasped her hands, 'we are wasting our time talking. It is not too late. It is *our* wedding they are preparing. . . . Your father will be good to us. . . . I'll take all the blame. . . Oh, just let us go. . .!'

But even if the angels from heaven had descended to help him plead his cause, it would not have moved Sofie.

Not frivolously, but with the whole deep seriousness of her soul, she had seized and become familiar with her new life, after she had succeeded in weaning her heart — possibly as her last act of self-mortification. She herself had held out her hand to the man to whom she was to belong, across the voluntary chasm he had created between them. This hand had been accepted with the same trust, the same gratitude, with which it had been offered. Her natural sense of justice revolted at the mere thought of disappointing such trust. But now her lover demanded that it be done in a sensational and truly offensive manner. Here, there was no longer a question of the sort of dismissal the world will sanction when it takes place within an acceptable period, and if it hides its barb in a small, dainty, carefully sealed and carefully franked piece of vellum. This was revolt, murder, arson; it was cowardice in the face of the enemy; it was a breach of promise the day before a wedding. She was to bring confusion into the house that was all decked out for the occasion; bring sorrow and consternation to all of her own family! This caught her too violently; found her too unprepared. Just as the first warm rays of the March sun are unable to penetrate and free the imprisoned life below ground, in the same way her lover's voice was unable to get through to her heart. The youthful bravery with which she at one time would have defended the birthright of love before the whole world, had been crushed, miserably crushed, along with courage, hope and trust. She had been seized with an infinite dread from the moment the first word had been spoken between them. It almost paralysed her ability to speak, or to comprehend what she later remembered with such dreadful clarity and detail. A voice within her drowned out everything else: if you engage in this battle, everything is lost — duty, honour, happiness all at one. Crush, annihilate — just do it quickly. She searched for the weapon that would deal the deadliest blow.

'But you do love me?' he said, appalled by her immobility.

She moved her lips, but there was no sound.

'You do love me?' He bent his ear down close to her lips.

What she said, they could scarcely have heard, those listening spirits of the mountains that spy so maliciously on the pitiful secrets of mankind, but *he* heard it. The next moment, he was leaning up against the rock wall with his hands before his face.

'Yes,' Sofie continued in a strangely hurried manner, 'yes, I was mistaken about myself. It was all a delusion that disappeared when your words penetrated my heart so painfully. We are not suited to each other! I am too naive, too serious for you ... to *him*, to the good, straight-forward man, I want to belong. He is fond of me; he has a high regard for me; and he would never deny this regard to someone else.... Yes, I am his; I have promised him that... I am to look after his home ... I shall take care of his children!... Oh, I'll be a good wife, I assure you.'

'I don't doubt that you will be a model wife,' he said without irony, but with stupefaction. 'And now you have sought this solitude to gather your thoughts before carrying out those duties.... And I! ... I have troubled you far too long.'

'Yes, yes, that's it; that's just why I was looking for solitude. To think over these duties.... Oh, on my knees I should beg Heaven to give me strength to carry them out! ... Yes, it's true, you ought not to have disturbed me; that was wrong of you, very wrong....'

He sank to his knees before her in unspeakable fear. 'Take back those cruel words; you don't know what you're saying; no, you don't know yourself. You're only saying those words; your heart doesn't recognize them.... After all, that heart is *mine*; I own it with a right more sacred than any other! Oh Sofie, do not repudiate me! ... My love ... my darling!'

'Be gone, be gone with such words!' Sofie cried, almost beside herself. 'One of us must leave this spot, and if you will not allow me to do so, then you must. . . . Or stay! Stay! But so help me God, no further word shall pass between you and me.'

She pulled her white shawl up over her head, wrapped herself in it as if it were a shroud, and remained seated.

It was absolutely quiet in the cave. At long intervals, there was just the sound of a drop falling into a little hollow with what sounded like a wailing sigh. There were many such sighs. It was so quiet in the cave.

Sofie looked up. As if coming out of a paralysed state, she jumped up, and with a subdued shout, almost as if calling out a name, she dashed outside. The light fell on her deathly pale face, one cheek of which agitation had marked with a dark, flaming spot. And she rushed forward, first hesitatingly, looking to all sides, as if she feared what she was seeking, but when she saw nothing, found nothing, she ran on with the growing speed born of anxiety.

She encountered nobody in the course of her singular hunt. Wait, yes, on the bridge she met an old tenant farmer with his son. They were both carrying heavy sacks of grain to the mill, and they had not intended to rest until they got there. But a little way up the hill the old farmer and his son had met a pitiable figure, whom they thought they recognized, and then they had put down their sacks and stared after the figure, after which they silently hoisted their loads back up on their shoulders and continued on their way to the mill. But when they saw this second apparition dashing past them, they again put down their sacks and stared after the sight for as long as they could, and then they walked on in silence. What was the old tenant farmer thinking as he looked after the apparition and reflectively turned his tobacco over in his mouth? Perhaps it occurred to him that such a sack was certainly a burden, but that not all burdens were sacks; that there might be many another heavy load to carry; and that the good Lord distributed these burdens more equitably among his creatures than a poor old man might sometimes suppose.

Outside her father's door, Sofie paused for a minute. She was listening. She cold hear nothing but the beating of her own heart. It was absolutely quiet in there. He was alone.

Alone! Why should he not be alone? She heard him calmly turning the page of a book. Poor Sofie! Don't waste your rekindled courage on this peaceful old soul! He only has a heart, a sigh for your great need, and that will be of no help at all. Down there is the roaring machinery that has seized the corner of your new hope — stop it, if you can.

Downstairs, they were preparing for a *wedding.*

A wedding! 'A ridiculous thing, when you come to think of it,' Müller had said. No, not ridiculous — dreadful is the celebration we call a wedding. We are not thinking of this exhibition of the bride's beauty and of her blushing cheeks: if his heart is in the right place and it can even be supposed he carries with him a mind that has not been completely dulled by convention, then anger and torturing jealousy must drown out all other sensations on such a day. Indeed, we will not speak of this, only of the entire banal show bedizening what is sacred, with which one goes to such trouble to deprive the sublime of its simplicity. *The consecration of marriage*, upon which God himself places his hand, was made for hearts that are already wedded to each other. The happy bride — but weddings were invented for the unhappy ones. No doubt they serve the same function as cymbals and kettledrums during the sacrifices performed by savages: they stun the victims and drown out their screams.

Confronted with the *consecration of marriage*, a reluctant heart might well find the courage to save itself — God is more merciful than man — but when confronted with a *wedding celebration*, there is no salvation.

Perhaps even our two lovers, who had found each other too late, might have been reunited; perhaps the two noble souls governing their fates might have been able to make up their minds to make the children happy, had it been possible to do so without undue notice. But it could not happen without undue notice. The wedding had been announced. The friends of the bride had already stitched their gifts. The guests had been invited, and from his spiritual herbarium the minister had extracted and memorized a sermon so old that it might be taken for brand new.

With a cry for salvation on her lips, Sofie had rushed downstairs. The anteroom was filled with fresh green branches and wreaths. Windows and doors were open, and in the room several servants were in the process of moving furniture about. It was not for any one of them that Sofie was looking. But from the kitchen Amalie came towards her, radiating joy. 'It has arrived! It has arrived!' she cried, pulling the passive Sofie with her.

The crate, the long-awaited crate from town, had arrived. The crate contained the wedding finery, which had been made by the best fashion house in Christiania, and it also held many other beautiful articles intended for the celebration. In the garden room, Mrs Ramm was busy unpacking. Her somewhat high colour suggested a great many things to do and a high degree of satisfaction. Tables, chairs, even the window sills were filled with articles that had been unpacked. The festive white sheen of soft silk, ribbons and veils was everywhere in evidence. Amalie ran admiringly from one object to the next. Sofie had collapsed on a settee. By chance, it was standing right underneath the unhappy Regina's portrait. Whether a silent anathema fell down upon the scene from this picture, as if it wanted to proclaim, 'Woe unto the daughters of my blood! I have never seen, I shall never see a happy bride!' is a thought and vision we shall have to leave to some future enlightenment to produce. Certainly in those days, by our calendar, such a thought would scarcely have occurred to any mother's soul.

'Oh, do look at the veils, Mother!' Amalie cried. 'How sweet! Are they both the same? Oh, you must see how it looks on Sofie!' She tossed the veil over Sofie's hair, whose abundant plaits had fallen down while she was running.

'Oh yes, I thank you,' said Mrs Ramm elatedly, 'that will be something to make them stare.'

'Mother,' Sofie said, but so softly, so brokenly that nobody heard it.

'And the dresses!' Amalie continued. 'How splendid they are! No, such soft silk dresses are really too elegant for a pair of village maidens like ourselves. I shall feel quite bashful in mine.'

'Oh, fiddlesticks,' said her mother. 'You will put up with it happily enough. For my part, I think that a wedding gown that isn't made of this heavy, soft silk is no wedding gown at all. *I* was a bride in such a gown, and I promised myself that if I could possibly afford it, my daughters would be, too.'

'Mother,' Sofie said again. It sounded like a faint cry for help, the last — like one of those inexplicable ones that sometimes reaches one's ear in the night, and about which one does not know whether to say they are real or not.

But yes, the cry reached her sister's ear. It went further — to her heart. Amalie was staring into the mirror. Her uplifted arms, with which she was just then fastening an ornament, paused in mid-air, and with an anxious cry of 'Oh God, Sofie is fainting!' she rushed over and caught the slumping form.

The usual remedies were resorted to. Mrs Ramm loosened Sofie's dress, but Amalie weepingly removed the veil and kissed the pale brow.

'Have no fear, Amalie, it will soon pass. I have been just that way myself. It just comes of walking about on an empty stomach. . . . And Sofie, dear! with such thin shoes in the dew! . . . There, you see, she's recovering. A cup of coffee will restore her — Amalie, a really good cup of coffee!'

'Madam mustn't depend on the Dean's not arriving until this evening,' the housekeeper called out from over by the door. 'Per says that the horses have been ordered at Brattli for one o'clock. So it will be best, after all, to do as I suggested and expect him for dinner.'

A stream of assorted instructions greeted this important piece of information.

'Are you better now, my sweet child?' Sofie's mother asked.

'Yes, much better.'

* * *

Our story ends here, and those readers who have had enough, perhaps more than enough, may certainly put the book aside at this point. But for those readers who have not had enough, but who are like children to whom one has told a fairytale and who always want to know more, we shall add a few words more, in an attempt to gather those few details from the subsequent fate of our characters that we may safely put down as absolutely reliable.

Georg Kold had returned to Christiania. It is an old saying that a man's heartbreak is more violent in its course, but also of briefer duration, than a woman's. Perhaps. He does not have the composure of disappointment at the decisive moment; he is not prepared for it the way a woman is. It is certain that Kold's suffering at having to give up his hope had none of that composure. He raged against himself and against Müller; he shut himself up for a long time and did not want to see anybody — he left for Stockholm. But even if this saying applies generally, we know from reliable sources that Kold's sorrow was deep and lasting in its vehemence; that for a long time this sorrow cast a melancholy shadow over all his pleasures; and that during the vicissitudes of his later life, in the course of which honour and fortune eventually became his constant companions, he never forgot his first love.

Of Müller we know only that he was obliged to stay for some weeks at the home of a civil servant in Trondhjem County in order to cure a dangerous condition from which the man was suffering. But here he himself fell victim to his philanthropic zeal, or, if you will, to the never-slumbering Nemesis. He fell in love with the daughter, became engaged, and was married. The wedding was splendid and gay. No formalities were left out. From the regular assurances he let fall in his letters to Kold regarding his authority as a husband, and from his anxiety that such a personality as his might crush such a frail and fragile instrument as a wife, Kold concluded that he had come to be henpecked — a supposition that is also shared by all those who have had the opportunity to observe Dr. Müller's domestic bliss at close quarters.

Sofie's first concern, when she found herself in possession of worldly goods and of her husband's trust, was Lorenz Brandt. She had long since got the Dean to take a lively interest in him. Another protector, however, more powerful than Rein, who endures more faithfully and who never asks for gratitude, had stolen the march on him.

Brandt had earnestly intended to mend his ways, and the change had really taken place, except he died from it. He did not have strength enough to go through what was perhaps the most difficult and painful process to which human nature is subjected. How many have truly endured the sufferings of a reawakened conscience, in which one has to add the contempt of others to the much more bitter contempt one feels for oneself — all the while martyring an already martyred body? Brandt tended increasingly to stay away from human habitation, and when other people sought shelter, he and his dog were not infrequently seen slumbering on the bare ground or under the hospitable roof of some spruce trees. A farmer driving home from the forest one summer evening with a load of freshly mown grass which he was going to spread out to dry in the fields, was followed part of the way by a grey dog that seemed noticeably upset. Guided by the dog, the farmer found Brandt a few steps from the road, lying in the middle of the heather with his arms under his head, with a peaceful, gentle expression as if he were asleep. He must have died very recently. The song thrush was singing a mellow cantata above his head. The farmer laid him down on top of the fragrant grass and drove him to Lorenz's mother's house, accompanied by the grieving Croesus.

Sofie mourned him with bitter tears. She treasured the small box he had given her as if it were a reliquary. Only the fortunate ones and the ones who spread the greatest happiness around are mourned by *all*. But more hotly and bitterly flow the secret tears for those who were doubly promising, but who betrayed everybody and themselves too — for those whose richest talents turned on them like a mockery and whose excessive demands on life were left unsatisfied thanks to the exigencies of reality, were swallowed up by debasement — for those unhappy souls, finally, whose unhappiness people shy away from mentioning on earth, 'the name of whose woes is but to Heaven known'.

And Sofie! . . . Reader, we have seen Sofie again in her own home. She has aged, while happiness has made her husband younger, with the result that the difference in their ages is no longer striking. Sofie seems to live for everybody else only. Not content with being the light and comfort of her closest family, her husband's admired ideal, and Ada's dearest friend, she attempts to pull all that suffer into the healing confines of her tenderness and care. It remains to be seen whatever *higher* life of light and peace is yet to rise within her, of which a powerful — albeit *invisible* — beginning may have been made during the many struggles and upheavals in that year of her life which these pages have but imperfectly accounted for, but the suspicion that such a life may be hers touches us soothingly as we are about to part from her.

Louise has become a widow, and the sisters visit each other often.

Amalie's second-hand romantic notions did not survive the union with Brøcher. They took flight without leaving a trace and were replaced by pure, unadulterated triviality. Whatever sweetness and seductiveness there had been in her manner gave way to a certain dry, domesticated sensibleness that is less than becoming.

The sisters' room upstairs has seen some changes. Amalie has had it wallpapered, and white linen curtains have indeed been put up. If we are not mistaken, these were tacked up with golden arrows. The poets of love have been taken down from the wall, however, and the old great-grandmother is looking grimly and triumphantly down upon her young descendants.